ACCLAIM FOR SA

"Cornwall's iconic sea cliffs are on display in *The Thief of Lanwyn Manor*, but it's the lyrical prose, rich historical detail, and layered characters that truly shine on the page. The story anchors the foray into Cornwall's copper mining legacy with historical accuracy and brilliant heart. Fans of Regency romance will be instantly drawn in and happily lost within the pages—this is Sarah E. Ladd at her best!"

—KRISTY CAMBRON, BESTSELLING AUTHOR OF THE
LOST CASTLE AND HIDDEN MASTERPIECE NOVELS

"*Northanger Abbey* meets *Poldark* against the resplendent and beautifully realized landscape of Cornwall. Ladd shines a spotlight on the limitations of women in an era where they were deprived of agency and instead were commodities in transactions of business and land. The thinking-woman's romance, *The Thief of Lanwyn Manor* is an unputdownable escape."

—RACHEL MCMILLAN, AUTHOR OF THE
VAN BUREN AND DELUCA SERIES

"Brimming with dangerous secrets, rich characters, and the hauntingly beautiful descriptions Sarah Ladd handles so well, 1800s Cornwall is brought vividly to life in this well-crafted tale that kept me glued to the pages. What a brilliant start to a new series!"

—ABIGAIL WILSON, AUTHOR OF IN THE SHADOW OF CROFT
TOWERS, ON THE GOVERNESS OF PENWYTHE HALL

"*The Governess of Penwythe Hall* is a delightful and emotionally gripping tale that will tick all the boxes for any Regency lover: romance, history, and enough unpredictable intrigue to keep you up past your bedtime."

—KRISTI ANN HUNTER, AUTHOR OF A DEFENSE OF HONOR

"Lovers of sweet and Christian romance alike will fall in love with Delia's strength amid the haunting backdrop of her tragic past and the Cornish coast. Throw in a handsome leading man willing to turn his life upside down for the children in Delia's charge, and you have a story you can't put down."

—JOSI S. KILPACK, WHITNEY AWARD–WINNING AUTHOR OF THE MAYFIELD FAMILY SERIES, ON *THE GOVERNESS OF PENWYTHE HALL*

"Absolutely captivating! Once I started reading, I couldn't put down *The Governess of Penwythe Hall*. This blend of *Jane Eyre*, Jane Austen, and *Jamaica Inn* has it all. Intrigue. Danger. Poignant moments. And best of all a sweet, sweet love story. This is by far my favorite Sarah Ladd book. Don't hesitate to snatch up this title!"

—MICHELLE GRIEP, CHRISTY AWARD–WINNING AUTHOR OF THE ONCE UPON A DICKENS CHRISTMAS SERIES

"A strong choice for fans of historical fiction, especially lovers of Elizabeth Gaskell's *North and South*. It will also appeal to admirers of Kristy Cambron and Tracie Peterson."

—LIBRARY JOURNAL FOR *THE WEAVER'S DAUGHTER*

"A gently unfolding love story set amid the turmoil of the early industrial revolution. [*The Weaver's Daughter* is] a story of betrayal, love, and redemption, all beautifully rendered in rural England."

—ELIZABETH CAMDEN, RITA AWARD–WINNING AUTHOR

"This novel reads well and fast. The well-crafted metaphors and tight sequences make for an absorbing read ... The style is fresh and the voice genuine."

—HISTORICAL NOVELS SOCIETY ON *A STRANGER AT FELLSWORTH*

"With betrayals, murders, and criminal activity disrupting the peace at Fellsworth, Ladd fills the pages with as much intrigue as romance. A well-crafted story for fans of Regency novels."

—PUBLISHERS WEEKLY ON *A STRANGER AT FELLSWORTH*

"An engaging Regency with a richly detailed setting and an unpredictable suspenseful plot."

—LIBRARY JOURNAL ON *THE CURIOSITY KEEPER*

The
THIEF
of
LANWYN
MANOR

BOOKS BY SARAH E. LADD

THE CORNWALL NOVELS
The Governess of Penwythe Hall

The Weaver's Daughter

THE TREASURES OF SURREY NOVELS
The Curiosity Keeper

Dawn at Emberwilde

A Stranger at Fellsworth

THE WHISPERS ON THE MOORS NOVELS
The Heiress of Winterwood

The Headmistress of Rosemere

A Lady at Willowgrove Hall

The
THIEF
of
LANWYN
MANOR

SARAH E. LADD

THOMAS NELSON
Since 1798

The Thief of Lanwyn Manor

© 2020 Sarah Ladd

Published in Nashville, Tennessee, by Thomas Nelson. Thomas Nelson is a registered trademark of HarperCollins Christian Publishing, Inc.

Published in association with the Books & Such Literary Management, 52 Mission Circle, Suite 122, PMB 170, Santa Rosa, California 95409-5370, www.booksandsuch.com.

Interior design by Lori Lynch

Thomas Nelson titles may be purchased in bulk for educational, business, fund-raising, or sales promotional use. For information, please email SpecialMarkets@ThomasNelson.com.

Publisher's Note: This novel is a work of fiction. Names, characters, places, and incidents are either products of the author's imagination or used fictitiously. All characters are fictional, and any similarity to people living or dead is purely coincidental.

Library of Congress Cataloging-in-Publication Data

Names: Ladd E. Sarah author.
Title: The Thief of Lanwyn Manor / Sarah E. Ladd.
Description: Nashville, Tennessee : Thomas Nelson, 2020. |
Identifiers: LCCN 2019031013 (print) | LCCN 2019031014 (ebook) | ISBN 9780785223962 (audio download) | ISBN 9780785223269 (epub) | ISBN 9780785223184 (trade paperback) |
Subjects: | GSAFD: Christian fiction. | Love stories. | Regency fiction.
Classification: LCC PS3623.I57778 (ebook) | LCC PS3623.I57778 T53 2020 (print) | DDC 813/.6--dc23

Printed in the United States of America

20 21 22 23 24 LSC 10 9 8 7 6 5 4 3 2 1

This novel is dedicated to K.J.N. – in loving memory

PROLOGUE

Cornwall, 1807
Tregarthan Hall

Isaac Blake regretted his actions, but had there been any other choice?

Even now, as censure brewed in Father's hard hazel eyes, Isaac tensed in anticipation of the inescapable reprimand.

Seconds passed.

Perspiration gathered on Isaac's brow, and he clasped his hands behind his back, resisting the itching urge to wipe it away. He wished his father would say something—anything. Even a sound scolding would be better than the deafening silence.

With his head still bowed Isaac snuck a glance at his twin brother, Matthew, who stood a few feet away from him in their father's study. Dirt smeared his tanned left cheek and clumped in his tousled fair hair, and already a bruise had formed beneath his bloodshot eye.

Guilt twisted Isaac's stomach. Now he had no choice but to take his punishment like a man.

Their father, Joseph Blake, stood from behind his heavy oak desk and squared his broad shoulders. As he rounded the desk and stepped closer, Isaac's courage and resolve faded.

"What were you thinking to strike your brother?" he thundered, his forthright stare uncomfortably direct.

Isaac bit his lip and focused on the rip in the knee of his trousers.

"Young man, you will look at me when I speak to you!"

Isaac jerked his face upward.

"I'm waiting for your answer."

Isaac swallowed the lump in his dry throat as a dozen explanations raced through his mind. His father would accept no less than the truth. Isaac had been angry, but his actions were justified. Yet Father would see any reason, however viable, as an excuse.

With a sharp inhale, Isaac straightened the full height of his fourteen years and lifted his chin. "I've no explanation, sir."

Father's square jaw clenched, and he stared down at Isaac for several unending seconds before he shifted to face Matthew. "Our copper mine provides work for more than half the men in this village. *Half.* One day when I'm gone, you'll both be leaders, whether you fancy the notion or not. No sons of mine will be sparring in the public lane like ragamuffins. I expect more out of you than this behavior. Much more. The two of you will work together to repair the fence you broke during your scuffle, and furthermore, you'll work in the stable for the groom until you earn enough money to pay for the repairs."

"But that's not fair!" Matthew's hazel eyes flashed. "Isaac attacked me. I did nothing wrong! I was defending myself."

"Your brother bears as many bruises as you," Father snapped. "You both fell through the church fence, and you'll both make reparations. My decision is final. Matthew, go. Isaac, stay."

With a huff Matthew whirled, aimed a red-faced glare at Isaac, and stomped from the chamber.

Isaac held his breath as the sound of Matthew's footsteps dissipated, his sweaty, dirty hands still clasped behind his back, turmoil warring within him as he waited for the unavoidable punishment that would be, he suspected, far worse than merely rebuilding a fence.

Father's voice lowered, but it did not soften. "Well? Are you going to tell me what happened?"

Isaac studied the mud-caked toe of his boot. He could tell him how Matthew had taunted Charlie Benson and poked fun at his poverty. He could tell him how Matthew had ridiculed Charlie's father and demeaned their way of life. Or that Matthew's words were so cruel that Isaac had to silence his brother any way he could.

But something held him back.

Seconds stretched out in the late-afternoon heat. The air he inhaled felt thicker and steamier with each breath. The sun must have retreated behind a cloud, for a shadow slid over the cluttered study. His father finally broke the stare and folded his arms over his barrel chest. "Ah, I see. I've demanded an explanation, but you don't wish to betray your brother. Or yourself."

Isaac swallowed and diverted his eyes. How his father always seemed to know what he was thinking never ceased to astonish him.

"The fact is, Son, I don't care why you hit your brother. Whether it was justified or not, it doesn't matter."

Isaac twitched.

"What concerns me is whether or not you learn a lesson. Violence may seem like a viable option, but it's never the right method with which to prove a point." He stepped to the large bank of leaded windows behind the desk and motioned for Isaac to join him.

Isaac did as bid, and for several seconds he surveyed Tregarthan Hall's broad green lawn, slightly tinged with brown from the recent lack of rain.

"Tell me." Father pointed his forefinger toward the north. "What do you see?"

Isaac lifted his gaze beyond the grounds and the tree line to the tall, redbrick stack of Wheal Gwenna's engine house. No smoke puffed from the stack. It emitted no sound. "I see Wheal Gwenna."

"That's all you see? A closed copper mine? Nothing more?"

Isaac squinted and studied the landscape—the blue Cornish sky, the gathering gray clouds, the cluster of white seabirds soaring above it all. But he saw nothing else.

"When you look at that, you shouldn't see just a closed mine, boy. You should see your future. One day that mine will be yours—yours and yours alone. There's copper in her yet, and it will be up to you to lead others to success."

Isaac huffed and sank back. He didn't want to hear about Wheal Gwenna. Wheal Tamsen, the family's main mine, was the only one that mattered. Matthew, older by three minutes, would inherit both it and Tregarthan Hall one day. He'd be responsible for carrying the family's rich legacy. Isaac, however, would receive the cast-off mine that had not been opened since before he was born, and yet Father spoke of it as if it were a great prize.

As if sensing Isaac's disbelief, Father grabbed his shoulder and forced Isaac to look him in the eye. "Don't scoff, lad. 'Tis an opportunity—a great one that many young men would risk life and limb for, and it's being handed to you. You must start preparing for such a responsibility now."

Isaac sniffed and swiped his ripped sleeve over his dirty nose. "How?"

"Everything you do enhances or tarnishes your reputation, including a brawl with your brother, regardless of the reason behind it. Others will judge you by your actions, even at your age."

The words rang harshly in Isaac's ears as he recalled the cluster of miners who had seen them arguing and the vicar who had pulled him off Matthew.

"Your reputation as a leader, as a good judge of character, and as a levelheaded man will be invaluable when you are older. I don't doubt that your brother probably did something unacceptable, but there is always another way to defuse a situation. Always."

Remorse surged in, bitter and strong. It warmed his face and tightened his throat.

Father was right, of course.

He was always right.

But why was it so hard to control his temper?

"Isaac—you possess a maturity beyond your years. I tell you this not to puff your pride, but rather to increase your awareness of it. If the only way we respond to anger is with our fists, the balance of life will never be steady. No, it must not be. You and your brother are very different souls, and you both have lessons to learn. But you are bound, and time must strengthen your bond. Do not let it weaken it."

The truth of his father's words struck more sharply than his brother's blows. Isaac could only nod in agreement.

His father squeezed his shoulder. "Hear me, Son. Family is the only thing on which you can rely."

CHAPTER I

Cornwall, 1818

J ulia Twethewey never considered what it would feel like to look down the barrel of a flintlock pistol.

Her blood froze. She could not move. She could not blink.

All she could do was stare at the metal barrel mere inches from her nose.

The masked man snaked closer, his narrow black eyes fixed on her, like a rabid hunter poised to pounce. "Where's your uncle?"

He knew Uncle William? But how?

She stammered, searching for a response. "I—I don't know."

"Ha!" The man, barely taller than she, sneered as he jerked his gloved thumb toward the chairs behind him. "Is he hiding like a thief under the table there? Wouldn't doubt it. 'Fraid o' what's comin' to him, and for good reason."

Two other men, masked and equally as filthy and gruff as the perpetrator before her, emerged from the Gray Owl Inn's darkened corners and approached them. She'd not noticed them before, when she had been sitting at the corner table, sipping her tea, but now the fire in the broad hearth cast flickering shadows over their sloppy forms, and they loomed larger than life.

She drew a sharp breath and scanned the sleepy, low-ceilinged taproom for someone—anyone—who could help her. Two elderly men sat at a table to her left, and a cluster of patrons gathered in the corner. All stared, wide-eyed and aghast, but without weapons they were as helpless as she.

The man drew even closer, and his putrid, unwashed scent encircled her. "Ol' Lambourne must be a bigger fool than we thought. What sort o' man would leave his niece—a *lady*—unguarded? Tsk, tsk. Somethin' bad might happen."

He nodded toward the small pouch clutched in her fist and stretched out his hand. "Your bag."

She clutched her reticule even tighter until her fingers ached, then slid her gaze from the dark-gray metal back up to the hard eyes of the man holding the weapon. She extended her reticule.

"Ah, there we are!" He snatched it from her, as if it were some great treasure. With a grotesque smack of lips from behind the sullied kerchief covering his face, he jingled the velvet bag before he tossed it to one of the other men, who ripped into the delicate woven fabric and dumped the contents on the table.

Her embroidered handkerchief and two coins tumbled out, clattering against the table's worn, pitted wood.

Her attacker's movements slowed as he assessed the meager contents, and then he whirled toward her. "You 'spect me to believe a lady such as yerself's got no money?"

She pressed her lips together. How she wished she had more to give him so he would go away, but all of her belongings were still in her uncle's carriage. Hot tears gathered in her eyes, and she struggled to control the quivering of her chin. "'Tis all I have."

He scoffed. "I'm sure you had some fancy teacher what taught you 'tis a sin to lie." He straightened suddenly and shifted his attention to her cloak's lacy trim.

Julia flinched as he reached out to touch it.

"Give me your cloak," he barked.

"Excuse me?"

"Your cloak! Or should I take it off you meself?"

With jittery fingers she loosened the satin ribbon at her throat to release the article. She couldn't pull it from her shoulders fast enough, and once it was free she hurled it in his direction.

He seized it as it dropped to the ground, rubbed the fine wool fabric between his dirt-caked fingers, then tossed it to the man behind him.

He stepped nearer still.

Uncontrollable trembling seized her. She had nothing left to give him.

Why was he not leaving?

She wanted to look away, wanted to look at anything besides the fearsome, ugly beast before her, but her gaze was locked on the man whose trigger finger could affect her mortality.

He lifted a hand toward her face, and Julia winced, as if bracing for a strike, but instead, he pinched a long, black tendril that cascaded from beneath her bonnet.

His eyes, their muddy depths invasive, were inches from hers as he studied the lock. "Yes, very pretty."

Julia refused to be a woman who succumbed to fainting spells, but at this moment, with this foul creature before her, she feared it would come to that.

Suddenly a baritone voice boomed from her left. "Enough. You've got what you wanted. Now go."

Julia gasped.

Her assailant released her hair and stumbled back, smacked by the interruption.

A tall, blond man stood paces from them, his stance wide, his shoulders broad, his hands fisted. The fire's light illuminated his jaw's firm set. No fear wrote itself into his features. Instead, annoyance and anger radiated from his eyes as they latched onto the robber.

And yet regardless of his bravery, the blond man was still at the mercy of the assailant with the pistol.

They all were.

The masked man aimed the pistol at the newcomer and swaggered toward him. He snatched a pocket watch from the blond man's waist, visible from beneath the cape of his greatcoat, held it up, flipped it over, and read the inscription. "Joseph Blake? That you?"

The blond man's shadowed eyes narrowed. "No. My father."

The thief looked over his shoulder. "D'ya hear that, lads? We got ourself a high-and-mighty Blake here." He chuckled and stuffed the timepiece in his own pocket and raised an unkempt brow. "There now, Mr. Blake. I know of you. The family what runs Wheal Tamsen. But I doubt you know who I be."

"No, I don't. And I'm not sure I want to."

"Soon you'll know my face well enough, and you'll not forget it either, especially when the day of reckoning comes and you and your kind rot for what you've done to decent, hardworking folk."

The hammer on a rifle clicked behind her. Julia whirled to face the sound. The gray-headed barkeep seemed to have materialized from nowhere and now stood behind his counter, rifle pointed at the man with the pistol.

Within seconds he took aim.

He fired.

A ball whizzed through the air—loud. Unearthly. Acrid. Julia screamed and collapsed to her knees, covered her head, and squeezed her eyes shut, as if by doing so she could shut out the sounds, the scents.

Shuffling. Screams.

More shots rang out.

White smoke choked her.

Strong arms shoved her the rest of the way to the ground, and a heavy weight covered her. At first she resisted, but as lead balls flew above her and glass shattered around her, she let her body go limp.

"Stay down," Mr. Blake ordered.

Then, as suddenly as it began, the shuffling stopped. The shouts and voices retreated.

Then everything was still.

"Stay here." The man pushed himself off of her.

She did not respond, she did not even move, until he was several paces away from her. She lifted her head in time to catch a glimpse of the back of his wide shoulders as he hurried into the gathering night.

Julia pushed herself up, there on the dirty floor of the Gray Owl Inn, and blinked as she looked around.

She was alone.

Abandoned.

And terribly, terribly frightened.

CHAPTER 2

Heart thumping, pulse hammering, Isaac burst from the confines of the low-ceilinged taproom out to the inn's muddy courtyard.

Dusk was falling, bringing with it a damp, thick mist that shrouded High Street running through the village of Goldweth. It mingled with the lingering smoke making it nearly impossible to see anything at a distance, and the sharp, bitter wind did little to dissipate the sulfuric scent of gunpowder burning his nose or the perspiration beading on his brow. Chest heaving, Isaac straightened his hat and looked left, then right.

But he was too late.

The three brigands were gone, and all was eerily silent. With the exception of the Lambourne carriage, the driver attempting to calm his harnessed horses, and a small gathering in the center of the courtyard, everyone else who'd been present had dispersed.

He expelled his breath in one swoosh of frustration. This was not what he'd expected when he and Charlie Benson left their work at Tamsen mine and entered the unassuming Gray Owl Inn for their supper. When they'd arrived at the narrow courtyard, Benson had been detained at the courtyard gate by a talkative friend, but Isaac had proceeded to the taproom and entered the inn at just the right—or wrong—time.

The wind caught the folds of his greatcoat as he approached his friend and the innkeeper, who stood at the courtyard's gate.

Benson's gruff voice cut the uncustomary silence, and his breath plumed white in the cold air. "Theivin' vagabonds."

"Did you recognize any of them?" Isaac turned his attention toward High Street, searching for signs of anything out of the ordinary.

"Not a one." Benson ran a thick hand over his bearded jaw. "Did ye get a good look at their faces?"

Carew, the innkeeper, shook his head. "Nay. They all had kerchiefs tied over their mouths the entire time I saw 'em, like a bunch o' cowards. But mark my words, I saw their eyes and I'll not forget them. Like a snake's eyes they were, beady and evil. If one of 'em dares to step foot inside here again, they'll be met with this rifle. And I'll not miss either."

"I'll go after them," interjected Isaac. "Join me, Benson?"

Benson burst out a laugh. "Yer daft. This fog's thick as mud, and they got quite a lead on us. Not much to be done now."

Isaac's gut sank. Benson was right, of course. The vagabonds would have cleared the village by now and could have fled anywhere. The murky fog would be in their favor, and now falling darkness shrouded all. Without hounds to trace their scent, pursuing them in such conditions would be futile. Irritation flaming, Isaac removed his hat and pushed his fingers through his thick hair.

They'd had enough trouble over the last six months over the closing of Bal Tressa, Lambourne's copper mine, and instead of getting better, the tension in the nearby villages was mounting to the point of attack. Isaac looked back through the inn's window. "Who's the woman?"

"Lambourne's niece, come o'er from Braewyn." Carew tucked his rifle under his arm, pointing the barrel downward. "Arrived about an hour ago with him. Lambourne said he had business with Rogers right up the street there and said he'd be right back. Left her sittin' all alone like too. No doubt the vagabonds saw Lambourne's carriage and thought to trap him. Surely if he was at Rogers's, he'd a-heard the shots and been here." Carew angled his head to peer through the window, where his wife could be seen wrapping a blanket around the niece's shoulders. "I bet she'll quit Goldweth before dawn's first light."

"Can't say as I blame her," Benson added. "Not exactly a welcomin' reception."

Isaac assessed the petite lady from a distance. Long, dark curls hung in disarray, blocking his view of her face, and the barkeep's wife was helping her to a table. He'd heard that the Lambournes were expecting a guest to stay with them at Lanwyn Manor, and evidently everyone in the countryside knew about it as well.

"Before you got out here, I sent my stable boy over to find Lambourne," Carew said, "and I sent Trent to fetch the constable."

"A lot of good a constable will do now," Benson scoffed. "Any thoughts on who the footpads might be?"

"Wish I knew, but one thing's certain—they were on the hunt for Lambourne. Heard 'em sayin' the name as they talked amongst themselves, and they knew she was his niece—asked for him right to her face, they did. I'd say they were hired, most likely. If they were from here, someone'd recognize somethin'."

"But who around here has enough money to pay for that?" Benson asked.

"Well, apparently they got paid with a timepiece." Isaac let out a sarcastic huff, patting the pocket of his waistcoat where his watch chain used to hang, careful to mask the gravity of the loss. To most, the piece would appear nothing more than a replaceable trinket, but to Isaac, the pocket watch was the last gift his father gave him before his untimely death. "If it was a targeted attack, can't say I'm surprised. The longer Lambourne leaves Bal Tressa closed, the angrier—and hungrier—the villagers will get. 'Tis a matter of time before they lash out."

A burst of laughter from Benson shattered the tension, and he slapped a heavy hand on Isaac's shoulder. "Can't believe you approached a man with a pistol with naught but yer bare hands to protect yerself. Carew here told me about it. Either you be a reckless fool, or yer the luckiest man to draw breath on God's earth. Can't decide which."

The rigidity in Isaac's back relaxed, and he shrugged. "Carew signaled toward his rifle as I entered, so I created a diversion so he could reach it without being noticed, 'tis all." He nodded toward the horses. "Come on."

"Where we goin'?"

"If they went to the north, we'll cut through the wold to try and cut them off at the crossroad. At least see where they're headed."

"You know me." Benson rubbed his hands together, his enthusiasm contagious. "Always up for adventure."

They bid farewell to Carew and mounted, but as they rode out of the courtyard, Isaac cast a glance back at the young woman still visible through the window. He thought he saw her narrow shoulders shake, as if she was crying, and anger at the fact that a man could treat a woman so horrifically welled within him.

He refocused his attention—and indignation—on the road stretching before him. He'd need a clear head in the coming days, for no doubt this attack was just a portent of things to come.

CHAPTER 3

J ulia gripped the threadbare blanket the innkeeper's wife had given her numb fingers and tightened it around her. Try as she might, she could not stop shivering.

She stared, unblinking, into the hearth's leaping orange flames. Surely the warmth should be enough to still her trembling limbs and chattering teeth, but shock and fear had left their icy fingerprints on her. Even though her mind knew she was out of danger, her muscles poised for peril.

She drew a deep breath and surveyed her surroundings with a cautious eye. Now the inn's taproom was relatively empty. No men wielded pistols. No blond man shielded her from danger. All that remained were the portly constable, the innkeeper, Uncle William, and a few unassuming-looking men.

She took a sip of lukewarm tea and then returned the cup to the table. The bitter liquid soured in her stomach, and nausea swelled. Oh, she wanted nothing more than to leave this little village inn, with its smoke-stained rafters and dense, musty air. Regret for having ever left her home at Penwythe Hall coursed through her veins, and her head throbbed with the unbelievability of it all.

She flinched as her uncle's sharp words echoed from the low ceiling.

"This is an outrage!" Uncle William's face flamed crimson as he stabbed his thick finger toward the constable. "I demand to know what's to be done."

The constable shifted, the wooden planks beneath his feet groaning with the weight. "We'll hunt 'em down. Such villainous actions will not be tolerated."

"That's supposed to satisfy me?" His throaty voice rose an octave. "They accosted my niece!"

The stoic constable slid a dark glance in her direction before he adjusted his dusty coat and returned his focus to her uncle. "With all due respect, your niece will recover from this episode. No harm's been done. I want to catch these men as much as you want me to. We'll find them, and when we do, justice will be served."

Uncle William thudded his walking stick on the floor.

Never had she seen him so irate.

"I will be satisfied, Constable Thorne. Since the magistrate did not feel this an important enough incident to warrant his presence, you be sure to communicate that I will expect his call tomorrow." Uncle William stomped over to Julia, reached for her elbow, and guided her to her feet.

Eager to be free of the pungent, poorly lit inn, she looped her hand around his offered arm and followed him toward the door and out into the damp courtyard.

Once she and her uncle were settled in the lavish Lambourne carriage, it groaned and lurched forward. The faint glow the village had afforded faded, and once they were under way, harsh slivers of fleeting light from the carriage lamps illuminated his full cheeks, robust side whiskers, and bushy gray brows.

As he stared out the window, he worked his jaw like a man contemplating his next move, and the drumming of his fingers on the seat's edge rose above the clamor of the wheels crunching over the rutted ground. He said nothing—no words of consolation, no words of comfort—but only stared into the night, the darkness of which emphasized the stormy shadows beneath his eyes.

Even though William Lambourne was her uncle, he was essentially a stranger to her. In all of her nineteen years, she'd only been in his presence a handful of times. It had been two and a half years since she last visited her relations at their London home to attend her cousin Jane's wedding, but he was rarely present. His stern expression and sharp tongue had frightened her as a child, but as an adult, she regarded him more with curiosity than uneasiness.

She had so many questions, and her mind, sluggish with exhaustion, struggled to organize them.

Where had her uncle gone that was so important he would leave her unattended at the inn?

Why would someone be so intent upon harming him?

Why had it taken him so long to return after the attack?

She doubted she'd have answers to her questions, at least at this moment, so she turned her attention to the landscape. The mist fully invaded the moors with frightful weight, as if it, too, were weary. Blurs of browns, blacks, and shadows swept past her on a fleeting journey of their own.

No doubt one day soon, these surroundings would be as familiar to her as Penwythe Hall's vibrant orchards and verdant meadows. But it would wait for another day. She slumped against the seat, permitting her body to sway with each rut and rift in the road. The carriage blanket covering her legs did little to curtail her shivering, and she let her eyes fall closed.

Aunt Delia, her guardian at Penwythe Hall, had cautioned her not to let her excitement consume her that morning as she bid her farewell. The words flared and echoed loudly in her mind. Julia had dismissed the advice, considering it overcautious. But who could have predicted a man would threaten her very life?

She'd been invited to Lanwyn Manor to be a companion to Jane, who was with child and confined to bed. At the time the invitation arrived, anything—and anywhere—seemed like a diversion from the quiet isolation at Penwythe Hall.

And a distraction from *him*.

Now, as she jostled in a carriage with her aloof uncle and the scent of gunpowder still lingering in her nostrils, she was not so sure.

"There, round this bend." His curt voice jarred her from her thoughts. "Lanwyn Manor."

Julia leaned forward and arched her neck, squinting to see out the window. She'd never been to Lanwyn Manor before. To her knowledge her uncle had only inherited the ancient estate two years prior, and even though it was not far from Penwythe Hall, she'd not made the journey.

She forced cheerfulness to her voice. "I'm eager to see it for myself. Jane speaks highly of it in her letters."

Her uncle grunted in reply and set about arranging his coat around his thick trunk. "No doubt your aunt will already know what transpired at the inn. She possesses the uncanny sensibility of unearthing every little detail of every little event. Prepare yourself, Niece. Your aunt already despises everything about Goldweth. This incident will fuel her fire like no other, mark my words. I need not tell you she's hardly a woman to take such things in passing."

Julia, surprised to hear of her aunt's opposition to Goldweth, stiffened at the warning in his voice. Aunt Beatrice's temper was well known, and Julia did not wish to be the source of a flare.

As the carriage turned the corner, the outer walls of Lanwyn Manor blazed into view. Its gray slate stone-castellated facade gleamed in the torchlight, and yellow light spilled from the mullioned windows of the gatehouse's upper levels onto the shadowed carriage turn below. The carriage slowed before the gatehouse's heavy wooden door, and Julia held her breath, noting the significance of this moment. Once she stepped inside this courtyard, everything would be different.

Or so she hoped.

She clutched the carriage blanket around her in lieu of a cloak, accepted assistance down the single step, and trod to the cobbled path. She passed through the narrow gate and into the inner courtyard, aglow with torches and a fire burning near one of the side entrances in defiance of the moisture misting down. The flickering glow cavorted around the large, square space, on arched wooden doors and great mullioned windows, but she focused her attention ahead. There would be time enough for exploring, and at the moment she wanted nothing but warmth and safety.

As she neared the main entrance, the ornate, timbered door flew open and Aunt Beatrice emerged.

Julia's shoulders eased at the sight of her aunt bustling toward her, hands outstretched and brows drawn. The torchlight lining the drive highlighted Aunt's graying hair as it danced about her face in a minuet with the wind. Caroline, Julia's cousin, followed close on her mother's heels, a crimson shawl whipping about her narrow shoulders.

Aunt Beatrice shooed her way past the footmen, and with determination emphasizing the lines on her full face, she gripped Julia's bare hands in her own. "Who can believe this? Why, you're frozen! Are you injured? Distressed?"

"No, Aunt, I'm well." Julia managed a convincing smile. "No harm's been done."

"No harm?" Aunt Beatrice's voice shrilled as she wrapped a warm, protective arm around Julia's shoulders. She then turned toward Uncle William as he traversed the stone path toward the door. "Jago Hugh was in the inn when it happened, and he came to tell me all. William, how could you allow such a thing to happen?"

Eyes fixed ahead and jaw clenched, Uncle William continued onward, ignoring his wife's question.

Aunt Beatrice huffed as she smoothed the blanket on Julia's shoulders. "Oh, bah. Men are so tedious when it comes to things such as this. Come, let's get you inside."

Julia allowed herself to be guided across the windblown courtyard, through two thick oak arched doors, and into a tall, broad foyer lit by two candles atop a side table.

Once they were all inside, her uncle stomped to the end of the foyer and paused to remove his gloves.

Julia bit her lip, shocked. He'd not even greeted his wife or daughter.

Aunt Beatrice's tight expression confirmed that the slight had not gone unnoticed.

Hoping to ease the uncomfortable situation, Julia placed a hand on her aunt's arm. "Please do not distress yourself on my account. I'm quite well, as you see."

"How could I not be angry?" she shot back, her cheeks flushing, her glare fixed on her husband. "My niece has come to visit us, and you leave her alone at a wayside inn and the worst happens? Julia is a lady," Aunt snipped, her face trembling with intensity. "*A lady*, William, and you treat her as if she were naught but a waif from the poorhouse. Talk of it will be all over the village by tomorrow morning, mark my words."

A darkness shuttered her uncle's eyes, and he still did not respond to his wife's harangue. Instead, he shrugged off his coat and deposited his belongings in the arms of the waiting butler. Julia almost felt pity for her uncle as he stood there, accepting his verbal lashing stoically.

After a few muttered words toward the butler, he turned and stomped up the stairs.

Julia looked to Caroline, who'd been standing silently behind her mother, hands clasped, eyes downcast.

If there was one nuance Julia remembered from previous visits, it was the ever-present tension threaded between her aunt and uncle, and nothing seemed to have changed on that count.

Aunt Beatrice's narrowed, pale eyes followed him up the great wooden staircase until he disappeared around the landing and the sound of his footsteps faded. Then, with a click of her tongue, she gripped Julia's hands in her own. "La, how cold your hands still are, but I'd imagine no less. What a rogue to take your cloak! How hungry and tired you must be. The footman will take your things up to your chamber straightaway, and Caroline will show you the way herself, for her own chamber is opposite yours. I'd take you myself, but you'll be on the second floor of the tower, and tonight my constitution cannot endure the climb."

As Caroline guided her through the foyer hall, Julia drank in the sights around her as her curiosity of her new dwelling intensified. The occurrence at the inn seemed almost a far-off, vague nightmare, especially now that she was safe and surrounded by comfort.

It was a different world here. Would she be able to adjust?

CHAPTER 4

What had started out as an ordinary day had become anything but ordinary.

When Isaac and Charlie returned from their search, they were wet and tired and had no more of an idea of who was behind the attack at the Gray Owl Inn than they did when they set out.

"What a waste of time," Charlie muttered as they turned from High Street onto Miner's Row—a long, cobbled road with dark-stone cottages flanking each side.

Many local mining families lived along this lane. It was a tight-knit community in and of itself, with shared spaces and gardens. The occasional bout of distant laughter rose above the steady patter of rain to crack the night's stillness.

Straight ahead of them stood the cottage Charlie shared with his wife and son. Light seeped through the linen curtains at the square front window, and Charlie nodded toward it. "Margaret's gonna wonder what I been up to. She don't like it none when I'm gone longer'n she thinks fittin'."

Isaac laughed, for Charlie's wife's temper—and expectations— were well known. "No doubt she's heard all the details of the events at the inn, for I'm certain the story's been told a dozen times over, up and down this row."

As if on cue Margaret opened the door, a dark wool shawl wrapped about her narrow shoulders, and she leaned her slender hip against the doorframe. "There you are, Charlie Benson. Come home to me at last, have you? I was beginnin' to wonder what it was you'd gotten up to."

"Couldn't be helped, Wife." The customary twinkle glinted in Charlie's eye as he leaned forward to kiss her cheek. "A bit of excitement at the inn been keepin' us busy."

She tilted her head to the side. "Eh, I heard all about your adventures. Trouble do find ye both, there's no denyin' that. Come in afore yer soaked to the bone. You too, Isaac. Got a stew on the fire."

Isaac dipped his head in greeting and removed his hat as he stepped over the threshold and ducked to avoid hitting his head on the low doorway. "Thank you."

The cottage's main room was small but homey. A cheery fire hissed and popped beneath the black iron pot, and the scent of potatoes and salt pork reminded him that he'd not eaten since midday. A modest settee faced the fire, flanked by two simple high-backed chairs, and a square table and chairs stood near the large cupboard against the back wall. A simple ladder led the way to the sleeping chamber above.

"Papa!" A ruddy-cheeked, black-haired boy came running from the corner and jumped up against Charlie. "You're home!"

With a husky laugh Charlie swept the boy up and swung him in the air, careful to keep free of the low ceiling. "There ye are, Jory. Give your papa a kiss now."

The boy wrapped his arms around his father's neck and kissed his cheek.

"Did ye help yer mama with the water, like I asked?"

The boy nodded energetically.

"Good boy."

Jory wiggled down and ran back to the corner where he was playing with a whittled horse, and Margaret shooed Isaac and Charlie to the table.

"Heard you went chasin' after them." Margaret retrieved two bowls from the cupboard and scooped stew into them. "Did you find anythin'?"

"Not a thin'." Charlie arched back to allow his wife room to place the bowl before him, then leaned his heavy elbows on the rough-hewn table. "Are ye still of the opinion it be the miners what worked Bal Tressa behind this?"

Isaac shrugged. "If they are trying to send a message to Lambourne, 'tis one way to do it. I didn't recognize any of them, from what I saw."

"If it was the miners, they'd have had to get someone else to do it for 'em. Everyone knows everyone 'round here. If I were Lambourne though, I might think about sleepin' with one eye propped open."

"Perhaps I'll find out more tomorrow." Isaac shifted in his chair. "Matthew and I are supposed to dine at the Lambournes with other mine owners, but in light of recent events, I'm not sure we are still invited."

"Hmm." Charlie spooned stew into his mouth before he turned to his wife. "Ye hear anythin'? Did ye say ye was over at the Jamesons' last week? He worked at Bal Tressa, didn't he?"

As a midwife Margaret tended to villagers from all over the area, not just those in their little community. She retrieved two pewter mugs and placed one before each man. "Yes, I saw 'em and delivered 'em a healthy baby boy with some of the blondest hair I ever did see. No one was talking much about mines."

Isaac stretched his long, booted foot over the stone floor. "If the unrest is leading to violence, I think we all have something to worry about."

"There ye go again." Charlie winked as he shifted to allow his wife room to pour cider into the mugs. "Borrowin' trouble."

"Sad as it is, it's a fact." Isaac folded his hands on the table before him. "When one mine closes, it affects everything, you know that. Prices. Workers. Wages. Nothing is spared."

"'Twould be easier for the workers if they knew why Lambourne closed Bal Tressa." Margaret sank into the chair next to Charlie. "As it is, it seems as if he closed it just to spite everyone."

"I told you both what I heard. He thought he was being swindled by the men providing the goods—the gunpowder, candles, fuses, things of that nature—and closed it until he felt he had a better handle on it."

"That was six months ago." Charlie heaved a dramatic sigh and leaned back in his chair. "Well then, when one mine closes, another must open."

Isaac read his friend's challenge. "You're talking about Wheal Gwenna."

"'Course I am." Charlie flung his arm out, his deep voice booming in the small space. "Big old mine, ripe for the pickin'. Won't be long now that betwixt the two of us we can get her runnin'."

"You make it sound simple." Isaac took a swig of the cider. "There's much to consider."

"Ah, nothing is simple, is it, friend? But I'm a simple man, and all I know is the longer the miners are out of work, the more restless they get. And if they have been driven to the point of holding Lambourne's niece at gunpoint, well then, I'll let ye draw yer own conclusions."

"You forget one thing." Isaac leaned forward. "Running a mine takes capital. Even with what you and I have scraped together, we are still hundreds short."

"Did you speak with Richards when you were in Plymouth?" Charlie smiled up at Margaret as she stood to retrieve a bundle of bread.

"I did. He said that with the current price of copper and with the economic decline, he passed."

"Even after telling 'im of the north lode?" Charlie leaned back to allow his wife to place the bread on the table.

Isaac laughed. "You know as well as I that the north lode is a legend. And if it were true, don't you think my father would have found it before he died?"

"Hmm." Charlie tore off a piece of bread with his thick fingers and popped it in his mouth. "I'm not about to give up. I may not have a mine to me name, but I'm ready to invest in yers. I've a mind to make something of meself, you know."

"Well then, you are as much a dreamer as I, my friend." Isaac accepted a piece of bread from Margaret. "But in the meantime we've got our hands full at Wheal Tamsen."

"Yeah, and that mine be belongin' to yer brother, and any profits line his pockets far more'n yers, and 'specially more'n mine."

"Well, that mine puts a roof over both our heads, as well as half the men in Goldweth. It's as just a cause as any."

After enjoying the company of his friends and then bidding his farewells, Isaac donned his damp felt hat, stepped outside, and walked down Miner's Row. The broad road gave way to the narrower lane that led to Wheal Tamsen. He traversed the familiar path, then paused at the main gate marking the mine's property entrance. Even now, in the black of night, workers were fathoms below the surface, seeking their fortune by lantern and candlelight.

It was a steady mine, and he was grateful for that. Since Bal Tressa's closing, the price of copper had improved, albeit marginally, which was good for Wheal Tamsen but devastating to the community. As it was, Wheal Tamsen could only afford to take on a handful of additional tributers, tut workers, and dressers, and with many of the other mines having closed down, villagers were scattered across Cornwall and Devon searching for work. Sadly, it did not surprise him in the least that someone would try to send such a message to Lambourne, for now he was one of the most hated men in the area.

Isaac continued on the road past Wheal Tamsen and followed it along the forest's edge to the fence that separated Tregarthan Hall land from moorland. On the other side of the stone fence was Anvon Cottage, his home. Whereas all of Tregarthan had been left to his brother, their father bequeathed the cottage, a bit of farmable land, and Wheal Gwenna to him. At the time Father had said it would be everything Isaac would need to be successful.

As the months dragged into years, Isaac was not so sure. It took every ounce of both Matthew's and his energy to keep Wheal Tamsen profitable. Surely Father would have known that. Would there ever be an opportunity to step away from Wheal Tamsen without abandoning those who depended upon him?

As he approached Isaac assessed the humble cottage. The structure—fashioned from granite, coated with white lime render, and capped with a slate roof—had been part of Tregarthan land for more than a century. In the night the outside walls glowed almost blue, and a pale light flickered from the ground-floor rooms. His housekeeper must have kept the fire kindled for his return.

He slowed his steps. What would it be like to retire to a home like Charlie's, with a wife and child? He and Charlie were the same age, both five and twenty, and yet aspects of their lives were so dissimilar. Whereas Charlie married early, Isaac's life hurled in a different direction when his father died four years prior and the responsibilities of running the mine fell to Matthew and him.

He pushed the gate open and stepped toward the door.

As the empty home loomed before him, Isaac could not help but wish he had taken a little more time to see to his personal life. But with the state of the economy, his focus was required elsewhere, and he needed to accept that.

CHAPTER 5

With a toss of her long blonde hair, Caroline looped her arm through Julia's and guided her from Lanwyn Manor's front hall toward the staircase. "Never you mind Mother and Father," she whispered, leaning close. "They're glad you're here, even though right now they are acting more like children than adults. Mother is always cross with Father these days for one reason or another."

Julia nodded but remained silent as they crossed the foyer.

Truly, this was not the reception she had anticipated.

Indeed, Lanwyn Manor was nothing like she expected.

Julia trailed her finger along the wooden banister as they ascended the stairs, noting the intricate scrollwork. At one time it must have been very grand. Now, dust gathered in the railing's carved nooks, and a fraying rug curled on the bowed steps.

She lifted her gaze from the dark paneled walls to the peeling plaster ceiling. The candle Caroline carried cast odd, bending shadows on the portraits and faded tapestries lining the staircase. Twice the uneven wooden stairs creaked beneath her boot, and each time Julia gripped the banister, uncomfortable as the stair gave slightly beneath her weight. She'd assumed her aunt would be satisfied with nothing less than marble halls and the finest furnishings, but while this hall was stately, it was far from the finery of the Lambournes' London home.

To her right, rain tapped and slid down the outside of the stair-stepped leaded windows. Surely by the light of day this would be an elegant and comfortable abode. Her nerves were just unsettled, but hopefully, within the hour she would be nestled in bed. Come the dawn, everything would surely seem brighter.

"What an ordeal you've had." Caroline squeezed her arm as they continued to climb higher. "Did a man really point a pistol at you?"

Julia nodded.

"How terrible!" Caroline tsked. "Goldweth is a lawless place, you'll find. I can't imagine why Father insists we remain."

Surprised, Julia slowed her steps. "I thought you were fond of it here."

Caroline tilted her head to the side, offered a weak smile, and then paused on the spacious landing. "We're on the first floor of the tower now. Mother and Father both have chambers on the ground floor below us. This floor is Jane's domain at present. Her sleeping chamber is to the left, and the lying-in chamber will be on the right when the baby arrives."

Julia sobered at the mention of her other cousin's name. "Is Jane asleep now?"

Caroline nodded. "She's always asleep by this time of evening."

"Is she very bad?"

Caroline lowered her voice. "She's been ill nearly every day since the beginning. It pains me to see her in this state, but what can be done? You will find her much changed, I think."

"There is naught her physician can do?"

"Mother has engaged one of the most highly respected accoucheurs in London, and he visits twice a month, but he says that some women are simply plagued with frail constitutions and are ill for the duration. He's tried bloodletting and every sort of remedy and concoction, but Jane can barely eat."

Julia's stomach tightened. She didn't like the thought of her bubbly, vivacious cousin unwell. "I have never really thought of Jane as having a frail constitution, have you? I do wish I could do something to help her."

Caroline gripped Julia's hand. "Your presence here will undoubtedly be the best medicine for her. And selfishly, for me as well, for I'm ever so glad you've arrived. It's been so dull around here with no company to speak of. Come now, our chambers are on the next floor, and I know you are ready to be settled."

Julia cast another glance toward the closed door, behind which Jane presumably slumbered.

Dear Jane.

After all, Julia's visit had been her cousin's idea. Jane had insisted there was nothing like a change of scenery to get one's mind off her troubles, and Julia hoped her cousin was right.

It was much easier to claim that she was coming to Lanwyn Manor to be a companion for her bedridden cousin than to reveal the truth.

They climbed another narrow flight of steep stairs. Once at the top Caroline swept out her arm and sighed. "Here we are—the second floor. The view is lovely from those windows over there, but the climb does grow tiresome."

Stepping up next to her cousin on the landing, Julia drank in the shadowed sight of the ornately carved chairs, unlit candle sconces, and heavy side table.

"That is my chamber there, and yours is on the left." Switching her candle to her other hand, Caroline opened the rounded door. "This is yours—the Tapestry Room."

Eager to see her new chamber, Julia followed. A gentle fire bubbled on the north wall. Opposite the door were two banks of three arched windows facing the west. A large walnut bed, curtained with heavy embroidered cream and light-green linen bed hangings, stood opposite the windows. A large carved wardrobe occupied the near wall, and a writing desk and three chairs with embroidered cushions filled the space near the fire. Her trunks had been placed at the foot of the bed. The most unique aspect of the chamber, however, were the tapestries hanging on the walls, covering nearly all the oak paneling.

"Will it do?" Caroline leaned against the threshold.

"Of course. It's perfect." Julia ran her fingers down the tapestry on the wall next to her. "My, there are a lot of tapestries in this house."

Caroline laughed. "Some of them are hundreds of years old, or so I'm told. This house is full of antiquities. Father wants nothing changed, much to Mother's chagrin." She stepped in farther and used her candle to light a few others around the room. "I'm so eager to hear your news, but I'll leave you to get settled, and then tomorrow we can have a long chat. I'll send up the maid to help you."

After kissing Julia on the cheek, Caroline quit the chamber, and Julia waited for the sound of her footsteps to vanish into nocturnal stillness. Exhausted, she exhaled and sank onto the high-backed chair by the fire. Her mind felt sluggish and cried for solace.

She stared up at the portrait of a stern woman with an exquisite black coiffure and an elegant blue dress from a bygone era above the mantel. A forlorn expression marked the woman's thin face and tightly drawn mouth.

How sad to be frozen for eternity with such a melancholy expression.

Julia swept her gaze to the left. Again, she was struck by the darkness of the room. It was night, of course, but the room itself, the colors, the heavy furniture, nearly blended into the shadows. She was used to her bright, airy room at Penwythe Hall, with its white curtains and vibrant views of lush gardens and delicious sea breezes.

The thought of home tugged at her.

Tears welled and she sniffed them away.

She would not give in to weakness. After all, this was what she had wanted—a new beginning. A fresh start. A new environment where every nook and cranny did not remind her of *him*.

Julia stood and pulled the thick woven drapes closed over the leaded windows. Tomorrow she'd be able to see the view that would greet her every morning, but for now, she would only be as happy as she made up her mind to be. She determined to put the day's events behind her and start new at dawn.

———◆———

By the time Julia awoke the following day, crisp autumn sunlight slid around the edges of the drapes. By its brightness she could only imagine she'd slept quite late.

After brushing her hair away from her face, she indulged in a yawn and stretched her arms over her head, extending her tight muscles. But as the memory of the previous night's events besieged her, she stopped midstretch.

The tiresome journey.

The ghastly incident at the inn.

The man shielding her from the pistol's fire.

The tension amidst her arrival at the manor.

She squeezed her eyes shut, as if to block out the gravity of it all.

She was safe now . . . comfortably tucked within the ancient guarded tower of Lanwyn Manor.

She opened her eyes and blinked. The chamber did not appear much different by daylight. The tapestries were more vibrant, more intricate than she'd first thought. Thick, delicately carved beams crossed the plastered ceiling, forming grids in the square chamber. The portrait of the woman in blue captured her attention again, and

Julia stiffened. She didn't like the feeling of the woman—whoever she was—watching her.

With a sniff she shook the blankets from her legs, stepped down the two steps that led to the tall bed, and shook out the folds of her white flannel nightdress. The planked pine floor felt cold against her stockinged feet, and she padded toward the closest bank of windows. She pulled back the faded velvet curtain, and her breath caught.

The view from this height was breathtaking. A broad lawn stretched out, a dormant shade of brownish-green, and a smattering of outbuildings, made of the same slate stone as the gatehouse, dotted the grounds. A gray drystone fence bordered the lawn's far edge, and beyond that a leafless tree line shivered in the gusty wind. Thick, silvery clouds churned and blotted out any trace of blue sky.

Her heart jumped at the sight. Already, she could imagine herself exploring the nuances of this expansive countryside, wild and new, with the bright Cornish breeze on her face and in her hair. She'd ask her aunt for permission to take a horse out riding, as was her morning habit at Penwythe Hall, for surely they had a spirited mare they could spare for her.

Julia turned back around. Someone had been in her chamber while she slept. The fire beneath the portrait had been tended recently, for it popped and danced, a lively contrast to the stillness of the room, and her pink wool gown, which the maid had unpacked the previous evening, now hung tidily in the wardrobe.

Footsteps followed by muffled voices echoed from the corridor and then disappeared.

At the sound, fresh excitement flooded her senses as the reason for her visit rushed to the forefront of her thoughts.

She'd almost forgotten. Jane.

Whereas Caroline would write Julia once a month at best, Jane wrote weekly without fail and had since they were children. Such steady communication cultivated a strong bond, and Julia considered Jane one of her dearest friends.

Julia reached for her heavy wrapper of pale-blue cotton at the foot of her bed, pushed her arms through the sleeves, cinched it tight at her waist, smoothed her hair from her face, and opened her door.

All was quiet on the landing. A generous mullioned window provided ample light, and a heavy oak cupboard displaying blue-and-white dishes along with two delicately carved chairs filled the landing. Opposite her, Caroline's chamber door was closed. Whoever had made the noises she'd heard moments ago was no longer here. Not wanting to draw any attention, she tiptoed her way to the narrow staircase and descended one level.

The layout of the first-floor landing and chambers was identical to the one above it, only instead of a cupboard, a table stood in the center of the landing, and instead of tapestries, rich, dark wood panels lined the wall.

She tiptoed over to Jane's bedchamber and tapped her knuckles on the door.

A soft voice called from within. "Come in."

Julia pushed open the door. There, abed, was Jane. Her appearance shocked Julia. Jane's gray eyes were far from vibrant, and shadows darkened the skin beneath her lower lashes. Her wan cheeks were slightly sunken, and her blonde hair was pulled back in a tight, low plait.

As their gazes met, Jane's eyes widened and a smile lit her face. "You're here at last!"

Julia pushed her shock to the back of her mind, closed the door behind her, and hurried toward the bed, accepting Jane's outstretched hands in her own before she leaned in to kiss her cousin's cheek.

"I've barely been able to remain still since I woke." Jane struggled to sit up straighter, and pink bloomed on her round face. "My maid told me what happened at the inn last night. Oh, Julia! How did you ever manage?"

"'Twas a blur, really." Julia sat on the bed next to Jane, determined not to distress her with details. "But I'm well, you see."

"If it were me, I should have fainted dead away, yet from what I hear, you were quite brave."

"I am not sure I'd call it brave exactly." Julia shrugged, her mind flashing back to how she screamed and fell to the floor at the sound of the pistol's fire.

"Well, that's what my maid said. Talk of it is all over the village, and she says it's all anyone can speak of downstairs."

"It is a sad thing to be known for." Julia drew a sharp breath. "But enough of me, I want to hear all about you. You look radiant."

"You are kind, but I very much doubt that." Jane smoothed a wisp of golden hair away from her face. "In truth, I must look quite different to you."

"The last time I saw you was your wedding day, remember?"

Jane gave a little laugh. "I do. Oh, but that seems like a lifetime ago. Can it really have been more than two years since I became Mrs. Jonathan Townsend? And now look at me." She placed a protective hand over her midsection.

Julia let her shoulders fall. There was no need for pretense with Jane. Her gaze fell to the basin next to the bed and then to the small collection of vials and powders on the table next to her bed. "Tell me, Cousin. How are you really?"

Jane flipped her long braid over her shoulder. "This season in life is much different—and more difficult—than I'd anticipated. I remind myself that this malaise is not permanent, and in about three months I'll have my precious child in my arms. And one day Jonathan will be home. Until then I am in a perpetual state of waiting. The hours do grow long being so confined, and I'm so grateful you are here. But I fear you'll grow quite weary. There's little distraction here at Lanwyn Manor."

Julia placed her hand over Jane's. "I'm here because I want to be here, and I shall keep you company until I wear out my welcome."

"That's not possible." Jane shook her head. "I must say I never dreamed that my husband would be serving in India and I would be living in my mother's home when I became with child."

"You said yourself that Jonathan will not be away forever." Julia tilted her head to the side. "Have you any idea of when he'll return?"

"None. His letters are few and far between." Jane reached to the bedside table and lifted a small framed portrait of her husband. She rubbed her thumb over the smooth glass overlay and then squeezed it in her hand. "Some days it seems he'll never return."

The sadness in her cousin's eyes tore at Julia. How vividly she could recall Jane's excitement at her upcoming marriage to the handsome soldier. She'd known at the time of her marriage that Jonathan's regiment was bound for India, but the reality of time and circumstance had taken its toll. Now a cloak of melancholy seemed to have settled over her countenance.

But then with sudden, perhaps forced, energy, Jane returned the portrait to the table, folded her hands atop the coverlet, and lowered her voice to little more than a hissed whisper. "I was sorry to read about your disappointment."

Julia straightened at the mention, as if stung.

The entire morning had passed, and she hadn't thought about *him* once.

Disappointment.

Her heart felt as if it would burst at the mere thought. How could one single word capture the sting of betrayal, the burn of humiliation, and the pang of regret?

No, the constant ache living within her chest was more complex, deeper than a few syllables. What had started as a secret attraction and stolen moments had ballooned to something unexpected and wonderful, and before she knew it, Julia found herself inexplicably in love. Then she was as shocked as anyone when he announced his engagement to another.

Despite her discomfort with the topic, it was right of Jane to inquire so bluntly. She'd been the one person Julia had shared all her thoughts and hopes with, chronicling them in her letters. She had shared the entire whirlwind journey, from the exciting beginning to the painful end.

"It wasn't meant to be," Jane continued, "and that means another gentleman will be the one to win your hand."

Julia squared her shoulders and forced a smile, her determination fueled by the pity in Jane's gray eyes. "There is absolutely nothing about which to be sorry. It was a girlhood fancy. And I daresay I've learned my lesson about letting my heart go before my head."

A wistful expression shadowed Jane's face. "Oh, you've so much ahead of you. I envy you. I do."

"How can you say that?" Julia shook her head at the odd statement. "You'll meet your dear child in mere months. I should think that more exciting than anything that could come my way."

Jane gripped Julia's hand. "It is, but think of what lies before you. You *will* fall in love again. Marry. You are still at the beginning of your journey. Even if your heart still aches at the thought of Percy, which I suspect it does, it will heal and fall anew. I only hope it happens while you're here at Lanwyn Manor so I may witness it all."

"I did not come here in search of a husband, Jane." Julia forced a laugh, hoping it would cover her lie.

Of course she was in search of a husband.

Every single lady of marriageable age was eager for security.

It was the ultimate goal, whether she chose to acknowledge it or not. "Indeed, I came with the notion of visiting my cousin and nothing more."

"Oh, Julia, you needn't pretend with me. Every woman wants to be married; there is no shame in that, and my mother's favorite hobby in the world is making matches. Now that all her daughters are either married or engaged, she will turn her attention to you. If a desirable beau exists within ten miles, she'll find him."

Julia wanted to receive the words of encouragement as intended, but at the idea of a beau, that familiar ache tightened her chest—the longing. The loss. The thought of embarking on another such journey filled her with trepidation.

Julia lowered her voice. "I wish it were already done. I wish I already had a husband and the entire ordeal was behind me."

"La, Cousin, that's naught but heartbreak talking, and nothing more. When the time comes, and it *will*, do not wish it speed. Enjoy it. Savor it, for time goes by so quickly, and soon, I daresay, you'll be in my situation with a child on the way."

Wishing to change the topic, Julia stood and crossed the room to the windows. This chamber was not nearly as dark as hers. The white plaster walls were almost cheery, and the flooding sunlight gave the illusion of warmth. She assessed the grounds below. Despite the airy brightness inside, a gray coldness covered the landscape. The wind's bitter fingers had whisked away all the leaves, collected them in the garden's corners, and assembled them at the base of the winding, low stone walls. Even now, the remaining leaves tossed and tumbled in harsh wind and flitted over the lane. Beyond the stone fence a redbrick tower stretched into the sky.

"What's that tower?" Julia asked, curious about the unique structure disrupting the pastoral landscape.

"That's the engine house for Bal Tressa, Father's mine. It has been closed for a few months now."

"I thought the mine was his main interest here." Julia turned from the window.

Jane huffed. "I thought so too, but no, it sits idle. The entire situation vexes Mother to no end, as I'm sure you can imagine. Father claims he's quite close to reopening it, so we shall see, but Mother longs for London. She's not meant for country life, and neither, consequently, is Caroline."

A maid entered the chamber and curtsied. "Pardon the interruption. Miss Twethewey, Mrs. Lambourne sent me to see if you were awake. Some visitors are here for you in the drawing room."

"Who has come, Evangeline?" Jane angled her head toward the door.

"Miss Prynne and Miss Trebell."

Jane chuckled and looked back to Julia. "Oh dear, I fear you are in for quite a treat."

"Shall I accompany you to your chamber and help you dress, miss?"

Julia nodded at the towheaded maid, smoothed the front of her wrapper, and faced Jane. "I suppose I should go."

"By all means. I'll not have you keep them waiting on my account."

Julia turned to go, but her cousin's words stopped her in her tracks.

"Oh, and Julia?" A playful twinkle glimmered in her eye. "Good luck."

CHAPTER 6

Julia dismissed Evangeline for a few moments of solitude to finish preparations to meet her new neighbors.

The previous day had been a blur, but today was the beginning of a new chapter—one Julia was fully ready to embrace, and meeting local residents was an excellent first step.

Once she was content with the tidy style of her hair and the fit of her pale-pink wool gown, Julia opened the door and stepped into the darkened corridor. Now that her mind was fresh and her body rested, a revived sense of adventure overcame her.

She placed a hand on the railing and descended several flights of stairs, and before long she found herself at the entrance to the great hall. Whereas most of the ceilings she'd encountered in the home were low, this room's was vaulted at least two stories, supported by great arched, timbered beams. The heavy paneling ascended a quarter of the way up the wall, and in sharp contrast, bright-white plasterwork and painted stone reached the rest of the way. Massive windows of stained glass cast a red, green, and blue glow over the smooth stone floor, and tarnished weapons and mounted hunting trophies adorned the walls, along with crossed rapiers and a tattered banner boasting a family crest.

"Good day, Miss Twethewey."

Julia, who'd become lost in her musings, jumped. She whirled to behold a slight elderly woman, clad entirely in black muslin, standing in a shadowed corridor just off the great hall. The woman, with her pinched lips and high cheekbones, appeared a rather frail sight, and her expression was as tight as the ebony fichu around her neck.

"Oh," Julia stammered, searching for words. "I wasn't aware anyone was in here."

The woman tilted her chin high and clasped her bony hands before her, appearing as confident as Julia felt uncomfortable. As she approached Julia, her austere gaze swept over her from head to toe, the scrutiny of which tempted Julia to smooth her gown. "I am Mrs. Sedrick, the housekeeper here at Lanwyn Manor. You appear to be searching for something."

Surprised by the unexpected raspy tone of the housekeeper's voice, Julia straightened. "So I am. My aunt wishes me to join her in the drawing room, but I'm not entirely sure where that is."

Nearly before Julia finished her statement, Mrs. Sedrick turned and stepped toward the pointed stone archway leading down a corridor Julia had not noticed before. "Follow me, Miss Twethewey."

Wordlessly, Julia followed the housekeeper through the low doorway and down a labyrinth of narrow stone halls and tight turns. She studied each passageway and deep-set window as she passed through, equal parts curious and determined not to find herself lost again, until muted feminine voices traveled out an open door.

Mrs. Sedrick stepped inside first and announced her, and Julia followed.

The brightness of the room was a pleasant surprise, with two large bay windows overlooking a great lawn. The plaster walls were painted a pale green, and a light-blue woven rug covered the flagstone floor, lending a great deal of color to the chamber. Atop it sat a settee, table, and two chairs.

"Julia, dear!" Aunt Beatrice exclaimed as Julia stepped through the doorway. "My, but you did sleep late."

Julia approached her and bent to kiss her cheek. "Good morning, Aunt."

Already, her aunt was as Julia remembered. Dressed in an elegant gown of iridescent indigo silk, not a hair out of place nor a ruffle errant. A glimmering crimson jewel hung about her neck, wildly audacious for the hour, and a small gray dog nestled on her lap. The anger she'd exhibited toward her husband the previous evening was absent, and instead, a placid expression dominated.

Julia shifted her attention to the two more simply clad ladies seated across from her aunt.

"As you can see, you already have visitors." Aunt Beatrice nodded to each one by name. "Miss Trebell and Miss Prynne have called to make you feel welcome in Goldweth. Ladies, may I present my niece, Miss Julia Twethewey, recently arrived from Penwythe Hall."

Julia began to curtsey, but before she could complete the act, the smaller of the guests—Miss Prynne—stood, approached Julia, and gripped her hands in her own knobby ones. With pale-green eyes sharp and unwavering, the wisp of a woman tightened her grip. "We've heard about your ordeal at the Gray Owl Inn and have come straightaway to inquire after you. Such a horrible introduction to our humble village. It's an abomination!"

"I thank you for your concern, but I'm well."

"Oh, I very much doubt that! You were physically assaulted! We're not disorderly people here, Miss Twethewey. Far from it, and yet I fear your experience will leave you uneasy."

"Truthfully, Miss Prynne, I'm quite comfortable and secure in my aunt and uncle's care." Julia moved past the women and sat on a low settee opposite her aunt.

Aunt Beatrice lifted her face and stroked the small dog's head.

"Rest assured, ladies, my husband has vowed to leave no stone unturned until the rogues are identified and held accountable for their actions."

Miss Prynne, in turn, regained her seat and the other, much more robust lady leaned forward, her faded curls bouncing with the motion. "And is it true? I heard that Mr. Isaac Blake came to your rescue."

At the mention of the name, the patchy memory of the man formed—her relief when someone stepped up to aid her. Her shock and gratitude as he shielded her with his body when the lead balls flew from the rifle. The sight of his broad shoulders as he raced to the door after she was safe. "Yes, Mr. Blake. I believe that was his name. It all happened rather quickly. I didn't have the opportunity to thank him for his assistance."

"For better or for worse, you'll not have to wait long to see him again." Aunt Beatrice fussed with the lacy fichu at her décolletage as annoyance furrowed her brow. "He is to dine here, along with others, this very evening per my husband's invitation. I have told my William that you're not strong enough for such company, but he insists. The dinner has been planned for some time, and he refuses to set another date."

Julia straightened and tried not to appear too eager. She loved company, and the thought of meeting new people appealed to her, especially the man who risked his safety for her. Jane was right. She needed to accept the idea that there was life beyond her disappointment with Percy. "I think a dinner sounds lovely."

"Well, if this dinner has any consolation, it is that Mr. Matthew Blake will be in attendance. You will find him to be much more suitable company than his twin brother."

"Oh, how can you say that?" Miss Trebell's pudgy hand flew to her chest, disrupting the modest lace trim adorning her tan gown's high neckline. "Mr. Isaac Blake is the best of men. One of the finest in our community, I'd venture to say. In fact, he gifted an entire basket of apples to the miners' children at harvest's end. Is that not a kind gesture? He told me he wished to remain an anonymous benefactor, but of course I could never honor that request."

Aunt Beatrice ignored Miss Trebell's words and turned her full attention to Julia. "Mr. Matthew Blake is quite accomplished. He owns Tregarthan Hall, which borders us to the north, not to mention Wheal Tamsen, a copper mine on the village's edge. He's the head of one of the finest families in the county. And he is unmarried."

Julia's jaw slackened at the openness with which her aunt addressed the topic.

The older ladies exchanged knowing glances.

"Do not look shocked, my dear." Aunt Beatrice placed her hand on Julia's arm, her light-blue eyes twinkling. "'Tis no secret. I'll not rest until I see you happily settled, and your dear sisters when they come of age. We shan't pretend otherwise, especially amongst friends. Your uncle Jac might be your legal guardian, but I've a much better eye when it comes to matters of the heart, and I owe it to your dear mother's memory to see that you're advantageously matched."

The directness of the guests' scrutiny pressed against her, forcing an awkward laugh to bubble up. "Aunt, I've only just arrived. Surely such talk can wait for another time."

"A young woman should always be on the lookout for a husband," Miss Trebell interjected with a firm nod, her expression quite somber. "Once an opportunity is gone, one never knows when another might come. Why, just look at Miss Prynne and me. Had we taken advantage of offers when we were your age, how different might our situations be."

Julia shifted self-consciously. She'd only just met them, and already they spoke of such personal topics.

"You're frightening the dear child, Miss Trebell," Miss Prynne teased. "If we cannot look truth in the face at our age, then what hope have we? Miss Trebell and I are spinsters. La, what a dreadful word! 'Tis not covetable, I'll admit, but it's a truth as sure as we're sitting here. So, let us be an example to you. Marry early. Marry young. Better to have such security than to lose all hope."

"Do not be so pessimistic, Miss Prynne." Miss Trebell tapped her friend's arm. "Miss Twethewey is as lovely as her cousins ever were. I've no doubt you will have a line of suitors, if you've not already."

Julia's stomach soured at the reference. What would they think if they knew one of the reasons she came to Lanwyn Manor was to recover from just that?

Aunt Beatrice pivoted to face her. "You've a duty, Julia, just as all young women do. A duty to marry well. You owe it to those who raised you, those who poured countless hours into providing for you and keeping you safe. By marrying well, you take the burden of your care from them. Your uncle Jac is a noble man, but his talent did not lie in amassing wealth. Oh no. So your dowry must be bolstered, and your uncle William and I will help with that."

For the first time in a very long while, Julia felt dumbstruck. Never had someone spoken so bluntly to her about such a personal topic, let alone in front of strangers.

Miss Prynne leaned toward Aunt Beatrice. "We do not mean to monopolize Miss Twethewey's time, but while we are here we must inquire as to whether or not you and your daughter intend to join us for the Ladies League this week? And Miss Twethewey, of course."

Aunt Beatrice's back stiffened, and she stroked her fingers against the dog's furry head.

Confused by the sudden change in her aunt's demeanor, Julia leaned closer. "If I may ask, what is the Ladies League?"

"Several ladies gather once a week to sew mittens and blankets for the miners and their children," explained Miss Prynne. "With winter at our doorstep, we must work quickly. We have so much, and the miners have so little, especially in the current landscape. Even the women in mining families work at the mine, and there is little time for such things."

"Women work at the mines?" Julia frowned. "I would have assumed that was a man's occupation."

"Yes, they're called bal maidens. The men bring the ore to the surface, and then the women break it up with hammers and the like. 'Tis long, hard work, and many of them are forced to leave their children at home in the care of other children for hours on end. It's really quite shocking."

"And we've ever so many poor, especially now with Bal Tressa closed." Miss Trebell shook her head. "The poor children."

Julia flicked her gaze to her aunt. It was the second time this day she'd heard of Bal Tressa's closure.

Aunt Beatrice pursed her thin lips and tilted her graying head to the side. "I care for the poor as much as anyone, but my eyesight can no longer endure the tedious attention of needle and thread. Julia, you may of course attend, if you wish."

Julia hesitated as all eyes turned to her. Her aunt's words said one thing, but her pinched brows and grimace communicated otherwise. It would be rude to decline after such freely given permission. Besides, she could not deny her growing eagerness to explore beyond Lanwyn Manor's walls. "Thank you. I shall be there."

After a fluster of polite farewells and much fuss over donning thick wool pelisses and voluminous bonnets, Julia found herself alone in the drawing room with her aunt.

Aunt Beatrice sat down again and adjusted the tiny dog on her lap. "I'm sorry, dear, to bombard you with guests on your first morning here. Miss Trebell and Miss Prynne are delightful ladies, but they often overlook basic social etiquette. They happened to arrive as I was passing in the hall, and they could not be put off."

"I like them," Julia announced as she returned to the sofa. "They are not afraid to speak their minds, are they?"

Aunt arranged her gown around her. "Regardless, they are pillars of Goldweth and have been here as long as anyone, from what I've been told. In fact, they're said to have been very thick with Mr. Rowe, my husband's late uncle, when he was master at Lanwyn Manor. Sometimes I think they believe their opinions hold as much merit here as when Mr. Rowe was alive, but they're harmless. I'll devise an excuse for you if you should change your mind. They've the uncanny tendency to coerce one into an activity before you truly know you've accepted."

Without waiting for a response, her aunt glanced at the small watch pinned to her bodice. "Are you certain you are ready to attend a dinner this evening? I fear you will overtire yourself, especially after yesterday."

"Of course." Julia's firsthand knowledge of Mr. Isaac Blake coupled with Miss Trebell's accolades made her curious to see him again. She could not resist confirming. "You said Mr. Blake will be among the guests?"

"Yes, but . . ." Her aunt hesitated and her voice dropped in tone. "Dear, I must caution you about the younger Mr. Blake. Miss Prynne and Miss Trebell may sing his praises, but he's simply not the sort of man a lady would associate with."

"I only intend to thank him for his assistance, Aunt."

"I'm sure that's understood. I—"

The housekeeper's appearance in the doorway curtailed her aunt's words.

"Ah, Mrs. Sedrick," Aunt Beatrice boomed. "Julia, I must tell you that Mrs. Sedrick has been an absolute necessity to me as we have relocated here. She's been a member of the Lanwyn Manor staff for decades and has been instrumental in helping us become acquainted with the area."

"You are too kind, Mrs. Lambourne." Mrs. Sedrick smiled stiffly before she shifted her gaze to Julia and back to her mistress. "And I am sorry to disrupt you, but there is a matter of great delicacy that must be discussed with you. Privately, if possible."

Aunt Beatrice frowned. "I can't imagine there's anything that cannot be said in front of Julia."

Mrs. Sedrick interlaced her long, bony fingers in front of her. "It seems there is a problem with some of the silver."

"A problem?" Aunt Beatrice smirked, jostling the dog that had just fallen asleep. "What could possibly be wrong with the silver?"

"Several pieces are missing. The teapot and some of the serving dishes."

"Good gracious." Aunt Beatrice's hand flew to her ample chest as concern replaced her previous sarcasm. "What do you think has happened to them?"

Mrs. Sedrick's jaw twitched. "I can't rightly answer that, Mrs. Lambourne, but I do know that in all my years here at Lanwyn Manor, we've not had items of such value go missing before. And it concerns me greatly. I'm concerned foul play may be afoot."

The apples of Aunt Beatrice's cheeks flamed, and she jerked in her seat, disrupting the slumbering dog. "Foul play? Are you referencing thievery? In our own home? I knew something was amiss. I knew it! And considering how horribly Julia was treated just yesterday, I cannot bear it. I warned my husband about this from the moment I set foot in this place. I sensed perfidy immediately."

Julia reached to take the dog from her aunt before it fell from her lap. "I'm sure it's only been misplaced. It will appear, I'm sure of it."

"I very much doubt that." Mrs. Sedrick cocked her head to the side. "That particular set of silver has been kept under lock and key, and the only key is in my possession."

"Mr. Lambourne must be informed the moment he returns."

Aunt Beatrice stood, and her full cheeks shook with every syllable. "And in the meantime, question the staff about it. Even the out-of-doors staff. I will not have a thief in my home. Oh, how I shudder at the thought."

With a nod and a glance toward Julia, Mrs. Sedrick curtsied and withdrew from the room.

Once the door closed, Julia stood and wrapped her arm through her aunt's. "Do not worry, Aunt. Please."

"You don't understand. This place, Julia." Aunt Beatrice freed her arm from Julia's and paced the rug. "This vile, decrepit house and its secrets! Everyone, with the exception of Mrs. Sedrick, stares at us with sly eyes, as if hiding something. Watching us. 'Tis a prison."

Taken aback but not altogether surprised by her aunt's outburst, Julia moved to pick up Oscar again and cradled him in her arms. Unsure of what else to say, she thought it best to remain silent until she knew more.

Yes, Lanwyn Manor was proving to have introduced her to a number of interesting characters, but she needed to be wary. It was still too early to know whom she could trust and whom she could not. As she had learned, placing trust in the wrong person could only lead to heartache.

CHAPTER 7

The early afternoon following the odd encounter at the Gray Owl Inn, Isaac sat in Wheal Tamsen's counting house with the mine's monthly ledger spread before him. He rubbed the back of his neck and leaned back in the creaky wooden chair.

Normally, Wheal Tamsen's counting house was a busy place, with people bustling in and out. Despite the constant whir of the pump from the engine house, the unmistakable ping of hammer against rock, and the occasional call from one worker to another, all was relatively silent.

The colorless sunlight, fleeting as it was, streaked in through the counting house's dirty west windows, illuminating the ever-present smoke and dust motes dancing in the air. He forced his attention back to the ledger in front of him, but racing thoughts and unanswered questions made his concentration unsteady.

Last night, a man had pointed a pistol at him.

What was worse, that man had also pointed a pistol at a woman whose crime was nothing more than being a relation to William Lambourne.

Was this what it had come to?

Unrest had been increasing for years, but when Mr. Rowe had died and his nephew Lambourne inherited his mine and then closed its doors months later, tensions mounted to an unprecedented state.

Lambourne claimed he'd reopen the mine quickly, but weeks spread into months, and the mine remained closed with little hope of opening anytime soon.

And the men who depended on the mines for their living were growing restless.

Isaac thought of the small woman from the inn. It hadn't been hard to figure out who she was, even before Carew confirmed her identity. Visitors were rare in Goldweth—especially ladies—and word had spread far and wide of Lambourne's niece's impending visit. With the exception of the fearful expression in her blue eyes and a mass of wild, dark curls, he hadn't really gotten a good look at her, and yet the vision of her, fearful and small, stuck with him. After the ordeal, though, he wouldn't be surprised to hear that she'd packed her things and left Goldweth without so much as a backward glance.

Approaching voices jarred his attention, and the counting house door creaked on its iron hinges and flung inward. The brisk air swooshed in from behind his brother's tall frame, disrupting the paper map hanging on the wall and causing the candles' flames to waver.

Isaac pressed his hand atop the paper to prevent it from blowing from its spot. "Where've you been? I was up at Tregarthan this morning and your butler said you were gone on business."

Matthew swept his beaver hat from his head and plopped it on the table inside the door, shook off his dark-brown caped coat, and raked his fingers through his pale hair. "Rode out to Falmouth yesterday to talk with Tom Sand."

"Tom Sand?" Isaac returned his quill to the inkwell. "What business did you have with him?"

Matthew stepped farther into the room to the sideboard, uncorked the glass decanter, and poured the amber liquid into a glass. "He's looking to take on investors for Wheal Hedra."

"The tin mine?"

"One and the same. Can't afford to keep it open much longer on his own, or so he says." Matthew drank the beverage, returned the empty glass to the cupboard, stepped to the broad fireplace, and extended his hands toward the heat. "Can't say I'm surprised. Haven't had a good pull from there in quite some time, and with tin prices being what they are . . ."

Isaac gave his head a sharp shake and stacked the papers in front of him. It was what every mine owner feared. "I suppose it was bound to happen sooner or later."

"We could be in the same situation if we aren't careful." Matthew leaned against Isaac's desk and crossed one leg over the other, his mouth curving in a lopsided grin. "Speaking of being careful, I heard you were quite the hero last night, stepping in to save the damsel in distress."

"Hardly," Isaac scoffed. "I offered a diversion tactic for Carew. Nothing more."

"Did you recognize the men?"

Isaac shook his head. "They all had kerchiefs tied about their faces. Heard a rumor this morning that Gaines and his men might have been behind it, but I can't be sure. None of them looked familiar, but you know how these men operate."

Matthew stepped away from the fire and pulled his snuffbox from his pocket. "I also heard that Lambourne was conveniently absent. That true? He left his niece alone in that inn?"

Isaac shrugged. "I didn't see him. Heard he left her there while he paid a call to Rogers, his solicitor."

Matthew clicked his tongue as he popped open the snuffbox. "Not true."

"What do you mean?"

"I've got it on good authority that he was speaking with Marcus Elliot, not Rogers like he claimed."

"Elliot." Isaac leaned with his elbows on the desk as he searched his memory. "Isn't he the miner from over near Falmouth?"

"One and the same. He was passing through Goldweth specifically to speak with Lambourne, and yesterday was the only day they could meet. Apparently they were discussing the possibility of Elliot buying Bal Tressa outright."

Isaac stood and crossed over to stand next to his brother near the mantel. "Well then, I don't see the harm in that. As long as he is a fair man, it would at the very least get our men back to work."

"Not necessarily. Apparently he has mining men—tutworkers, tributers, even carpenters and surface workers—that he'd bring with him. It could bring an entirely new problem to Goldweth and the surrounding villages." Matthew pinched the black snuff between his fingers and extended the box toward Isaac as an offering.

Isaac waved his hand in refusal and considered what he had just been told.

Matthew was right.

At least now there was the hope of reopening Bal Tressa. If someone else came in with their own workers, not only would the price of copper go down, but many would not have the hope of employment.

Matthew held the snuff to his nose, inhaled deeply, and returned the snuffbox to his pocket. "The worst thing that could happen is for Lambourne to sell it to an outsider like that. It's more important than ever that we convince him to lease the land to us."

Isaac nodded.

His brother had spoken often of trying to persuade William Lambourne and reopen the closed mine, but every other adventurer and mine owner for miles around was trying to do the same thing. No one could afford to buy it outright, and at least if one of the local adventurers were running it, there could be collaboration.

"And the lady?" Matthew inquired. "Lambourne's niece?"

"What of her?"

Matthew raised his brows. "She might actually be the key to our success."

Isaac moved to stoke the waning fire. "What makes you think a relative of Lambourne would have any interest in assisting us?"

"Think on it. You've done a service for Lambourne, have you not?"

"I'd hardly call it a service."

"What else would you call it?" Matthew rubbed his palms together, like a man hatching a great scheme. "Listen to me. Bal Tressa sits empty. Lambourne hasn't the first idea what to do with it, so we must convince him not to sell it to this Elliot fellow, but to allow local adventurers, hopefully us, onto the property. It's money ripe for the picking. Everyone knows the copper's there, but Lambourne fears being taken advantage of. We've been looking for the perfect way to get on old Lambourne's good side, to gain his trust, to separate us from the other adventurers wishing to do the same. And now that you've offered his niece protection, the scales might be tipped in our favor. Well done, Brother."

Isaac scoffed and returned to his chair and straightened the ledger. "Always the opportunist."

"We need more money coming in, as you well know. Like everyone else, our dividends here have slowed. Unless we want to end up like old Sand, polling others for money, we need a plan of some sort, and I can think of none better. Things are progressing nicely enough here. We could spend time away to establish processes. Then, not only would we have additional revenue coming in, but the locals would be back at work."

"That also could mean more copper for sale, which would deflate prices."

"So tell me about this niece of his." Matthew ignored Isaac's comment, snatched the ledger Isaac had been reviewing, and closed it. "Is she pretty?"

Isaac pushed his chair away from the table and stood to his full height, which was only slightly taller than Matthew. "The man had a pistol pointed in her direction and then at me. Assessing her charms was hardly my top priority."

"Ah, doesn't matter. You saved his niece. The way I see it, he's in our debt. Well, at least *your* debt. We'll use it to our advantage."

Isaac huffed, took the ledger book from Matthew, and returned it to the desk drawer. "That's a terrible idea."

"Terrible? Why?"

"Because those men were angry enough at Lambourne to point a pistol at an innocent woman. I can't help but wonder whether, given enough time, they would have fired it. We don't want to get involved. Not in that. We've enough trouble on our hands keeping our own employed and money in our own pockets."

"No need to be so fatalistic," Matthew exclaimed, his expression injured as he straightened his waistcoat. "Besides, I fancy a challenge. I'm sure I could sway her."

"Sway her?" Isaac raised a brow. "I suppose she will just throw herself at you, will she? Why? What have you to recommend yourself?"

His brother chuckled and waved a finger in the air. "A great deal. Don't I? I'm young. Own an estate, and I own this mine."

"A mine whose business rises and falls at the whims of the metals buried beneath the surface. It's hardly a steady income. Perhaps in our father's time it was, but not now. And what of Miss Davies?"

"Miss Davies?" Matthew's smile faded ever so subtly at the mention of the brunette beauty. "She's naught but sport."

"I daresay she, not to mention her papa, would disagree."

"I'm not a married man, Isaac. Egad, I'm not even a betrothed man. What harm could come of a little innocent flirtation?"

"A great deal."

"Business alliances are forged all the time because of marriage relationships."

"Marriage?" Isaac reached for his hat and lifted his coat from the hook. "I'm afraid you're getting ahead of yourself."

"Need I remind you of how angry the miners are?" Matthew's lighthearted tone sobered. "Maybe after last night's events Lambourne will take things more seriously, and this could give us the foothold we need. I'll bring it up tonight at the dinner. Besides, aren't you the least bit curious about her?"

Isaac considered the frightened expression in her eyes. The feel of her in his arms as he shielded her. It had been an awkward, unusual encounter, and if it were up to him, he would walk away from the entire situation and leave it at that. But Matthew was right. The Lambourne mine was inactive, and there was copper beneath the ground—he knew it. Everyone did.

Matthew slapped a heavy hand on Isaac's shoulder. "You've already done your part, Brother, stepping in and saving the day. I'll oversee the matter from this point forward."

CHAPTER 8

In spite of her discomfort at the talk of marriage and suitors, Julia decided that she liked Miss Prynne and Miss Trebell.

They were opinionated and slightly overbearing, but this was what she wanted, was it not? Anything that would distract her from the heartbreak was favorable in her eyes.

And now she had a dinner to anticipate.

Eager to return to Jane after her conversation with the women, Julia followed Aunt Beatrice's directions to take another route to the family bedchambers in the tower. Instead of turning right out of the drawing room to go through the great hall, she exited, turned left, and continued down the broad corridor. To her left, windows set deep into walls of thick painted stone overlooked an overgrown, dormant garden. Benches and chairs lined the walkway, and beneath her slippers a faded carpet softened the stone floor. As her aunt had indicated, a narrow staircase appeared at the hall's end. She approached it, but then the sharp echo of masculine voices drew her attention and slowed her steps.

A door at the far end of the corridor, just before the stairs, was ajar.

"We believe it to be an isolated attack," said a muted yet distinguished voice. "Most likely personal."

"Personal?" Her uncle's guttural response seemed more of a growl, gritty and low. "What am I supposed to do? Fear that every time I or my family step from the house we might be accosted?"

"As I said, I believe it to be an isolated event intended to convey anger, not cause injury."

Uncle William huffed. "And how do you know that? A wild guess? Or perhaps you have information you're not sharing with me."

"You have been apprised of everything we know," said the unfamiliar male voice.

"I don't care if he intended to harm anyone or not. He threatened a member of my family. Justice must be served."

Julia stiffened. She did not need to see her uncle's face to know he was angry. It was the same tight, high voice he'd employed with the constable the previous evening. Curious, she glanced both ways down the corridor to ensure she was alone and leaned closer to the door.

At length the other man said, "You've not asked for my advice, but I'll share it nonetheless. You own the largest producing mine in the area—a mine that employed nearly half of the villagers. You closed it, leaving them no choice but to scatter far and wide to compete for work. They are hungry and growing desperate. I fear that attack at the inn might be the first of others that come to push you out. I can't do anything until they are caught in the act. My advice? Open the mine or consider returning your family to London."

"Bah! I will not be pushed into doing anything, especially by vagabonds intent upon tomfoolery and uproar."

"It's your decision, but I'd hate to see something happen. Perhaps you'd be more confident if you hired your own man to sort things right."

Hasty footsteps pounded toward her, and Julia withdrew behind a tapestry on the far side of the door. She held her breath and waited until the footsteps subsided before she poked her head around the tapestry's edge.

Quietude once again reined.

The stranger's words echoed in her head: *My advice? Open the mine or consider returning your family to London.*

Were the Lambournes in danger?

Was she in danger?

Julia stepped out from behind the tapestry, tiptoed toward the room the man had exited, and tapped her knuckles on the open door. All remained silent.

She nudged the door open and looked around the room that was undoubtedly her uncle's study. But he was nowhere to be seen.

"Uncle?"

Still no response.

Where had he gone?

Another assessment of the room confirmed that three doors led from this chamber. All of them closed. He must have departed through one of them.

With a sigh she withdrew back to the corridor and tried to forget what she'd heard.

She had hoped the attack the previous night had been a case of mistaken identity.

But perhaps it was not.

There would be plenty of time to learn more, and she intended to do just that.

———◆———

Later that evening as a purple dusk descended over Lanwyn Manor's frosty grounds, Julia sat at the dressing table in Caroline's chamber, examining her reflection in the gilded mirror. Satisfied, she lifted her hand, barely touching the curl that escaped the chignon at the base of her neck.

Her hair looked so elegant. She tilted her head right and then left, examining how her cousin's maid had woven the silver satin ribbon through her dark locks.

"Do you like the style?" Caroline inquired eagerly, nudging past her maid and tucking a wisp of hair beneath the ribbon.

"It's incredible. Truly lovely."

"Did I not tell you that Evangeline is the most accomplished hair-dresser? She knows all the latest styles from London, although I fear such talent might be lost here in Goldweth."

"I've never had my hair dressed before, not like this. My aunt Delia or sister always styled it."

"Well, I'm glad to have someone here who appreciates such things." Caroline dropped to the chair. "Jane is not interested in dressing hair at the moment, especially not confined to bed, and few other ladies in the area concern themselves with such finery."

Julia turned as Aunt Beatrice, clad in a fresh gown of gold bombazine with a dazzling ruby pendant at her neck, breezed through the doorway, a large wrapped parcel in her arms. A giddy smile toyed with her thin lips, and she lowered the box atop the bed and faced Julia. "What a surprise we have for you!"

"Oh, Aunt, that's not necessary." Julia stood from the table and dropped her gaze to the box. "You've already been so kind."

"No, no. None of that. You're a brightness to us during Jane's dark time, and the least we can do is offer you a favor in return."

With a ceremonious wave of her hand, Aunt Beatrice lifted the parcel's lid, unfolded the thin paper within, and removed a gown of pale blue.

Julia could only stare at the elegant billows. "A gown?"

Her aunt scurried toward her and held the gown's bodice up to

Julia's shoulders. "Jane selected the fabric. She thought the blue would accentuate your eyes. I wholeheartedly agree. Caroline and I worked with the seamstress on the cut."

Lace trim adorned the neckline, and tiny silver flowers were embroidered in the bodice. It really was beautiful, but new gowns were expensive, especially this lavish silk. Even at Penwythe Hall a completely brand-new gown was truly coveted, for they were always deconstructing existing gowns to reutilize the fabric, ribbon, and lace and altering them to fit the next sister.

But this one was perfection. And no doubt costly.

"It's lovely, Aunt, truly, but I cannot accept it."

"Nonsense. It has been such fun for us, has it not, Caroline, selecting every embellishment? I even wrote to your aunt Cordelia so we could make sure it would fit you exactly."

Her aunt's contagious excitement transferred to Julia. Pushing hesitation aside, she accepted the gown. "You are quite generous."

"And you will look exquisite in it, my dear." Aunt Beatrice clasped her hands before her and gazed at Julia with such pride, one might have thought the woman crafted the gown herself. "I see Evangeline has already seen to your hair, and she'll help you dress as well. We want you to present your finest to the guests and, of course, Mr. Matthew Blake."

Julia's spine stiffened at her aunt's comment. Her gaze fell to her own gown of pale-lavender muslin with ecru lace adorning the sleeves and hem. She'd always thought it pretty, but now it seemed inadequate. Perhaps this new gown was just that—a gift from her family to welcome her to their home. Perhaps it was a way to improve her country appearance, so they'd not be embarrassed to present her to Goldweth society.

Either way, her stomach churned and her heart raced. This was what she wanted, wasn't it? New people? New surroundings? A new situation?

Nay, it went beyond that.

She wanted to *be* someone different.

Before long, the gown had been donned over Julia's linen petticoat and chemise, and she turned to allow Evangeline to fasten the row of satin-covered buttons between her shoulder blades. After giving her approval on Julia's attire, Aunt Beatrice departed, taking Evangeline with her and leaving Caroline and Julia alone in the chamber.

Caroline, already clad in a gown of buttery satin, stepped behind Julia and beheld her image over Julia's shoulder. "Don't let Mother fluster you." Caroline smoothed the lace trim of Julia's gown at the base of her neck. "She is all bluster, as you well know. Now that I'm betrothed, I fear she's desperate for another young soul on whom to bestow her matchmaking talents. Unfortunately, that's you."

Julia smiled. Her visits to London had been few and far between, but even during those memorable visits, she could recall her aunt commanding attention and arranging those around her like toy soldiers. "Your mother does enjoy being in society."

"I hardly call the Goldweth residents *society.*" Caroline smirked and sank onto the bed. "There are times I still can't believe Father moved us here."

Julia turned. "You aren't happy at Lanwyn Manor?"

"Here? In the middle of nowhere?" Caroline huffed. "I'm counting down the days until I am married and my husband sweeps me off to London to set up a household of my own."

The harshness of her cousin's words sobered Julia. It was not the first time she had heard the Lambourne women voice their displeasure with Lanwyn Manor. She adjusted the small bead necklace around her throat. "Your mother doesn't seem very content here either."

"She tolerates it, for Father's sake." Caroline glimpsed her own reflection in the mirror and bit her lower lip for color.

"And your father?"

"Oh, you know how he is." Caroline waved a dismissive hand. "He's determined that his fortunes lie in those dirty mines. But he's away from Lanwyn most of the time, to London or Plymouth or some such place seeing to his other investments, and he doesn't endure the day-to-day trials of living in such a place."

Julia swallowed. Her uncle had been known for his risky ventures. She repeated what she'd overheard earlier that day, hoping to glean more information. "I thought that his mine had been closed."

"It is. When Father inherited the land, the mine was being run by a man who Father thought was cheating him. As the landowner he had the right to cancel the arrangement. I believe it was his intention to let the land to another miner to operate it, but as of yet he has made no arrangements."

"How long ago was that?"

"Six months or so." Caroline shrugged. "I think the truth is that mining is a much larger venture than he thought it would be. But let's not think on that now. Such dreary talk. Besides, you'll hear your fill of mine talk tonight with all the adventurers in one chamber. Father seems to think that if he surrounds himself with others, he will become like them."

Julia's brows drew together at the unusual term. "Adventurers?"

"Ah. Yes. From what I have learned, an adventurer is a miner who pays the landowner for the right to work his land, and then, in turn, the landowner receives a portion of the mine's earnings."

"Will there be any ladies in attendance?"

"Yes. Mrs. Davies and their daughter, Miss Eleanor Davies, will be here with Mr. Davies. And two of the other miners are married, but their children are grown now and will not be with them." Caroline patted her hair into place one last time. "Well, are you ready?"

Julia followed her cousin's lead and cast one last glance in the mirror, then pinched her cheeks for a blush. "I am as ready as I'll ever be."

CHAPTER 9

Isaac slowed his horse as he and Matthew approached Lanwyn Manor's arched gatehouse entrance. Already, carriages were arriving for the evening's event.

Thick clouds blotted out any trace of the moon. Despite the intermittent drops of rain, torches lined the circular drive before the gatehouse, casting their vibrant orange glow on the activity. Footmen in fine livery assisted guests from their vehicles, and stable hands directed carriages and assisted the men who had arrived via horseback.

After handing their horses to the stable hands, Isaac and his brother stepped through the gatehouse arch and into the grassy courtyard. It was a broad, impressive space, with a long cobbled pathway that parted the lawn and veered off to various torch-lit doors and passageways.

Before them, light from the great hall filtered through the stained-glass windows, painting the courtyard in shades of green, blue, and red. How different it felt from the unassuming, sleepy Lanwyn Manor he remembered from his boyhood, when Mr. Elon Rowe reigned as master and the Lambournes had not yet descended upon Goldweth.

Matthew lowered his voice as they crossed the courtyard to the main entrance. "Impressive. Lanwyn looks fit for a ball instead of a dinner among friends."

Isaac raised his eyebrows. "Friends, indeed." He nodded at the elegantly clad Pennas, and he and Matthew stopped to let them pass before them.

'Twas no secret that none in attendance was here for the sake of friendship.

Every guest was from a long-established mining family.

The Pennas. The Dunstans. The Davieses.

And each desired access to Bal Tressa.

Lambourne might be the most despised man in the village, but he could also make one adventurer potentially very rich. It was a game, pure and simple, and every person present played a role.

Once the Pennas were out of earshot, Isaac jerked his head toward the line of torches. "If he's making a point to declare his wealth, he's succeeding in abundance."

Matthew chortled. "At least someone in the county is prosperous."

"Yes, and everyone already knows it. Now, if only he'd invest it in his mine or allow someone else the opportunity to do so, it might be worthwhile."

"He will." Matthew puffed out his chest. "Give me time."

"Don't do anything ill advised," Isaac warned under his breath. "Need I remind you, Miss Davies will be in attendance. We can't afford to make an enemy because you decide to strut around like a peacock."

Insincerity dripped from Matthew's wry smirk. "I'll be the model of polite behavior."

They entered Lanwyn Manor through the impressive great hall's arched stone entrance. Gargoyles hovered above the stone threshold, which boasted a massive wooden door with intricate floral carvings and heavy iron nails. As Isaac handed his greatcoat and hat to the butler, Mr. Lambourne stepped near to greet them, his deep bellow filling the vaulted foyer.

"Gentlemen, come in. So good of you to venture out on such a dreary night. Pity the weather did not pay heed to our little party, eh?"

Isaac extended his hand to shake Mr. Lambourne's pudgy one.

Matthew followed suit, his expression bright. "I'm told I missed a great deal of excitement last night at the Gray Owl Inn."

"I'll say!" Lambourne guffawed as if the event had been entertaining instead of frightening. "But your brother did you proud, and I'm sure you heard the account." Lambourne pivoted to face Isaac. "I've not had the opportunity to convey my gratitude. You'd departed by the time I arrived. So you stepped in front of a pistol on my niece's behalf? Quite the noble deed."

Isaac nodded. "I hope she's recovered from the ordeal."

"I've not seen her yet today, but my wife tells me Julia is quite recovered and will be joining us this evening."

"Then I shall look forward to making her acquaintance," Matthew interjected.

Isaac cast a sideways glance at Matthew. He knew that glint in his brother's eye all too well—and rarely did a venture that began with such a twinkle end pleasantly.

"Well then, come into the hall, out of the rain and wretched wind. You're hardly the first ones here. The Pennas and the Davieses have preceded you."

Isaac turned into the great hall and took in the beamed arched ceiling and the weaponry displayed on the walls. He tried to remember the last time he was here. Surely it was before his father died. The plaster walls had been painted bright white since his last visit, and now ornate wooden chairs lined the walls beneath the leaded windows. A fire blazed in the broad stone hearth.

Familiar faces glanced in their direction with nods of welcome.

How many times had he been in this very situation? This very night, under the guise of a social gathering, bargains would be struck, deals made, advice shared. A specific kinship connected the people in this room. They all spoke the miner's language and lived the miner's life. Had Lambourne not inherited such a prime piece of land, he would not be included among this sort, but now he was suddenly everyone's friend.

Isaac was about to say something to Mr. Dunstan when a silence fell over the room. He turned to follow the other guests' line of vision.

And there she was. Miss Twethewey.

His breath caught in his chest at the sight.

No longer was she the frightened young lady huddled in her cape, defiantly arguing with her attacker.

Far from it.

A gown of pale blue hugged her curves. Dark curls, which last night tumbled in disarray over her shoulders, now adorned her head like a crown. Wispy tendrils framed her face, and a healthy rosy glow on her high cheekbones replaced the previous night's pallid complexion. Elegant arched eyebrows framed eyes the color of bluebells that graced the forest floor in the warmer months to come, and a sweetly sloping nose drew his attention to her parted lips.

Matthew nudged his shoulder. "Ah, Brother. Now I see."

"See what?" Isaac regained his composure.

"No wonder you were in such a hurry to dismiss any idea of my wooing Miss Twethewey. And who could blame you? I suppose you had an idea to do the same."

———◦———

Julia was not timid by nature, but such direct, unwavering attention was unnerving.

All eyes were on her.

She managed a smile and scanned the unfamiliar faces until she saw the face she sought.

Mr. Isaac Blake.

He stood on the chamber's far side with a small cluster of guests. Even though their interaction had been fleeting, she recalled his light-blond hair and broad shoulders. He stood next to a man who was almost identical, but whose hair was a shade or two darker. It had to be the twin Aunt spoke of.

Somehow his presence eased her in spite of—or perhaps because of—their odd encounter. Yes, they were strangers, yet an unmistakable bond drew her to him. She could not help but wonder what sort of man would face such danger to intervene on a stranger's behalf. What must he think of her, after seeing her crying, hair wild, and unmistakably frightened?

Once inside the great hall, Aunt Beatrice nudged her toward the nearest guest, a short, rotund man standing next to a tall woman with an ostentatious green gown. Introductions began immediately. Julia smiled, answered polite questions, and tried to commit names to memory.

Together, she and her aunt made the rounds until, at last, they had arrived at the gathering of guests with the Blakes. A flutter quaked inside her stomach, and a strange sense of vulnerability settled on her shoulders. Mr. Blake had seen her in a way no other person ever had and, hopefully, would never have reason to see her in that way again.

As she drew nearer, Mr. Blake's features came into sharper focus. His snowy-white cravat highlighted a square, clean-shaven jaw, and dark lashes framed green—no, hazel—eyes.

The other man was slightly shorter and his focus was already on her, a bright smile lighting his face.

"Ah, the brothers Blake." Aunt Beatrice approached the twins, interrupting their conversation with two other gentlemen. "How pleased we are that you were able to join us tonight."

Aunt Beatrice managed to maneuver herself into the group to separate Mr. Isaac Blake from them. Then she wrapped her fingers around Julia's arm and guided her closer to Mr. Matthew Blake.

Julia resisted the urge to frown at her aunt's blatant rudeness. After all, Mr. Isaac had been the one to rescue her. She at least owed him gratitude. But then, her aunt was determined to the point of tactlessness.

An ardent smile creased her aunt's face, and a look of triumph lit her round features. "You have not met my lovely niece then, have you, Mr. Blake?"

"No, ma'am. I've not had the pleasure." He turned toward Julia and bowed. "Welcome to Goldweth, Miss Twethewey."

She curtsied, taking a moment to study the man, from the fine cut of his dark-blue broadcloth coat to the intricate tie of his cravat.

"Mr. Blake is our neighbor." Aunt repeated the information she had shared that morning. She pivoted toward Julia. "His estate meets ours to the northeast."

So this was the man her aunt had thought would make a match for her. With hair the color of sand and ample dark lashes, he certainly was handsome, and judging by his interested expression, quite attentive.

Determined to rectify her aunt's rudeness, Julia turned her attention to the younger brother. "Good evening, Mr. Blake. We meet again, sir."

If he was surprised at the directness of her statement or at her aunt's oversight of him, he gave no indication. He bowed low. "We do. I'm happy to see you are settled well."

"I am." She raised her chin. "Thank you."

"Do excuse us, gentlemen." Aunt Beatrice's nose twitched, and she fluttered her fan with one hand and placed the other on Julia's shoulder, turning her away from the men. "Dinner will begin soon, and others are eager to make Julia's acquaintance."

Obeying her aunt's bidding, Julia dipped her head in farewell and allowed herself to be led away, resisting the urge to glance back at the two seemingly very different gentlemen.

CHAPTER 10

Julia lowered her napkin to her lap as she sat at the table in the dining hall. Candlelight and polite conversation filled the high-ceilinged chamber, and a lively fire in the stone hearth added energy to the room. Curiosity about all of the new faces around her commandeered her senses to the point she had to remind herself to eat.

Uncle William sat at the head of the long, ornately carved oak table, which stretched from one end of the long room to the other. Aunt Beatrice occupied the opposite end, like a queen on her throne, and was much engaged in conversation with an elderly gentleman seated to her right. The men far outnumbered the ladies in attendance, and as a result of Aunt's meticulous planning, the women had been evenly dispersed around the table. Most of the feminine guests appeared to be around her aunt's age, but other than Caroline, only one other young woman, a Miss Davies, was present.

Julia found herself sitting between two gentlemen—Mr. Matthew Blake to her left and Mr. Andrew Dunstan to her right.

"I consider myself the most fortunate man in attendance tonight."

She cast a sideways glance at Matthew Blake and found his gaze on her. "Oh?"

"Can it be any wonder?" He grinned, his hazel eyes catching the light with a mischievous twinkle. "I'm seated next to the guest of honor. A true privilege."

"I'm hardly the guest of honor, Mr. Blake." She laughed with a shake of her head. "A visitor, nothing more."

"Visitor or not, I still consider it a privilege." He sobered and then lowered his head, as if taking her into his confidence. "But I must say, I'm outraged at what happened at the inn last night. Absolutely reprehensible."

How she wished the unfortunate event never happened, and now every person she came into contact with knew about it. So many questions darted around her mind, and even though she'd sought her uncle several times throughout the course of the day to ask him about them, she'd never found the opportunity.

Julia shifted in her chair, adding to the distance between Mr. Blake and her that seemed to be closing. "I was grateful your brother was there to offer assistance."

Mr. Blake looked past her and down the table at his brother, seated near her uncle. "He's quite the man. I'm proud to call him family."

Isaac Blake was seated next to the pretty Miss Davies, and their heads were tilted toward each other in conversation.

She watched the pair with interest for several moments. "I hope to be able to thank him in person this evening."

"I am sure you'll have the opportunity. You know how parties like this go. He's a modest man, though. I doubt you'll get much conversation from him."

Julia returned her full attention to her neighbor, determined to change the conversation. "My aunt mentioned that you and your brother are twins. I've never met anyone who was a twin before."

"You haven't?"

"Not that I can recall."

"Yes." He leaned back in his chair. "I'm a whole three minutes Isaac's senior. A great feat indeed."

She laughed at his little joke and then lifted her gaze to the lock of blond hair that fell over his forehead. "You bear a strong resemblance to one another."

"You think so? We've often been told that, but the older we become, the less we look alike." He paused. "Do you have siblings, Miss Twethewey?"

"I do. I've four siblings. Two brothers and two sisters."

"A large family, then. Are you close?"

"Very. Our parents died when we were children, and my aunt and uncle raised us."

"Ah yes, at Penwythe Hall."

"You know it?" She raised her eyebrows. "I'm surprised. It isn't extraordinarily large."

"I confess, I peppered your uncle with questions about you prior to your arrival. You see, we don't have many visitors in this part of the country. It's quite an anticipated occasion."

"Ah, Mr. Blake, I am sure to disappoint."

"You have already surpassed every hope, Miss Twethewey."

She flushed under the praise and obvious flirtation. "Really, Mr. Blake."

"You doubt my sincerity?" He laughed, his expression playfully injured.

"No, sir, I don't doubt it. But now I'm at a disadvantage, for you know various details about me, but I know naught of you, other than you're my uncle's neighbor and have a twin brother who's but three minutes your junior."

"What would you like to know?" He laced his fingers together on the tabletop. "I have no secrets."

"Tell me about your industry." She considered it a safe topic. "How do you occupy your time?"

He shrugged and nodded at the other guests. "My business is the same as every other man in attendance. Mining."

"I know very little of mining," Julia divulged, fidgeting with the food on her plate. "My uncle tends apple orchards on his estate, and there's little room for any other occupation."

"Apples, eh? Well, spend a little time in Goldweth and you will be an expert in mining in no time."

"What's the name of your mine?"

"Wheal Tamsen. It's a copper mine just over the hill from here. Isaac and I work it together. I own it, but I also act as the purser, meaning I care for the finances, and he's the mine captain and manages all the operations. My father ran it before us, and his father before that."

"I understand my uncle inherited a mine," she offered, curious to learn more about the venture that brought her aunt and uncle to Goldweth.

"Bal Tressa." His good-natured expression subsided. "The largest copper mine in the area. At the moment it stands still."

"So I've heard." Sensing her opportunity to learn more, she tilted her head toward the side. "Can it not be reopened?"

Mr. Blake shrugged. "Of course, but even though your uncle owns the land, he lacks experience to run it. He needs someone to help him—or to do it for him. Often landowners like him make agreements to have their mines run by men called adventurers—men who know how to make mines successful and who are willing to pay to work the land."

"I see."

"Tell me," he said with renewed vigor, "what do you think of Lanwyn Manor?"

She drew a deep breath and surveyed her surroundings anew. "It's impressive."

"Have you seen the ghost yet?"

"A ghost?" She laughed. "You jest."

"No, no." His eyes sparkled. "I'm in earnest. A ghost—or should I say ghosts—reside here. Ask anyone."

She eyed him, as if waiting for him to admit the folly in his statement. "Not a single soul has said anything about it."

"Well, your family may not be aware of the stories, but ask any of the servants here. I'm sure they could tell you dozens of accounts of unexplainable occurrences. Inquire after the treasure while you're at it."

"Treasure?"

"'Tis a well-known truth that there is a treasure hidden somewhere within these walls. The only issue is that no one knows exactly what is hidden or where."

"And pray, how did you become such an expert on Lanwyn Manor?"

"Time. I spent a great deal of it here as a boy. Isaac and I both did. Our father and old Mr. Rowe were good friends and often collaborated on mining projects." Matthew wiped his mouth with his napkin and studied her for several moments. "I can tell by your expression that you're surprised to hear that."

"Not at all." She searched for words, recalling her aunt's not-so-favorable comments about the local residents. "It's just that I know so little of this area."

"Well, allow me to enlighten you with a little Goldweth history. There was a time, a couple of decades ago actually, when Rowe was the most profitable miner in this area."

"What happened to him?"

"A tragedy. His only son was killed in an accident. An unprecedented rainstorm flooded the shaft his boy was in and killed him. After that Rowe never visited the mine again, and he let it to adventurers—the very ones your uncle broke ties with."

She stiffened at the unexpected sadness in the tale. "How tragic."

"It is sad." He nodded. "But it lends credence to the myths surrounding this old house. The legend is that the family who lives here is cursed."

She huffed. "You're not serious."

"I am! Quite."

She eyed him, fighting not to show her skepticism.

"Is it any wonder?" He shrugged and lifted his eyes to the molded ceiling above him. "This building is ancient—hundreds of years have passed since this very room was built."

She considered his words but remained silent.

"Don't take my word for it. Ask anyone." He leaned so close she could smell his scent of tobacco and port. "But you've been warned."

The clink of silver against crystal captured her attention, and she pivoted to see her uncle standing at the table's end, his glass extended in his hand. The candlelight shining behind him accented not only his gray hair and side whiskers, but the billowy folds of his cravat and the gold piping on the trim of his double-breasted coat.

He cleared his throat. "I thank you all for coming this evening, and the event is made even richer by the presence of my niece, Miss Julia Twethewey. We are so pleased you have joined us." He lifted his glass higher. "To a long and happy visit."

She smiled as warm murmurs of agreement circled the table. Indeed, it was a kind welcome. But as she looked at the strange faces, there was so much she did not know.

Geographically she was not that far from home, but indeed, there was no denying she was in a very different world.

CHAPTER 11

Lively conversation echoed and laughter abounded as Isaac remained with the male guests in the dining room. The ladies, led by Mrs. Lambourne, had retreated to Lanwyn Manor's drawing room, leaving the men to drink their port and discuss mining business. Smoke puffed from clay pipes and cheroots mixed with that from the hearth's fire. To an outsider the assembly might appear nothing more than a comfortable gathering of friends with nary a care in the world.

The pretense of camaraderie made Isaac uncomfortable.

He cherished his genuine friends, such as Charlie and Margaret, and pretending to be otherwise was difficult. Regardless, it was important to play the role he'd inherited—a miner who needed to manage the interest of his own undertakings.

Isaac moved to stand next to the window and stared into the rain-smeared black night. As he listened to the men's chattering of hunting and pistols, his frustration grew. Gathered here were the best minds in mining, and not a single soul had the courage to bring up last night's events. Instead, laughter and gaiety ruled the room, and his brother was at the heart of it. Just as Isaac had made up his mind to be the one to address it, footsteps sounded.

He glanced over his shoulder to see Dunstan approaching, port in hand. "Heard about your experience at the Gray Owl last night."

"No doubt everyone's heard about it."

Dunstan regarded the laughing guests, joking and making merry, behind him. He heaved a sigh and shook his graying head. "These are precarious times. There's a great deal at stake. But I don't have to tell you that."

"No, sir, you do not."

"Look at them all." Dunstan set down his glass on the side table next to the window, retrieved a lacquered snuffbox from his waistcoat, and opened the lid. "All hoping to gain access to ol' Bal Tressa, but I daresay Lambourne's playing them all for fools." He pinched the black powder between his fingers and inhaled before he extended the box to Isaac.

Isaac waved off the gesture and with a shrug Dunstan returned the box to his pocket. "You've heard Lambourne's been in talks with Marcus Elliot?"

Isaac folded his arms over his chest. "Yes. Apparently that is why he was absent during his niece's distress."

Dunstan gave a dry laugh. "Speaking of Lambourne's niece, your brother seemed quite enchanted by her charms during dinner."

Isaac chuckled at the change of topic. "Noticed that, did you?"

"I gather everyone did. Not a bad tactic, I suppose. If I wanted a shot at Bal Tressa and I were twenty years younger and unmarried, wooing the owner's niece might seem like a valid approach."

"I'm not sure the Davies family would agree." Isaac shot a glance over to Mr. Davies, whose scowl during dinner signaled his disapproval of the budding friendship between Matthew and the guest of honor. Isaac had been seated next to the discarded Miss Davies at dinner, and despite his best efforts to be an amiable dinner neighbor, her lack of interest in this Blake brother was evident.

"True." Dunstan retrieved his port. "But Lambourne is so unaccustomed with the workings of a mine that it just might work."

"Have you interest in Lambourne's mine?"

Dunstan drew an exaggerated breath, turned his back toward the window, and assessed the group. A hint of a smile quirked one side of his mouth. "No, I don't. I've set my sights in a different direction."

"Oh?" Isaac raised his brows. "And what's that?"

Dunstan leaned closer and lowered his raspy voice even further. "I've heard chatter that you might consider opening Wheal Gwenna again. About time, says I."

Isaac jerked, shocked to hear his mine mentioned. "Wheal Gwenna? Where'd you hear that?"

"Charlie Benson. Said he was working with you to gather capital."

"Ah." Charlie was his good friend and a most loyal comrade, but he often had a hard time keeping his own counsel. "Wheal Gwenna's closed and will likely stay that way. Even if I did plan to open her, it'd take a great deal of time, not to mention funds. With my work at Wheal Tamsen, I'm not sure how I'd manage."

Dunstan drew a deep breath and rubbed his hand over his cleanly shaven chin. "Tell me, young Blake, do your plans include Bal Tressa like every other man in the room?"

Isaac shrugged. "Running a mine like Bal Tressa takes a great deal of money. You forget Matthew owns Wheal Tamsen, not me. His financial and business decisions are his. I manage his mine, and nothing more."

"Yet you profit from it."

Isaac nodded. "Yes, I do."

"Let me ask you this plainly." Dunstan shifted his ample weight and squared his broad shoulders. "Are you seeking investors?"

Isaac widened his stance as he considered the question. True, he and Charlie had been talking—dreaming—about opening Wheal Gwenna, but frustration crept into his countenance. Charlie was eager, almost too eager, to secure investors. Wheal Gwenna was still Isaac's mine, and he'd decide who'd have influence and who would not. But now wasn't the time. He didn't have sufficient funds, nor did he want outside investors affecting the mine operations. He wanted to be master of his own.

Then again, every man in the room wanted to be master of his own destiny, and unfortunately, very few were.

"Not at this time, no."

Dunstan narrowed his eyes. "Have you considered that if other mines were finding success, the hullabaloo about Bal Tressa would cease?"

They stared at each other for several moments, the truth of the statement hanging heavily between them.

"I, for one, would be eager for such a venture, especially if I were young and unattached. You've much to gain," Dunstan said.

After a pause, Isaac finished his sentence for him. "And not much to lose."

Chapter 12

As Julia sat in the drawing room with the other ladies after the meal, she looked to Oscar, Aunt Beatrice's little gray dog sitting on the settee next to her.

He looked as bored as she felt.

Julia lifted Oscar to her lap, mindful not to catch his nails on the delicate folds of her gown. He grunted with the disturbance but quickly nestled into place.

Absently she stroked the dog's head, observing the other ladies assembled. Aunt Beatrice led three guests in a game of whist. Two others, nearly asleep, sat on either side of her, and Caroline was conveniently absent. Julia found herself slightly envious that her cousin had found a way to elude the dull party. How she wished Jane were well enough to join the gathering, but with the exception of their talk earlier that day, every time Julia had visited her, she'd been asleep.

Julia let her posture droop ever so slightly. Selfishly she'd hoped to meet ladies who were as friendly as Miss Prynne and Miss Trebell, but in truth, these ladies present seemed to want to know nothing of her. She'd especially hoped that Miss Davies, the pretty brunette who appeared about her age, would become a friend to her while she was in Goldweth, but as it was, she said little and stayed close to her mother.

Suddenly the sound of heavy footsteps and deep voices invaded their interlude, and Julia lifted her head. Finally the men were to join them.

Julia straightened her posture anew and smoothed a curl away from her face as they filtered in. They brought a certain vitality that her female companions had lacked, and within minutes, conversations flared and laughter once again filled the space.

She held her breath until the Blake brothers at last entered. She was already certain she had, at the very least, a friend in Matthew. Their amusing conversation at dinner had confirmed it, and the knowledge that her aunt believed him to be a viable suitor recommended him that much more.

Matthew entered first, with Isaac right behind him. Even though Matthew had been so attentive and even flirtatious, she could not deny her interest in the younger brother. She needed to find a way to speak with him, to thank him for his intervention. She smoothed her skirt and lifted her chin. Fortunately, she was not prone to shyness—a trait that, at times, had the tendency to lead to a downfall.

Mrs. Davies, in a flash of dark-purple silk, jumped from her chair and was at Matthew's side, taking his arm to capture his attention. Isaac escaped the ambush and skirted around them to the back of the room and stood near the garden doors.

With a glance to ensure her aunt was engaged in conversation, Julia tucked the tiny dog under her arm, stood, and, careful not to draw attention to herself, stole across the room along the back wall.

At first he did not notice her. She drew closer. "Mr. Blake."

He turned, appearing almost shocked at her approach. His gaze flicked from her to his brother, shifted to Oscar, and then met hers once again. "Miss Twethewey."

She smiled her sweetest smile and adjusted the dog in her arms. She'd probably be wise to rely on her aunt's guidance in this matter, but her curiosity got the better of her. "I was hoping to speak with you. I owe you a debt of gratitude for your assistance and have not had the opportunity to thank you."

His expression softened. "I'm only sorry it happened at all. Have you recovered from the ordeal?"

"I have, as you can see. I looked for you after things settled down to thank you, but the innkeeper said you'd tried to find the thieves."

"A few of us did try, but to no avail."

"'Tis a shame."

"It is, but all's not lost. We've ways of finding information. All in good time and we'll bring them to justice."

She considered him for several moments. He did not shy away from the conversation, and he seemed to have a good grasp on the landscape.

She stepped closer and cast a glance over at her aunt. "I've been so curious about something, but I am not sure if it is quite appropriate for me to ask."

"If it is of any help, you may ask me whatever you wish, and I will do my best to answer."

In that moment, she decided to trust Mr. Blake. "Does someone wish my uncle harm?"

———◆———

Miss Twethewey fixed her intent eyes, blue and wide, on him.

And she was waiting for his response.

It would be difficult to deny this woman anything, especially the answer to such a simple question, but it wasn't his place to divulge family matters, especially to a woman he hardly knew.

Isaac cleared his throat and shifted, casting a glance toward his brother. He'd decided earlier to avoid Miss Twethewey, even before Matthew made a fool of himself flirting and fawning over her. Just because he'd assisted this young lady, he had no right to expect anything from her.

But now she sought him out and still awaited an answer.

She adjusted the small dog in her arms. "Please, Mr. Blake. I would not ask unless I felt it absolutely necessary. Earlier today I overheard a conversation that suggested my uncle might be in danger, and it concerned me."

He drew a deep breath. He could get lost in those bewitching eyes—that alluring expression—if he was not cautious.

He should tell her he knew nothing.

It would be best not to get involved.

But perhaps it was already too late. They'd experienced the attack together, and after what had happened to her, she deserved to know the truth.

He selected his words with care. "When your uncle inherited one of the most profitable mines in the area, he canceled the contract with the adventurer running the mine, which put a great many miners out of work. Times are difficult, and my suspicion is that the miners have a notion to take matters into their own hands to pressure him to reopen Bal Tressa."

Knitting her brow, she pressed her lips together before speaking. "Then I overheard correctly. My uncle is in danger."

"I don't think it's as dire as all that. I'm sure your family is quite safe here, but there's a great deal of uncertainty afoot, and uncertainty breeds mistrust."

She pivoted and leaned closer. "But do you think that I—?"

"Julia?" a sharp voice trilled from across the room. "Julia!"

Beatrice Lambourne dashed toward them, her face flushed from the room's heat, her bosom heaving with each breath.

He almost laughed at the expression of near horror on her face. He could hardly be surprised. By her actions this night alone, it was clear she viewed Matthew as a possible suitor for her niece. Isaac, clearly, was not permitted to be near her, so here she was, sweeping in to save her niece from the undesirable younger brother.

"Aunt Beatrice! You startled me."

Mrs. Lambourne wrapped her hands protectively around Miss Twethewey's arm and tugged. She lifted her chin and looked down her nose at Isaac for several seconds. "Now that the men have rejoined us, it's time for the music, and as our guest, I should like for you to entertain us first."

Miss Twethewey's pleasant smile faded, and she shook her head. "Oh, Aunt, I—"

"Oh, fie, child. Your aunt Delia gave you the finest pianoforte instruction. Surely she'd be proud to know you have entertained us so splendidly. Give me Oscar and prepare yourself." She released Miss Twethewey's arm long enough to settle the dog in the crook of her arm and then clapped to garner the attention of everyone in the room. "Come all. Come over to the instruments. Julia has graciously agreed to play for us, and you will not be disappointed."

Miss Twethewey offered him a wary smile before she obeyed her aunt. Beatrice Lambourne made a great show of ushering her niece to the pianoforte positioned in the room's corner, ordering chairs to be drawn close and for all to be silent.

From his spot against the far wall, Isaac observed the activity. Each lady in attendance would present a talent. Mrs. Lambourne would play the harp. Miss Davies would sing. Caroline Lambourne would also play the pianoforte. Everyone in attendance would listen politely and praise extravagantly. It was a charade—a parade of accomplishments that could, at times, be painful to endure.

Normally his interest would fade at this point in the evening and his mind would wander.

But not tonight.

As Miss Twethewey lifted her fingers to the keys, his focus narrowed. The music, haunting and soft, seemed to materialize from the air. And then she started to sing.

He was not sure if it was the bizarre nature of recent events or his desire for something different, but he could not look away from the lady. He'd never seen anyone like her. Did she know how alluring she was, with soft tendrils escaping their pins and cascading to her shoulders? His brother had been right—not many strangers came to their town, much less beautiful ones. Isaac knew nothing of her other than her relations, but he did know how she felt in his arms as he pushed her to safety, and that alone invaded his thoughts.

Motion beside him caught his eye. Not far from him Matthew leaned forward in his chair. Isaac recognized the look of conquest on his brother's face.

She'd prefer Matthew, of course. He possessed the family fortune. The business. The estate. His brother was the heir and, as such, held a special place in society—a fact Isaac had come to peace with a very long time ago.

Her music soared, soaking the room with a melancholy sweetness. He held his breath as he watched her hands move over the keyboard, bathed in warm candlelight. An ache, all too familiar, all too poignant, settled in his chest as he watched her. A longing for something—or someone—to round out the rough corners of his life.

Yes, he wanted the type of relationship that Charlie and Margaret had. Only one or two young ladies in the past had caught his eye, but regardless of anything he'd do or say, they'd been drawn to Matthew—or at least to what Matthew had to offer.

He'd grown used to it. But now, this inexplicable discomfort battled for attention.

Perhaps it was that he, in some way, felt responsible for her.

Perhaps it was the confidence in her voice or the shape of her mouth that made her appear to always have a hint of a smile.

He glanced around at the other faces. Miss Davies glared at Matthew from the corner, as did her mama. Next to her sat Mrs. Lambourne, an expression of smug satisfaction curving her lips, and next to her, Caroline oozed boredom. If the death of old man Rowe disrupted the balance of life in Goldweth, the arrival of Miss Julia Twethewey, he surmised, would unsettle it that much more.

The door of the next room flung open, and footsteps pounded in a riotous manner across the floor.

The music stopped. All turned toward the clamor.

There stood Timmy Beale, an underground captain at Wheal Tamsen. His dark eyes were wide, and with his working clothes—dirty trousers and dirt-smeared coat—he appeared utterly out of place.

There was only one reason he would interrupt such a gathering.

Isaac jumped to his feet, his breath lodged in his throat.

Gasping for air, Beale swept his hat from his head and fixed his wild gaze on the Blake brothers. "There's been . . . an accident. You're needed . . . at Wheal Tamsen."

CHAPTER 13

Julia dropped her hands from the keyboard, shocked to see the filthy worker in the elegant drawing room, and even more shocked at his declaration.

Isaac flew from the room. Mr. Dunstan, Matthew, and Uncle William followed.

Murmurs and whispers raced around the high-ceilinged chamber. For several moments none of the other guests moved. Then Aunt Beatrice stood from her chair, her cheeks flushed a vibrant pink. A forced laugh bubbled from her. "My. This is unusual, to be sure, but I'm certain all will be well. The men have it in good hands, I daresay. Julia, dear, please, continue."

Julia bit her lip, unsure of what to do. An accident had just sent guests running from the room, and her aunt wanted her to continue?

"Julia," Aunt Beatrice repeated with greater force. "Play."

Uncomfortable heat crept up her neck, and Julia returned her fingertips to the smooth, cool keys. She glanced up at the eyes on her—unfamiliar eyes—and she wished she were tucked safely in her tower chamber.

She pressed her fingers in the familiar pattern—one note after the other. After several bars and a smattering of finger slips, the song concluded.

As the accolades commenced, nausea swelled. How could anyone remain calm and be entertained by her meager melody at such a time? An accident had sent four men running from the room. Did such an event have no effect on them?

As the room once again fell silent, Julia retreated to one of the rear chairs and Miss Davies took her turn at the pianoforte. Julia found it hard to remain still and listen, but everyone else seemed unruffled. At length, Matthew and her uncle slipped back into the room and waited silently near Julia. Isaac and Mr. Dunstan were noticeably absent.

At the conclusion of Miss Davies's performance, Aunt Beatrice stood and approached the returning men. "What has happened?"

"An accident, at my mine," Matthew said, his face very grave.

Those around her exchanged knowing, tentative glances that seemed to have a language the others understood.

"One dead, at least two injured," Mr. Blake continued after a pause. "Isaac's left to assess the situation. I daresay it will be grave indeed. Sadly, as we are all aware, mining is not without incident, but every man who descends the ladders knows the danger."

"Should you not go as well?" Julia stood, surprised at his lack of urgency.

All eyes turned toward her.

She stiffened. Perhaps she should have held her tongue. She was speaking into a world of which she knew nothing. Of mines, of deaths.

Perhaps they'd consider her as ignorant as her uncle.

Matthew's somber expression softened. "You're good to be concerned, Miss Twethewey. It does you credit. And you are correct. I should be on my way, and I'll be following my brother shortly. I merely came back in to bid our hostess farewell."

"I will come with you and do what I can." Her uncle stepped forward.

"That's kind, but this could be of a sensitive nature. However, if you would like to come out to Wheal Tamsen, I would be happy to show you how our operation works. Later this week, perhaps? The sooner we can resume normal activity, the calmer the men will stay."

Conversation swirled. Tones of renewed disbelief and words of shock echoed around the space.

Julia wondered at the seeming heartlessness of it—as if such an event was business as usual.

Maybe it was.

Matthew turned to Julia. "Perhaps you'd like to join your uncle, if the weather is more pleasant."

Julia caught sight of her aunt's eager gaze and subtle yet insistent nod of encouragement. "Thank you, Mr. Blake. Weather permitting, I will."

He bowed and then moved to another group to bid his farewells.

Caroline, who had been noticeably absent for a great deal of the evening, came up and looped her arm through Julia's.

"This is a sad business," Julia said softly to Caroline. "Lives have been lost."

Caroline sighed and tilted her head. "I don't know much about mining ventures, but I know there've been a handful of deaths since we moved here. I've heard Father and the servants talking about it. It happens with regular occurrence."

"Have you been to visit a mine?"

"Me? Heavens, no. But I daresay Mr. Blake did not invite you to Wheal Tamsen *just* to see the mine."

Julia drew her brows together.

Caroline gave a little huff. "Come now, Julia. He's not taken his eyes off you, and that is flattering for any woman. But . . ." Her voice faded away, and Caroline tossed a nod across the room. "You'd have no way of knowing this, but normally Miss Davies is quite the amusing guest, but she's particularly quiet this evening. She fancies Matthew Blake as her beau, and I daresay he is. But perhaps not for much longer."

Caroline raised her brows and gave Julia a half smile before she swept over toward her mother, leaving Julia alone in the center of the chamber.

She looked at the young brunette at the pianoforte. No wonder her manner had been so cold. Julia felt almost ill and her shoulders slumped. The last thing she wanted to do was make an enemy.

Music sounded, so she returned to her chair, grateful that for the moment, she did not need to interact with anyone.

So far, her time in Goldweth had been a whirlwind. First the attack and now this. Her intention had been to come and care for her cousin and seek a diversion. Unfortunately, these were not the diversions she had in mind.

CHAPTER 14

Isaac knew what catastrophe awaited him at the mine.

He'd seen rock falls before. There'd be chaotic piles of rubble. An endless hovering of dust and bits of earth. All would be made worse by the dark of night. He urged his horse faster over the meadow, and Dunstan and Beale were close behind him.

With every breath he recounted what he knew and struggled to make sense of what he had heard. Danny Williams dead. Two were injured. And Charlie Benson was one of them.

Isaac may not know all the details, but he did know exactly where the miners had been working—and exactly who'd been present. With naught but tallow candles as their guide, the tributers often worked during the midnight hours, and it was always dark beneath the surface. This particular pitch had been a tricky one. The workers had been instructed to stay away until further exploration could be done, but apparently eagerness to find and follow the lode had interfered with common sense.

And now it was too late.

He could recall several times when he'd accompanied his father on a ride like the one he was making now.

"People. People make a mine, Son."

But Charlie was not just any person. Not just an underground captain who contributed to Wheal Tamsen's success. He was a trusted friend—perhaps his greatest friend.

Isaac's arm muscles tightened as his horse thundered beneath him, traveling a familiar, worn path they could traverse in their sleep. The appearance of the inky outline of Wheal Tamsen's engine house against the charcoal sky urged him to move faster. Torchlight and fires cast eerie, dancing shadows on an area that should have been quiet and tranquil. Tragedy always summoned the curious and concerned, and men, like shifting black shadows, lurked about like ghostly vapors.

Once through the mine's iron gate, Isaac rode to the small courtyard and slid from his horse. Each step toward the mine shaft's entrance was faster than the other, half fearing, half anticipating what he would see.

Nate Minear, one of the men who'd been working the pitch, met him. "Derwin's going to be fine, but Benson's in a bad way. Bal surgeon's on his way."

The men who'd been standing at the shaft's entrance stepped back as he approached, and Isaac dropped to his knees next to Charlie's slumped form, close enough that he could see the blood streaking down his friend's face and the rips in his linen shirt.

Threatening darkness lingered, and that combined with the fog and dust that hovered in the air produced the ambience of a nightmare.

Isaac tried to force lightness to his tone. "Thought we agreed to stay away from falling rock."

Charlie's gritty voice was barely audible above the torches' crackling and the men moving about the courtyard. "My luck's run out, ain't it?"

Isaac touched Charlie's shoulder. "'Course not. Let's move you inside. Everything will be fine."

"Don't lie." A throaty, forced chuckle burst out. "You've more respect for me than that."

"Aye, I do." Isaac looked up as two men approached with a stretcher. "They're coming to take you to the counting house now."

With sudden desperation Benson grabbed Isaac's sleeve. "My wife. She'll be alone."

"Don't say that. The surgeon will be here soon, and—"

"I know what's happening. I seen it a'fore, just not from this side."

Isaac had never seen Charlie so pale. Never had he seen the beads of perspiration so thick or the anguish of pain so intense.

Isaac could argue. He could fill these final moments with talk of hope. But they both knew the truth and Charlie was right—Isaac had too much respect for him to pretend something was other than it was.

Isaac swallowed, his throat tight. "What can I do?"

"Margaret. I promised her everythin'. Gave her nothin'. Get her Wheal Gwenna. Like we talked."

"Charlie, I—"

"Promise!" Intensity radiated from Charlie's eyes, and fear poised in his expression.

Isaac could only nod.

Several men lifted Charlie onto the stretcher. Isaac gripped one end of the stretcher's handles, clenching his jaw as his friend's groaning met his ears.

CHAPTER 15

The morning after the dinner, Julia awoke early, as she did every morning at Penwythe Hall. Dawn had not broken yet, and a cold, murky blue light was just beginning to glimmer to the east. A steady, chilly rain pinged against the leaded windows and pelted the dormant grounds below.

In her dark-paneled bedchamber a lethargic fire simmered in her fireplace. It felt more like the dead of night rather than the start of a new day, but eager to be about her normal activities, Julia rose from her bed and rang for Evangeline.

As Julia stood still, waiting for the maid to dress her in a long-sleeved gown of light-brown wool, she revisited the previous night's events in her mind. Still, a sense of shock sobered her at how nonchalantly many of the guests responded to the tragedy.

Julia pivoted to allow the maid to fasten the back of her gown. "Have you heard any news about the men at Wheal Tamsen?"

"No, miss." Evangeline tightened the bodice's lacing between Julia's shoulder blades and secured it snugly. "I ain't 'eard a word."

Evangeline stepped back, and Julia turned to face her. "And my cousins? Have they awoken yet?"

"They sleep quite late. Mrs. Lambourne too. I wouldn't expect them to be up for several hours."

"So long?" Julia frowned, disappointed but not altogether surprised to hear of her cousins' hours.

"Yes, miss." Evangeline scurried around the space, retrieving Julia's night clothing and tending the fire. "Shall I bring you some coffee or something to eat? Cook won't serve the morning meal for a few hours yet, but I could find you something if you're hungry."

"That's not necessary." Julia forced a smile. "I can wait."

Evangeline departed, and Julia turned to watch the rain pelting the earth. Silence ensued, and the first bits of homesickness crept in. She thought of her aunt Delia and uncle Jac, her siblings. How she missed them, and how she missed the things that were familiar. How would she fill the time—the hours until her family would wake? At Penwythe Hall responsibilities and activities busied her from morning to night, but here, she felt useless.

She pressed her lips together. It would do no good to wallow in such thoughts. It might be early, but she needed to find something to do. Aunt Beatrice had mentioned in passing that there was a library off of her uncle's study.

Julia decided to find it.

As she descended the dim, narrow stairwell, the steps creaked beneath her slippered feet, as if hinting at secrets, and the banister groaned under her grip, as if the house were as alive as she. The sounds combined with the testy rumble of the late-autumn thunder, intensifying the mysterious symphony. Matthew Blake had spoken of ghosts that roamed Lanwyn Manor's halls, and while she didn't believe in tales, she had to admit that the ancient halls and archaic artifacts lent themselves to such lore.

She made her way toward her uncle's study—presumably the one she'd passed the first day of her arrival when she overheard the magistrate and her uncle talking. The corridor seemed a forgotten part of the house, used only by her uncle and the servants as a short-cut to the tower staircase. No candles winked from this hall, and she wished she'd thought to bring one.

She was almost content with letting her imagination run away with her until she turned a corner.

There stood Mrs. Sedrick.

Julia jumped at the suddenness of seeing the woman, clad in black, there in the morning shadows. The woman seemed to materialize in the oddest places, at the oddest times. It was as if she was watching her.

Or following her.

The housekeeper pinned a dark glare on Julia. "Looking for something, Miss Twethewey?"

Julia blinked, taken aback by the sharpness of the question. "I—was looking for the library."

"It's an old house, Miss Twethewey. Lots of twists and turns. One could get lost here."

They locked eyes for several moments—an unusual battle. Julia resisted the urge to shrink back, as if she'd done something wrong. Neither spoke, and then the housekeeper relented. "Follow me."

Wordlessly, Julia followed Mrs. Sedrick down the narrow hall, taking note of the gray streaks in the housekeeper's dark hair. Her curiosity about the woman was increasing. Why was she so cantankerous? Why did she dislike Julia so? Or was it just visitors in general she detested?

After a sharp corner, Mrs. Sedrick turned into the study through a different door than Julia had used before. The chamber looked as it had the previous day, with dark-green walls and a large desk anchored in the center of the room.

They crossed over the plush rug to yet another smaller painted door that had been closed on Julia's previous visit and stepped through it. Her breath caught at the sight. Gray morning light filtered through tall windows along one wall, illuminating a layer of dust atop the room's single table. The entire opposite wall was covered with books from floor to ceiling. Still, straight, silent, like soldiers guarding some sort of secret. But what?

She almost laughed. She was letting Mr. Blake's stories affect her, and with little else to occupy her mind, she was giving them far too much credence.

"This room does not get a great deal of use. You'll excuse the dust."

"I find it hard to believe this chamber is neglected." Julia stepped forward to get a better view. "There must be hundreds of books here, if not thousands!"

Mrs. Sedrick did not look at the shelves. Instead she clasped her hands primly before her. "What are you seeking?"

Julia did not take her eyes from the books. "Merely something to read, and Aunt said I was welcome to whatever I found in here."

"Will you be wanting a fire?" Mrs. Sedrick gestured toward the carved stone mantel above the hearth that stood on the wall opposite the door.

"No, I shan't be in here long enough for that." Julia pulled a book from one of the shelves by its spine.

"Very well." Mrs. Sedrick nodded toward the bellpull on the wall. "Should you need any further assistance, just ring for us and someone will help you." Then she turned on her heel and vanished, as quietly as she had appeared.

Julia dismissed the odd experience and breathed a sigh of relief as the woman's footsteps turned into the corridor.

A chill lingered and Julia rubbed her arms, wishing she'd brought a shawl, but at least now she was free to explore at her leisure. With the exception of two portraits hanging on the near wall, bookshelves covered every open wall. She walked along the rows, pausing to peruse the titles.

She continued along until a door broke the row of bookshelves. It was a narrow door, apparently disguised by paneling, barely as wide as her shoulders. She noted its odd location.

Curiously, she placed her hand against it and pushed. The iron hinges creaked loudly as it gave way. Dust swirled with the door's movement, and she coughed as motes took flight, dancing and darting around her. The door opened to another, smaller chamber. A long, narrow table in the center of the room, which must have once been quite handsome, was covered with grime. Half-burned tallow candles still stood in the candelabra atop it, and upon closer inspection, she noticed the dust was disrupted in areas, as if someone had been in here recently.

More books and rolled maps were stored haphazardly on shelves, and even in this forgotten room, tapestries adorned the walls. She approached the space between the chamber's two windows and looked down to the small courtyard—an enclosed bit of land that contained the sleeping kitchen gardens. From what she understood, it was often used as a servants' pass-through from the kitchen to the dining room and gave the windows of interior rooms access to daylight.

"How curious," she muttered as her attention shifted to the map hanging next to the window. It was a rendering of Cornwall, but odd markings and lines on it meant nothing to her. As she leaned toward the map to get a better look, she stubbed her toe. At her feet was a trunk as grit-covered and forgotten as the rest of the room. She knelt to lift the lid, but it was locked.

Glancing around to confirm no other doors existed, she shivered. A gust of wind slammed the pane and slid through a crack in the window. As Julia returned to the library, she glanced back at the curious little space. She had the nagging suspicion that there was more to this room than what met the eye, and she decided that, in time, she would learn its secrets.

CHAPTER 16

After Julia's odd experience in the library, she retreated to her tower chamber with a couple of books tucked in her arms. With the Lambourne women still slumbering, she called for Evangeline to bring her a quill and inkwell so she could write to her aunt and sisters with details of her first days at Lanwyn Manor, careful to omit the news of the attack at the inn for fear of inciting unnecessary concern.

When Evangeline notified her that Jane had awoken, Julia set her letter writing aside, grabbed the book she had selected for her cousin, and made her way to Jane's chamber. She found her cousin propped against her pillows, needlework in hand.

Jane's expression brightened, and she lowered her sewing to her lap. "Julia! Evangeline tells me you have been up for hours. I'd expected you would sleep later after last night's dinner."

Julia shrugged and sat on the settee next to the bed. "I hardly ever sleep late. I'm a creature of habit, I suppose. Besides, the rain woke me. Tell me, how are you feeling this morning?"

"The same as I feel every morning." Jane smiled. "Large. And quite sluggish."

"Well, you are one day closer, and tomorrow you will be closer still." Julia squeezed her cousin's hand. "I brought you this. I found it in the library. I thought you might enjoy it."

Jane accepted the book. "So kind. Poetry. I've not yet been down to the library. The accoucheur insists that I remain abed, and Mother enforces his instructions to the letter. I'm not even permitted to walk to the window to look at the lawn. To be honest, I'm growing weary of staring at these four walls."

Julia gave her cousin a quick overview of her morning's experiences, from her interaction with Mrs. Sedrick to the door that led to the tiny chamber. They talked and laughed like they had done as children. Jane returned her attention to her needlework, a small smile curving her lips. "Now, tell me all about the dinner last night."

With a sigh Julia leaned against the tufted back of the settee. "It was pleasant. I do wish you could have been there."

"Well, I could not, so I must live it through your account. Caroline did sneak away to see me while everyone was gathered in the drawing room. She said Matthew Blake was quite smitten with you." She arched her blonde eyebrow. "And that you have been invited to visit his mine when Father does."

Julia thought back to the handsome man, with his dark-blond hair and hazel eyes. His attention had been flattering, but it was his brother and his quieter, subtler style that intrigued her more.

But there was one thing that bothered her.

She could not shake the memory of Miss Davies's cool expression. Yes, it would be exciting to have a beau—someone who was fond of her—but at the expense of another woman's heart? "Are you acquainted with Miss Davies?"

"Not personally. I know the name, but that is all."

"Caroline told me Miss Davies believes herself soon to be betrothed to Mr. Blake. And if that is indeed the case, surely I could not look on him in that way."

"Surely there is a mistake, then."

"I had a man treat me as such, and I could not bear to be the source of another woman's pain."

"I daresay you are only hearing one side of the story. Surely he would not come into this house and behave in such a way. She'd not be the first woman to feel more strongly for a man than he felt for her. I'm sure it is a mistake."

"Perhaps. Do you know much about the Blake brothers?" Julia asked.

"Not a great deal. But I have heard a little from Mrs. Sedrick and Evangeline. You can barely see their estate from that window there."

"So close?" She knew they were neighbors, but she was surprised the house was so near to this one. Julia stood and looked out the window. Sure enough, gray stone chimneys rose into the morning mist and fog. She'd seen the same home from her window but never considered that it might belong to the Blakes.

"Mr. Matthew Blake owns it now."

"And Isaac Blake?" Julia could not resist the question. "What do you know of him?"

"I believe he owns a small bit of land on the edge of the estate. I cannot be certain."

Julia chewed her lower lip as she considered Jane's words. "Isaac Blake was the one who came to my aid, you know, the night of the attack at the inn."

Jane nodded. "I've only heard positive things about him. Well, except from Mother, but she rarely has anything positive to say about a second-born son."

Julia gave a little laugh. "Yes, she has made it quite clear that Matthew Blake would be a good match."

"I used to think that Mother was all stuff and nonsense about such things. If you remember, she did not want me to marry Jonathan. She wanted me to marry Mr. Ichabod Cruthers." Jane wrinkled her nose. "He's the heir to a large estate in Scotland of all places. I tried to be fond of him, for Mother's sake. Really I did. She was mortified to learn that I had given my heart to a soldier. But the heart's desire cannot always be dictated."

Julia nodded. "Aunt Beatrice informed me it was the duty of a young woman to marry well, if nothing more than to ease the minds of those who raised her."

Jane laughed. "That sounds like Mother, but she's always been more interested in advancing her social status than forging real relationships, and I don't think she'd contradict me on that statement. Even so, I sometimes wonder what would have happened if I had followed my mother's bidding. How different it would be if I had a house of my own and a present husband instead of one who is so far away."

The sincerity in the words took Julia aback. Was it possible her cousin regretted following her heart? Marrying for love?

Aunt Delia had voiced her concerns about the whirlwind nature of Julia's courtship with Percy, and she'd ignored them. Even Uncle Jac had made a comment or two about Percy's haughty tendencies. Julia dismissed them as quickly as she'd dismissed her aunt's comments. Had she heeded their warning, she could not help but wonder what would be different.

Now Jane's words stung, and that familiar pain, which for the last day or so had been relatively quiet, stabbed.

She'd thought she'd find happiness with Percy. Theirs had been a fast love. He was wild and impetuous. Ardent and headstrong. She'd have sacrificed almost anything to marry him and become his wife, but then the shock of sitting in church one Sunday morning and hearing the banns read for him to marry another had unsettled every hope, every dream she thought they had built together. And then, as if by some nightmare, rumors of their attachment began to filter through the parish. Mortification hardly described her state.

Trusting another man—laughing with another man, enjoying another man's company—seemed like an impossible endeavor. She'd try to consider Matthew Blake that way. After all, that's why she was here. To move on with life and find new direction. Perhaps her cousin's suggestion was right—it was best to leave such things to the women who knew better and abandon her budding infatuation with Isaac.

"Oh, I am so envious of you," Jane declared. "So much life lies ahead of you."

Julia laughed at the absurdity of the statement. "I'd much rather already be settled. I've had enough excitement."

"But don't you see? You have so many things to explore. A betrothal. Marriage. Love. Children."

"And do you not have those things? You're living them."

Jane's face fell, and the fleeting vibrancy fled her gray eyes. "Yes, but it is far different than I thought. My husband is gone, and I don't know when, if ever, I shall see him again. I am confined to a bed. I am living under my mother's roof, for heaven's sake."

"But your baby will be here soon, and surely that must give you a measure of anticipation."

"You've hit it exactly, dear cousin. Anticipation. Oh, delicious anticipation. And you have so much room for it."

Julia chuckled. "It's been my experience that infatuation with the opposite gender results in stomachaches and restless weariness. I wish I already knew what my place in life will be."

"You would take it all out then? The bloom of new love?"

"I suppose I haven't experienced it. I thought I had, but no. If I had, perhaps I might feel differently."

Jane patted her hand. "Finding love is the single most exhilarating experience I have had in my life. Its power was so great that it blinded me to the thing everyone warned me of—marrying a soldier. And yet, the memories of those times are enough to sustain me. They must be. For what choice do I have? Do not be overly eager to be settled.

Do not overlook the glorious feeling of being pursued and desired. For when it is over, it's gone. And it shall never be experienced again."

Julia's stomach fell, for something was different in her cousin's tone with these last words. Did she regret her decision to marry Jonathan? Was she sorry to be with child? It dawned on her at that moment . . . Julia had thought her cousin's world so enviable—a husband. A child. Security. But now she wondered if her cousin's suffering was not greater.

CHAPTER 17

Isaac stood at the gates of Wheal Tamsen and looked down Miner's Row. A steady, cold rain fell to the earth, just as it had all morning, muting the colors of the landscape even more than the sneaky arrival of winter already had.

In front of him a boy of four or five ran across the narrow road, chasing a dog, and farther down the lane, two adolescent girls, clad in heavy gray capes, carried large baskets toward High Street.

After shifting his gaze to Charlie's cottage, Isaac shivered and blinked away the moisture that found its way beneath his hat's brim. He needed to visit Charlie's widow—the task he was loath to do.

He'd encountered Margaret a couple of times during the midnight hours at the mine's counting house. She'd arrived shortly after he did, frantic and fearful, and she'd been at Charlie's side when he breathed his last. The horror painted on her face would haunt Isaac for months—nay, years—to come.

He trudged down Miner's Row to the familiar cottage that felt almost like a second home. Could it really only have been two days since he last sat in this home with Charlie and Margaret, laughing and talking? Now, everyone's worlds were different.

A light shimmered from behind the cottage window's thin linen curtain. He knocked on the door. At length, it creaked open. Warmth and the scent of smoke wafted out.

How many times had she welcomed him into this home, always cheerful, always smiling?

But today Margaret's auburn hair hung unruly and wild over her shoulders. Dark patches beneath her red-rimmed eyes stood out in sharp contrast against wan cheeks. She appeared battered and frail—and simultaneously young and old.

The words caught in his throat. "May I come in?"

At first she did not respond; her expression did not change. Then she inched back to give him room to pass. He removed his coat and stomped the moisture from his boots before he stepped inside.

He assessed the space, from its simple stone floor to the narrow wooden staircase leading to the first floor, to the herbs hanging from the hand-hewn rafters. A low-burning fire simmered in the small hearth, and a black pot hung over it. He'd heard from the miners that someone had been with her constantly, and true to the stories, Miss Harriet Prynne sat in a chair near the fire, cradling Charlie's slumbering son.

Isaac cleared his throat, placed his satchel on the table, and withdrew two loaves of bread. "My housekeeper sent these to you."

Margaret sat at the table, leaned her elbows on the top, and only stared at the offering.

He searched for words that would be appropriate, but none came. They remained silent for several moments, bound in a grief that, while each felt it differently, was raw and real and fresh.

He'd promised Charlie he'd watch out for her.

But what did that mean?

He sat next to her and then he covered her still, cold hand with his own. She drew a deep breath and, as if it took all of her energy, lifted her head to look at him. "Can you believe it?"

"No."

She slid her gaze over to her child, and fresh tears filled her eyes. "Charlie always warned this could happen. I never believed him."

"It is a risk every miner understands, but . . ."

The silence resumed as his words faded.

Over the next hour a handful of concerned neighbors and friends filtered in. The vicar, the apothecary, but mostly mining folk. Margaret was in no mood to receive them. And he could not blame her.

Isaac said little while he was at the cottage, but as dusk began to fall, the church bell chimed, marking the lateness of the hour. After a guest departed, he stood, reached for his satchel, and approached her. If it was possible, she looked even paler, frailer than she had when he arrived.

There was one more task he needed to tend to before he departed.

It was customary for a mine to offer monetary support to a widow following her husband's mine-related death. As the captain of the mine, he needed to give Margaret what was rightfully hers.

He opened his satchel and retrieved a smaller pouch.

Margaret's wide-eyed gaze snapped to the small leather purse. Before he could even fully extend it toward her, she snipped, "I don't want it."

They locked eyes for several moments, and then he placed it on the table. "It belongs to you."

She folded her arms over her chest, her eyes teared afresh, and she jutted her chin in the air. "I'll not take it."

Isaac softened his tone as much as he could. "Charlie worked for this. It's his. He'd want you to have it. He'd want Jory to have it."

"My husband wanted one thing." Her chin trembled as a tear escaped her lashes. "He had but one dream. And you know it full well. Wheal Gwenna."

He swallowed dryly. "Now's hardly the time to—"

"It was his dream!" Her lip trembled. "Take that money and put it toward opening it. He'd want it that way."

Her round face reddened, and he feared she might make herself ill. He'd not contradict her. Not now. Instead he stepped forward. "If that's what you want, but I'm going to leave it here until a more suitable time. You keep it safe. We can revisit the topic at another time."

As Isaac prepared to depart, Miss Trebell arrived to relieve Miss Prynne and stay with Margaret and Jory, and Isaac offered to walk Miss Prynne back to her cottage. The hour had grown late, and after the incident at the inn, he didn't feel comfortable with anyone walking alone after dark, especially not someone he revered as much as Miss Harriet Prynne.

Besides Matthew, Isaac had little family in Cornwall, but he'd known Miss Prynne his entire life. She felt like family. His mother had regarded her as a great friend, and after she died, Miss Prynne took both Matthew and him under her wing. She shared his passion for those in the community, and often they'd work together to help the miners.

They walked along High Street, both feeling the loss of a great friend and grieving for the pain of the family he left behind.

Miss Prynne placed her hand on Isaac's arm. "I do worry for her."

Isaac winced as he recalled the pain etched on Margaret's face. "She's a strong woman."

"But she is still that—a woman. A mortal woman, with thoughts and feelings and emotions and limits. Be it a strong person or weak, a loved one's death could cause anyone to crumble."

He sobered. Miss Prynne had never married, but she knew the loss of love—and everyone in Goldweth knew it.

"Do you remember when David Coryn was killed at Wheal Tamsen when the old shaft flooded?" he asked. "I recall being in awe of my father. He always knew what to say to ease the pain of those around him."

"Your father was a remarkable man, but, Mr. Blake, you are like him in many ways. Can you not see? There is a way you can fill your father's place and comfort your community."

He slowed his steps. Time and experience had taught him Miss Prynne's insight usually had merit. "How so?"

"You'll forgive this old woman the offense of eavesdropping, but I overheard you and Margaret speaking of Wheal Gwenna."

He drew a deep breath. He didn't want to discuss it, yet so many seemed to know of it.

"I think it's a fine idea. One that your father would be proud of. Our community is hurting. Like your father, you see a need and you meet it."

He chuckled uncomfortably. "It's not that simple."

"Not much in this life is simple."

By the time Isaac delivered Miss Prynne to her door, darkness had closed in completely. She paused at the threshold and turned to fix faded green eyes on him. "Good night, Mr. Blake. And think on what I said. You know how fond I was of Mr. Rowe. There's a hole in our little community now that he's gone. Everyone is looking for someone to smooth the way—not necessarily someone to replace him, for he could never be replaced. But we need someone to champion the likes of the lowly, and I think you could be that man."

Isaac bid her good night, and as he walked home, he considered Margaret's request and Miss Prynne's words. How his heart ached for the loss of his friend, but seeing the fire lit in those remaining— the fire for him to continue to fight—ignited fresh purpose and determination within him.

CHAPTER 18

Nearly a week later, Julia rose early, dressed in her dark-blue riding habit, and made her way to Lanwyn Manor's stable. The groom had paired her with a gentle white mare, aptly named Snow, and as soon as he helped her onto her sidesaddle, she set off to the west lawn.

She turned her face toward the cool breeze. A predawn mist hovered over the ground, and the gray sky promised rain. Even with the threat of precipitation, the icy air invigorated her senses, and the broad, open lawn reminded her of the freedom she enjoyed at Penwythe Hall.

Other than two brief visits from Miss Trebell and Miss Prynne, Julia had seen no other people besides the servants since the night of the dinner. Uncle William had departed for business in the south a few days following her arrival, and the family did not even venture out for church, since Aunt Beatrice had a headache on Sunday. In fact, once the excitement of the first few days subsided, life settled into a steady, predictable pace. By nature Julia preferred company over solitude, and several days with no new faces wore on her.

She'd not been out long when she spotted a horse and rider approaching along the opposite side of the drystone wall that separated Lanwyn Manor from the public road. Normally she'd pay such a sight little attention, but something familiar about the broad shoulders and distinctive profile made her look twice.

Was that one of the Blake brothers?

The man raised a hand in greeting.

Curious, she guided her horse to the wall's edge.

"Miss Twethewey," called the rider, "this is a surprise."

"Mr. Blake!" A little thrill shot through her when Isaac's features became clearer. "I thought that was you."

He stopped his gray horse on the opposite side of the fence. "I didn't realize you were a horsewoman."

She smiled and rested her crop over her lap. "Oh, I am. At home I ride nearly every day. Besides, if I wanted some fresh air this morning, I needed to take it now. It looks like rain might keep us indoors later in the day."

"I think you're right." He lifted his hazel eyes heavenward before he returned his attention to her. "But is your uncle comfortable with you being out alone?"

"Uncle William has gone to Plymouth. He will return later today. Prior to his departure he gave me permission to ride Snow here on the grounds whenever I'd like."

It had been nearly a week since she had last seen Mr. Blake, and Julia had overheard the servants discussing the death of his friend. She sobered and tilted her head to the side. "I was sorry to hear about Mr. Benson. I understand he was a friend of yours."

She did not miss the twitch of his freshly shaven jaw, nor how his gloved grip tightened on his reins. No doubt he was surprised to know that she had heard such information, but there was no use pretending she hadn't.

"He was," Mr. Blake responded at last. "A very good friend."

"I also understand that he had a wife and child," she said hesitantly, for she was treading on conversation that was not really any of her affair.

But Mr. Blake only nodded.

"I cannot imagine her pain."

"Margaret Benson is a strong woman, but the sting of grief is a relentless burden, even for the strong."

"I couldn't agree more." Julia forced lightness to her voice to combat the conversation's heavy turn. "So, are you coming or going?"

He gave a little chuckle and adjusted the tall hat atop his head. "I am on my way to Wheal Tamsen now, and I'm coming from my home, Anvon Cottage, which is down that lane."

She followed his pointed finger to where the public road split to the north and a small path disappeared into a copse of trees. "I see."

His horse tossed his mane, and Isaac reached forward to pat the animal's neck. "We did not have the opportunity to finish our conversation the night of the dinner. How are you settling into life at Lanwyn Manor?"

"Very nicely."

"It's an impressive home, is it not?" He lifted his gaze past her to the tower portion of the home, reaching four stories into the heavens.

"It is indeed, although I confess, it's not at all what I expected."

"And what were you expecting?"

She sighed, considering her answer. "My aunt has very particular tastes—ones more suited to the drawing rooms of London. In fact, I was surprised to hear they'd left London at all."

"How long do you intend to stay in Goldweth?"

"I came to Lanwyn Manor to be a companion for my cousin who's confined to bed. So I will stay for as long as I can be a comfort to her. I should think until after the baby arrives."

The wind swept down from the woods, giving a sharp whistle through the bare branches and carrying with it the first bits of moisture.

"I think the rain you referred to earlier is about to arrive." He gathered his reins again. "I'd best be on my way."

"Will I see you at church tomorrow?" she asked, wishing he did not need to hurry off and that the rain would stay at bay.

"I do hope so." He tipped his hat. "Good day, Miss Twethewey."

She dipped her head in parting and watched for several seconds as he continued down the road. Then, with a click of her tongue, she patted Snow's neck with her gloved hand and urged her into a trot. Unable to resist one final glance, she looked over her shoulder.

Mr. Isaac Blake.

A very interesting man indeed.

———◆———

Julia adjusted her position on the hard pew and fixed her gaze on the intricately carved pulpit at the front, resisting the urge to look around the vestibule. Parishioners clad in drab cloaks of brown, gray, and black bustled in and out of the morning wind. They chattered amongst themselves, their whispered words echoing from the great wooden beams above them and the stone walls.

And Julia could not have been more curious.

The Lambournes, however, did not join in the pre-sermon conversations. They sat stiffly in their family pew. Eyes forward. Silent. They'd arrived early—a tactic Julia soon realized her aunt employed to avoid speaking with anyone. Earlier that morning, Julia had thought they might neglect services—again. Aunt Beatrice complained of a headache, and it was only at the last moment that she declared it her duty to set an example for the community by attending.

Grateful for any opportunity to learn more about her surroundings, Julia smoothed the lavender wool of her new pelisse, then touched the satin ribbon cascading from her new bonnet. Since her cloak had been stolen at the inn, Aunt had given her this one. Julia shouldn't have been surprised, not really. Especially after her aunt had purchased a new gown for a simple dinner.

As she demurely glanced around the dimly lit space, she recognized a handful of attendees from the dinner, but most were strangers. This was a modest yet ancient church, airy and cold, constructed of the same slate stone found in Lanwyn Manor. All around her parishioners filed into the oak pews with high sides and backs. Judging by their simple clothing, most of them were the miners the staff had talked about.

But really she was looking for *him*.

She'd been surprised to see him out the previous morning, but what surprised her most was how often he occupied her thoughts.

It was normal, she supposed, to romanticize someone who had helped her so selflessly. But day by day as thoughts of him increased, thoughts of Percy decreased.

Maybe there was something to Jane's words of anticipation after all.

"There," Caroline whispered, leaning near. "That's the widow you asked about, entering now. In the black pelisse."

Julia slid her gaze to the woman as best she could without drawing attention.

So that was Margaret Benson.

Empathy seized Julia's heart as the woman looked around, as if searching for someone.

She was a slender woman, with auburn hair that was shockingly bright against her pallid complexion. She clutched a small boy's hand in hers, and a hooded black cape draped her from head to toe.

She and Caroline were not the only ones to notice her entrance, for hushed voices sounded from the pew behind them.

"I have it on very good authority that Charlie asked Mr. Blake to take care of her—asked him as he lay on the ground dying, God rest his soul."

At the mention of the names, Julia stiffened and held her breath to hear the whispers.

"They'll be married within the year," muttered a deeper voice. "Mark my words."

Commotion sounded, and at this Julia could not remain still. She pivoted as the Blake brothers paused in the doorway.

It amazed her how two men could appear so similar, but even with their striking resemblance, they each possessed qualities that made them unique. Isaac was the taller of the two. Both had hazel eyes, both had blond hair, but Isaac's jaw was squarer, and Matthew's left cheek dimpled when he smiled.

Matthew entered with a hearty laugh as he greeted a group of men.

Isaac, however, entered more subtly, reverently, and after a few quick greetings, he stepped to the pew where the widow was sitting. He smiled down at them and ruffled the boy's hair. Then his expression sobered.

Julia shifted her attention forward but cut her eyes to watch him. She could not hear what they were saying, but the sympathetic draw of Isaac's brows was telling, intimate in its focus.

Mr. Blake left Mrs. Benson, and as he straightened he looked in Julia's direction.

Heat flushed her. She'd been caught watching him.

The corner of his mouth twitched in a smile. He nodded in her direction, then moved to a pew near the front.

After the service, the Lambournes greeted the vicar before they moved out to the churchyard. Julia spied Miss Trebell and Miss Prynne, and she excused herself from the family to go speak with them.

"My dear Miss Twethewey!" Miss Trebell's blue eyes widened, and her cheeks flushed pink in the cool air. "I am so delighted you were able to come to our humble service this morning. We hope this is the first of many you will attend."

"I intend to be here every Sunday I am able." Julia allowed the woman to take her gloved hands in her own.

"Oh, how lovely. And will you join us for the Ladies League this week? 'Tis a shame we could not meet this week, but with the accident, I fear no one was quite in the right frame of mind."

Eager to make plans to see the ladies again, she nodded. "Yes, I will be there."

After a brief conversation, Julia caught sight of Miss Davies near the stone fence, watching as her mother stood across the yard in conversation with a lady Julia did not know.

Here was an opportunity. The woman was alone. She stepped toward her. "Miss Davies?"

Miss Davies pivoted, but as her gaze fell on Julia, her eyes narrowed and she offered a stiff curtsey.

Her own hurt at being betrayed fueling her courage, Julia forced a smile. "Miss Davies. I was sorry that we did not have much of an opportunity to speak the other night."

A flush crept over Miss Davies's smooth cheeks, and her lips twitched. "I fear your attentions were much occupied."

Julia resisted the urge to wince at the sharpness of her words. If this woman was indeed in love with Matthew Blake, it was no wonder her manner was so cool. Even so, Julia would try to mend a bridge before it became irreparable.

"I do wonder if you would care to join me for tea one afternoon this week. Perhaps Wednesday? I know my aunt and cousin would enjoy it very much."

Miss Davies inhaled sharply and cut a glance toward Aunt Beatrice. Julia followed her gaze and was distressed to see her aunt speaking to Mr. Matthew Blake.

"I thank you for your kind offer, Miss Twethewey, but I fear I will be unable to join you this week. Perhaps another time. If you'll excuse me." The tall woman turned and walked away, leaving Julia alone in the courtyard.

If there had been any question about Miss Davies's feelings, this awkward conversation confirmed it.

Julia glanced toward Matthew.

Oh yes, he was handsome. Animated. Full of life and charm. She watched him for several seconds and was about to join her family when the sound of her name from a nearby conversation snagged her attention.

"Julia Twethewey's from Braewyn. She is Mrs. Lambourne's sister's child. Came to be a companion for one of the Lambournes' daughters."

Julia's heart raced. Someone was talking about her.

She gathered her courage to look in the direction of the voice but only saw the tops of two bonnets over the hedge.

"Can't say I'm surprised," the other voice hissed in a whisper. "They say her husband's serving in the army."

"Likely story. Perhaps Lambourne moved his family here to avoid scandal and has no intention of mining. Why else does she never show her face?"

"Apparently she's ill and is confined to her bed."

"Be it scandal or curse, that house isn't doing them any favors. No child born under that roof has survived."

Alarm trickled through her. Had she heard that correctly? No children survived?

The voice huffed. "'Tis naught but lore."

"Is it? There's a curse on that home. Can you recall hearing of a child born there living to adulthood? I cannot."

Nausea swirled within her. Curses weren't real. Were they?

Surely not. But talk of ghosts and mysteries would wreak havoc with her sensibilities. Her enthusiasm for learning all she could about her new surroundings was vanishing as completely as the sun behind the persistent clouds, and Julia wanted nothing more than to be tucked inside her tower chamber.

But clearly there was one more encounter she needed to endure. Ahead of her, just outside of the Lambourne carriage, Mr. Matthew Blake spoke with her aunt and uncle. She gathered her skirts and hurried toward them.

"Julia, there you are! Where did you get to?"

"I was speaking with Miss Prynne and Miss Trebell."

"Well, never mind. Mr. Blake is here, and I daresay he would much rather speak with you than with me, my dear."

Matthew bowed. "Miss Twethewey. I was just telling Mr. Lambourne that we must get him out to Wheal Tamsen, and he has agreed to come tomorrow. Will you join him? I should so like to show you a bit more of Goldweth."

She caught the enthusiasm on her aunt's face. Regardless of Miss Davies's coolness, regardless of the unsettling words she'd heard, there was no reason she should not accept Mr. Blake's eager invitation.

She glanced over as Isaac opened the church gate, allowed Mrs. Benson to pass before him, and then swept the Benson boy up to sit on his shoulders.

No, there was no reason she should not accept Mr. Matthew's invitation. She smiled up at him. "Thank you, Mr. Blake. I should like that very much."

CHAPTER 19

Matthew was making good on his plans to endear himself to the Lambournes.

Even now he stood by the Lambournes' carriage, his head thrown back in laughter.

Isaac's gaze fell to Miss Twethewey. She stood next to Matthew, clad in lavender—a refreshing feminine color in the midst of the bleak grays and browns surrounding her. The top of her beribboned bonnet came only to Matthew's shoulder. Dark tendrils escaped from beneath her bonnet and danced in the wind. Even from this distance, her cheeks glowed pink and her vibrant blue eyes struck him.

There was no denying her loveliness. But did any of that matter? Matthew had clearly set his claim on the beauty. She'd prefer him. There was nothing left to do or to say.

Besides, Isaac had more important things on which to focus. Like keeping his promise to Charlie.

Jory squealed in delight on his shoulders and clutched Isaac's hat. Margaret fell into step beside him, and together they left the churchyard.

"I'm glad that's over." Margaret wrapped her arms around her waist as she walked, paying little attention to the mud splattering her hem. "I cannot abide the looks of pity."

"I'd say it is concern rather than pity. Everyone loved Charlie."

After turning onto High Street, the crowd thinned and they shared the street only with those headed to Miner's Row. They walked in silence for several moments before he asked, "How are you, really?"

Margaret squinted into the breeze and tucked a loose strand of hair behind her ear. "I should be stoic and tell you Jory and I are well, but the truth is, we're livin' in a nightmare."

Isaac adjusted Jory on his shoulders. "Is there anything I can do to help you?"

"Actually, yes." She slowed her steps. "Our cottage. I don't want to be there anymore. If you want to help Jory and me, you can help me find another place for us."

A little stunned at her request, he said, "But it's your home. And the only home Jory's known."

"It's a miner's cottage." Forcefulness flared in her tone. "We're no longer a miner family. Not anymore."

The thought of the Bensons leaving Miner's Row did not bode well with Isaac. "As your friend, I'd advise you not to make any rash decisions, Margaret. Not yet. Give yourself time. Everyone here cares for you and Jory, and it's been but a week."

"I don't want time, Isaac," she snipped, impatiently swiping a tear away. "What I want is to be away from here—away from where I see his ghost around every corner."

Drawing a deep breath, Isaac looked to the modest row of cottages. Yes, Charlie's ghost was around every corner.

He had lived on this row since he was a child, first with his father and now his family. There certainly were plenty of vacant homes in other parts of the village, especially since so many families had to leave to find work elsewhere. Charlie's raspy request rang in Isaac's ears, clanging loudly and demanding attention, like a mine's bell orchestrating the day.

If this was what she wanted, who was he to deny her? "If you're certain, then I can make arrangements."

"Thank you."

They continued on in silence until they reached the cottage door. Isaac lifted Jory from his shoulders and set him on the ground. Isaac propped his hands on his hips as he watched Charlie's dog trot from around the cottage and greet the boy.

She stepped to his side. "There's one more thing. Wheal Gwenna—"

Isaac stiffened. "That can wait until later."

"Can it?" Margaret sniffed. "'Tis all I can think about."

"Fulfilling Charlie's plans will not bring him back, Margaret. You must look to Jory and your needs now."

She folded her arms across her chest. "Are you sayin' you'll not open it?"

"Not necessarily, but in good conscience I cannot see you invest your money in something that might fail."

"It was the one thing he wanted. Ever since he got that inheritance, albeit modest, from his uncle, he was determined that you two have enough to make a go of it. He spoke of it daily."

"But you will need that money for the future. For Jory. I—"

"You forget I'm a midwife. I can support myself. I need not be reliant on anyone. I want to proceed, Isaac. You'll not change my mind. If that is what he wanted, then that is what we'll do."

Isaac nodded. "If that is what you wish, but the details will have to wait for another day and will come in good time. Just don't forget that a mine—any mine—is a gamble, pure and simple. I'm not sure I am comfortable risking your security on something that is uncertain."

"That is for me to decide, I suppose." She offered a shaky smile. "I never did like to be told what to do."

———◆———

The next afternoon, sunlight filtered in through Lanwyn Manor's great hall's stained-glass windows, painting colorful patches on the flagstone floor and reflecting from the silver urn on the side table. The rain and drizzle of the past few days had subsided, and now the sun, with its vibrant white light and its appearance of warmth, beckoned Julia to join it.

At Penwythe she was rarely indoors. She'd pass her hours riding, visiting the village, walking on the moors or along the seashore, regardless of the weather or clime. But here, her aunt and Caroline were content to sit in the drawing room, and poor Jane was confined to a single chamber. Initially Julia felt duty bound to stay in their company, but now sheer boredom convinced her to venture off on her own.

The time had almost arrived for her visit to Wheal Tamsen. Julia stiffened as Aunt Beatrice fiddled with the collar of her emerald-green riding habit, and she winced as the older woman tugged a lock of hair back into place.

"Oh, Mother, let her be," Caroline entreated as she swept into the hall, clad in a gown of yellow muslin with vivid white Vandyke points along the hem, her thin eyebrow raised in amusement. "She's lovely as she is."

"It doesn't matter if I'm lovely or not." Julia flinched as her aunt pinched her cheeks to add color. "I'm going to see the mine, nothing more."

"Nothing more? La, Julia Twethewey." Aunt Beatrice pinned her with a warning glare. "He'd be an advantageous match, and don't forget it for a second. One never knows how many opportunities may come one's way."

A breeze swept through the open door to the main foyer, and Uncle William stepped in. The wind had disrupted his thinning shock of gray hair, and the ruddiness of his cheeks suggested it was colder outside than it appeared. "Are you ready, Niece? Blake should be arriving soon."

"Yes, I'm ready." Julia was grateful for the interruption as she pulled away from her aunt's fussing fingers and moved toward him. "And I must thank you for agreeing to ride instead of taking the carriage. I feel as if I've not seen the sun in days, and I'm desperate for open air."

Her expression rich with disapproval, Aunt Beatrice tsked before Uncle William could respond. "Let's hope Mr. Blake doesn't think you indelicate. Riding horseback when one could be taking the carriage—I've never heard the like. I've often questioned your aunt Delia's decision to allow you to be such an outdoorswoman and roam about the countryside as you do, but I suppose there is naught to be done about that now."

Caroline and Julia exchanged amused glances, and Julia stepped to the window and looked to the bright, sun-drenched lawn. She was eager to see the mine, and in truth, she was eager to see Matthew again. At dinner he'd proven himself an amusing, attentive companion. After contemplating all that she discovered while at church the previous day, Julia decided that her initial interest in Isaac was in response to the incident at the inn, and now it was clear his intentions were elsewhere. She had no real proof that Matthew had treated Miss Davies unfairly. So why should she not enjoy his company? What harm could an afternoon's ride possibly do?

She turned to her cousin. "Caroline, will you not change your mind and come?"

Caroline smirked. "I've no interest at all in looking at a dirty mine. Besides, Father is a suitable chaperone. You don't need me getting in the way."

Uncle Lambourne retrieved his leather riding gloves and lifted his left hand, preparing to don them. "I've been very impressed with the Blakes of late. I find Matthew to be a first-rate man, and his brother did us a great service the night of your arrival. He might be a good business partner, but I want to see him in his element before I follow that thought too far."

By the time Matthew arrived, Julia was almost bursting at the seams for someone new to talk to. She withdrew from the window, lest he think she was waiting for him.

He swept into the foyer, a contagious laugh preceding him. As he rounded the corner, the sight of his easy smile and bright eyes reminded her of how pleasant his company could be.

"Are you certain you will not join us, Mrs. Lambourne?" Matthew teased Aunt Beatrice, taking her hand in his and bowing over it. "The day is fine, and I should so enjoy your company."

Aunt Beatrice tittered, basking in the attention, and waved a dismissive hand in front of her. "Horseback? Me? Heavens, no. I haven't ridden in I can't recall how long. My nerves do not stand for it anymore, but you all go." Her gaze flicked from her husband back to Mr. Blake. "I know my niece is in good hands."

Once outside, the invigorating breeze grazed Julia's flushed face as she stepped from the arched entrance to the courtyard where the horses were waiting. The blue sky beckoned, and the birds swooping overhead implored her to remain out of doors. She accepted the groom's assistance to mount Snow, and within moments she was settled and arranged her skirts modestly over her legs.

"A horsewoman, eh?" Matthew smiled as he circled his own bay horse, his admiration evident. "An equestrian and a talented musician? It seems your niece is quite accomplished, Mr. Lambourne."

Julia beamed under the praise. "I'm not sure I would say that, but I do enjoy riding."

"Have you been to the village yet, Miss Twethewey?" Mr. Blake inquired as they cleared the gatehouse arch and crossed the carriage turn to the main drive.

"Not really." She swept a tendril from her face. "Of course, I saw the church yesterday and the inn the first night I was here, but I haven't seen much beyond that."

"Well, we must remedy that, and perhaps show you another side of Goldweth. What say you, Mr. Lambourne?" Matthew looked over his shoulder toward the older man riding behind them. "With your permission we can cut through the forest there and go to the mine via High Street."

With her uncle's consent they veered the horses from the main drive toward the trees separating the property's edge from the village. Julia had been told that the fastest way to Wheal Tamsen was to cut through Lanwyn's east meadow and pass Tregarthan Hall.

Once they were in the forest, the path narrowed. Matthew and Julia rode next to each other, and Uncle William followed. Julia cast a glance at the man riding next to her. The sunlight filtered through the barren branches, dappling his broad shoulders and catching on a piece of golden hair that happened to escape his hat.

It could be worse than to be courted by such a man.

"I do wonder that my wife or Caroline did not take you to the village in my absence, even if for nothing more than to make you acquainted with your surroundings," her uncle mused as they traveled the worn, uneven path. "They do their best to avoid it, I suppose. It pales pitifully in comparison to the elegance of London."

"I've not spent a great deal of time in London, so I can't compare it," she said.

"You strike me as a lady who is happiest in nature and the country."

She turned to Matthew, almost suspecting his comment was made in jest, but his content, happy expression suggested it was meant as a compliment.

Martins and swallows rustled and called to each other from the boughs overhead. Julia lifted her face to the sunlight. When the wind calmed, it almost felt warm, and she smiled under the sensation of it.

Despite the tranquility around her, she jumped when a twig nearby snapped. She jerked her reins sharply, causing Snow to toss her head and whinny. "What was that?"

"Only a rabbit or some such creature." Matthew leaned over to grab her reins and help settle Snow. "Did it startle you?"

Feeling foolish, she forced a smile and regripped her reins. "No, I suppose I am a bit jumpy, 'tis all."

"Well, you are completely safe with us, Miss Twethewey." Matthew lowered his voice, his hazel gaze fixed on her. "I'll not let anything happen to you."

At length, they emerged from the forest and made their way over the bridge. "This is High Street," Matthew said. "It isn't much, I fear, but 'tis home to us."

"It's much larger than the village outside of Penwythe Hall." She took in the tidy stone shops and cottages and a broad, cobbled street, surprised to see so many people bustling about.

"There's the shop where the ladies buy ribbons and such things, and the butcher, the apothecary, and the baker are over there."

She slowed her horse and assessed the bustling town.

"The church is there, which you of course know, and just beyond it is where Miss Prynne lives. I believe you've met her."

"Indeed. Miss Prynne has invited me to her house later this week for a sewing circle."

"So Miss Prynne wrangled you into helping her?" He laughed, a twinkle glimmering in his eyes. "She's very good at that. But in all seriousness, Miss Prynne prides herself on seeing that the poor are well provided for, especially in cold weather, and she will recruit any person willing to help her cause." His smile faded. He cast a glance back at her uncle and then lowered his voice. "You'll not think that I interfere if I offer advice?"

"Depends on the advice," she teased.

"This will sound odd. Everyone loves Miss Prynne and Miss Trebell, but I still would like to caution you." He tilted his head toward her. "They are well intentioned enough, but they have the tendency to provide a great deal of town gossip. Even the best intentions sometimes take a wrong turn, so be careful how much you reveal about your life, lest you find it the focus of every conversation in town the next day."

Julia raised her brow. "Spoken from experience?"

He shrugged. "I've lived here all my life, and I never remember a time when Miss Prynne and Miss Trebell were not present. I've lived here long enough to see more than one cruel round of gossip, and in case you haven't figured it out yet, I hold you in esteem, Miss Twethewey, and I would hate to see you fall prey. Friendly advice, after all."

Heat flooded her cheeks, no doubt adding to the pink already there from the cold air. "I consider myself warned, although I doubt anything I would have to say would be the cause of gossip. I admit I lead a rather uneventful life."

"Well, that remains to be seen, does it not?"

They continued down High Street, and Mr. Blake slowed his horse and nodded toward a cobbled street with modest cottages of stone and thatch lining either side. "That's Miner's Row. Many of the miners who work regularly at Wheal Tamsen live here."

He did not slow his horse as they crossed the lane and kept his eyes forward as they rode down the road. Curious, Julia shifted her gaze. People along the road were staring in her direction. She was not sure if they were looking at her uncle or Mr. Blake. Perhaps they were looking at her.

"Ah, we're here."

Julia was not sure what she'd expected. A large stone building with a chimney stood at the edge of the property, and another house stood close to it. Smaller buildings stood scattered around, but all in all, it was not as grand as she'd anticipated.

"What do you think, Miss Twethewey?"

She blinked, assessing the area. "I hardly know. I've never been to a mine."

"It's far from impressive from this vantage point. The bulk of the work happens underground. Certainly not as idyllic as orchards and farmland, but we find beauty in it."

People nodded and bowed toward Blake, but he did not seem to notice. Instead he offered to help her from her horse. "Let's go inside the counting house. It is not as elegant as you are used to, but it will give us a chance to warm up. I'm eager to show you my world."

CHAPTER 20

Isaac stomped the mud and debris from his riding boots before he opened the door to the counting house.

The morning had been a long one, and now, with the day nearing a close, he was eager to finish his tasks and return home. He'd just completed his assessment of the northern shaft, and he had dirt on his coat to prove it. Setting day—the day on which men bid for work—was coming, and he'd been underground to determine exactly what work was required.

He ducked under the counting house's low, rustic doorframe, and his eyes adjusted quickly to the dimly lit foyer. Directly before him a narrow staircase led the way to three upstairs bedchambers, used in case of an injury or if he or Matthew decided to stay on the grounds. To his left a door led to an office, and to his right another door led to a sitting room.

He was about to turn into the cluttered mining office when rustling from the sitting room drew his attention. From the low doorway firelight gleamed, brightening the fading day. No doubt it was Matthew settling the day's count in the books. Good.

Despite the fact that Matthew had attended church the previous day, he and his brother had spoken only briefly following Charlie's death. The morning after the accident, Matthew had departed for Falmouth. He'd not even been present at the burial. Even so, Isaac was not surprised that Matthew was avoiding him. It was times like this when his brother disappeared—times when tragedy struck and answers were needed.

Isaac pressed his lips together, preparing what he would say to his brother. A conversation like the one that was required was never easy.

He stepped over the planked floor and ducked through the threshold. "Matthew, I need—"

But who he saw made him stop short.

Miss Twethewey, clad in a riding gown of dark green and a black hat with a matching ribbon, stood at the fire. Dark tendrils framed her cheeks, and dark lashes accented brilliantly blue eyes.

"Miss Twethewey." Isaac straightened, surprise nearly robbing him of speech. Almost as an afterthought he remembered to bow. "I was not aware you were here."

"Mr. Blake." She returned the greeting with a curtsey, a sweet smile on her full lips. She tilted her head to the side and clasped her gloved hands before her. "I wondered if I would see you."

He deposited the rolled maps he was carrying on the table. He removed his hat, placed it next to the maps, and raked his fingers through his hair, conscious of how he must appear. Even so, he smiled. "I'm always here."

It was rare to have a lady in the counting house, and now that he was in the sitting room, her scent of lavender—alluring, intoxicating, and thoroughly feminine—surrounded him. Her dainty appearance seemed wildly out of place.

"I apologize for my appearance." He attempted to brush the stone dust from his coat. "I've been underground. It's not the tidiest of places."

"Do not apologize, sir. This is a mine, after all."

"To what do we owe the pleasure?"

"Your brother invited my uncle and me to visit. He wanted to show Uncle William the operation, and I've never been to a mine before."

Isaac's spine stiffened.

Of course. *Matthew.*

"They're at the pump house now, or at least I believe that is the correct term," she continued. "My uncle and your brother think me too delicate to accompany them. So I'll have to observe it from the window."

"Quite right. It's very noisy. And dirty."

She smirked. "And I'm far too fragile for anything dirty and noisy."

Isaac chuckled at her unmasked sarcasm. "I doubt that."

He moved a lantern from the hook to the desk and tugged on the hem of his striped waistcoat to straighten it. "Please." He extended his arm to the settee by the fire, and once she was seated, he sat on the settee opposite her. Unsure how best to welcome their visitor, he stammered, "Have you been offered tea?"

"I believe your maid has gone to make some." She leaned forward as if taking him into confidence. "I must say I believe I caught her unawares. I don't think she was expecting guests."

Relaxing in her company, Isaac shrugged. "Eliza does not often have the opportunity to make tea for ladies. Miss Prynne and Miss Trebell call quite often, but other than that, few ladies come to the counting house."

As if on cue Eliza entered the sitting room from the kitchen entrance, awkwardly balancing a tray, panic twisting her young face. Steam curled from the piping-hot liquid, and she placed the tray on a table at the end of the settee, poured the tea with a shaky hand, and extended the teacup to Miss Twethewey.

Miss Twethewey thanked the maid, took a sip, and returned the cup to the tray.

He had to admire Miss Twethewey's tact. With Eliza making the tea, there was no telling how it actually tasted.

"Tell me, Miss Twethewey," he said, attempting to divert her attention from the undoubtedly bitter brew, "now that you are here, what do you think of Wheal Tamsen?"

"I hardly know what to think." She laughed. "I've not seen much of it."

"I'm afraid there really isn't much to see. Engine house for the pump, counting house, not all have a stable, but we have one here. Some of the other buildings are for surface work, but most of the work takes place beneath the surface. Under our very feet, even."

"I've seen the engine houses and their chimneys on the moors, but I never knew much about them."

"Are there not mines close to where you are from? You're from Cornwall, are you not?"

She nodded. "Yes. My paternal uncle, Jac Twethewey, owns a small estate west of here. Penwythe Hall in Braewyn. But his business is orchards and agriculture."

"Braewyn? Oh yes, you have mines around you, both copper and tin. Wheal Tilly and Wheal Thomas are both on the coast not far from there."

"Have you always been around mines, then, Mr. Blake?"

"All my life. My father owned a handful of mines to the east, and some of my earliest memories were there. Tregarthan Hall, our family home, is a short ride from here to the north."

"We can see Tregarthan Hall from Lanwyn, if I'm not mistaken."

"I believe so."

"Uncle Jac was of the firm belief that a woman should, in the very least, be well acquainted with the methods that support one's family. I fear I know more about apples and orchards than I care to admit."

He smiled. "But then, apples are cultivated in the sunshine, not buried fathoms below the earth's surface. I doubt your uncle would feel the same about mining and you going underground. Truth be told, I am surprised Lambourne consented to allow you to visit our humble mine."

"If that is the case, then I'm sure the only reason my uncle desires my company is to vex my aunt." A twinkle sparkled in her eye. "She wants to know nothing of his ventures."

"Ventures?" He didn't like the suggestion in her expression.

"Yes. Mining. In a general sense, of course. Over the years Uncle William has had several different financial pursuits, and Aunt Beatrice believes his interest in the mine will soon pass." She angled her head to look out the window on the far side of the mantelpiece, as if looking for him. "But perhaps he has more interest than I give him credit for."

The knot in Isaac's stomach tightened. He'd hoped—they'd all hoped—that William Lambourne would be a positive force in this area and help bolster mining endeavors, especially with so many needing work. Her words confirmed the fear that perhaps he was not serious about the business.

Unaware of her comment's impact, Miss Twethewey stood and moved to the window. "How many employees do you have?"

He joined her and gazed down onto the courtyard. It was busy this time of day, with the shift about to change. The men would be coming to the surface soon. "Well, they aren't employees. Not exactly. We do have a few employees—the underground and surface captains, the smith, engine-men, binders, carpenters, and even a mine barber, but the majority of the workers are here by contract. Every two months we have a setting, which is, in essence, an auction for the upcoming work. There are two types of workers below the ground. The tut workers dig the shafts and the tunnels, and the outworkers extract the ore."

Suddenly she whirled around, interest arching her brows. "Are those the bal maidens?"

He looked down at the row of women standing at a long table. "Yes."

"Miss Prynne told me about them. Do they always work outside like this? Even in this weather?"

"Yes. They're breaking down the ore to separate the good from the bad."

He couldn't help but notice how her soft, elegant fingers showed no sign of hard work.

She pivoted, noticed the items on the mantel, and picked up a piece of ore. "Is this what it looks like?"

"Yes." He took it from her, careful not to touch her hand with his dirty one. "This is a piece my brother and I extracted with my father when we were boys."

"How interesting." Her attention turned to the portrait above the mantel. "What an exquisite painting."

He stepped up next to her and beheld the image, even though he did not need a painting to recall the merry blue eyes and ruddy cheeks that always seemed to be windblown. "That's my father. He died nearly four years ago now."

"Your father?" She appeared to examine the image more closely. "Is it a good likeness?"

"A very good likeness. Matthew painted it."

"That's remarkable," she muttered.

"Yes, Matthew's the artist in the family. He traveled abroad for two years before he came home to run this mine when Father fell ill."

"Do you paint as well?" She faced him.

She was quite close now, and they stood shoulder to shoulder.

He paused before he responded, a bit taken aback by her steady stream of questions. He'd have thought she'd have no interest in the workings of a mine, but from what he observed, quite the opposite seemed true.

And now, she seemed interested in his family.

In him.

She looked toward him, eyebrows raised. "Mr. Blake? Do you paint?"

Oh yes. She'd asked him a question. "Uh, no. No, I don't."

He cleared his throat and returned his attention to the painting. He needed to look away from the soft ringlets framing her face, the gentle slope of her slender nose, and the subtle cleft in her chin.

Matthew had said he intended to court her. No doubt that was what he was doing now. She was here to visit Matthew. Not him.

Footsteps and laughter sounded outside the door. Isaac turned, disappointment dripping through him. His time alone with Miss Twethewey was coming to an end.

Matthew and Lambourne strode in.

"Ah, Isaac, you're here. Good." Matthew motioned toward Isaac, his broad smile and boisterous voice reaching to every corner of the low-ceilinged sitting room. "I've just been showing Mr. Lambourne the engine house and pump." He turned his attention to Miss Twethewey. "I hope you were not too lonely while we were away?"

"Of course not. Eliza has brought me tea, and Mr. Blake has been excellent company."

Isaac stepped back, allowing Matthew to move next to Miss Twethewey.

"Impressive." Lambourne clicked his tongue, ignoring his niece's statement. "You gentlemen have quite an operation."

"Your Bal Tressa used to be very like it, you know, if not larger," Matthew said. "And she could be again."

As if finally taking notice of Miss Twethewey, Lambourne extended his arm toward his niece, which she accepted forthwith. "I'm sad to see our visit come to an end, but I must get Julia home. Her aunt will be wondering where she is."

"I'll accompany you." Matthew reached once again for the hat he'd discarded. "We should continue our discussion about improvements for Bal Tressa another time. What say you to dinner at Tregarthan Hall in the coming days? Your entire family, of course, is welcome. Isaac will be there as well, won't you, Isaac? No one in the whole of Cornwall knows as much about mining as my brother."

Isaac lifted his head at the mention of his name and nodded. He had no idea what the men had talked about when at the pump house, but if a meeting at Tregarthan Hall would allow him to be in Miss Twethewey's presence, he'd be there.

Lambourne dipped his head in agreement. "We shall look forward to it."

CHAPTER 21

Julia walked into Lanwyn Manor, rubbing her gloved hands together, grateful for the warmth. The sun had begun its descent on their ride home, and with it went all semblance of heat.

Once inside the great hall, she hurried to the low window and looked out at her uncle and Matthew Blake. A smile toyed with her lips. Every expectation for the day had been met—and some had even been exceeded.

Leaving Penwythe Hall for a fresh residence was the best cure for a broken heart. She was certain of it now. Percy had not crossed her mind all afternoon, and now as she thought of his name, no sting of pain emerged.

She whirled from the window, appreciating that for the first time in a very long while the weight of pain and regret seemed to lift from her shoulders.

Perhaps Jane was right—anticipation was the key. Glorious anticipation.

Julia tucked her riding crop under her arm and pulled her glove from her left hand, a little astonished Aunt Beatrice was not waiting in the hall to hear every little detail of the day. Caroline, too, for that matter.

She'd tell them of their ride into the village. Of Mr. Blake's attentions. She would omit the part of him leaving her in the counting house, however. She'd thought that a bit odd, especially since he'd invited her to see the mine.

Although, the slight had afforded her the opportunity to visit with Isaac.

Her conversation with him had been pleasant. His gentleness, his humility, appealed to her. Then again, perhaps she was drawn to him simply because he had rescued her. What girl would not want to be rescued by such a handsome man?

But Isaac was tied to Margaret Benson. Yesterday she had seen it with her own eyes in the churchyard. She was determined to follow Aunt's guidance in this matter.

Yes, Matthew Blake was the man for her.

Deciding to go tell Jane about her day, Julia stepped toward the main staircase when a sharp voice caught her attention.

Aunt Beatrice.

Concerned at the alarm she heard in the tone, Julia dropped her riding crop and gloves to the side table and followed the sound of her aunt's voice to the drawing room, where her aunt spoke with Mrs. Sedrick.

"We've looked everywhere, in every nook, every cranny." Mrs. Sedrick's raspy voice rang harsh in the silence. "'Tis as if it simply vanished."

"This is getting quite out of hand." Aunt's voice was high as she paced over the rug, wringing her hands more tightly with each step. "And you have questioned the servants? All of them?"

"I have worked with this staff for years, Mrs. Lambourne. It was not one of them. I'd stake my reputation on it."

"But circumstances have changed here, have they not? Can you be certain they're as loyal as they once were?"

Determined to help calm her aunt, Julia stepped into the drawing room to make her presence known. "Good afternoon, Aunt."

"Ah, Julia, my dear." Aunt Beatrice rubbed her forehead. "It seems more silver is missing. Again."

Julia moved closer. "Perhaps it has just been misplaced."

"Perhaps." Her aunt looked back to Mrs. Sedrick as she returned to her seat on the sofa. "Keep me abreast of any developments you uncover. That will be all."

Julia took a quick step back to avoid being trampled by Mrs. Sedrick as she exited the room, then hurried to the brocade-covered settee, picked up Oscar from where he'd been sleeping, and sat next to her aunt. "Don't worry, Aunt. I'm certain it will be discovered. Things go missing all the time."

"Oh, it isn't merely the silver, dear." Aunt Beatrice's face reddened, tears welling in her eyes. "It's this horrid place. These people. This dreadful house!" She swiped her nose with a lacy handkerchief. "When we first arrived here, your uncle was emphatic that we keep the staff in place. We did not even bring our own housekeeper. Can you imagine? Fortunately, Mrs. Sedrick has proven valuable, but the rest of them are against us, I know it."

Aunt continued, her face flushing deeper with each syllable. "You know that my heart is in London, but your uncle is determined to be here, and a woman's place is with her husband, but he follows every whim, caring not what is best for his wife and daughters. I call it selfish."

Julia, unsure how to respond, adjusted the dog on her lap and tried to make her voice soothing. "It pains me to see you so upset, Aunt. It's a beautiful house, really. Such charm. I've never seen a house its equal."

"And now to think there is a thief among us? It is not to be borne!" Aunt Beatrice burst out, ignoring Julia's attempt at comfort. She jumped to her feet and resumed pacing. "How glad I will be when this whim of his passes. He'll tire of this mining pastime, as he does with every scheme he chases down, and then where will we be?"

Initially Julia had thought it a whim as well, but the interest she'd seen in her uncle's face when he spoke with Matthew had been unmistakable.

"Speaking of your uncle, where is he? Did he not return with you?"

"He did. When I saw him last, he and Mr. Blake were still speaking in the courtyard. Shall I fetch him?"

"With Mr. Blake? Then no, no. Do not disrupt him."

Julia studied the blue ribbon tied about Oscar's neck and straightened it. She wasn't sure what to think. If her family was not happy here, surely the best solution would be to leave. But then Mr. Blake's words about the village resonated. If Uncle left without opening the mine, how would that affect those who had relied on it for so long?

With a sudden sniff Aunt Beatrice pivoted. "Well, we must find joy and happiness where we can, I suppose. Joy is in the people around us, is it not? I have two of my daughters with me, and you, of course. Oh, I don't want you to think it all bad, for I want you to stay here with me—with us—as long as possible."

"I have no desire to depart Lanwyn Manor. I like it here, truthfully." She reached to grab her aunt's hand. "Plus, there is so much to anticipate. Caroline is to be married, and of course Jane's baby."

"And Mr. Blake? With the ridiculous nonsense of the silver, I almost forgot about your outing. Tell me all about it. Omit nothing."

Julia allowed her thoughts to turn to the afternoon's events. "It was interesting. And you will be happy, I think, to know that Mr. Blake invited us to dine at Tregarthan."

"A dinner invitation! Well." All trace of misery vanished. She tapped her finger to her lips, and her eyebrows rose. "Oh, my dear. If our presence here means you have the chance to be courted by a man such as Matthew Blake, then it is not in vain."

CHAPTER 22

A misty drizzle was falling as Isaac returned to his home from the mine. Gathering clouds had eclipsed twilight's purple glow, and now a thin veil of rain added darkness to the landscape as a cold, hard wind snapped sharply through the otherwise quiet night. Winter would be fully upon them soon.

Through the copse of bare trees, lights winked from the narrow leaded windows.

Anvon Cottage.

Home.

Tipping his hat lower, he nudged his horse to a trot. A gray squirrel scampered through the undergrowth, and a gust of wind swirled dried leaves on the path before him. He inhaled the crisp, fragrant air, enjoying how the freshness filled his lungs and awakened his senses. For the moment all was peaceful, and after the difficult days since Charlie's death, peace was all he desired.

Through a clearing in the trees, the sharp outline of Wheal Gwenna's tower jutted into the murky night sky. Nearly every day of his life he had passed that structure, and more days than he cared to admit it had been empty. But for some reason, tonight of all nights, it beckoned for him to slow his horse and study it further.

The mine and the land on which his cottage sat were not part of the original Tregarthan estate. His grandfather purchased this portion separately, so when it came time for the bequest, his father split this piece of land from Matthew's inheritance. It was not nearly as large or as fine as Tregarthan Hall, but it was his.

As he approached the cottage's courtyard, he saw Marco, Matthew's bay horse, tethered to the hitching post near the door. Matthew was nowhere to be seen.

Curious as to what would bring his brother out to the cottage, Isaac slid from the saddle, secured his horse next to Marco, and stepped beneath the elms and oaks toward the door. He was glad his brother was here. They still needed to discuss the accident at the mine, and he'd not seen Matthew since he'd left the counting house to escort Mr. Lambourne and Miss Twethewey to Lanwyn Manor.

With a turn of the iron handle, Isaac opened the timbered door, and his eyes quickly adjusted. There on the settee perpendicular to the simmering fire sat Matthew, the orange light glowing against the angles of his face.

Matthew jumped to his feet at the door's creaking like a spring, loaded and ready to uncoil. His normally calm countenance flared, and his eyes narrowed.

Isaac pushed the door closed, taking a moment to loop his satchel over the hook next to the door to afford himself time to address his brother.

Matthew, by most accounts, possessed a nonchalant if not aloof manner. Rarely vexed, he tended to find the humor in all. Such mannerisms endeared him to many, especially during times of uncertainty and strife, but there was another side of Matthew, one not often seen, where anger ruled every action and a temper flared beyond control. It was a family trait, one passed down from one man in the family to the next, and one which Isaac, unfortunately, shared.

Judging by his brother's pressed lips, this was one of those times when the tendency would blaze.

"Good evening, Matthew."

Matthew stepped forward, his expression tight. "When were you going to tell me about your plans for Wheal Gwenna?"

"What plans?"

Matthew scoffed. "I spoke with Dunstan today. I know you've been considering opening it."

Isaac stifled an inward groan as he shrugged his coat from his shoulders. He wasn't ready to talk to his brother about the possibility of opening Wheal Gwenna. Not yet.

"He said you and Benson were seeking investors."

"Benson's dead." Isaac removed his hat and set it on the table. "And no, I've not taken on any investors."

Matthew speared him with a glare. "You'd do that to me?"

"What exactly would I be doing to you?"

"Leaving my mine without a captain. Becoming my competition when times are uncertain enough as it is."

Isaac raked his fingers through his hair. "I've always planned to open Wheal Gwenna—ever since the day Father died. You know it to be true. I've never professed differently."

Matthew huffed again and shook his head, looking more like their father with each second that ticked by. "Why would you abandon a lucrative post for a mine that ran out long ago?"

The brothers stared at one another, frustration hovering precariously between them.

How could he make his brother understand? Matthew had been handed a successful mine. He'd never had to toil and slave to make it profitable. If their situations were reversed, Isaac doubted Matthew would feel the same.

"You're needed at Wheal Tamsen, Isaac. It takes both of us. You know that."

Both of us.

It was well known that the mining knowledge and expertise their father possessed went to Isaac. Matthew had a way with people, but Isaac understood copper—where to look for it, how to organize and inspire the tributers to work and be prosperous, and how to keep spirits high when profits—and morales—were low.

A coolness glinted in his brother's eyes—a look Isaac knew well. "I needn't remind you that the amount of money required for you to make her operational is astronomical."

Isaac determined to stay calm. "Be that as it may, 'tis still my mine. The only thing that truly belongs to me."

"Everything you learned about mining you have learned from Wheal Tamsen," Matthew hissed.

"No, Brother. Everything I've learned I learned from Father. He left me Wheal Gwenna fully intending me to do right by it. No time will ever seem right, but consider. I'm not married, have no one dependent upon me."

"Wheal Gwenna was closed for a reason," Matthew fired back. "Only a fool throws good money after bad. Would you abandon Wheal Tamsen, then? Everything our entire family has worked so diligently to build?"

"I'll not abandon Wheal Tamsen or the people there, but I will make my own path. Make no mistake. Perhaps if you spent more time at the mine tending to actual business, you would feel more comfortable when the day comes that you are left to tend it on your own."

CHAPTER 23

Julia was late. She hated to be late. No doubt Miss Prynne expected her a half hour ago for the Ladies League meeting. Julia had no desire for her first impression to be that of a tardy guest, and yet it could not be helped.

She smoothed her lavender pelisse and straightened her bonnet before she lifted her gloved hand to knock on the cottage door. She looked toward the narrow window flanking the door, searching for a sign of movement. After several moments, muffled footsteps echoed, and a young girl with black hair and dark eyes, who could be no older than thirteen, answered the door.

"Miss Twethewey to see Miss Prynne, if you please."

The girl did not take her wide, curious eyes from Julia but stepped back to allow her to enter. Almost immediately, Miss Prynne, clad in a gray high-necked gown with a white cap over her fading auburn hair, appeared. "There you are, my dear! I was beginning to fear something may have happened to you."

"I'm terribly sorry to be so late." Julia removed her gloves and pelisse and handed them to the servant girl. "My cousin has not been feeling well and I was hesitant to leave her."

"Don't give it a thought." Miss Prynne gave a dismissive wave, her expression kind. "The important thing is that you are here now, and I'm ever so glad for it. Come in and meet our neighbors and friends.

We haven't a large gathering today, but every little bit of progress is helpful, is it not?"

Julia allowed herself to be ushered into the modest parlor. A cheery fire glowed in the grate, and two worn settees covered in faded, embroidered cushions flanked the carved mantel. Three women sat in wooden chairs near the fire. At their feet were baskets brimming with fabrics and yarn. All three glanced up from their sewing.

Miss Prynne wrapped her arm around Julia's. "Ladies, Miss Twethewey, the Lambournes' visiting niece, has joined us to aid in our cause. Isn't that wonderful? Miss Twethewey, you must allow me to introduce you to Mrs. Finn, Mrs. Bray, and Miss James."

Julia straightened and smiled, hoping she did not look as sheepish as she felt. She'd not really considered the other women who would be present, but these women eyed her coolly.

Nerves tightened within her. Was it possible these were the women she'd overheard in the churchyard gossiping about her family?

Miss Trebell, also seated next to the fire, pushed up the small, round spectacles on her nose. "Miss Twethewey, you join us at last! Do be seated, and I'll pour you some tea. It's still hot, I believe."

Within moments Julia was settled in a tufted chair next to the fire with a cup of tea in her hand and a basket of sewing supplies at her feet. Before she even had time to get settled, the other women had returned to their sewing.

Miss Trebell patted her arm and pointed toward the basket. "There's a scarf that's been started but abandoned. Would you like to try your hand at completing it?"

With a nod Julia picked up the half-finished piece and assessed the stitching on the garment of green and gray wool, feeling clumsy and awkward. True, she had done this sort of work before, but it had been a long time.

She'd figure it out as she went.

The conversation resumed, and Julia glanced around Miss Prynne's parlor. It was much smaller than she had anticipated. Given that Miss Prynne visited with her aunt, Julia expected the older woman to have greater means, but her surroundings suggested the opposite to be true. Two candles added their light to that from the fire. Sparse furnishings dotted the chamber, and a single painting of a jovial-faced man hung on the wall. Despite its plainness, a sense of cheeriness prevailed in the space. Striped curtains of pink and blue hung at the windows, filtering the day's bright sunlight. To look out the window one might think it a warm day, but the cold air seeping in told another story.

Julia's attention shifted once the women's chatter resumed.

"She's faring better than one would dare expect," Mrs. Finn said, whose light-brown hair was pulled back tightly from her face. "Who would have thought that a miner as experienced and dedicated as Charlie Benson would perish in such a way? 'Tis nothing short of a shame. How quickly one's life can be altered completely."

Mrs. Bray nodded. "I heard the timber gave way, but they aren't sure why."

"Sometimes we never know the reason for such things." Mrs. Finn pulled an errant stitch. "Poor dear has suffered so much heartache. First her mother, now her husband."

"Well, you know Charlie and Mr. Blake always were on friendly terms." Miss James reached for the scissors on the table next to her. "There was a rumor they had been planning to reopen Wheal Gwenna."

Julia's interest piqued as she heard the Blake name. She slowed her stitching to listen.

"But Charlie's gone now. I have no idea if Mr. Blake plans to continue."

Mrs. Finn's eyebrow rose. "Mr. Blake may have other plans now."

"Meaning?"

"He was observed walking Mrs. Benson home from church recently. I've heard she no longer wants to live in Miner's Row and has asked for his assistance, and you know they've always been quite friendly. Perhaps a bit too friendly. It's almost scandalous, if you ask me."

"Gah, Mrs. Finn," protested Miss James. "He's only offering assistance, surely."

"Maybe, maybe not. All I'm saying is that it's quite suspicious."

Julia shifted uncomfortably as the women discussed Isaac Blake. Would she ever be able to hear his name and not think of the day he rescued her?

Time and time again she'd convinced herself that Isaac was not the man to catch her eye and that Matthew was the more suitable match. But for the past two mornings, she'd encountered Isaac on her morning rides. Their talks had been brief and they'd spoken of little more than the weather and the landscape, but it had been enough to set her imagination flying.

But now, after hearing the women talk, perhaps she had misinterpreted the situation. He might be a kind man simply in the habit of rescuing ladies in need, whose interests were firmly with the widow.

Regardless, they'd spoken a name she'd not heard. "What's Wheal Gwenna, if I may ask?"

The three other ladies jerked their heads up in unison and stared, as if she had asked for the moon.

Miss Prynne leaned forward. "Wheal Gwenna is a copper mine owned by Isaac Blake. It has been closed for decades, but rumors abound that he might reopen it."

"Oh." Julia returned her attention to the scarf in her hand, trying to ignore the heat of embarrassment flaming her cheeks. She looked up to see Miss Prynne watching her, and she gave a nervous laugh as the yarn she was holding tumbled to the floor. "Perhaps I'm a bit out of practice."

Miss Prynne leaned back and offered a reassuring smile. "You are doing just fine. Isn't she, Miss Trebell? After all, it is the thought and intent behind the actions, dear. Surely you're aware of that fact."

"Yes, but it would be even better if what I make is actually useful to someone."

"So it shall be."

Julia was about to show the women her progress when a childlike giggle caught her attention. She looked toward the door to discover the source. She had not been aware that there were any children in attendance, but a fair-headed girl, who could be no older than six or seven years of age, peeked around the corner. A single, long golden braid fell over her shoulder, and freckles dotted her upturned nose.

"Oh," Julia exclaimed. "Who's this?"

"This is Sophia." Miss Prynne extended her arm toward the child and motioned for her to draw closer. "She's staying with me awhile, along with her brother. Are you not? Come in, child."

Sophia eyed Julia thoroughly before she tiptoed into the room, then in a sudden burst of energy, she ran toward Miss Prynne.

Once the child was settled, Julia put her work aside and leaned forward. "How do you do, Sophia? I have a sister named Sophia. It's a very lovely name."

Instead of responding, the child reached out a tiny finger and touched the blue ribbon on Julia's skirt.

"Sophia!" Miss Prynne pulled the child back. "Please, keep your hands to yourself."

The child's eyes grew wide, and she bit her lower lip.

"That's all right. Do you like that ribbon? I think blue is my favorite color."

Sophia did not break her gaze, but she leaned back against Miss Prynne, who smoothed the child's hair away from her face affectionately and whispered to her. With a smile Sophia reached for a biscuit on the side table and ran from the room.

"What a lovely child." Julia watched as the little girl disappeared around the corner. "I don't know when I've seen such large brown eyes before."

"She is lovely. And her brother is just as charming. It's a sad story, though. Her mother is a dear friend of mine, but at the moment she's very, very ill. We all pray for a miracle, but her recovery is doubtful."

"And their father?" Julia furrowed her brow. "Is he living?"

"He is, but he took a position at a mine in the west when your uncle closed Bal Tressa. He's been gone ever since. To my knowledge they've not heard from him in months."

Julia's stomach tightened at the mention of her uncle.

Then it struck her.

No wonder the other women did not seem to warm to her.

Julia tucked a long lock of hair behind her ear. "I know very little about mining, yet it seems the mine closing has had an immense effect on a great number of people."

Mrs. Finn cut a glance toward Miss James.

"You're very perceptive, Miss Twethewey," Miss Prynne said. "There are dozens of mines around, of course, but none as large as Bal Tressa. There are just not enough mines to employ everyone. Mr. Rowe was a great champion of the working miner, and his presence—and his attitude toward his workers—is dearly missed."

Julia fixed her eyes on her work and pulled a stitch. "What will happen to Sophia and her brother?"

Miss Prynne sighed and shook her head. "Hopefully her mother recovers. If not . . ."

"'Tis sad to think of a child losing her mother." Julia straightened, understanding her meaning fully. "Did you know that I am an orphan?"

The women blinked at her.

It was a personal tidbit to share, but it was true. There was nothing to be ashamed of. "My mother died when I was a bit older than Sophia, and my father died when I was twelve. After that my brothers and sisters and I went to live with my paternal uncle at Penwythe Hall."

"No, I did not know that," Miss Trebell said. "How interesting."

"I was fortunate to have so much family. My uncle took in all five of us and made us feel quite at home, and we've been happy there ever since. I'll always be grateful to him, just as I'm certain Sophia and her brother will be grateful to you. Life often calls us to step out of what is familiar and comfortable to help those around us, does it not? But the rewards far outweigh the pains along the way."

"We do what we can, but unfortunately there are stories like this in villages all over the area, and not just in Goldweth. It's a pitiable state of affairs, to be sure. But now, look at how much progress you've made!" Miss Prynne pointed to the scarf.

Julia lifted it, allowing it to dangle freely. The first rows were crooked, but the farther she progressed, the straighter and tighter her stitches became.

As time ticked past during the afternoon, the iciness she had felt from the other ladies melted. Julia liked the Ladies League and looked forward to attending their meeting again.

CHAPTER 24

Julia bolted upright in bed.

She blinked in the darkness.

Something—or someone—was banging against her bedchamber door.

Springing to life with all the alarm of one yanked from the depths of slumber, Julia thrust the bed curtain out of her way and stumbled to the floor, her muscles sluggish with sleep's effect.

Before she could step to it, the door flung open. Caroline stood in the threshold. A single candle clutched in her slender fingers illuminated a face pale as the linen of her nightdress.

"Caroline?" Julia gasped, still unsure if she was awake or dreaming. "You scared me half to death! What is it?"

"Do you not hear that?" Caroline's light eyes widened.

"Do I hear what?" Julia strained to hear.

"Oh, bother." Caroline scurried closer and reached for Julia's hand. "You can't hear it here, can you? Come with me. Quickly."

With surprising insistence Caroline half dragged Julia from her bedchamber across the small landing that connected their rooms and into her own. Caroline stopped suddenly and stood very still. Her long blonde plait swayed as she angled her head to listen. "There! Do you hear it?"

Julia sighed, prepared to hear nothing. If anything, perhaps a mouse had found its way behind the bureau, or a bird had perched on the ledge just outside her window.

Then Julia heard it—scratching, coming from above.

At first she thought she might be imagining the sound.

"What in heaven's name?" she whispered.

Caroline tightened her grip on Julia's hand. "The staff always say there's a ghost in this house. Of course, I never believed it."

"That's ridiculous." Julia tilted her head to hear better.

The scratch sounded again, followed by a thud.

"Perhaps we should get your father," Julia suggested, concern mounting.

"He left for London last night, remember? He won't be back for days."

"Ah, yes. Your mother, then."

"No. She already hates Lanwyn Manor, and something like this would put her in hysterics."

Julia raised her eyes toward the beamed ceiling. "What's above this room?"

"Attic space, I think."

"Do any servants sleep up there?"

"Not in this tower. Their quarters are in the attic above the kitchen."

"Well then." Julia grabbed Caroline's hand. "Let's investigate."

"What?"

The scratching intensified.

The cousins froze.

The scratching stopped.

The women gaped at each other.

"Have you another candle?"

"You can't be serious." Caroline snatched back her hand. "It could be a wild animal. Or a person."

Julia propped her hand on her hip. "If it's an animal, then it probably isn't a very big one and nothing to worry about. And what person would make that noise?"

"No." Caroline shook her head emphatically. "I'm not going."

"Well, I shan't sleep a wink knowing something or someone is up there." Julia took up a candle and, using the fire in the grate, lit it. "There. Now, are you coming with me, or not?"

"Oh, Julia. I don't think this is a good idea."

"Come on." Julia stepped back into the corridor. "Where's your sense of adventure?"

"Wait, where are you going?"

Julia did not stop to respond, and yet she heard the pattering of her cousin's feet behind her.

Together they made their way to the staircase. With Caroline clutching her arm, Julia could not help but smile. Growing up, her brothers would often play tricks on her, and now she felt quite fearless, and Caroline's extravagant dramatics were almost amusing.

The moment her foot fell on the attic landing, damp coolness surrounded her.

Perhaps she was not as brave as she thought.

Julia lifted her candle, and with the aid of a tiny sliver of moonlight coming from a window at the corridor's far end, she attempted to assess the space.

Like the floor below it, the rooms were positioned on either side of the corridor, but instead of the spacious rooms present below, these appeared much smaller. No doubt, at one time they had been used for storage or servants' quarters. Some of the doors were open, some were not.

A sharp scratching noise halted her observation, and fear prickled her back. But she had come this way under the guise of bravery. She'd not fall short now.

She walked to the space above where she estimated Caroline's chamber to be and put her hand on the doorknob, turned, and pushed.

Empty.

Julia frowned. "Surely this is above your chamber, but nothing's here."

Caroline dragged the toe of her stocking across the uneven layer of dust on the floor. "How odd."

Growing more confident that no person was present, Julia explored the other rooms. They contained a few trunks and a few pieces of furniture, and even on this floor, tapestries hung on the walls and covered the floors. She stepped to the window and looked out.

They were in the highest part of the tower. Frost had covered the surrounding land with a silver shroud in the cool moonlight. She was about to turn from the peaceful sight when something caught her eye. She squinted. A dark figure raced along the edge of the woodland, away from the house and toward the forest.

Alarm tremored through her.

Surely whatever that was, *whoever* that was, was not related to this noise.

She watched until the figure was no longer visible, and then she stepped away. The same sense of fear she'd felt that night at the inn returned, only this time, Isaac Blake was nowhere around to intervene. With her uncle out of town and her cousin prone to dramatics, she decided to keep this sight to herself. It would do no good to point out something like that to Caroline, not in her current frame of mind. After all, what could be done?

Julia forced confidence to her voice. "Well, whatever was making that noise is no longer here."

Caroline snipped, "I can't abide it here. I cannot wait to marry and return to London."

"Well, that isn't tonight, so try to put it past you and go back to bed," Julia said as nonchalantly as she could. But as she stepped down the tower steps, she could not shake the uneasy feeling that something was amiss at Lanwyn Manor.

CHAPTER 25

Isaac whistled a tune as he guided his horse from Anvon Cottage's courtyard. A gray, ethereal mist hovered over the muddy lane and faded grasses, and above him, thick clouds churned, blocking out the morning sky.

Despite the gloomy weather outside, today would be busy, for it was setting day. This afternoon all the local miners would gather and bid on the work that needed to be done at Wheal Tamsen for the next two months. And he was ready.

One day, with any luck, he'd be holding such meetings for Wheal Gwenna.

As he turned from the narrow lane to the main public road, Isaac slowed his horse and surveyed the Lanwyn Manor lawn that ran along the road. For the past several days he'd encountered Miss Twethewey on her regular rides. Each morning, their talks grew longer. More meaningful.

As he'd hoped, he saw her sitting atop her white horse, straight and elegant, clad in a habit of brilliant green. The wind whipped her hair about her face with untamed abandon, and it tugged persistently at her skirt's hem. Instead of walking, the horse stood motionless. Miss Twethewey's back was to him, and she appeared to be looking down at the ground.

At the sight of her his heart felt light.

Even though Matthew had made his plans to woo her clear, Isaac found it difficult to take his brother's intentions earnestly, for he suspected that Matthew's interest did not lie in Miss Twethewey, as he professed. His interest was solely in Bal Tressa and the money it could generate.

"Miss Twethewey," he called, directing his horse closer to the stone wall as he approached her.

She lifted her head and guided her horse toward him, and as she did something seemed different. Normally, her face was bright and her lips held a smile. Today, her expression was tight, almost nervous.

As their eyes met, he tipped his hat.

She smiled at last. "Mr. Blake."

Isaac drew his horse to a halt and waited for her to do the same on the other side of the drystone wall. He glanced toward the sky. "It's not a very nice morning for a ride. I fear we are in for more blustery weather."

She looked upward, squinting at the muted light. "You're right."

He frowned at her uncustomary demeanor. "Is something the matter?"

"No. I mean, yes." She fussed with her reins and bit her lip. "Well, I'm not sure."

He stiffened his spine. In the time he'd known her, he'd found her to be direct, and this new side of her was concerning. "You're not sure if something's wrong?"

She shook her head, her distracted gaze fixed hesitantly on the horse's milk-colored mane. "The oddest thing happened last night. I wouldn't bother you with this, but after what happened to us at the inn, I thought you might have some insight."

She proceeded to tell him about strange scratching noises, and a shadowy figure on the midnight lawn, and about how she'd spent the morning thus far looking for clues at the tree line. Her words spilled out, a jumble of confused thoughts and possible explanations. "I can't help but feel as if something is amiss here."

He switched his reins to one hand and crossed his other hand over his arm as he considered her story. As much as he would like to calm her fears, he was too well acquainted with the current mood of the local population to discredit her. "I think it best you inform your uncle. It could be quite serious, especially considering what happened at the inn."

"Uncle William's away from Lanwyn. I'm not certain when he'll return. As it is, Jane is ill, Caroline is frightened and will barely step foot from the tower, and I worry that if I tell Aunt, she'll descend into hysterics."

"If it would make it easier, I will engage a handful of men to stand guard at the property line. At least until your uncle returns."

She shook her head. "I would hate to put you to such trouble. After all, no harm was done. Let's hope it was just an odd occurrence and nothing more." She forced a rigid smile and looked him in the eye for the first time that morning. "You must think I bring trouble with me wherever I go, Mr. Blake. I just didn't know who else to tell, and I felt someone should know."

"You may tell me anything, Miss Twethewey. And you are not trouble. Not to me."

A sharp breeze gusted from the tree line, and her horse whinnied and pawed at the earth. Rain was imminent, and the horses seemed to know it.

She adjusted the reins in her gloved hands to still her animal. "Let us not linger on such dull topics. Tell me, have you a full day, Mr. Blake?"

He nodded, relieved to see a glimmer of her normal vibrancy return. "Very. Today we'll conduct the setting at Wheal Tamsen. 'Twill be a full day. It just pains me that we do not have more work to offer.

We've opened a handful of new pitches, but it will hardly meet the need."

She toyed with the end of her riding crop, as if considering her words. "At the Ladies League meeting earlier this week, the women were talking of Wheal Gwenna and wondering whether or not you intend to open it."

He gave a little laugh, careful not to lace it with too much sarcasm. "I wish I could open it."

"Why can't you? If more work is needed, then it seems a viable solution."

"Viable, yes, but not simple. You see, at this very moment, it's flooded. It's been empty for decades and must be drained before any work can be done. That alone takes time. And money. My father sold the pump after closing the mine, and a great deal of capital would be required for a new one. But the greater gamble is the mine itself. My father said the ground still held copper, but others have said she's run dry. I'm afraid that even if Wheal Gwenna were to open, it might not produce the way we'd need it to in order to really make a difference."

She swiped a curl away from her cheek and straightened her shoulders. "I met a child named Sophia at the sewing circle this week. Do you know her?"

"I do."

"Is her mother really as ill as Miss Prynne led me to believe?"

He nodded.

"I can't help but wonder if Uncle William is aware of all the anguish that closing Bal Tressa has caused."

Her words surprised him. He expected Lambourne's niece to side with her uncle on all things, but the opposite seemed to be true. She had an uncanny insight to put compassion for those around her above the comfort of her family. It appealed to him, almost as much as the small dimple that formed at the side of her mouth with each smile.

"And where has your brother gotten to?" she asked suddenly. "He called at Lanwyn Manor for several days in a row, but then his visits stopped. Aunt enjoyed his company a great deal."

The reference to Matthew caught him off guard, and he tensed. It always came back to Matthew.

"Falmouth," he muttered. "He left two days ago. I expect him back this morning for setting day." His brother had so much to offer, but Julia had come to Isaac. She'd brought her questions, her fears, to *him*. Such trust had to count for something.

It was lovely, he supposed, to believe she might consider him in a romantic way. Her sweet smile and spirited demeanor attracted him, and she already occupied his thoughts much more than she should.

He was not the sort of man to give up without a fight, and he had a feeling that Miss Twethewey—or at least the chance to win her attention and affection—would be worth fighting for.

A bit of rain blew in on the breeze, and he lowered his hat. "I must be going, but will I see you out riding tomorrow morning?"

She jerked slightly.

He knew what he had just asked. It was one thing for them to encounter one another by accident. It was another thing entirely to plan to meet her, or at least set the expectation.

She lifted her chin. The breeze caught the tendrils around her face. Her cheeks were pink—whether from the cold or his question he might never know.

A captivating smile curved her lips. "You will, Mr. Blake."

CHAPTER 26

Julia studied the lanky Mr. Cornelius Jackaby with skepticism. This was her first time to meet the accoucheur, or male midwife, who would attend Jane's birth, and she was far from impressed.

"The bloodletting should help ease the general discomfort." Mr. Jackaby's voice was unusually high for one so tall. He pressed his bony fingers against Jane's wrist to check her pulse before he placed a cloth in the crook of her arm to stop the bleeding. "There's nothing like draining bad blood to restore one's constitution."

Despite the tightening of Julia's stomach, she smiled reassuringly at Jane, who was propped up in her bed, pillows and coverlets tucked all around her. Julia resisted the urge to wince at the sight of Jane's pale complexion and the layer of perspiration dotting it.

As Mr. Jackaby returned to his bag to pack his things, Julia looked to her aunt, who stood by watching with an approving smile. After refusing to consider a local physician, Aunt Beatrice had engaged Mr. Jackaby to tend to Jane as soon as it was confirmed she was with child. Her aunt seemed to accept everything Mr. Jackaby said without question.

Frustrated, Julia stepped forward and addressed Mr. Jackaby. "Surely there is something else you suggest for us to do. Jane is ill all day long, and she's so weak she can barely keep her eyes open."

The man slowed his movements and fixed beady eyes on Julia.

He adjusted the spectacles high on his nose and assessed Julia for several moments. "My dear, I appreciate your concern, but it is not uncommon for women in her condition to be ill, and it does happen that some women experience severe sickness throughout. That is the case here. 'Tis nature's way, I'm afraid."

Julia resisted the urge to roll her eyes. She certainly knew very little about such things, but she did pride herself on her common sense.

Mr. Jackaby retrieved a glass jar from his bag, pushed past Julia, approached Aunt Beatrice, then lowered his voice. "Your daughter is weak but the babe remains strong. As far as timing, I do not see any reason to adjust my estimation on the delivery date." He handed the jar to her aunt. "See that she eats vegetables every day, if she can manage, and stay away from meats and spices. Dissolve this powder in her drink twice a day. I should like to see the lying-in room before I depart. I trust it's prepared."

"It is." Aunt Beatrice accepted the jar, eagerness brightening her round face, and she handed it to Evangeline before she swept her arm toward the door. "It's through here."

Jane had shared with Julia that she disliked Mr. Jackaby, but what could be done? Sensing her cousin's discomfort, Julia offered her a reassuring smile, reached to squeeze her hand, leaned near, and whispered, "I'll find out what they say. I'll return shortly."

With her hands clasped behind her, Julia followed nonchalantly into the corridor and trailed her aunt and the accoucheur into the lying-in chamber directly across the corridor.

"This should do nicely." Mr. Jackaby stepped to the window, lifted the curtain to look to the grounds below, and then walked around the space, assessing the furnishings. "The windows will need to be sealed, of course. We don't want any drafts affecting the new mother during her confinement. And you have secured a monthly nurse?"

"Yes, we have. A respected one by the name of Mrs. Meyer. She is scheduled to arrive on the same day you will be here."

"I know Mrs. Meyer. Excellent choice." He looked back to the chamber. "Considering your daughter's condition, a wet nurse is advisable. Write to Mrs. Meyer on that count. She might have a recommendation."

At the conclusion of his visit, Julia and Aunt Beatrice escorted Mr. Jackaby back down the tower and through the foyer, and watched at the window through the steady rain as he retreated from the courtyard. Julia wrapped a shawl around her shoulders, and the women were silent until no sign was left of him.

"What a remarkable man." Aunt Beatrice lifted her chin, admiration shining in her pale-blue eyes. "So much knowledge."

"I don't know," Julia said slowly, turning away from the window. "Something about his manner is concerning."

"Concerning?" Aunt Beatrice's voice rose in pitch, and a flush reddened her cheeks. "He's highly recommended—the very best London has to offer. Honestly, Julia, you can't possibly consider yourself well educated on such a topic. You shouldn't offer your opinion on things you know nothing about." With a huff she flounced from the room.

Aunt hated to be questioned. In hindsight Julia would have been wise to keep her opinion to herself. Despite the fact they were family, she was still a guest. But didn't being a companion to Jane include trying to do the best for her?

She bit her bottom lip, wringing her clasped hands. The words she'd heard at the church about births at Lanwyn Manor being cursed washed over her. How she wished she could forget them, but they were burned into her consciousness, and fresh fear for her cousin washed over her.

Many hours later, after the day's tasks were complete, Isaac sat alone in Anvon Cottage's modest, low-ceilinged sitting room, staring into the fire, clay pipe in hand. With the exception of the occasional pop of the fire, silence prevailed.

The setting had gone well, and Wheal Tamsen had firm plans for the months to come. Matthew had arrived about an hour prior to the setting, but neither had spoken of the argument over Wheal Gwenna. Their interactions were normal, as if no argument ever occurred. That was Matthew's way.

Despite the day's general success, a nagging sense of discomfort flooded him.

So many workers had been turned away. Men with families to feed and needs that only steady work could meet. Even now, in the solace of his comfortable, warm home, their disappointed expressions and downcast eyes haunted him.

If only more could be done to provide for them.

Isaac glanced over to the meal his housekeeper had laid out for him. It remained untouched.

In the past Isaac would customarily dine with Charlie after the setting was complete. It was always a celebration of sorts, but now his friend was gone and not many felt like celebrating.

His thoughts turned to Margaret.

He'd made inquiries about a new cottage for Charlie's widow and son, but he was also aware of the gossip intensifying with each passing day. Several village women had decided that he and the widow should become more than what they were.

And that he could not do.

Isaac was not a man given to emotion. Emotions were rarely to be trusted. His father had taught him that. But mostly, he attributed the ache in his chest—this nagging restlessness—to mourning his friend and the loss of their plans together. They'd planned to do so much good with Wheal Gwenna. Now, there was no one else he trusted with whom to undertake such an endeavor—not even Matthew.

The orange kitchen cat slinked in from the doorway and brushed up against his leg. He leaned over to pat the animal's head when the door creaked open.

Matthew stepped across his threshold. Anvon Cottage was not part of the Tregarthan estate, and yet Matthew always walked in as if he owned it. Normally, it didn't bother Isaac. He needed little privacy and had little to hide. But Matthew was changing, and the sight of his brother in the door made Isaac's defenses rise.

Perhaps it was *he* who was changing.

Isaac did not stir as Matthew shrugged off his coat. "The housekeeper left stew over the fire in the kitchen. You're welcome to it if you're hungry."

"Ah, Mrs. Odgers's stew. Always was the best." Matthew's countenance was calm, almost jovial. Everything from the cadence of his gait to the looseness of his jaw suggested that the argument was behind him, and true to Matthew's nature, he naturally assumed that if he had put it behind him, then Isaac had as well. "It still irks me that she would rather keep house for you than at Tregarthan."

Isaac raised his eyebrow. "Perhaps she considers you a terrible master."

Matthew scoffed, swept his hat from his head, and dropped it unceremoniously to the table. "I do like to insist on things being accomplished a certain way." He trudged toward the fire and sat on the high-backed settee against the side wall.

His light hair was cut shorter than normal, and a new blue double-breasted waistcoat peeked from beneath the worsted wool coat. Isaac swiped his hand over his own tan waistcoat, mindful of the dust still there from the afternoon's work, and propped his booted foot up on the footstool. "What brings you to Anvon Cottage tonight? Surely it is not just because you desire my company."

"Actually, I've two things to share with you." Matthew reached into his pocket and pulled out a rock. "This was found at the mine this afternoon. I told Beale I would bring it by to show you."

Isaac's interest focused on the glittering item in his brother's hand. "Where'd they find it?"

"Two fathoms down, on the west end. Looks promising, no?"

Isaac pivoted the stone in the light, studying the color and the way the firelight reflected from the surface. "It does."

"I thought we would pull some of the men to do a bit of exploratory work over the next couple of weeks."

Isaac stood and put the rock atop the mantel and then returned to his chair.

Matthew retrieved his enameled snuffbox from his waistcoat, opened it, pinched the black powder between his fingers, and inhaled.

Seconds stretched to minutes, and they sat in comfortable silence. In times like this, when all was quiet, it almost seemed as if they were boys again, and the cares and realities of their world did not weigh on their shoulders. Matthew did not seem to share the sentiment. He jerked suddenly and returned the snuffbox to his pocket. "Do you never grow weary of it?"

Isaac lifted his head at the odd statement. "Weary of what?"

"Of stones." Matthew threw his arm out, motioning to the collection of oddly shaped ore that had been collected on the mantelpiece over the years. "Of mines. Of dark tunnels and the sound of pick on stone."

Isaac shrugged. "Weary or not, 'tis our way of life."

"And is it so easy for you to just accept it? Do you never give a thought to what else could be done?"

"Father left us with a duty."

Matthew huffed. "Duty indeed. He left us more with a stone tied about our necks, threatening to pull us underneath. We've one life to live, and is this how we are to live it?"

Isaac sobered at his brother's unusual countenance, and yet somehow he was not surprised. Matthew had been avoiding the mine as of late. His travels had increased, and an obvious thread of discontent wound its way through his words and actions.

Matthew jumped to his feet, as if unable to contain the emotions warring within him. "Sometimes I've half a mind to sell it all, but who would buy into such a fickle thing? Even if I did sell it, I doubt I could even cover my debts."

Unsure of how to respond, Isaac leaned with his elbows on his knees and stared at the toe of his boot for several seconds. "What brings this on?"

"I understand your desire for Wheal Gwenna and a mine of your own. I do. I felt the same way when the reins of Wheal Tamsen were handed to me. But I can't understand why you would wish this uncertain, thankless life for yourself and simply accept it without as much as a thought of what else you could do. I don't believe I was meant for a life like this."

Isaac scoffed. "A life where you own an estate and have funds at your disposal? A life where you own a thriving mine and have influence in the community? A life without want?"

Matthew shot him an irritated glance. "I see you don't share my opinions."

"I see it differently. I'm grateful for this life. This little cottage. Feeling like I am making some sort of contribution."

"*Contribution*," Matthew muttered as he stood, moved to the mantel, and looked to their father's weapon hanging there. "You were always more like him, you know."

Isaac sobered. Yes, he was more like his father than Matthew.

Much more. They had gone outdoors together. Underground together. Fishing. Hunting.

Isaac cleared his throat. It was not like Matthew to show emotion or be reminiscent. It would not do to linger on the things that had at one time divided them so fiercely. "You said you had two things to share with me. You've only told me one."

"Ah." The brightness returned to his eyes, and Matthew reached into his coat pocket. "Look what I stumbled upon at the peddler in Wheyton." He removed his hand, and dangling from a long chain was a watch.

Isaac's watch.

"Is that . . . ?" Isaac's question faded as he reached toward the gold timepiece.

"Yes. Father's watch. Or your watch, I should say. Seems like the vagabond who stole it from you decided to sell it."

Isaac arched his eyebrow. "You just happened upon this?"

"That would make for a great story, but no. Daniel Lobby told me he saw it there and thought I would like to know, so I paid a call on my way back from Falmouth. Sure enough, I looked in on it, and there it was. Nothing like paying good money for something our family already owned."

Isaac cracked a smile as he wrapped his fingers around it. He was not a sentimental man, but this watch reminded him of his father in a way nothing else did. "Thank you."

"You can thank me by coming to Tregarthan Friday evening. Remember how I invited the Lambournes to dinner? I received a note today from Mrs. Lambourne that they have accepted the invitation, and I need your help."

"Help with what?"

"Convincing Lambourne that we are the adventurers to run Bal Tressa."

"I thought you were weary of mining?" Isaac quipped.

"Weary, yes, but I still need money, like we all do. Besides, Miss Twethewey will be there. I need you to occupy Mr. and Mrs. Lambourne so I can woo their niece. I think Lambourne was impressed with Wheal Tamsen, but we must secure every foothold we can."

Isaac shifted. Perhaps now would not be the best opportunity to share his growing sentiments toward Lambourne's niece with Matthew, or to reprimand his brother for considering such a deception.

After a bowl of stew and conversation, Matthew departed. Isaac stood at the door as his brother and Marco disappeared into the woodland that served as Tregarthan's border.

Matthew had made no reference to their argument from a few days prior. Instead he'd extended his olive branch in the form of a lost pocket watch. The thought was kind, but there was so much about Matthew's actions of which he could not make sense. Isaac wrapped his fingers around the timepiece, wishing he could be happier in the moment.

CHAPTER 27

Julia placed a book in the basket atop her bed and looked to Caroline. "I do wish you'd come with me. I think you'd be surprised."

Caroline crossed her arms as she stood in the threshold and gave a little huff. "You're a much more charitable person than I. Besides, you know how Mother feels about us interacting with the miners."

"For heaven's sake, they're just children." Julia added two more books to the basket and tucked a blanket over them. "You'd be doing them a service."

"Just children?" Caroline raised an eyebrow in amusement. "I thought I heard you say that Mr. Isaac Blake was to attend."

Julia ignored the implication and looked away, feigning indifference, but she had spoken to him just that morning when she encountered him on their morning ride, and he had assured her he'd be present. She'd told no one at Lanwyn Manor of their morning meetings, not even Jane, who was the person she spent the most time with. The lie slid easily—and perhaps a little too quickly—from her lips. "I'm not certain he'll even be in attendance."

"Perhaps if Mr. *Matthew* Blake was going to be there you'd have just cause to attend, at least in Mother's eyes. Is she aware of this excursion you've planned?"

Julia looked to the basket, fighting embarrassment. No, she hadn't told her aunt or asked her permission. She fussed with her gloves.

"She gave her permission for me to attend the sewing circle, and this is but an extension of that. Miss Prynne and Miss Trebell will both be in attendance. Besides, Aunt is away having tea with Mrs. Penna. She'll not miss me."

"I don't see how reading with children can be an extension of sewing, but your decisions are your own. Far be it from me to interfere." Caroline smirked and turned from the door. "But as for myself, I fear it might rain. I've no desire to fall ill from being out in the elements. Besides, I need to write my Roger. I'm sure he's impatient to hear from me and to drink in every word I write."

Grateful for the change in topic, Julia lifted her eyes. "And what of this fiancé of yours? A Mr. Tremaine, if I'm correct? When shall I meet him?"

"Oh, he'll be down anytime now for a visit, and you shall meet him then. He's not fond of the country, and we are well suited in that respect."

Once Caroline withdrew, Julia set several tarts wrapped in paper, which she'd talked Cook into baking, into the basket. She moved to her wardrobe, opened it, and retrieved a blue ribbon hanging on a hook. Young Sophia had admired a similar ribbon trimming on her gown on Julia's first visit to Miss Prynne's cottage. Perhaps she'd like this as well. With a smile she pinched it in her fingers, turned, and dropped the ribbon on top.

Julia slung her basket over her arm, then made her way to the courtyard to where Snow was saddled and waiting for her. She mounted, crossed under the gatehouse arch, and headed toward the village. She was quite accustomed to the ride through the woods now, even though she carried with her Mr. Blake's words of caution and a watchful eye. The event the night of her arrival was weeks removed and seemed so distant now—more like a bad dream that would occasionally pop into her consciousness but then dissipate as soon as it did.

Miss Prynne had instructed that they were to meet at the second cottage on the left in Miner's Row for the day's lesson. According to the older woman, this gathering was a weekly event where Miss Trebell, Miss Prynne, and other learned adults of Goldweth would share their time with the miner children in the hopes of imparting to them the skill of reading, since most of their parents were illiterate and there was no school to teach them. Julia took High Street and located the cottage without trouble, dismounted and secured Snow, and then stepped toward the cottage, optimism swirling within her.

She knocked on the door, and Miss Prynne opened it. "Oh, my dear, come in. Do come in."

Julia ducked through the doorframe and looked around, surprised to see so many people in a small space. The ceiling was low and the light was dim, but happy tones and laughter put her at ease.

Perhaps a dozen girls, ranging in age from five to nine, gathered around her. True, they seemed much more interested in her riding habit and the feather in her bonnet than her books, but their enthusiasm was endearing.

A table over she noticed Mr. Isaac Blake.

So he *had* come.

He was sitting with several young boys, showing them a piece of ore. She watched for several moments as he held the stone up and pointed something out with his finger. He handed it to one of the boys. Across from him sat the widow Benson with her son on her lap.

Julia had been in Goldweth several weeks now, and even though she'd seen the widow at church each Sunday, she'd not been formally introduced, and her curiosity about this woman was increasing.

Julia watched them from the corner of her eye. Mrs. Benson leaned forward and must have said something amusing, for Isaac threw his head back in laughter.

Julia had to admit that Mrs. Benson was very attractive, especially when a smile dimpled her cheeks and her eyes sparkled instead of dimmed with despair.

Was there really an attachment as she'd heard rumored?

How she wondered that very thing so many times. During their morning rides Mr. Blake never spoke of the widow, and she never asked. But surely he would not be so engaging with her if his attentions were elsewhere.

Would he?

But then she thought of Percy—Percy, who was far more flirtatious than Mr. Blake had ever been.

But she'd been wrong about him and misjudged his character sorely.

Who else could she be wrong about?

It was then Mr. Blake noticed her. He caught her eye from across the room, and he smiled.

She smiled back, trying to calm the flutter in her stomach and the sudden lightness in her head.

How that smile had the power to disarm her, she was quickly coming to realize.

The feeling was alarmingly similar to how Percy had made her feel, but it was just that—*a feeling*. An emotion and nothing more. It was one thing to enjoy his company on misty morning walks or to capture his attention, but she must not read more into it than what was there.

Julia shook the thoughts away and gathered with the girls near the fire. Dusk was still hours away, but with only three windows the cottage was quite dark. When they were settled around her, Sophia among them, Julia began to read aloud.

Time passed quickly with the young girls, and homesickness's familiar pang stabbed afresh. She missed her own sisters. The mining children's vitality was something she missed while at Lanwyn Manor, and she felt her own vitality increase with their company and influence. Her heart went out to them. They were so hungry to learn whatever she could share with them.

She sobered. How easy it was to take the advantages she'd been given for granted.

At length the group thinned, and the hour was growing quite late. Aunt Beatrice would miss her if she remained much longer. As she packed her things back in her basket, she sensed someone watching her.

She turned. Sophia's brown eyes were fixed on her.

Julia waved for the girl to draw near. "I have a present for you." She put her hand in the basket. "Close your eyes and hold out your hands."

With a little jump of excitement, the child squeezed her eyes shut and cupped her hands.

Julia pulled the length of blue ribbon from the basket, rolled it into a ball, and placed it in Sophia's hands. At the touch Sophia's eyes widened and she gasped. "Is this for me?"

"It is. And it will look beautiful on you." Julia took the ribbon back, motioned for the girl to turn around, and tied it at the end of the girl's long plait. "There you go. So lovely."

Sophia threw her arms around Julia's neck and then ran to show Miss Prynne.

Satisfied with the girl's happiness, Julia returned her attention to the rest of the children and dispensed the remaining tarts. Mrs. Benson stood not far behind the children. Her long auburn hair was in a loosely bound plait down her back. Every time Julia had encountered her, Mrs. Benson had been quite pale, but today color highlighted her high cheekbones, and she even smiled.

Feeling confident after so many pleasant interactions, Julia stepped toward the widow and extended a pastry. "Would you care for a tart, Mrs. Benson? I fear it's grown cold, but I am sure it's still delicious."

A sudden shadow darkened Mrs. Benson's expression, and she pivoted to face Julia fully. "You may bring tarts and gifts for the children, that is one thing entirely, but I do not need, nor do I want, your charity."

Taken aback by the sharp tone, Julia drew in a sharp breath. "I—it isn't charity."

"What is it, then?" The midwife braced her hand on her hip, tilting her head to the side.

Her defenses rising, Julia tucked the basket on her arm and lifted her chin. "It is a token of goodwill, nothing more."

"Goodwill?" Mrs. Benson huffed. "Do you suppose that you can move to the large house on the hill and imagine you are the benefactor of us all, of these children, when it is the master of the very house you call home who has brought the trial on our heads?"

Mr. Blake, who'd been standing nearby, stepped forward. "That's not fair, Margaret. Why don't we—"

"Nay." Margaret crossed her arms over her chest. "What's not fair is that my husband's dead. What's not fair is that there are children who this very eve are hungry or away from their papas, while the Lambournes pretend to offer their charity and goodwill to the very people they are hurting. *That* is what's not fair."

Isaac took her arm again, his voice low. "You might come to regret the sharpness in your tone."

"Oh, I do have regrets." Mrs. Benson jerked her arm free and pinned her hard gaze on Julia. "But I'll not regret saying what needs to be said."

Julia blinked and glanced around the room. Disapproval dented Mr. Blake's forehead. Miss Prynne held her hand to her mouth, and Miss Trebell, for once, was speechless. Several children still remained, and for the first time, they were all quiet.

Julia was certain she had never felt so out of place in her life.

Mr. Blake seemed to be defending her, and yet she could not bring herself to look in his direction.

No good could come from arguing.

Somehow she managed a weak smile. "It was not my intention to upset you. I apologize if I caused offense." Fighting tears of frustration and embarrassment, she reached for her cloak and turned to the girls she'd been reading with and managed a little smile. "Thank you, ladies, for allowing me to spend a lovely afternoon with you."

Without another word she left the cottage.

The cool air whipped around the corner and collided with her as she exited, burning against the tear tracks on her cheeks. She'd never been spoken to in such a manner, especially never with such vehemence and what could only be perceived as hatred.

What was worse, Isaac Blake had witnessed the entire ordeal.

With each step the tears clouding her vision grew thicker, and their heat pricked stronger. Oh, what was she thinking, coming here and trying to insert herself into village life as if she were some sort of benefactress? Had she learned nothing? The villagers at Braewyn were proud, she knew. It had taken her years to be truly welcomed among them. Did she really think these villagers would be much different?

She quickened her steps to where she had tied Snow and stepped on the mounting block. Gripping her reins and crop in her left hand, she used her shaky right to hold the iron stirrup steady to put her left foot on it. But tears blinded her vision, and her boot was wet from the ground. She gripped the sidesaddle to pull herself up, but her foot slipped from the iron and she nearly fell.

Disheartened, she tried it again.

A sharp, deep voice called her name.

Mr. Blake.

Increasing her pace, she fumbled with the iron. Frustration flared. She'd never had trouble mounting before. Why now?

"Miss Twethewey, wait! Please." His footsteps were coming behind her more quickly.

She'd not try to mount again, not when he was so near. She wiped her eyes, stepped down from the mounting block, and turned to face him. "Yes?" Her words snipped sharply with injured impatience.

"Are you all right?"

She did not answer.

He reached around her to take the horse's head collar and hold it steady. "I'm sorry for that. It wasn't deserved."

His arm blocked her from attempting to mount. She was trapped between the horse and him.

"I do not wish to make excuses for Mrs. Benson," he continued. "All I can say is that she's grieving and wants to blame someone."

Julia huffed a weak smile. "So that someone is me."

"I don't share this sentiment." He fixed his hazel eyes on her. Intently. Intimately. "Far from it."

"Whether you do or you don't, it's becoming increasingly clear that I don't belong here. I don't know what I was thinking to come."

"I think you thought you were doing a kindness."

"A kindness," she repeated as she adjusted her crop in her hand. "And yet one cannot force kindness where it is not wanted."

He reached forward and gripped her hand, commandeering her attention. "I—I want you here."

Her stomach twisted as she looked into his eyes—a familiar ache—one she'd experienced not too long ago.

How she wanted to believe him.

But he was so connected to Mrs. Benson. And had not another man said something similar?

It had been a lie when Percy said it, and perhaps it was a lie now.

She did not respond. Instead she brushed his arm away and gripped the saddle.

This time, he did not try to stop her. He formed a cup with his hands to make it easier for her to mount. "Allow me."

At first she hesitated. She didn't want help. But the sooner she was mounted, the sooner she could return home.

She accepted his assistance and was quickly settled in the sidesaddle.

Without another word she urged the horse forward. She could not leave Miner's Row fast enough.

CHAPTER 28

Mrs. Sedrick informed her that Mr. Blake had called and was waiting for her in the great hall. Julia could not bring herself to ask which one.

It would not do to delay the inevitable. If it was Matthew Blake, he would be a pleasant diversion. If it was Isaac Blake, well, she'd have to see him again at some point.

She stepped through the passageway to the great hall.

There stood Matthew Blake.

Her stomach sank with unexpected disappointment.

And the very fact that she should care so much annoyed her.

It had been several days since the incident at the cottage on Miner's Row. She'd told no one at Lanwyn Manor about it. Fortunately, persistent morning rains had kept her indoors and Snow in her stall, so she'd not encountered Mr. Isaac Blake at all. She made no trips into the village and stayed behind from church. Additionally, Jane's condition had worsened, so Julia made a greater effort to spend as much time as possible keeping her company.

In surprising contrast, Aunt Beatrice spent little time with her daughter, claiming that her knees could not take the walk up the stairs, and Caroline seemed wholly indifferent to her sister. Julia feared the bloodletting and strange, foul-smelling concoctions were doing more harm than good.

But that was not what concerned her at the moment.

She paused. "Mr. Blake. What a surprise."

"I didn't see you at church yesterday. And when I wrote to your uncle and heard no response, I became worried." He extended his hands, his grin broad, his cheeks ruddy from the cold. "So here I am."

She smiled, ignoring the little flutter in her chest. It was lovely to be flirted with. "Uncle did not respond because he's not here. He's away. I'd wager your note is sitting in his office untouched."

"But he'll be back in time for our dinner at Tregarthan Hall later this week, will he not?"

Julia's stomach tightened. The fluttering ceased.

The dinner at Tregarthan Hall.

Isaac would be there. She'd almost forgotten. "Yes, Uncle should return in the coming days, weather permitting."

Matthew toyed with his hat in his hands. "I was worried that one of you ladies had fallen ill. This weather will do that to one."

"You are kind to be concerned. We are all well, with the exception of Jane, of course."

"Is her condition much worse?"

Julia shrugged. "The accoucheur assures us that she will be fine, but she's so weak."

"Have you garnered a second opinion? I'd happily call on my family's physician. He's a great friend and I'm certain he'd be happy to pay a call."

"You're kind, but Aunt has placed her full confidence in Mr. Jackaby, and I'm afraid she'll not be dissuaded. Apparently he's quite the rage in London."

"You don't share her opinion?"

"I fear it matters little what I think."

"And Mrs. Townsend's family? Surely they have thoughts on the matter."

"Her husband is away fighting, and his family is from the northernmost parts of England and are quite removed."

"How difficult it must be for Mrs. Townsend to be apart from her husband now."

"It is."

"When I marry, I shan't leave my wife's side," he declared, confidence dripping from his tone. "No doubt she'll grow weary of my company, but I don't understand how one can be away for so long."

It surprised her, a little, to hear him speak so openly of sentiment. "Well, Jonathan will do his duty to his country and then return to his wife and child very soon."

There was no denying the flirtation in his words or the intent expression on his face. Had Isaac told him about what happened with Mrs. Benson? If he had, she suspected Matthew would have brought it up and vocalized his outrage on the matter. The relationship between the brothers remained a mystery to her. They seemed close. Their professions were intertwined, and yet a distance remained. Two people could not be more different. Ironic, considering they looked so much alike.

Matthew widened his stance and cleared his throat. The volume of his voice lowered. "I am happy to encounter you alone, for there is something I—"

Commotion at the door stopped his words.

They both turned to see Mrs. Sedrick. How long had she been standing there? Had she been eavesdropping? Watching? Whatever she'd been doing, her tight expression screamed of disapproval. "Mrs. Lambourne is in the sitting room and will receive you now, Mr. Blake."

He smiled at Julia, a boyish, almost apologetic grin, and waited for her to precede him into the corridor.

Once in the sitting room, Julia saw that Aunt Beatrice was seated like a queen on her throne, bejeweled in dazzling gems at a time of day when it might be considered audacious. Yet they suited her. "Sit down, Mr. Blake, next to Julia on the sofa there. How nice to have a visitor. It's such a shame that this part of the country is woefully lacking in such graces."

Before obeying her direction, he took her hand and bowed low over it. "I was telling Miss Twethewey that I was concerned since I didn't see you all in church Sunday. I was worried you or one of the other young ladies had fallen ill."

Julia observed the conversation with incredulity. Oh yes, he was charming, with his dimpled cheek and the lock of pale hair that fell so carelessly over his forehead. And judging by the flush on her aunt's cheeks, his words and charisma were having the desired effect.

She tensed, aware of the conflict brewing within her. Aunt was right. Matthew Blake was aptly suitable for her. In so many ways. Why did she always have to complicate things? Why could she not put all thoughts of Isaac out of her head and focus on Matthew? He'd made his intentions clear. If she were to offer the least bit of encouragement, no doubt her life could take a very dramatic turn.

So what could be done? At what point should one allow one's head to rule over one's heart?

Hours after Matthew's impromptu visit, Julia reclined on the settee in Jane's chamber. Jane's illness intensified earlier that afternoon, and Julia had promised that she would not stir from her side, lest she should fall ill again, but the longer she sat in deafening silence watching her cousin sleep, the more her stomach churned.

How much longer could Jane continue in this state? She grew weaker by the day, and regardless of any prompting from Julia or Caroline, Aunt Beatrice refused to summon the accoucheur for a return visit.

When Jane woke an hour later, she requested Julia write a letter for her, and Julia complied. It felt horribly intrusive to be writing words of affection and dreams of the future a wife intended for her husband, but what else could be done? Julia could not help but wonder what it would be like to write such a missive to her own husband.

Husband.

For so long Percy's face had filled that space in her imagination. Her sense of sadness turned into anger. The last face she wanted to see in that role was Percy.

But now, in spite of her better judgment, another face was taking that place.

She could not deny it.

A bloodcurdling scream shattered the night's stillness.

Julia jumped, nearly upsetting the bottle of ink. She whirled to face Jane's ashen countenance. "What in heaven's—?"

A sharp shout, followed by a cry, echoed.

Julia dropped her quill and raced to the corridor. More muffled cries echoed from the floor below. Julia hastened down the stairs to the ground-floor level, where her aunt and uncle's chambers were.

Wide-eyed and breathless, Caroline rounded the corner from another direction. "What is it?"

Julia shrugged. Together they scurried into Aunt Beatrice's open chamber door.

The older woman was still dressed in her shimmery wrapping gown around her full form, her light hair loose around her shoulders.

"Aunt, what is it? What has happened?"

"They're gone! My emerald-and-diamond brooch, my ruby necklace, my amethyst pendant—they're all gone!"

Eager for more information, Julia whirled to Aunt Beatrice's lady's maid, who was stammering, grasping for words. "I—I always put them in the top drawer there."

Julia's muscles tensed. Not again. Not more items missing.

"Isn't it clear? They were stolen!" cried Aunt Beatrice, tears streaming down her cheeks. "Is this what this place has come to? No longer content to be stealing our silver, but now my jewels? Oh, this is not to be borne. Fetch Mrs. Sedrick, quickly!"

The horror-stricken lady's maid bustled from the room, and Aunt Beatrice returned to the jewelry box and yanked open drawers.

"Please, Aunt, do try to stay calm," Julia implored, gaping helplessly as her aunt continued to tear through the jewelry chest. "Caroline, help me convince her!"

Caroline placed her arm around her mother's shoulder, turned her from the box, and guided her to the settee. "Mother, please, we don't know what has happened. Let's not assume the worst."

Julia retrieved the smelling salts from the dressing table and held them to her aunt's nose.

Mrs. Sedrick and the butler appeared in the doorway, and Aunt Beatrice pushed past Julia and hurried to the housekeeper. "I should have taken your words of caution more seriously, Mrs. Sedrick. Now look what has happened!"

Caroline drew close to Julia and lowered her voice. "I don't think it is a coincidence. Do you? Surely this has something to do with what we heard in the attic."

Julia pressed her back against the wall as her cousin began to pace. The memory of the figure flashed in her mind. "We are not even sure what made that noise."

"But strange noises? The missing silver, and now Mother's jewels are gone? It is far too coincidental. Perhaps I should send word to Father to urge him to come home as soon as possible. I know he is due home shortly, but he knows of none of this. Perhaps it is time he did."

Julia could not deny that this went far beyond coincidence. "Yes, I agree. I'll find a footman and send him to Uncle with a message right away."

CHAPTER 29

The night of the dinner at Tregarthan Hall, Julia along with her aunt, uncle, and Caroline bundled into the Lambourne carriage. It was not a far drive, but it was a cold one. The errant wind seeped in through the windows and cracks at the door. Even the foot warmers with heated coals did little to ward off the icy winter chill.

The bitterness in the air, however, was no match for the frigid tension between Aunt Beatrice and Uncle William.

As the carriage rumbled over the rutted roads, Julia studied her uncle's profile against the day's fading light. Uncle William returned the day following the discovery of the missing jewels, but instead of bringing comfort to the situation, he'd been frustratingly dismissive, suggesting they'd overreacted and imagined the events. In turn, Aunt Beatrice blamed him for every recent ill that had befallen them, and she did not hold back.

If any opportunity remained for Aunt Beatrice to accept Lanwyn Manor as her home, this incident erased it completely. It was one thing to have silver stolen; it was another matter entirely to have her personal property invaded.

If this evening's excursion offered any reprieve from the heaviness at Lanwyn Manor, it was that the black cloud hovering over Aunt Beatrice seemed to lift at least momentarily. The anticipation of dining at Tregarthan Hall seemed to raise her spirits and create a much-needed diversion for them all.

Aunt leaned toward Caroline and patted her leg. "Did I not tell you all that Mr. Blake would take to Julia quickly? Mark my words, we'll have a proposal before the winter's out. Although I do worry about setting you up to live here in Goldweth. Wretched countryside."

Aunt Beatrice waved an authoritative finger in the air. "I've told you before, dear Julia, 'tis a woman's duty to marry well. Now, we will have no more talk of it for now, but I expect you to be encouraging and kind to Mr. Blake. He's been most affable to come and visit us and to be so very concerned for our welfare."

"I haven't been anything but kind." Slightly offended at the implication, Julia sank against the seat and looked to the window, trying to push the family frustrations aside and focus on the evening.

The carriage turned a sharp corner, and a tall house of gray stone loomed before them. She'd only seen Tregarthan Hall from a distance, and it was much larger than she'd anticipated. Instead of possessing a full courtyard like Lanwyn Manor, the house itself formed a U-shape, with two wings that jutted forward of the main entrance. The building rose three stories, imposing and stately, and boasted banks of tall leaded windows overlooking the broad grounds below.

She lifted her gaze to the tops of the numerous chimneys as her foot hit the drive.

So, this was where the Blake brothers grew up.

This was where Matthew Blake still resided.

The woman who eventually married Matthew would be mistress of this mansion.

Now that she beheld the home, her head understood her aunt's insistence. But even so, as she looked to the door and saw Isaac just inside, her heart told her something entirely different.

CHAPTER 30

Isaac had to hand it to his brother. If there had been any question, it was now answered: Matthew Blake was a mastermind at getting his way. His shrewdness and cunning were beyond anything Isaac would have suspected him capable of.

Over the past several weeks, Matthew had worked his way into the affections of an entire family.

Mr. Lambourne trusted him.

Mrs. Lambourne adored him.

And, no doubt, Miss Twethewey had to be aware of his intentions by now, and there was no reason for Isaac to believe that she did not return his attentions, especially after how things had been left at the cottage on Miner's Row.

Almost immediately upon Miss Twethewey's arrival, Matthew ignored all other guests and focused on none but her. He sat by her at dinner. Praised her. Flirted with her.

Once Isaac caught Miss Twethewey's eye while everyone was seated for the meal. At the subtle interaction her cheeks flushed to match the salmon color of her lace-trimmed gown, and she quickly looked away. Isaac had attempted to speak with her twice upon her arrival, but Beatrice Lambourne was determined that she speak with no other man besides Matthew.

After dinner, the ladies retreated to the parlor, and as the men lounged around the dining table, Isaac sat amazed.

Matthew had made clever, intentional invitations for the night's festivities. Not a single other mining man was in sight, just the vicar, the physician, and a solicitor. With such guests Matthew could control any potential mining talk that might arise and steer it to his benefit.

Almost amused to see how his brother would direct the conversation, Isaac sipped his port as Lambourne apprised the men of the odd occurrences at Lanwyn Manor. Isaac already knew about many of the happenings, for Miss Twethewey had shared them with him, but even so, Lambourne's version of the same stories proved interesting.

Lambourne paced the room with animated gestures, his full face florid and flushed as he relayed details. "All the women in my family are frightened of our very home! Somehow, in the last six weeks, the place has gone from a diverting retreat from the hassle of London to a frightening house of horror. If it weren't for Jane requiring bedrest, I think I should be forced to return all the ladies to London."

The vicar, Mr. Bequest, a tall, lanky man with thinning hair and gray side whiskers, leaned forward, folding his hands atop the table. "Have you informed the magistrate?"

"Oh, of course," Lambourne snipped, his blue eyes popped wide. "Several times. But the blackguard takes nothing I say to heart. Not a single word."

"Let me ask you this." Matthew stood from his chair, commanding the attention of the room, lifted the decanter of port, and moved to refill Lambourne's glass. "Have you considered that the magistrate is from a mining family?"

Lambourne's head jerked up. "What's this?"

Matthew shrugged and returned the decanter to the table, his voice smooth as the liquid he'd just poured. "The magistrate is a man of the people, so to speak. His brother is a principal investor in Bal Anne Marie not ten miles north of here, but of course, you'd have no way to know that. Furthermore, he had family—two cousins, I believe—who worked at Bal Tressa."

Lambourne's countenance darkened, and his lips flattened to a thin, unflattering line. "No, I wasn't aware of his mining connections. Are you suggesting he's purposely turning a blind eye to the happenings?"

Matthew eased back down to his chair, leaned back comfortably, and crossed one long leg over the other, pausing to swipe a bit of dust from his tall, polished boot. "It's a sad state, but the mines are taken very personally around here—but I needn't tell you that."

"The uprisings are due to lack of employment," Mr. Bequest interjected matter-of-factly with a sharp shake of his head. "Everyone's frightened of the unknown. Even the other mine owners. These are precarious, uncertain times."

"Unemployment, you say?" Lambourne growled, his cheeks darkening to an angry purple. "Bah. The employment status of the miners in the area is not my concern. I've nothing to do with it. I'm well aware they think if Bal Tressa were to reopen it would solve all their problems. If that's the case, let them put their own money up against it. The land is mine, and I'll do with it as I please, just as any of you would do. Do you think I got to where I am by acting rashly? Of course not. None of us have. My predecessor may have been seen as somewhat of a saint around here, but he ran his business into the ground."

"I understand," Matthew soothed, his calm voice a sharp contrast to Lambourne's passionate declaration. "I do."

"Do you?" Lambourne pointed his thick finger in Matthew's direction. "You own your land *and* work it. There's a great difference. I own the land, but before I make decisions on its future, I must be more informed. I'll not be taken advantage of, and I'll not be pushed into making a decision by those who feel they've a right to be employed by my land."

"Well said, and I daresay there is not a man in this room who disagrees with you." Matthew retrieved his snuffbox—slowly, methodically—from his pocket and placed it on the table before him. "I admire you for refusing to be made a fool of. Mining is tricky business, and there's a great deal of the unknown. But you do have options."

"Such as?" Lambourne dropped into his chair, breathing heavily like a man who had just run a race.

"Well, you could contract with adventurers, as Rowe did. It would be the easiest for you but perhaps not the most profitable. You could join forces with investors and open it yourself. Of course, there would be a certain bit of education you would need, and you'd need to partner with men who share your vision for the future. Or you could sell the land outright, gather your profits, and be done with it once and for all."

"I've no wish to sell," blurted Lambourne. "Even in spite of all the odd things that have happened. But I do need income to justify my presence here."

Matthew reached for the port bottle once more and swirled the liquid. "I feel I must inform you of something. Rumor has it that you intend to sell your property to Marcus Elliot. Now, I do not buy into idle gossip, but I also believe a man has the right to be informed when his name is being bandied about."

"Bah. Elliot." Lambourne snorted, extending his glass for another refill. "He's even a bigger fool than I thought. He offered me half of what the land is worth. Half! Nothing short of insulting. But if things continue as they have in Lanwyn Manor, I might be forced to cut my losses."

Matthew swiped his tongue over his lips and cut his eyes toward

Isaac before he spoke. "Come now, no man should be forced into selling when he hasn't a mind to, nor should he be coerced into accepting a farthing less than what his property is worth."

Matthew stood and paced the space for several moments before he clapped a hand good-naturedly on Lambourne's thick shoulder. "You know what you need? Someone who can reevaluate your mine. It's been closed for a while now, hasn't it? Have you been down there?"

"Me?" Lambourne scoffed, his face reddening with each second. "No."

"I know the basics of it, but most miners in the area do. You should let Isaac here go down and assess it. He is the best mine captain I know of, and he will tell you straight what you are dealing with, friend to friend."

Isaac stiffened at the mention of his name. He was not sure he wanted to be drawn into his brother's game. Even so, he leaned forward. If assessing the mine would help it reopen, he'd do what he could.

Matthew returned to his seat and drummed his fingers on the table before a grin creased his face. "There *is* another tactic."

"And that is?"

"You must get the community on your side. The miners are angry. Bitter. It would not hurt for you to offer some sort of goodwill."

Lambourne laughed. "'Tis an impossible tide to turn."

"Difficult, but not impossible." Matthew cocked his head to the side. "Have you considered hosting a gathering, a ball or dinner of some sort?"

"What? For the miners?" A throaty laugh rumbled from his chest. "I doubt they'd come."

"Oh, I think they could be persuaded. We had our setting day at Wheal Tamsen a while back. Normally, the miners would celebrate the day afterward. 'Tis a typical occurrence, but with the recent death of one of our beloved miners, they didn't feel much like celebrating.

But now, time is passing, and a bit of merrymaking could be just what this lot needs. Think on it. In the meantime, let's go to the ladies and enjoy the evening."

———•———

Isaac shook his head in amazement. By the time the gentlemen arrived in the drawing room with the ladies, Matthew had completely convinced Mr. Lambourne that a ball was the best way to connect with the miners.

He followed behind his brother and Mr. Lambourne—close enough to overhear their conversation, yet far enough away not to be a part of it.

"Mr. Blake has given me the most wonderful idea," Lambourne announced as they entered the drawing room, capturing the attention of all in attendance with his booming voice and grandiose sweep of his arm.

"Well, I, for one, am not surprised." Mrs. Lambourne lowered the cards in her hand and lifted her gaze to the men. "Tell us, what have you gentlemen concocted?"

"A country dance." Mr. Lambourne beamed with pride. "At Lanwyn Manor. For the villagers."

The other ladies at her card table smiled at the news, but Mrs. Lambourne's mouth dropped open in horror. "Oh posh. Why?"

"Goodwill, my dear." Lambourne placed a thick hand on his wife's shoulder and glanced down at the cards she held. "It's been brought to my attention that closing Bal Tressa has caused grief for many local workers, and unfortunately that breeds negative rapport." He paused to reorder the cards in her hand. "I'm not ready to open the mine at this point, but this gesture might smooth ruffled feathers and buy me a little more time."

Mrs. Lambourne jerked her cards from her husband's reach. "I don't like the thought of all those strangers in my house, especially with everything that has been transpiring."

"My mind is made up. This is how we'll proceed."

Beatrice Lambourne shook her head, causing the cluster of jewels around her neck to shake. "Mr. Lambourne. I—"

"If I may, Mrs. Lambourne." Matthew stepped forward, interrupting the couple. "I believe your husband's idea to be a splendid one. The miners are a fickle lot, and if they are acting out their frustrations, it pains me to see you under such duress."

Color saturated her face. "But what makes you think they would actually come? With the exception of the handful of people here, I've never seen such an unwelcoming lot of people in my life."

"I'm certain of it."

"Why?"

Matthew grinned and raised his brows. "Because everyone knows of the treasure."

At this Isaac could not help but huff.

Mrs. Bequest laughed. "Ah, but that is naught but a legend, Mr. Blake."

"Quite right, Mrs. Bequest. It is a legend, of course. We know that, but the miners are superstitious. Lanwyn Manor is ancient, and with a house that old, tales are bound to accompany it. You see, Mrs. Lambourne, it's rumored that a treasure was built into the very stones of Lanwyn Manor hundreds of years ago. The story states that an ancient spirit guards the house, and when one is brave enough, clever enough, and cunning enough, the secret location will be revealed."

"Why, that's ridiculous." Mrs. Lambourne fluttered her fan in front of her face, disrupting the faded, forced curls at her temples. "Who'd believe such nonsense?"

"Nonsense or not, it's the legend that has surrounded that home for centuries, and one of the main reasons old Rowe stopped entertaining. He grew tired of people trying to deconstruct his house."

"How remarkable." Fresh interest lit Mr. Lambourne's expression. "How were we not aware of it?"

"Because in reality, it's just a story, folklore, and holds no merit," responded Matthew. "But these are simple people who are curious."

Isaac glanced up to see Miss Twethewey sitting next to Miss Prynne, drinking in the conversation with her head cocked slightly to the side. He liked the way she looked in his family home. A small smile curved the corner of her lips as she listened to the banter, and she exchanged glances with Miss Prynne.

Isaac took advantage of Mrs. Lambourne's divided attention and strode over to her side.

Miss Prynne shifted her position to face him as he approached. Instead of showing amusement, her expression hardened. "So there is to be a ball at Lanwyn? Did you have anything to do with this, Mr. Blake?"

He held his hands in the air, declaring innocence. "Solely Matthew's idea. But I support it. Don't you? The miners suffer as a result of Bal Tressa's closure."

Miss Twethewey looked up at him, amusement brightening her blue eyes, and she didn't give Miss Prynne a chance to respond. "Do you think there's really a treasure? How interesting."

He shrugged. "I suppose it depends on your definition of treasure."

"Folklore," snipped Miss Prynne with surprising forcefulness, her face growing pale. "I'm shocked he'd mention it and encourage such talk. 'Tis shameful and disrespectful."

Miss Twethewey sobered. "My, Goldweth seems to be full of secrets."

Miss Prynne stood, her jaw twitching. "I don't think it a good idea at all."

"Why not?" Miss Twethewey asked.

"It's trickery, plain and simple. Yes, it might appear on the surface a gesture of goodwill, but as soon as the memory of it fades and reality resumes, the kind sentiments will be for naught." Miss Prynne excused herself in a huff, leaving him alone with Miss Twethewey.

She frowned and also stood. "I wonder what has upset her?"

Isaac waited until Miss Prynne was completely out of the chamber before he spoke. "She has a very long, very personal history with the past residents of Lanwyn Manor. I'm sure it stirs memories she'd rather forget."

He was acutely aware of Julia standing near him in his childhood home. He'd sought out her presence, and now that he was alone with her, he was not sure what to say. Her scent of rosewater was refreshing—a bit of summer in the midst of winter, and the soft rustle of her gown seemed to disrupt any thought.

The memory of their last conversation haunted him. The tears in her eyes. The anger in her expression. He wanted to right any wrong that might have passed between them. True, Matthew had sights on her, but Isaac was not ready to admit defeat. Not yet. He stepped closer to her. "I missed seeing you at the wall the past mornings."

She remained silent for several moments, leaving him to wonder if she was going to respond at all. Then she said, "The rain kept me indoors."

"The rain?" He glanced over his shoulder to see Mrs. Lambourne drawing Matthew into a game of whist. "Is that the only thing that kept you indoors?"

She fidgeted with the lacy cuff of her sleeve.

"I would hate to think that something I said or did made you upset with me."

She absently bit her lower lip a few seconds prior to responding. "You've done nothing. It's just that I—"

"Was it Mrs. Benson? She was out of line, but I think—"

"It is a number of things, Mr. Blake." She inhaled deeply, and then her expression softened. "I came to Lanwyn Manor to be with my family and to keep Jane company. I expect nothing more. From anyone. Be that as it may, I can't help but feel like I owe you an apology."

"An apology?" He frowned. "I don't see why."

As she leaned closer a tendril swept her shoulder, and the soft rose fragrance enchanted him anew. "You are right. The interaction with Mrs. Benson did upset me. But you only tried to be helpful, and I was rude to you."

Isaac held up his hand. "There's no need. I—"

"Please, Mr. Blake." Her words silenced him. "You were attempting to be kind to me, I see that now. I didn't respond well. Either way, I want you to know that I value your friendship, and I would hate to think that something would come in the way of it."

"Friendship?" His brow ascended at the word.

"Yes, for are we not friends?" Her brilliant gaze pierced him. Surely this woman must be able to see right into his mind and read his every thought.

"I like to think so." He nodded toward her aunt, uncle, and Matthew, who were now laughing with the other ladies at the card table. "Although I do not think your aunt approves of such a friendship."

Miss Twethewey's shoulders relaxed slightly. "My aunt has my best interest at heart. It would probably be wise to follow her guidance and yet, in some instances, we simply do not see eye to eye."

He tried not to read too much into her words, for perhaps they were just as she said. Or perhaps he was interpreting the glint in her eye properly. Perhaps there was more to her statement.

In that moment, in that simple interaction, he knew what he needed to do.

He stepped closer to her.

She did not retreat.

He lowered his voice. "Will you be at the wall tomorrow?"

She looked to her aunt. The corner of her mouth twitched in a smile. "Weather permitting."

"You must know it is one of my favorite times of the day."

Isaac was so lost in conversation that he did not notice Matthew had approached. His brother placed a heavy hand on Isaac's shoulder and nudged him to the side to give himself room to join the conversation. "You two appear to be discussing something quite interesting. Do tell me what it is."

Miss Twethewey looked toward Matthew, tilting her head to the side. "We were speaking of treasure."

"The Lanwyn Manor treasure?"

Miss Twethewey raised a brow. "Indeed."

"Well, I do hate to interrupt such an enthralling conversation, but I had hoped that you might entertain us." Matthew gestured toward the instrument. "Our pianoforte is quite old, and it hasn't been played in years, but I'm certain with your talent, you will be able to make it sing."

She cut her eyes toward Isaac before she responded. "I should be happy to."

Isaac stepped back as Matthew offered her his hand and led her to the pianoforte. He instructed all to be silent, and Miss Twethewey was seated at the keyboard. She lifted her fingers and began to play, but Isaac was not sure he heard the melody.

He marveled over their conversation. He searched it. Evaluated it. Dare he hope that she would consider him over Matthew?

What a lovely picture she made, the candlelight bathing her in soft light. It caught the glint of her dark curls and shimmered against her gown. It was dangerous to entertain such thoughts, but with every note that sounded, the idea became planted more firmly in his mind.

He could not let Matthew use her as a pawn. He *would not* let Matthew use her as a pawn. If he thought for a moment she returned any regard for him at all, he'd do whatever necessary to protect her from getting hurt.

Her song ended, but at Matthew's bidding, she started a new one. He was surprised—nay, shocked—when Mrs. Lambourne came and stood next to him near the back wall of the drawing room. Her lily-of-the-valley scent was as nauseating as Miss Twethewey's rose scent was alluring. Normally, the prideful matriarch would not even acknowledge his existence, but now she leaned close, her throaty voice only loud enough to be heard above the music. "I am so pleased that Julia chose to come and stay with us."

Curious, he nodded. "Yes, she is a charming addition to Goldweth society."

Mrs. Lambourne's gaze did not leave her niece and Matthew, whose hand was on the music, poised to turn the page at the appointed time. "She and Matthew look fine together, don't they?"

The brazen, bold comment took him aback. He had heard that Mrs. Lambourne was a doggedly determined matchmaker and opinionated beyond measure. He swallowed. "They do."

"Your brother seems quite enchanted, does he not? And I can hardly wonder why. She would make an excellent match for him. Imagine, uniting two of the prominent families in the area."

This topic was hardly proper, and yet he was well aware of what she was doing.

By all accounts, Matthew did look every bit the doting suitor. His eyes were fixed on Julia's every move. But what would Mrs. Lambourne say if she knew the truth behind his brother's attentions toward her niece? Then again, perhaps that would not deter her.

The music stopped, and Mrs. Lambourne finally turned to look him in the eye. "You never know, Mr. Blake. You could have a new sister very soon. She is the very thing needed to make this house into a home. Wouldn't that be lovely? Surely you can see how advantageous that would be for everyone all around."

CHAPTER 31

The hour was late when Julia and the Lambournes returned from Tregarthan, but Julia was not tired.

Far from it.

The night's events swept through her mind with blinding speed, and her heart struggled to keep up.

She'd barely spoken with Isaac over the course of the evening. Nearly every moment was spent with Matthew. But it was the few slivers of time with Isaac, and the unmistakable attraction pulsing between them, that dominated her memory.

Even so, it was evident. Isaac Blake had feelings for her.

For *her.*

The few words that had been said during their brief conversation and the subsequent glances had been as full of meaning as any hour-long conversation.

Once the carriage drew to a stop in front of Lanwyn Manor, Julia scurried through the darkened hall, down the narrow corridors, and to the tower where she encountered Evangeline.

The blonde lady's maid curtsied. "Mrs. Townsend asked me to tell you she is awake and hoped you wouldn't be too tired to pay her a visit when you returned."

With renewed energy Julia hurried to Jane's chamber. Candlelight glimmered from the space. She entered to see Jane abed, book in hand.

"What on earth are you doing awake?" Julia stepped closer. "I would have thought you'd been asleep for hours."

"I can't sleep. That's the danger of sleeping during the day." Jane tossed the book aside. "Besides, every time you return from an encounter with Mr. Blake, I expect to hear an announcement of your engagement."

"Surely you know me a bit better than that, and if tonight confirmed one thing, it is that Mr. Matthew Blake is not the man for me."

"Why do you say that?"

Julia thought back over the night's subtleties. Matthew had been at her side all evening, but tonight his intentions were abundantly clear. He was wooing her aunt and uncle, not her. "He's much more interested in gaining access to Bal Tressa than courting me."

"Oh, I doubt that, but one must be practical, I suppose. Matches are made all the time to align with business relationships. It is the way things have been done for centuries."

"Yes, but I'll not marry for a business advantage."

"You sound awfully firm on that count."

"You refused to marry for a business alliance," Julia challenged. "You married for love, remember?"

Jane's smile faded. "Yes, I did, but look at me now. Alone. Unable to rise from bed. A prisoner in my mother's house."

Julia jerked at the acidic tone of her cousin's words. "Do you really feel that way?"

"I love Jonathan, with all of my heart I do, but I never see him. Sometimes, I wonder if Mother was right. If I had married Ichabod Cruthers as she'd desired, my husband would at least be by my side, and I'd have a secure home of my own." Jane, as if regretting the bluntness of her words, forced an awkward smile. "But enough of me. Since you came bouncing in here with a grin on your face, I must assume the evening had some redeeming points. And I can't help but wonder if Mr. Blake's younger brother had something to do with that."

Julia locked eyes with her cousin.

Part of her wanted to share every detail of her blossoming feelings for Isaac, but another part, a more injured, sensitive part, was hesitant. She'd been overly forthcoming with Jane about her relationship with Percy. Surely she learned her lesson.

Jane fixed her dark eyes on Julia and patted the bed next to her. "Sit. I have a confession."

"A confession?" Confused, Julia followed her cousin's bidding and sat next to her. "What is it?"

Jane took Julia's hand in her right one and covered it with her left. "I may be stuck here, but I have been paying attention, you know. I can see the meadow wall from my window. I've seen you talking with him. At first I thought it was Mr. Matthew Blake you were speaking with, but then I began to figure things out."

Uneasiness flared. Julia was not embarrassed for meeting with Isaac in the mornings, but she'd thought everyone asleep, and never did she dream her cousin could see out her window from bed.

"You're blushing, but there's no need to be embarrassed," soothed Jane. "Just make sure you aren't trading the excitement of the moment for future troubles."

Julia pulled her hand free with a bit more force than she intended, stood, and stepped back. She bent and kissed her cousin on the cheek. "I am tired. I think I'll retire. Try to sleep." Eager to be alone with her thoughts and free from the opinions of others, Julia retreated, climbed the staircase, and stepped onto the landing.

A gentle light emanated from her own room, and Evangeline's

voice could be heard coming from Caroline's chamber. Julia tugged at the pins that held her curls away from her face, but as she stepped into her chamber, she started.

For there sat Aunt Beatrice in a chair by the fire, still dressed in her gown from dinner, Oscar at her side.

Julia's blood seemed to slow as she beheld her aunt's bothered countenance. In her weeks at Lanwyn Manor she'd only seen her aunt climb the tower to Jane's chamber a handful of times, and she had never seen her on this floor, and never had she seen her aunt's face twisted in such an odd expression.

"Aunt, what a surprise to see you here. How did you manage the stairs?"

Aunt Beatrice nodded at the chair across from her with the silent instruction for Julia to sit. "Julia, I must speak with you."

Julia tensed.

What had she done wrong?

She lowered herself to the chair. Oscar trotted toward her and put his paws up on the chair, and Julia lifted him into her arms, grateful to feel as if one living, breathing creature might be on her side.

Aunt Beatrice's iron glare speared her. "Have you or have you not secretly been meeting Isaac Blake?"

Julia jerked, unable to blink at the shock of the question. Jane's admission of seeing them echoed in her mind. "Secretly meeting Isaac Blake?" she repeated, buying herself time.

"Matthew told your uncle that you and Isaac have been meeting on your so-called morning rides. So I ask you again, have you been meeting him?"

Julia shook her head, searching for words. "I have encountered him several times while on my morning ride, but I've not gone out to specifically meet him."

"You are a lady, Julia," Aunt Beatrice seethed, "not a common girl who meets men at fences. Why, the idea!"

"Aunt, you misunderstand. I assure you, I—"

"This must cease."

Julia winced at the sharp words. The bubble of elation she felt at their conversation in the Tregarthan drawing room popped.

"You've no business being out early in the morning as it is. From now on you will only ride out when accompanied. Am I clear?"

"But I ride every day, Aunt. I have for years. I—"

"Your uncle Jac has entrusted you to my care," Aunt Beatrice snapped, slicing into Julia's words. "I'd never dream of allowing my daughters to behave in such a way, and I'll no longer permit you to do so."

"But I enjoy riding, Aunt."

"If there is anywhere you need to go, the driver can take you in the carriage," Aunt Beatrice declared. "I don't know what distresses me more, whether you have been meeting him behind my back or if you have given Mr. Matthew Blake the wrong impression."

"Matthew Blake?" She winced.

"He is very fond of you; he told your uncle so himself."

Charismatic, charming, entertaining Matthew Blake.

Julia's face flushed with the unfairness of it all.

But then Percy flashed before her.

Perhaps if she had been a little more careful, the entire ordeal never would have happened.

Aunt Beatrice knocked her fist against the chair's arm to recapture Julia's attention. "Do I have your word that these morning rides and secret meetings with Isaac Blake will cease?"

Julia drew a shuddering breath. Had she any other choice? At the end of the day, she was a guest at Lanwyn Manor. Whether she liked it or not, she needed to behave like it. "You have my word."

Her aunt pointed a thick finger in Julia's direction. "You will stay indoors and not leave unless you have my explicit permission. Is that clear?"

Julia nodded and then watched, defeated, as her aunt lumbered from the room.

Suddenly cold, suddenly overwhelmingly sad, she scooped up Oscar and hugged the tiny dog to her, mindless of how his toenails might snag her dress, and lifted her gaze to the portrait above the fireplace.

The same woman, frozen in time, with her tightly curled hair. Her blue gown. Her forlorn expression. Julia had awakened to this woman's image every day since her arrival. She still did not know her identity, but she was beginning to understand the melancholy in her eyes.

Had she been under this house's spell? Did she know of a treasure? Did she hear sounds in the midnight hours? Was she one of the women whose child never survived birth within these walls?

After several moments, Evangeline entered, her voice cheery, unaware of the turmoil churning. "Are you ready to prepare for bed now, miss?"

Julia, ignoring Evangeline's question, answered it with one of her own. "Who is that woman in that portrait? Do you know?"

Evangeline propped a fist on her hip. "That's Mrs. Rowe. The former master's late wife."

Julia's blood slowed. "What happened to her?"

"She died before I came here. Died in childbirth, if I'm not mistaken."

Fear gripped Julia. "Did the child survive?"

"He did. 'Twas before my time, though. But he died in a mining accident as a young boy. Broke the master's heart, it did."

Julia was quiet as the maid helped her into her nightclothes, and once she was finally alone, she blew out the candles, snuggled the dog in her arms, and climbed into her bed.

"Broke the master's heart, it did."

The words echoed in her mind. Curses. Sorrow. Disappointment.

At the moment it was all too much. Maybe this house was cursed after all.

CHAPTER 32

Several mornings after the dinner at Tregarthan Hall and her uncomfortable discussion with Aunt Beatrice, Julia sat in her bedchamber on the small tufted settee beneath one of the banks of leaded windows. Oscar was curled up at her side, and she absently stroked his fur. From her vantage point she looked out over Lanwyn Manor's west lawn, the drystone wall where she would have had her morning chat with Isaac Blake, and the public road beyond.

Had she her choice, she'd be out riding at this very moment, amidst the frosty grass and barren trees. It was just dawn still, and the day promised to be fine. Soon the sun would crest over the east tree line and burn off the low-lying fog settling over the lawn.

But it was not to be.

Yes, she was disappointed.

The first day after her aunt forbade her to go riding, she'd watched for him from her window. He arrived, as usual, and waited for her for several minutes before he continued on his way.

The second day he did the same.

But as the days passed, his waiting times decreased, until now he did not even stop.

Her shoulders slumped and she leaned her head against the wall as she looked out the window. What he must think of her, especially after the moment that passed between them in the drawing room at Tregarthan Hall, and after her promise to meet him there.

With the exception of the lack of her morning rides, the days at Lanwyn Manor settled into a predictable routine. She still was permitted to go to the Ladies League, by carriage. Miss Prynne and Miss Trebell still called and chattered about Goldweth events. Julia still sat with Jane daily, and she worked on her needlework with Caroline. In addition to their normal activities, preparations for the country dance also added to their day. The seamstress visited frequently to make sure the Lambourne ladies had new gowns, and the servants flitted about, moving furniture, preparing food, and making certain that the house was ready for the whole of Goldweth to descend upon it.

One afternoon, after a fitting with the seamstress, Julia visited the library to select a new book to read with Jane. As always, she walked through the dark study and turned into the library, where a figure made her jump.

She cried in alarm, and Matthew's strong arms steadied her.

"Mr. Blake!" she gasped, gripping his coat's lapels as she found her footing. Realizing she was holding on to him, she dropped her hands and took a large step back, forcing him to remove his hands from her arms.

"Are you all right?" He stepped forward, arms still outstretched. "I didn't mean to frighten you."

She retreated farther.

Upon her arrival all those weeks ago, she'd have no doubt been pleased to encounter him. But somehow he had managed to be at Lanwyn Manor nearly every day since the Tregarthan dinner. At one time she might have thought his persistent attention flattering, but now she was growing to dread their encounters. The more she resisted, the more intent he became.

"I'm here to speak with your uncle," he explained. "He'd asked for some maps, and I've brought them with me."

Julia sighed, attempting to catch her breath from the sudden shock. "Have you not heard? He's out of town. He left for London this morning."

"Did he?"

"Yes." She furrowed her brow. "Did the butler not tell you when you arrived?"

"I confess I came in through one of the back entrances through the stables. I thought he was here and didn't think he'd mind my sneaking in."

She shook her head, trying to make sense of what he was saying. Was he in the habit of letting himself in the house?

It seemed odd to her, but then again, Matthew and her uncle had become good friends, and they seemed more congenial with every interaction. "I'm sure you can leave whatever it is on his desk for when he returns."

With a smile he removed several papers from a satchel and placed them on the desk. He retrieved a quill and ink and wrote a quick note, then left it on top of the papers. He returned the quill and corked the ink.

"Would you care to stop for some coffee or tea?" she offered out of duty, stepping back toward the corridor. "I know my aunt would like to see you."

Instead of accepting without reservation, his eye twitched oddly. He appeared almost uncomfortable, and he shuffled the papers on the desk once more before he slid his finger between his neck and cravat. "Normally, nothing would prevent me from spending time with you ladies. But previous obligations forbid it."

He said nothing else. No words of excessive praise. No flowery sentiments. He simply bowed and departed.

Dumbfounded at the uncharacteristic exit, she returned her attention to the library and tried to remember why she'd come here in the first place. No one else was there. Nothing was out of place. She strolled over to the desk and lifted the note he'd written, but nothing was odd about it. She returned the letter and bit her lip.

Julia was not exactly sure what she had encountered.

Abandoning her original plan, she made her way up to Jane, who had spent the morning hunched over the chamber pot, unable to keep even water down. It had been a taxing morning of tears and fitful crying. Sobbing. Aunt Beatrice was frustratingly absent, and Caroline was out.

Julia, herself, felt weary. At length Jane's sobbing ceased and exhaustion took over, and she fell into a fitful sleep. Once she was certain her cousin was asleep, Julia slumped against the sofa and looked out to the drystone wall where she had met Isaac so many mornings.

Everything seemed backward.

Jane should be happy and anticipating the arrival of her child. But she was ill. Weepy.

She should be with her husband, but he might never return.

Julia should be entranced by a handsome, wealthy man such as Matthew Blake, but she wasn't.

She should look past Isaac Blake but could not.

Bal Tressa should be open, providing work and incomes, but it wasn't.

The injustices swirled, haphazardly and bitterly. And what could be done to change any of it?

She lifted her gaze from the drystone wall to the colorless sky above it. It had been cloudy for so long it seemed that a reprieve would never come.

When would lightness return?

Would it ever?

A dark, sobering melancholy seemed to reach inside her very heart and mind. This was a different melancholy than any Julia had ever experienced, even after her cruel disappointment with Percy.

Feeling the need to be surrounded by those who truly loved her and had her best interest at heart, Julia moved from the sofa to the writing desk and pulled a fresh sheet of paper from the drawer. She lifted the quill, dipped it in the small inkwell, and began to write Aunt Delia.

She wrote general greetings and then updated her aunt on Jane's condition.

There is a sadness with watching someone you love be ill for so long. Even though I hope and pray that at the end of this journey she and her baby will be whole, I cannot be certain of it.

It is frightening, to think that life might not turn out the way we had hoped. I tasted only a morsel of that disappointment with the ordeal with Percy, but I will recover. I have recovered. But the pain Jane experiences—will it ever dissipate? The fear of not knowing is stifling her. I fear it might be killing her.

My pain is nothing compared to hers. I remind myself of this and am very grateful for my health. But uncertainty plagues us all, and mine comes to me in a different light.

CHAPTER 33

Isaac leaned with his elbows on the desk of the counting house and looked into the sitting room. Outside, men shouted and called to each other. The pump engine whirred, and a cart rumbled past. The bal maidens sang as they tended their work, and before him sat an untouched, lukewarm cup of Eliza's bitter tea.

It had been weeks since Miss Twethewey first visited their counting house and he encountered her in that very sitting room. The teasing memory of her smile, the curve of her full lips, and the warmth in her radiant eyes lingered. Thoughts of her were becoming more and more frequent, although he'd not seen her at all since the dinner at Tregarthan.

She'd told him that night that she would meet him at the wall.

He'd believed her fully, and yet she never came.

He consoled himself with the fact that she had an overbearing, very disapproving aunt. Normally that would not bother him in the least. But Matthew's constant comments about his visits to Lanwyn Manor and the progress he was making with the family did.

What a fool he'd been in that moment.

He'd misread the expression on Julia's face and the meaning in her words.

Perhaps he should have heeded Beatrice Lambourne's haughty declarations and taken them for what they were—a warning.

He returned his attention to the letter before him, but even as he wrote the words he could not pin down his thoughts. His normally focused mind seemed thwarted, and he knew why.

He missed her.

He'd grown used to seeing Julia there in the morning light, offering a bright smile, a cheery word. The anticipation of it made him eager to leave the house and eager for the next day to arrive. What was more, he enjoyed her company, and he respected how she worked with the children and helped with the Ladies League.

He wouldn't have to wait long to see her again, despite her absence at the drystone wall. The country dance at Lanwyn Manor would commence in a few hours. As a leader in the community, he had to set an example of acceptance and tolerance. The invitation confused the miners, and Isaac knew full well that if he did not attend, many would follow his lead.

After completing his letter and sealing it with wax, he reached for a stack of missives that still needed his attention. He flipped through them, and one in particular caught his eye.

He separated it from the stack, slid his finger beneath the wax, and popped it open. Elwin Richards, the investor from Falmouth, had originally declined Isaac and Charlie's invitation to be a silent investor for Wheal Gwenna.

Isaac read the letter. And then he read it again, focusing on a section in the middle.

After considerable thought, I've reconsidered your suggestion of investing in Wheal Gwenna. I am prepared to personally cover the cost of the pump and remain silent on matters related to the running of the operation. In return, I expect all supply purchases to be made through me.

Isaac drew a deep breath and dragged his hand over his face as the meaning of Richard's terms sank in.

The tributers and tutworkers required certain objects to do their work: Rope. Candles. Shovels. Gunpowder. Coal. All these items could be difficult to come by in a remote village, so the mine would buy them and turn around and sell them to the workers. Wheal Tamsen did not make a profit off of these sales, but it happened quite often—an investor or adventurer would supply all the needed materials at an outrageously inflated price. With such an arrangement Richards could demand any cost he wanted for the merchandise and still be paid, regardless of how much that cut into the profits of the miners. And with most mines not seeing profits for months or even years, it could be disastrous.

The pump was key to reviving Wheal Gwenna. Isaac wanted nothing more than to accept this offer, but the price was far too high.

"You look glum."

Isaac was wrenched from his thoughts. Matthew entered the counting house, whistling, and tossed his hat on the table.

"I do?" Isaac folded the letter and tucked it in his coat. "Well, you seem quite happy."

"I am." Matthew shed his caped greatcoat and pulled an apple from his satchel, tossed it in the air, caught it, then turned to Isaac. "You've not asked me why."

"I assumed you would tell me."

"I've just come from Lanwyn Manor. As you know, the dance is tonight, but I managed to talk with Lambourne for a few minutes. We had a very interesting conversation."

Isaac's already frustrated mood soured further. "About Bal Tressa?"

"No. About Julia."

The use of her Christian name stabbed like a knife. Isaac held his breath as he waited for an explanation.

"He's given me his blessing with regards to her. It's perfect."

"As in marriage?" Isaac jolted. "Are you serious?"

Matthew whistled, tossed the apple again, and then took a bite.

Isaac tensed, preparing himself for the answer to his next question. "Do you love her?"

"Bah, love." Matthew waved a dismissive hand. "Love's nothing to do with it."

A thread of anger tightened in Isaac's chest, and he stood from behind the desk. "I have to wonder if Miss Twethewey feels the same way."

"This isn't about her, as you well know. 'Tis all about Bal Tressa. Our plans."

"*Your* plans. And I thought mining didn't suit you."

"It doesn't. But the only way to get out of it is to work through it—make enough money so I never have to set foot in the counting house again. There are a couple of ways to do that. Marrying his niece, for a start."

Matthew threw his head back in hearty laughter. "Oh, don't look so disapproving. You look just like Father with your brows scrunched like that. Besides, you know me. I've no intention of actually marrying anyone. It won't come to that, you can be sure. As long as I can get into Bal Tressa, I can find a way to break things off after that. Lambourne just needs to *think* I've got marriage on my mind."

Needing to redirect his frustration, Isaac snatched the stack of letters and flipped through them. The next letter was addressed to Matthew. Isaac extended the missive to his brother. "Here."

Commencing his whistling again, Matthew leaned over the desk, lifted the letter, and then popped the seal and walked to stand next to the sitting room fireplace while he read it. His smile faded. The whistling stopped.

Intrigued by the sudden change in demeanor, Isaac glanced up.

Matthew stared at the page for several moments, flexed his jaw, then crumpled the letter and threw it in the fire.

"What was that?"

"That? Nothing." Matthew wiped his hands together and turned back to Isaac. "I'm going to Tregarthan to prepare for tonight. Do you still want to attend together?"

Isaac nodded, eyeing his brother warily.

"It could be a late night. Best to take the carriage. I'll be by the cottage for you."

Isaac nodded again and watched as his brother exited. He was about to turn back to his letter when something caught his eye.

The letter Matthew had thrown into the fire had not reached the flames. It rolled out and now sat crumpled and charred on the hearth.

Curious, Isaac retrieved the missive. He held it up. The edge had been singed, but the letter was still readable.

Study

12 tonight

HP

He flipped it over, but there was no other sign. Matthew was always up to something strange, but this was odd, even for him.

Isaac tucked it away in his pocket, determined to find out what it meant.

CHAPTER 34

Trepidation hovered over Lanwyn Manor the day of the country dance.

For the past few weeks, everyone's attentions—from the master to the servants—had been focused on this night, but no one quite knew what to expect.

Even so, Julia knew what was expected of *her*. To be a charming hostess and to encourage the attention of Matthew Blake. Her aunt had been abundantly clear.

The thought tore at her.

She'd only seen Isaac from a distance in the weeks since the Tregarthan dinner. What he must think of her. With any luck, to-night she'd finally be able to speak with him.

Julia pinched her cheeks for added color and paused to assess her reflection in her looking glass. She smoothed her gown of ivory silk and ran her fingertips over the shimmery, finely netted overlay. The seamstress had spent hours embroidering tiny violet flowers on the high, corseted bodice and hem. At the bustline the bodice gave way to a gauzy skirt of sheer ivory silk, embroidered with the same violet flowers over a silk underskirt. She ran her finger along the gold necklace about her neck and adjusted the golden ribbon woven into her upswept hair.

Caroline entered Julia's chamber, running a long pink ribbon through her fingers. "You're not hiding up here, are you?" she teased. "Don't you dare. If the rest of us must endure this night, then you must too. And isn't this what the Penwythe Twetheweys are all about? Community and such?"

Julia could not help but smile. Yes, this would be a common occurrence in her home. But then she sobered as she remembered whom she would likely encounter. "I'm ready, I suppose."

"Well, you look lovely, even if you don't sound very enthusiastic." Caroline stepped forward to adjust the sash at Julia's empire waist. As if reading her mind Caroline said, "I saw Matthew Blake down in the great hall. He looks as handsome as ever."

Julia stepped away from her cousin and leaned down to put on her slippers, then moved closer to her looking glass. Caroline had adopted her mother's sentiments on Matthew Blake, and the constant reminder of him was wearing.

Caroline stepped behind Julia and looked over her shoulder, patting her own golden hair into place. "Are you not eager to see him?"

Not knowing how to respond, Julia pressed her lips together.

When Julia remained silent, Caroline clasped her hands before her. "Ah, I see. I should not tell you this, but I will."

Finding the lilt in her cousin's tone alarming, Julia whirled around. "Tell me what?"

Caroline fixed her gaze on Julia. "Mr. Blake has asked for Father's permission to properly court you. Officially."

Julia stiffened. "What?"

"Yes. All of his flirting seems to be leading to something more meaningful. He said he hoped one day to unite the families. Is that not exciting?"

Julia groaned and sat on the bed.

"I must say." Caroline's hand flew to her chest, as if she were shocked, and then she pivoted to assess her reflection in the looking glass. "I thought your response would be happier."

"Oh, Caroline, Matthew Blake is not the man for me. Surely you see it. I *hope* you see it. I wish Uncle would have at least discussed it with me."

Caroline leaned her shoulder against the bedpost. "If you don't want that to happen, you should probably make it quite clear, and the sooner the better." She tilted her head to the side, her tone softening. "If I'm not mistaken, I believe there is a certain reason why you are not interested in a union with Matthew Blake. Or perhaps I should say a certain *person*."

Julia huffed, shook her head, and busied herself fussing with the ribbon on her bodice.

"Oh, come now." Caroline straightened. "You've been moping about, staring out the window every morning since Mother forbade you to go on your morning rides, and I don't believe for a single moment that the reason for that is because you really enjoy riding all that much."

Heat crept up Julia's neck. Her cheeks. But she could not deny it.

Caroline's eyebrow rose. "He's downstairs too."

Julia snapped her eyes upward toward her cousin.

"He is, and he looks handsome. Well, they both do since they look exactly alike, but you understand my meaning." Caroline stood and shook the folds out of her gown. "I'm going back down, but only because I'm worried that Mother is going to faint with the thought of the miners in her drawing room. Don't be too long. It might take both of us to keep her calm."

Caroline withdrew, leaving Julia alone with her thoughts.

Perhaps she had not done as good a job as she'd thought masking her feelings about the younger Blake brother.

But that did not matter now.

What mattered was that he was here, and now she could finally explain what had happened.

She lifted her candle and began to descend the stairs. Music and laughter could be heard even at this distance from the great hall. She took the back stairs. It was quicker, and if her aunt really was hysterical in the drawing room, she would arrive there faster.

But as she reached the ground floor and traversed the corridor, she slowed her steps.

No one was supposed to be in this part of the house, and yet light glimmered from the study.

Curious, she stepped into the room.

Miss Prynne stood in the middle of the room, her thin back to the door and a delicate lace shawl draped over her shoulders. She held a candle and stared at the portrait above the fireplace.

"Why, Miss Prynne." Julia stepped in farther. "Whatever are you doing in here?"

Miss Prynne did not move. She didn't even flinch when Julia said her name.

Concerned, Julia stepped closer and placed her hand on her friend's shoulder. "Miss Prynne?"

As she turned to her, candlelight glimmered off the tear tracks on the older woman's cheeks.

"What's the matter?"

Miss Prynne still did not respond. Instead, she turned her gaze back to the painting and held a shaky, thin hand over her mouth.

Julia beheld the portrait of a woman in old-fashioned dress. Auburn tresses flowed over her shoulder, and her bright-green eyes were vibrant. The woman did not smile, but her eyes sparkled, as if she held a great secret.

"This house holds a great deal of memories for me," Miss Prynne whispered at last, her gaze unwavering. "I've spent a great deal of time here over my life. Sometimes happy, sometimes sad."

Julia had heard that Miss Prynne had been close to the previous residents, especially Mr. Rowe, but not much had ever been said about it. She struggled to make sense of it. "But surely that is not something that should upset you?"

"No, it doesn't upset me." She forced a smile and reached for Julia's hand. "Don't mind me. I'm an old, foolish spinster, merely reliving a memory, for you see, I am that lady in the painting."

CHAPTER 35

Julia did not feel right about leaving Miss Prynne alone in the study, but it was what the older woman had wanted.

A dozen questions swirled in Julia's mind after the odd interaction.

What was a portrait of Miss Prynne doing in Lanwyn Manor's study? Furthermore, were her aunt and uncle aware that she was the subject? And what of the painting of Mrs. Rowe? Why would that not have been in Mr. Rowe's study?

Julia thought of all the times Miss Prynne had been within Lanwyn Manor's walls and never said a thing about it. None of it made sense. Rumored treasure. A painting of a village spinster. Stolen items. Curses and secrets. Noises and shadows in the night.

It all had to be connected.

Didn't it?

Trying to put the interaction behind her, she followed the music and the chatter to the great hall. When she arrived, her breath caught at the sight and she stopped midstep. She'd seen the hall decorated before everyone arrived, of course, but with dancers swirling and musicians playing and dozens of candles lighting the space, it really was a sight to behold. Garlands hung from the rafters. A jaunty, lively tune echoed from the walls. Candles hung from the ceiling in round, iron chandeliers and were positioned around the room in freestanding candelabras.

But as she adjusted to the magic of seeing the space alive with dancers, she wrung her hands before her. She needed to find Miss Trebell. The women were the best of friends, and perhaps she would know how best to comfort Miss Prynne.

Then a voice sounded very close to her ear. "You look distressed."

She turned around.

There he was. Isaac Blake.

She'd not expected to see him so suddenly. Perhaps after a few minutes of mingling. But it was more as if he had been waiting for her.

Her heart thudded within her chest.

He looked so much like Matthew, but instead of the ominous feelings of dread that often curled through her when she saw the older brother, her heart soared.

He appeared as if nothing odd had transpired between them at all—as if no time had passed.

Nay, he did not seem annoyed in the least.

His clean-shaven cheeks dimpled ever so slightly with his easy smile. His fair hair curled over the high wool collar of his frock coat, and the lighting made his hazel eyes appear even brighter. There was so much she wanted to explain to him—starting with why she had not met him at the wall—but in that moment, with him staring at her so intensely, words would not form. She'd anticipated seeing him for days, and now that she was standing so near to him, she felt almost stunned.

"Distressed?" She gave a nervous little laugh. "No, not distressed. It-it's just that I saw the oddest thing."

"Here?" His eyes twinkled, and he scanned the rough crowd. "I find that hard to believe."

She smiled in spite of herself, relaxing in his presence. "No, not the miners. I passed my uncle's study and saw light inside. Miss Prynne was in there. She was crying."

"What?" His brows drew together in concern.

"I asked if she was all right, but she said she was merely reliving a long-forgotten memory and that she was the woman in the portrait hanging above the mantel."

"Ah." His shoulders relaxed.

"You're not surprised by that?"

He leaned his head closer. "Do you remember at Tregarthan when I told you she had strong ties to Lanwyn Manor?"

She nodded, unblinking.

"It's not my place to share her stories, but you should know. Miss Prynne and Mr. Rowe had a very interesting relationship—a relationship beyond the bounds of mere friendship."

"I-I thought Mr. Rowe had a wife."

"He did. She died in childbirth many, many years ago."

Julia widened her eyes. "I wonder if my uncle is aware that Miss Prynne's portrait is hanging in his office."

"I doubt it. I suppose it isn't something that comes up in everyday conversation. Everyone who has lived in Goldweth for any length of time knows of it and it is just accepted."

"How odd that she should be crying."

"That is the greatest question, is it not? They'd been friends since they were children and were always together. But they never married. It's quite sad, really."

She let out a little laugh, thinking of all the uncomfortable conversations she'd had with the older woman about marrying young. "No wonder she is always speaking of marriage and so forth."

"She speaks to you of marriage?"

When she realized what she had said, warmth flushed her cheeks. "She has strong opinions on it, 'tis all."

"He married his first cousin at his family's urging. It really is no secret that theirs was not a match of love, and when she died, it was always assumed that he and Miss Prynne might marry, but they never did. It was said that on his deathbed he called for her, but by the time she arrived, it was too late. By all accounts it was a devastating scene. She wept over the body as if she were his widow.

"I never understood it. I would think that when a man finds a woman he loves, he would do whatever necessary to keep her by his side, regardless of circumstances and obstacles. Rowe had money and power. But on his deathbed, nothing could be done to change the past, and none of that money or power meant a thing."

"So that's why she never married." Julia breathed deeply, almost in relief, as one who'd finally unscrambled a riddle.

"Yes."

She forced a smile, attempting to keep the conversation light. "Perhaps your brother was right. Perhaps whoever lives in this house is cursed."

At the reference to his brother, his smile faded and his countenance darkened. "Oh, I don't know."

"Don't you believe in curses?" She tilted her head to the side.

He drew a deep breath, looking around the hall. "Curses are only true if you believe in them. I much prefer to think a man has more control over his outcome than to let it be affected by a ridiculous curse."

She liked his answer. He was ruled by common sense. "You and your brother are very different men, aren't you?"

"Matthew is drawn to the dramatic."

"And you?"

"The practical, I suppose. Not very exciting, I fear."

She looked back toward the entrance to the hall, to the corridor that led to the study. Miss Prynne finally appeared, but she seemed more like a lost child than a woman who had been at the heart of the community for so long. "My heart aches for her now. I wonder if she misunderstood his intentions, or if she was content to have things the way they were."

"A misunderstanding?" he repeated. "I wonder, Miss Twethewey, if there has been a misunderstanding between us."

She trembled under the weight of his gaze. "Us?"

"Yes." He took a small step toward her. "I did wait for you at the wall the morning after the dinner at Tregarthan Hall. I'd hoped to see you there."

"I know. I saw you. And I did not come. I'm so sorry." She bit her lip, searching for words. For how could she explain it? "I would have come, but my aunt, you see, she . . ."

"I can finish that for you, I think." He gave a slight chuckle. "She would prefer you not spend your time with the younger brother of a man who would be such an advantageous match."

She almost laughed at his tone. But then she sobered. "There is really nothing to laugh at in that, is there? You must know, surely you know, that I do not agree with my aunt on such matters. There are more important things that come into the factor."

He stepped closer to her, so close she could feel the heat from him. "I would like it very much if we could prevent any future misunderstandings."

She looked up to him. At his nearness she felt weak and could barely speak above a whisper. "Well then, so we are clear and there are no misunderstandings, it was my intention to meet you that morning, and I'm very sorry to have spoiled our plans."

CHAPTER 36

She was so close to him that he could have reached out and touched the glossy tendrils that framed her face so perfectly. It was as if they were the only two people in the great hall. Everything else faded into the background. The effect was intoxicating.

She *had* intended to meet him the morning after the dinner at Tregarthan Hall. The simple realization both erased the weeks of wondering and frustration and intensified his desire.

They were no longer strangers.

Nay, not anymore.

So many things could be said in such a moment, and the ensuing conversation had the potential to change both their lives. This was not how he intended to speak of such things, in the middle of a noisy, crowded hall, in plain sight of everyone.

But then again, maybe it was perfect.

Something happened in that flash of a second—in that singular breath. A million words were communicated without a single one having been spoken.

He'd always wondered if he would realize when he'd met the woman who captured his mind. His heart. He'd always thought himself immune to it. But now, as he watched her tuck a wayward curl behind her ear, he knew she was that lady.

Rowe had let many things stand in the way of his romantic happiness.

Isaac refused to follow in the man's footsteps and wait too long to act.

But there was another situation that needed to be dealt with—Matthew and his intentions toward her. His brother's callous words about wooing her without intending to marry her bordered on vulgar. If he read Miss Twethewey properly, there would not be much damage to her heart, but her reputation could be tarnished, and that he could not allow.

The sudden urge to speak compelled him, and he further closed the space between them. "Miss Twethewey."

She focused expectant eyes on him.

Oh, how those eyes had the power to stop him in his tracks, to clear his thoughts and make him forget what he was going to say.

"Julia."

At the sound of her Christian name, a pretty flush colored her cheeks. But then her gaze shifted slightly over his shoulder. Her smile faded and she stepped back. He turned to identify the source of her discomfort.

There, behind him, stood Matthew, eyes wide, smile broad.

"Ah, there you both are!" Matthew slapped a heavy hand on Isaac's shoulder. "Look at the two of you huddled over here. Isaac, it isn't fair of you to keep Miss Twethewey to yourself like this. She might misinterpret your attentions."

Isaac expelled his breath in a swoosh and ran his fingers through his hair.

"Miss Twethewey, have you forgotten?" Matthew extended his hand toward her. "You promised me this dance."

"I did?"

"Yes. Oh, don't tell me you've forgotten! Before I left for the coast.

When we were speaking with your aunt in the drawing room, you said I could have the first dance, and I've not forgotten, you see."

She gave a weak smile. She avoided making eye contact with Isaac. "And so I did."

———•———

Julia could not look back at Isaac. How could she? Every thought was surely written on her face. Her heart was so full, she feared that if he were in her line of vision, she'd not be able to bear dancing a single step with Matthew. Yet she could not refuse him. Not and expose every emotion in her heart.

Isaac had called her by her Christian name. How sweet it sounded coming from him.

It was a word she heard daily, and yet the tenderness in his voice when he half whispered it had stolen her very breath.

Furthermore, he'd been so close to saying something momentous. She sensed it, as surely as one could sense the rain coming on the cusp of a summer storm. Nearly floating through the motions, she lined up with the dancers. There was no need to force a smile, for she felt almost giddy.

Isaac Blake cared for her.

For her!

The dance, at least, was a lively one. She turned and twirled when required, clapped and hopped. Music mingled with laughter and voices, and she wove in and out of the other dancers, feeling light for the first time in weeks, and it had nothing to do with her partner.

At the dance's conclusion she allowed Matthew to lead her from the dance floor. She expected to be free, but he tucked her hand in the crook of his arm and slowed the pace of his steps.

She tried to pull away, but he held her hand firm. "I was just in proximity to your home, Miss Twethewey."

"My home?" She drew her brows together at the odd statement.

"Only yesterday I was at Wheal Tilly, very near to Braewyn, I believe."

"Is it?" Her stomach tightened. She did not like the direction the conversation was taking.

He shifted and positioned himself between her and the gathering, blocking her against the wall. "On my return journey I had half a notion to visit Penwythe Hall, for I understand I was only a few miles from it. But I thought better of it. I'm a stranger to them, after all."

She glanced around for a familiar face, hoping to find someone to add to their conversation to prevent them from speaking alone. She ignored the alarm tremoring through her and forced her voice to remain steady. "I'm sure they would have welcomed you with open arms."

"I like the thought of that . . . of your family welcoming me. What are their names? Uncle Jac? Aunt Delia?"

She winced at the boldness of his statement and snapped her gaze upward.

"You can hardly doubt, Miss Twethewey, that I've developed strong feelings for you. But I have to say the news I received from my colleague at Wheal Tilly was not pleasant. News I wished I had not heard."

The rumors that had been swirling about prior to her departure clanged loudly in her head. "Oh?"

"Yes, for I was informed that you came to Lanwyn Manor to recover from a broken heart."

Anger blazed in, scorching any awkwardness or bashfulness. "What did you say?"

"A broken heart." His smug expression appeared almost proud to know such an intimate detail about her life. "Oh, don't look shocked. Of course it pains me that you had feelings for another, but I hope those feelings are changing, as mine are. Please, don't be embarrassed."

She pulled her hand free and could not keep the curt tone from her voice. "I'm not embarrassed. At the moment I am too exasperated to be embarrassed. And I'm not sure where you heard that from, but my personal life is nothing that need concern you."

He smirked. "Percy Broaden is a fool."

She clenched her fist.

The insolence.

His smile was annoyingly calm. "Don't be exasperated. I only was interested to learn more about you."

"If there is anything you want to know about me, sir, you need only ask me, not ask questions of people from my home."

But his eyes had traveled upward to her hair, examining it. He reached up and touched one loose curl. "I thought you'd be flattered that I'd want to know more of you."

She smacked his hand away. "Flattered?"

He looked injured. "Why are you so angry?"

She narrowed her gaze and lowered her voice. "Let me be clear, Mr. Blake. No aspect of my life is of your concern. Not now, not ever."

Julia pushed her way through the crowd, cheeks flaming, muttering invectives under her breath. With a glance over her shoulder to make sure Matthew was not following her, she stepped from the great hall to the corridor that led to the drawing room and the study. Once she was away from the crowd, she stopped, and only then did she realize tears were burning her eyes.

Percy.

What a fool she had been with him. She saw it so clearly now.

And so many people knew. The thought of it getting out amongst her new friends sickened her.

Most of all, she did not want Isaac to know.

A small group of women walked past her, and she wiped her eyes with the back of her hand. It would not do to stand here crying in the corridor. She sniffed, pressed her hand to her stomach, and calmed her breathing, then stepped back out into the party.

Almost as soon as her foot fell on the stone floor, a servant was at her side. "For you, miss."

With a frown she took the letter from the tray and held it up in her gloved hand. Her name was written on the outside. "Who asked you to bring this to me?"

"'Twas a boy. I didn't recognize him. He said it was urgent."

"Thank you."

Curious, she popped the wax seal and unfolded it.

> You are not welcome in Goldweth.
> Leave, or you will wish you had.

CHAPTER 37

Panicked, Julia gaped around the room. Who would send this to her? She stood there dumbstruck, alone, in a room brimming with laughing, dancing strangers.

She had no enemies.

Did she?

Uncle William had enemies. Plenty of them.

"There you are." Isaac approached. As he drew near, his smile faded. "What's the matter?"

She shook her head in contemplation as she stared at the note. She could read the words quite plainly but could not make sense of them. They seemed foreign and cold, as if they were not intended for her at all. And yet they'd been handed directly to her. "I-I—"

"Julia, you're pale." He stepped closer. "Maybe you should be seated."

He was speaking, she knew, but she could hardly hear. For her eyes were focused on the words.

A warning. A threat.

Never had anyone addressed her with such animosity. Not since the night at the inn. Was it that person? Could it be?

Mr. Blake touched her arm, and the warmth of it drew her attention. "What has happened?" Urgency now tinged his voice.

This time, she handed the letter to him.

As he read it his face reddened, then he nodded over his shoulder. "I'll fetch your uncle. He will want to know of this."

"No." She clutched his arm. "No. Please."

"No? Julia, in addition to what happened to you on your arrival, this is not to be borne."

"But it's my decision whether or not to tell him, Isaac." His Christian name slipped from her lips easily and without thought. "Please. Not now. Not here."

He lowered his head near hers. "You must know I can't—I won't—stand by and do nothing. You're being threatened. Come with me. Let's talk over there." He guided her from the crowded space to the privacy of a corridor just beyond the foyer.

They were alone now, as alone as they could be in a home full of dancing and laughing guests. Even though they stood in silence, she drew strength from the man who was standing so near.

How could this be happening when she was finally finding her place here? "I just don't understand why someone would send this to me."

He placed his hands on her shoulders and ducked his head to look at her at eye level. "I'm convinced this has nothing to do with you. Someone's toying with your uncle, and you're caught as a pawn. He needs to know."

———◆———

What could this woman possibly have done to provoke anyone to write such words? Furthermore, what benefit could come to anyone if she left?

As they stood in the corridor's privacy, Isaac rubbed his thumb against her arm. She did not pull away. In his other hand he lifted the note, assessing the unfamiliar handwriting and sinister message more closely. "You must know that I don't feel this way."

She sniffed. "Quite possibly you're alone in that sentiment."

"I doubt that. The children. Miss Prynne and Miss Trebell. Your cousin. Your family."

"Anyone could have sent that note." She folded her arms over her midsection.

He softened his voice. "I wish you'd tell your uncle."

She shook her head intently and took the note back from him.

"I meant what I said, Julia." He looked at her more closely. "Are you crying?"

"No, of course not." Even as she spoke, moisture glittered in her eyes.

"You belong here."

"It's just that—I don't know where I belong." She stepped back, widening the space between them. "After what happened at Penwythe Hall, I'm not certain I belong there. Despite what you say, I clearly do not belong here. It's as if I am waiting for something to happen, and I don't know how to proceed."

"What happened at Penwythe?" He could see the battle warring within her—her reluctance to tell him something. His imagination rapidly fired dozens of possible scenarios. "Why don't you belong there?"

She drew a steadying breath. "If you'd have asked me a year ago what I would be doing this very day, I thought I'd be engaged to a certain gentleman, but it turns out I was quite mistaken, and quite taken for a fool. Not only that, but everyone knew it. I claim to have come here for Jane, but I suppose by coming here I was running away from the stares and comments, looks of pity or satisfaction. It's a shortcoming of mine—I detest being seen as weak. So I left, as if by putting the entire ordeal out of sight, it would flee my mind as well."

He could not deny a stab of jealousy over her affection for another man. He pushed it aside, trying to focus on the conversation at hand. "And has it?"

She nodded. "I see a different future for myself now, even though I am not entirely confident what it encompasses. But now, my presence here is upsetting someone to such an extent that they would send me a note like this. Oh, is there a place to settle and feel at ease, free in one's own self?"

He stepped closer—so close that the hem of her gown swept against him. He opened his mouth to speak when footsteps approached from the servants' entrance.

Frustrated, confused, and suddenly desiring solitude, she whirled to leave and he caught her arm. "When will I see you next?"

She did not answer his question. Eyes wide, she stepped back and put her forefinger to her lips. "Remember, not a word."

CHAPTER 38

The night of the country dance seemed endless. The miners made merry, the cider flowed freely, and candlelight glimmered on the faces of the people Isaac had known his entire life. Such an event should have been comforting and optimistic—an opportunity for the miners and the wealthy to align.

And yet, it was not right. None of this was right.

Anger simmered in his chest. He was ready to act. To intervene. But she'd asked him not to.

Someone was taunting the Lambournes. In all likelihood it was a subgroup of the miners, perhaps even some in this very chamber. For now it was a faceless foe, and that made it all the more unnerving.

Despite his best efforts to seek her out, Isaac did not see Julia again after their moment in the corridor. She'd all but disappeared. He could hardly blame her. He'd seen the fright in her eyes. But he also worried for her.

Yes, their bond was deepening, but he didn't want to overstep his bounds. He respected her and her space, yet he also felt compelled to act.

At the moment Isaac stood in Lanwyn Manor's billiards room with Matthew. The gentlemen who generally considered themselves above the miners had gathered in this room, and card tables had been set up. He stood next to the table where Lambourne and Dunstan played a hand, not really watching.

Matthew nudged Isaac with his arm. "You look bored to tears."

"Do I?" Isaac leaned his shoulder against the dark-green wall.

"Yes, and I wish you'd stop, because I need diversion." Matthew reached for his glass on the side table and took a drink.

Isaac bit on the leading statement. "Why?"

"Oh, I've vexed Miss Twethewey. Now she's nowhere to be found." Matthew huffed and tugged at his cravat. "She's all but accused me of meddling."

Isaac folded his arms over his chest. "And were you?"

"No. Maybe. I don't know."

"I thought you didn't care about Miss Twethewey. I believed you referred to her as the means to an end."

Matthew snorted and took a swig of his beverage. "Well, at any rate, it's certainly not the worst thing I've been accused of. She'll get over it."

"How can you be so sure?" Isaac scoffed. "Miss Twethewey seems the sort of woman who knows her mind."

"Miss Twethewey is like any other woman, especially one with little dowry who is looking to capture a good match. She'll do as she's told. Of course, 'twould be helpful if she'd just fall for my charms, but sometimes women like her need a bit of persuading."

Isaac clamped his jaw shut—tightly—to prevent criticism from spilling out.

He wasn't sure what to make of this sensation—of seeing her in a new light. And seeing a different side—a cold, calculating side—of his brother.

Isaac folded his arms over his chest and didn't take his eyes from the card table. "I hate to be the one to tell you, but perhaps you ought to prepare yourself for the possibility that she might not return your affection."

"Not possible."

The game of cards ended in a loss for Lambourne, and Isaac made his way out to the great hall, where the mining men mingled and the bal maidens danced. A layer of smoke from the fireplace and candles hovered over the guests, thin as gossamer, and warmth thickened the air. Despite the smokiness, he could breathe more freely here. There was no need for pretense here—no need to watch what he said or how he said it.

Daniel Lobby, one of Wheal Tressa's underground captains, stood to his left. He'd not had the chance to talk to him privately since Matthew returned the watch to him. Now was as good a time as any.

"I've been meaning to thank you," Isaac said as he approached the tall, wiry man.

"Me?" Lobby jerked his head around. "Why?"

"For telling Matthew about my pocket watch." Isaac retrieved the shiny watch from his waistcoat pocket and cupped it in his palm. "I'm glad to have it back."

Confusion darkened Lobby's brow. "What are you talking about?"

Isaac extended his open palm before him. "Matthew said you told him you saw my watch at a peddler's in Wheyton."

"What, me?" Lobby burst out a laugh. "What would I be doing in Wheyton?"

Isaac frowned. "So you did not tell my brother about it?"

"Not me, friend. Wish it were. But what a stroke of luck that was, finding that with a peddler, eh? Like a needle in a haystack, if you ask me. Bless me, everyone knows someone stole that from you. What fool would try to sell something like that so close from where it was taken?"

Isaac gritted his teeth and stared down at the watch shining in the candlelight.

Matthew had lied to him.

What else was Matthew lying about?

As he stared at it, Isaac noted the time. It was a few minutes past twelve. It was the time mentioned in the odd little crumpled note Matthew had tried to burn.

Isaac glanced up and looked around.

Matthew was nowhere to be found.

CHAPTER 39

Still clad in her gown of ivory silk, Julia locked her bedchamber door, removed her slippers, yanked a coverlet from her bed, and sat in a heap on the floor next to the fire.

After receiving the threatening note, she'd managed to convince her aunt that she'd developed a dreadful headache and really was quite ill. It was a lie, of course, but what other choice did she have?

Fear—and frustration—held her captive. No one but Isaac knew of the note, and she wanted to keep it that way—at least until she sorted out her thoughts.

Ghosts and gossips, secret letters and hidden motives—all seemed to be as much a part of Lanwyn Manor as the tapestries hanging on the paneled walls. She'd not believed in the notion of curses, but it was becoming harder to convince herself of its folly.

A bitter, driving winter rain pelted the earth, and the wind whistled in the cracks of the window. It would be a frigid ride home for the guests as they departed, but judging by the music and loud voices echoing from the lower levels, she expected the revelry would continue for quite some time.

She settled back farther into the blankets, trying to fix her mind on the pleasant part of the evening—Isaac Blake and his gentle smile.

His soft touch. Time slipped past and her breathing slowed. All of the anxiety had exhausted her. Her eyelids grew heavy. Perhaps she'd be able to escape into slumber after all.

Then footsteps—heavy, like a man's—plodded along the wooden floor. Whoever it was, was coming from the south and getting closer.

She stumbled to her feet, pushed the blanket away, and snatched the candlestick on the desk, ready as a weapon if needed. No men should be in this part of the house, especially at this hour. Her heart pounded as the footsteps drew closer.

Then they slowed.

She thought of the rumored hidden treasure, and how the guests might go wandering in search of it.

Flickering light inched along the narrow crack beneath the door. The sound of paper scratching against wood pricked the silence, and something white and square slid beneath her door. Then the walking resumed in the same direction.

Pulse hammering, she froze as she waited for the night to fully absorb the footsteps' echo.

With stockinged feet she tiptoed over to the door and lifted the paper, hesitantly, as if at any moment it might burst into flames. She turned it over. It had been carefully folded but was not sealed. Biting her lip, she hurried over to the fire to glean whatever light she could and unfolded the paper.

Her hand shook, causing the paper to tremble as she read it.

You've worn out your welcome. Go.

She pulled out the note she'd received earlier and compared them. They were written by the same hand, of that she was certain. Julia pressed her hand to her mouth, as if fearing saying something out loud would make this more real. Tears, hot as fire, blurred her vision, and that combined with the fire's flickering light made the hastily written words seem as if they were leaping from the page.

The first letter was unnerving enough, but this letter—and whoever delivered it—had tracked her to her chamber, where she was alone. Vulnerable. The hiding spaces and empty shadowed rooms she'd seen in the attic chamber above haunted her. She shuddered as her own imagination fanned the flames of her fear.

The sudden onset of tension formed a real headache. She had half a notion to feed the fire with the note, but fear was giving way to anger. How could someone write to her this way? She was a lady and a guest in this house.

No, she'd not throw it in the fire.

She moved to her desk, put the note in the drawer with the first one, and turned the tiny key. Absolutely nothing could resolve this issue tonight. In fact, she wasn't certain anything could be done about it ever.

She could return to Penwythe and leave this place forever.

But Jane was still ill. And Isaac . . .

She moved to the door. After taking several seconds to garner her courage, she opened it and looked into the dark hall. The carpet appeared dark in the dead of night, with naught but a sliver of rain-soaked moonlight peeking through the window at the end of the hall. She closed her door and turned the lock.

Satisfied nothing more could be done, she moved to the bed, placed the key on the table beside her, and slipped beneath the smooth bed-covers. Not even the memory of Isaac's warm smile could put her at ease now.

CHAPTER 40

The afternoon following the Lanwyn Manor ball, Isaac stepped toward Miner's Row, gripping a sack of peppermints. He'd promised Charlie he'd watch out for Margaret and Jory, and he intended to make good on his word. He lowered his hat against the wind, crossed the broad muddy street, and tapped his knuckles on the Bensons' cottage door.

Margaret appeared almost instantly, her wild auburn hair bound at the nape of her neck, a smile on her face. "Isaac. Come in."

He removed his hat as he ducked to fit through the doorframe. During the weeks immediately following Charlie's death, Margaret's eyes would be rimmed in red when she answered the door, but now, every so often, he would catch a glimpse of the Margaret he'd known for so long.

Jory trotted up to meet him. In a single motion Isaac swept him up in his arms. "Aha! There now. What do you suppose I brought with me?"

Giggling, Jory reached for the sack, and after a quick game of holding the treat just out of reach, the boy snatched the sack and threw his dark head back in laughter. Treasure in hand, he wriggled from Isaac's arms to the floor.

Jory skipped toward the warm fire and dropped next to the dog sleeping in front of the hearth, and at Margaret's invitation, Isaac settled in the chair at the table, as he had so many times.

Margaret retrieved two mugs and a jug of cider and joined him.

"You did not come to the dance at Lanwyn last night," he said, watching her pour the liquid.

"Nay. I'd no desire to." She scooted one of the mugs closer to him. "Besides, Charlie's only been dead a month. It would hardly be respectable."

"Well, you were missed." He wrapped his fingers around the mug. "More than one person asked if I'd seen you."

A sigh whispered from her lips. "I was in no mood for such a gatherin'—especially at Lanwyn Manor. It's a farce, if you ask me. It's shockingly obvious what Mr. Lambourne's attemptin' to do. I can only wonder how so many of the miners are buyin' into it. Goodwill, indeed."

He masked a smile. She might be in mourning, but her fight—her sass and vivacity—was returning. However, there was more than one side to the issue. "Maybe they are tired of the way things are and are willing to step out in good faith in an effort to change things."

She did not respond, only sipped the cider and returned the mug to the rough tabletop. She watched Jory for several seconds and then looked back to Isaac. "Or maybe they went to partake in a cheap night of merriment."

"So skeptical. And that's not quite like you."

She huffed. "I'll never be the same as I was. How could I?"

"You've experienced a great loss. We all have, but you and Jory most of all." The fire popped and sizzled in the grate. "I do wish you would have come. I don't think Charlie would like for you to be lonely."

She shook her head and tightened the shawl around her shoulders. "I was alone, but I was not lonely. At least, not lonely for the sort who'd be at Lanwyn Manor. I know you don't believe me, but I was in earnest when I said I'd no desire to attend. I've never been fond of that place. Something is amiss with it. Always has been."

He frowned at the strength of the emotion behind her words. "I guess I wasn't aware you'd ever been on the property."

"Oh, aye." Margaret nodded, pushing her hair from her face. "You know my mother was a midwife. When I was around fourteen, I assisted her with a birth there. A servant girl. A surprise to everyone—I don't think her employer knew she was with child. The baby was stillborn."

Isaac winced. How had he never heard such a tale? "I didn't know."

"I don't think anyone knew. 'Twas Mr. Rowe himself that dismissed her. Horrible, to send a young girl out into the cold world after something like that. I often wonder what happened to her. It's cursed, you know. The house. The land. Too much has happened within those walls for happiness to truly abide there."

"Curses are all folly, Margaret, and you're too practical to believe otherwise."

She tossed her hair and shrugged. "Think what you will."

Isaac stiffened at the mention of a curse. Talk of it seemed to be everywhere. "Come now. You don't really think that—"

"Decades, nay, centuries of bad and evil people have plagued that house, and the current occupants are reapin' the harvests of those who lived there before them."

"Mr. Rowe wasn't evil." Isaac leaned his elbow on the table.

"Are you sure?" she challenged, her green eyes ablaze. "Regardless, I know what I saw, and I'll ne'er step foot again in that house."

They sat in silence for several moments before she tilted her head to the side. "This sudden interest in Lanwyn Manor wouldn't have anythin' to do with a certain guest under its roof?"

He took a drink of his cider. "I assume you're referring to Miss Twethewey."

"Rumors are rampant regardin' both you and Matthew. As one friend to another, I'd caution you against gettin' involved in anythin'—or anyone—pertainin' to the Lambournes. It would be a lapse in judgment."

His spine stiffened at the words. "You judge her harshly."

"She's related to the Lambournes, Isaac. By blood. There's no way to judge her but harshly."

Wishing to change the subject, he retrieved the letter from Edwin Richards and placed it before her. "Let's talk of something else, shall we?"

She lifted the letter. "What's this?"

"From a man interested in investing in Wheal Gwenna."

A glow of anticipation replaced the angry fire brimming in her eyes. "This is wonderful, is it not?"

He shrugged. "I'd temper my excitement if I were you. It's dangerous territory to agree only to buy supplies from one merchant. Something similar is going on at Wheal Tamsen with another merchant. His prices for basic supplies are ridiculous, but he's the third largest shareholder and possesses a great deal of weight. I'm concerned that if we agree to these terms it could be months, perhaps years, before the mine yields a profit—if it ever does. Richards is a smart businessman—this agreement would allow him to eventually recoup his investment by overcharging us for supplies, and you and I might never see a farthing."

Her shoulders slumped, and a slight pout curved her lips. "So you suggest we wait?"

"I'll not negotiate on certain aspects, and we'll only encounter men like Richards, who's intent upon lining his pockets at our expense." Isaac folded his hands before him and fixed his gaze on her directly. "Margaret, you mustn't continue to wait for something that may not come to fruition. You must put this thought from your mind."

"You can't mean not to open the mine." Anger brightened her eyes. "You can't mean that! This is what Charlie wanted. It's what he wanted!"

"But things have changed. Everything's different. You've got Jory to think of, and—"

"But Goldweth needs another mine. Bal Tressa is not going to fix the problems we have. Wheal Tamsen may not be able to sustain itself for much longer either, from what I've heard."

This was the first time he'd heard Wheal Tamsen mentioned in such a light. "What?"

She crossed her slender arms over her chest and lifted her chin. "It's Matthew. People are talking."

"I don't care for gossip."

"This is not just gossip, Isaac."

They stared at each other for several moments. There was no reason to doubt her words. "What are they saying?"

She hesitated, almost as if she regretted addressing the topic. She unfolded her arms. "Word is he's fallen in with some dubious folks in the south. Even worse, he is defaultin' on his loans. There's even talk of him lookin' to sell his shares of Wheal Tamsen."

Isaac stood, dumbstruck. "Who'd you hear this from?"

"Is it true?"

"No, it is *not* true." He squeezed his hand into a fist, then released the pressure.

"Well, you'd better be sure, because if Goldweth loses control of Wheal Tamsen and there are no other operatin' mines to support the folks around here, I fear the worst."

CHAPTER 41

The clock struck a late-afternoon hour, and Julia looked up from her needlework. Next to her, Jane slumbered and a steady rain tapped on the windows.

Two days had passed since the dance at Lanwyn Manor, and Julia still hadn't told anyone about the threatening notes. Both Miss Prynne and Matthew had called to speak with her, and she'd claimed yet another headache and refused to come down to the great hall. Julia had sequestered herself in Jane's room and spent the days doing needlework.

Only when she received a letter from Aunt Delia did Julia's tension ease. The very sight of her aunt's handwriting warmed her. How good it was to feel connected to one she loved so dearly. With a glance at Jane to make sure she was still asleep, Julia returned to the sofa, tucked her legs beneath her, slid her finger under the wax seal, and unfolded the letter.

My Julia,

It is hard for me to know you're so far away and that you are hurting. I wish I could be there by your side and help you face every difficulty. But you are finding your way, my dear one. Oh, the journey can be difficult, but it is one that will shape your future. Furthermore, it is one that only you can navigate.

When I read your letter, I saw fear written in between your words, and I could almost hear it in your voice. But, child, do not let it rule your decisions and guide your tongue. Darling girl, you know this to be true. You had your heart broken, but I promise you, it will mend. Your aunt Beatrice has much to offer you in the way of guidance, but God has given you your own intuition and has already sent tests to strengthen and refine it. Learn from what has happened in the past. Trust the man who will not break it again, and your aunt Beatrice cannot tell you who that man is, no matter how much she may want to. You are the only one who can reason that for yourself.

I am proud of your decision to be by your cousin and not to leave her during her lying-in. She may not be able to verbalize it, or even realize it now, but it is giving her strength. And it is good for you—when one learns that serving another person diminishes one's own pain. In the long run, the giver always becomes the receiver.

How I long to see you again, but how I am eager to see how you will grow. You are giving to another and growing your character. You will never regret such actions.

Tears formed in Julia's eyes, not tears of sadness but of relief—relief that someone desired the best for her. In a world where no one seemed to care about her—the real her—it was a treasure indeed.

As Julia returned to her chamber to prepare for dinner, her steps slowed. The sliver of light coming from the cracked door was not unusual, but the whispered voices emanating from the space gave her reason to pause.

She approached the door with caution. She used her fingertips to nudge it open. Julia stopped short.

Aunt Beatrice, Uncle William, and Mrs. Sedrick all stood within her chamber.

She fought the sense of betrayal that her privacy had been invaded. "What's going on here?"

Uncle William extended his hands. "I'd ask you the same question." In one hand he held a brooch. In the other the corner of a tapestry. Just beyond him, where the tapestry had hung, was a small open door.

Immediately panic battled confusion. She moved past him to get a closer look. Sure enough, a small door built into the paneling opened to a large closet of sorts. Inside lay several treasures. A silver candlestick. A piece of jewelry.

"Why are those there?" she blurted.

Her aunt's watery stare pinned her. "Perhaps there's something you would like to tell us."

Breathless from shock, Julia shook her head emphatically. "I don't know what you are talking about."

"We thought all of these had gone missing." Aunt Beatrice stepped forward, a silver bowl in her hand. "Did you take these things? And hide them?"

"*What?*" Julia hurled back, hurt exploding into anger. "Of course I didn't take these things! What on earth would I do with your brooch and candlesticks? Surely you do not think me capable of stealing!"

"I don't know what you're capable of." Her aunt sniffed. "I confess that after your recent behavior, I am not sure I know you at all."

"My recent behavior? And to steal? Honestly. I had nothing to do with this. I didn't even know a door was here!"

"Then how did these items get here?"

"I haven't the slightest idea." Suddenly she recalled the note. Perhaps if they read it, they would realize someone was out to harm her—that she was a victim in this, not the culprit.

"I've something to show you." She reached for the key on her dressing table and opened the desk. Her hands trembled as she fumbled through her papers. Nausea swirled, and perspiration dotted her brow. "It cannot be. They're gone!"

Aunt Beatrice's eyes narrowed as she stomped to peer over Julia's shoulder. "What's gone?"

"I received a note—multiple notes, actually—warning me to leave Lanwyn Manor. Can you not see? Someone wants me gone from here."

"What a ridiculous notion." Aunt Beatrice sneered. "Honestly, child, this is most unbecoming and unexpected."

"You must believe me! And the greater concern here is that someone else is stealing these things and sneaking into my chamber. Does that not concern you? Who else knows of these hiding places?"

"How could I possibly know the answer to this question?" Aunt Beatrice snipped.

"Well, someone had to tell you of this. Who was it?" Julia demanded.

At length Aunt drew a sharp breath. "I was alerted by a member of my staff that these were here."

Julia jutted her chin upward and slid her gaze to the housekeeper. Of course. Mrs. Sedrick.

"You are mistaken if you think I had anything to do with this. I'm offended you'd even suggest such a thing," Julia said, with confidence much fiercer than she actually felt.

"Come now," Uncle William soothed. "This is very unusual, and we're all upset."

Aunt Beatrice retrieved her jewelry from the shelf right inside the small door and gathered the pieces to her chest. "So you know nothing of the rest of it? The topaz piece? The emerald?"

"I didn't take them, so I don't know," Julia seethed. "Perhaps Mrs. Sedrick might be able to find those for you as well."

Without another word, Aunt Beatrice sniffed and stomped from the chamber, followed by her husband. As Mrs. Sedrick turned to leave the room, she and Julia locked eyes before the housekeeper finally jerked the door shut behind her.

Julia whirled around, propped her hands on her hips, and huffed in the sudden silence. The nerve!

There could be no doubt now. Someone did not want her here. They hid things in her chamber. Looked through her personal papers and took the incriminating evidence.

So many people had been in the house over the last several days. But who would do this? And why?

She stomped to the desk and checked again. Her notes were gone.

In the time since her arrival, she'd been attacked, made to look like a thief, and robbed of personal documents. Yes, she should be frightened, but it was not in her nature.

Her first thought was to pack her bags and leave in the dark of night. She'd been accused of something quite horrific. She flung her wardrobe open, assessing her belongings, and determined to take only what she needed. She could be home tomorrow if she so desired.

But what Aunt Delia referred to as her stubborn streak challenged the thought. If she left, would it be seen as an admission of guilt? As giving in to fear? Her pride, wounded as it was after the incident with Percy, would not allow it.

And then she thought of Jane, lonely, sad, and broken. The friends she'd made in Goldweth—Miss Prynne and Miss Trebell. The children. The other ladies in the sewing circle.

And, of course, Isaac.

For the most part she'd been happy here. Happier than she thought she would be. And if she returned home—no, she'd not think about it.

Someone was threatening her, and she'd not stand for it.

She stomped over to the secret door, yanked it open, then slammed it shut again. When closed, it disappeared completely into the paneling. Only when she held the candle very close did she notice the tiny slot in which to insert a finger to unlatch the door so it would swing open unhindered.

Curiosity took hold. With candle in hand she stepped into the secret closet and poked and prodded the other panels for some sort of opening. She found none. A few more items were in here—dusty clutter and items from a bygone era. Several pieces of fabric hung from a hook, and determining that they must be dresses, she lifted her hand to look at one, but when she did, a flash of metal caught her eye. She angled her candle higher to illuminate an old-fashioned lever. She pulled it and another door swung open to a narrow passageway.

The slight forgotten, she found her adventurous side dominating. Pushing aside the dusty clothing, Julia followed the tunnel, careful to keep her hair away from the candle's flame. The tunnel led to a steep staircase, which was more like a ladder. She paused, assessing where she must be in relation to her room. She had to be in a narrow space between the exterior wall and the interior chambers.

She descended one step and then another. With each step she grew more nervous. She was not sure how many floors she'd descended, and the stairs had twisted, making her uncertain which direction she faced. Her muscles tensed, and her heart raced as the walls seemed to grow too tight, the ceiling too low. Should her candle go out, she'd not be able to see her hand before her face.

Gripping the railing for orientation, she made her way to the foot of the stairs, where she found a door. She held her candle to it and nudged the handle. Locked. She may not know exactly where the door led to, but now she did know that someone had hidden access to her chamber.

And it unsettled her.

Julia tucked away the knowledge, lifted her candle, and climbed the narrow stairs back to her chamber, but she knew full well that sleep would not come to her that night.

CHAPTER 42

Isaac left Anvon Cottage at dawn, as he did every morning, and guided his horse down the lane. He turned onto the public road and glanced toward Lanwyn Manor, which still slumbered in the morning stillness.

He'd not seen Julia in the few days since the ball, but he'd not expected to. Even if he called on her, he doubted her aunt would grant him admittance into the house, and he fully expected that Julia would not be allowed out without a chaperone. Still, he could not help but scan the lawn for a sign of her, and as he assessed the misty horizon, his breath caught.

A woman's form, clad in a dark hooded cloak, was at the tree line on the far side of the drystone wall.

Julia's report of spotting a mysterious figure along the tree line came to mind. He squinted and slowed his horse.

It *was* Julia, but she was not on horseback.

His senses jumped to life. What was she doing out now, and after what had happened? He didn't stop to consider it. He urged his horse into a canter and hurried down the lane to her.

Even from a distance he could see that her face was pale, her blue eyes red-rimmed and shadowed. She didn't smile as he approached, as per her custom, but she kept her gaze low and met him halfway, casting a glance over her shoulder with every couple of steps.

Once she was within earshot he called, "What is it? Is everything all right?"

Julia did not respond right away. The wind caught her long, loosely bound tendrils and whipped them free from her hood.

He slid from the saddle, gathered his reins in his gloved hand, and walked to the drystone wall. He waited to speak until she was just on the other side of the wall so he could keep his voice low. "Has something happened?"

She bit her lower lip and nodded. She'd been crying.

The urge to protect her, to shield her, flooded through him. "Are you hurt? Did someone—"

"No, no, nothing like that." She swallowed and looked back to the house. She stepped closer. "Do you remember how I told you items were missing? Someone put several of them in my bedchamber. Well, not in my chamber exactly, but behind the hidden door we found a tunnel, and I followed it, and—"

"Slow down." He furrowed his brow, not sure he understood her. "A tunnel? Inside Lanwyn?"

She nodded. "Yes, I had no idea it was there. Apparently neither did Aunt or Uncle."

Isaac sobered. There were always rumors about old passageways in that house, about secret rooms and the sort, but didn't every house have such rumors? "Start again, from the beginning."

She summoned a deep breath. "Items have been missing, like I've told you. Random items. First small ones, like a piece of silver or something along those lines, but recently the items have been increasing in value, and lately my aunt's jewels have been the perpetrator's target. Whoever it was must have wanted to make it look like I was the thief, for someone stashed them in a hidden chamber in my room."

"And you have no idea who the culprit is?"

"No, not exactly. Several of the servants are not fond of me, but I don't think they would stoop to such a thing."

"And they found a hidden chamber off of your room?"

"Yes, a small chamber behind a hidden door. I was investigating it and found a staircase that descended to a locked door."

Isaac frowned. "That's very odd."

"It gets even more unpleasant." She gripped her gloved fingers before her. "Whoever put those things there must be behind the letters."

"Plural, as in more than one?"

She nodded. "I received a second one the night of the ball, a few hours after the first one. Someone slid it under my bedchamber door after I retired. The handwriting appeared to be the same. I'd show it to you, but it's gone. Someone took it out of my writing desk drawer." A sob cracked her voice. "Someone's been in my chamber, and I don't know . . . I-I don't know—"

He had to do something—anything—to erase the fear he saw in her expression.

He released the reins, braced his hand against the top of the drystone wall, and vaulted over it. When he landed on the other side, he was quite close to her.

A tear dropped from her lower lash and trailed down her cheek. He reached out to take her hand in his.

"I'm so sorry." She shook her head, staring at their joined hands. "I don't mean to burden you with this. It's just that I'm not sure where to turn, and Aunt and Uncle think I stole their jewelry, and I—"

He drew her into an embrace. For so long he had wanted to do that—to hold her in his arms, to feel her against him.

But not like this—not when she was frightened and vulnerable.

She leaned against him, her head dropping against his shoulder, warm and intimate, and then she drew a steadying breath and stepped back.

Begrudgingly he let his arms fall to his sides.

She was right to be conservative, of course. They were near a public lane. She was an unmarried woman, and he just a mining captain.

"Come." He wrapped her arm around his and guided her back down the lane, under the cover of the wintering elms. Once they were under the shadows, he turned to face her but did not release her hands. "Tell me."

After another deep breath, she told him of her aunt's anger. About how she forbade Julia to meet him. Of her distrust of Mrs. Sedrick. Of the odd rooms off of her uncle's library. Details tumbled from her, surprising ones and others he could have easily guessed.

Sharing her thoughts seemed to help, for after a while she managed a little smile. "I'm beginning to think your brother was right. Lanwyn Manor is cursed."

"Matthew is all bluster, Julia. Give no credit to his stories. They're tall tales, nothing more. He's eager for reaction."

"But it isn't just his stories, Isaac. It's a collection of things. The attack at the inn. The stolen items. The threatening notes. The strange sounds. I've tried dozens of times to put it together, but I can't. What do you make of it?"

He considered his reply. "I'm sure you're right to think it all connected, but I'm not sure I have the answers."

He reached out his gloved hand and brushed a lock of hair from her face. His finger lingered on her cheek. "What do you want to do?"

"I know I don't want to leave Jane. I promised her I would stay until the baby is born. But after that, I don't know."

"Selfishly I'm quite glad to hear you're going to stay, but I don't want you to be afraid. Do you feel unsafe at Lanwyn?"

"Not unsafe, but I feel as if Aunt and Uncle believe me to be a criminal."

"I will look into things more on my end. Let me make some inquiries. I know a lot of miners. If anyone knows anything, they might talk. But you must make me a promise. If at any moment you feel unsafe or if something further happens, send me word, or even come to my house. It's right through that grove of trees."

She gave a little laugh. "That would really set tongues wagging."

But he did not laugh at her little joke. He let his gaze drift from the small curls at her temples, to her darkly lashed eyes, to her full, parted lips. "I wonder if you know how deeply you've touched me."

She jerked, seemingly surprised at the sudden depth of his words.

Before she could speak, he stepped closer and took her in his arms. He lowered his lips to hers.

She did not pull away. Instead, she melted against him. Her warmth, her scent of lavender, the softness of her lips beneath his.

He moved his lips to her ear. "I promise you, Julia, I will keep you safe."

CHAPTER 43

Isaac tried to concentrate on his work at the mine, but thoughts of Julia—and all the odd occurrences all over Goldweth, including Lanwyn Manor—stole his focus. The beauty of the memory of her lips on his, the sensation of her in his arms, battled with the ugliness of the reality of their situation.

For the first time he could see—and truly believe—that a future with Julia might be possible, but nothing would ever come to be if they didn't settle the unrest. For the Lambournes would always be her family. And he would always be a Blake—a miner and a part of the Goldweth community.

The difficult situations were piling up. Not only were the villagers facing hunger and cold as winter deepened, but his brother may or may not be in dire financial straits and up to mischief, and someone was targeting Julia.

The longer he sat in the mine's counting house, the more restless he grew, until he could take it no more. Not much could be solved this very moment, but one thing could—he could get answers from Matthew about how he found their father's watch. Lobby had no reason to lie about his role in the strange transaction. Furthermore, Margaret referenced rumors about Matthew's financial instability. Isaac was not willing to risk his own future on his brother's business whims, and if Matthew was considering selling the mine, Isaac had a right to know.

The idea that Tregarthan Hall could potentially be at any type of risk sickened him. His father—and his grandfather before him—had endeavored to leave a Blake legacy.

As the clock struck the noon hour, Isaac jumped from his chair, grabbed his coat and hat, saddled his horse, and set off for Tregarthan Hall. When he arrived, he did not knock or wait to be let in.

"Matthew!" he bellowed. His voice echoed from painted plaster and bounced from the planked floor. No response came. "Matthew!"

The aging butler appeared, his bushy eyebrows raised in surprise. "Mr. Blake. We were not expecting you today."

"Where's my brother?"

He shook his head. "He's out. I expect him to return later today. Shall I tell him you called?"

"No." Isaac walked past the butler. "I'll wait in the study. When he arrives please let him know I'm here."

Still fueled by the heat of frustration, Isaac marched down the corridor and into the study where he'd spent so much time with his father. The room was cool and dark. No fire lit the grate. No candles offered light. Clutter, paper, books, and maps littered the space. He stepped to the window and looked out at Wheal Gwenna, recalling the days when he'd stand by his father's side at this very window and talk about the future.

Isaac set his jaw as the memories intensified. Whereas Matthew had been determined to separate himself from Tregarthan, explore the world, and leave for school as soon as Father permitted it, Isaac embraced his heritage. He'd spent every day in his father's company, learning. Observing. And when he grew from adolescence to manhood, his father became his mentor. His trusted advisor. His best friend.

All that ceased for him when Father died. Matthew, of course, had been devastated at their father's early demise, but Isaac's entire world was shaken. He hadn't been able to cry for several weeks, for it was not real. Surely it couldn't be real. And he hadn't even been able to step foot in this room for a full year following his father's death.

But reality crept in as it always did, and now being in this study, in his private space, was still too much, and he suspected it would always be. And he couldn't help but wonder if his father would be proud of the man he had become.

Using the flint atop the mantel, he lit several candles and sat in the chair.

Unable to sit still, he jumped up again and perused the items on the desk. Letters and ledgers were strewn about. He set about shuffling through them when a door creaked.

Isaac jerked his head up.

There was a door off of his study that tradesmen used to use when they would visit his father, for his mother never wanted them tracking mud through the house. It was that door he heard, and it had to be Matthew.

Isaac braced himself, mentally preparing what he'd say to his brother. But the form that filled the doorway was not Matthew.

A tall, wiry man with greasy, long, unbound black hair and a dirty coat appeared. An eerie grin slid across his face, revealing several missing teeth. "Yer surprised to see me, I can tell."

Isaac blinked, not sure what to make of this man.

But the superior manner in which the man walked into the room, the air that he had the right to do so, was disconcerting. "I know, I know. Ye told me ne'er to meet ye here no more, but I knew ye'd be wantin' this."

Clearly, this man thought he was Matthew. In the room's faint light, the mistake would be an easy one to make.

Isaac leaned forward to accept the packet. He loosened the leather strip binding the portfolio and opened it. Inside was a stack of papers. "What's this?"

"Those? Why, they be the travel arrangements ye asked for. Took some work, but me men got it, quiet like, just like ye said. Travel to set sail to the East Indies, fortnight hence."

Isaac stiffened. The East Indies? What on earth would his brother do there?

Determined to show no response, he closed the portfolio and set it atop the desk. "And?"

The wooden planks squeaked as the man shifted. He gave a nervous laugh. "Beggin' yer pardon, but there be the matter of payment."

Isaac speared him with a hard stare. "Come back for it later."

The man opened his mouth to protest.

"I said come back for it later," Isaac snapped in his best impression of Matthew. He repeated the visitor's words back to him. "I told you not to come here. You'll get your money. Soon. You can go."

The man hesitated, as if prepared to argue, but then he tipped his crumpled hat. "Ye know where to find me." And with that, he withdrew through the same door he entered.

Isaac searched his memory, hard and fast, to see if he knew this man, but surely he'd remember one with such a lack of teeth. No, he did not know him, but apparently Matthew did.

The minutes slid into an hour. And Isaac grew angrier with each moment. Fuming, he began to pace the crowded space. If his brother was in dire financial straits, how was he buying expensive passage? There was one way to find out.

The family strongbox.

It was behind a low-hanging portrait of a hunting dog. Everyone in the house knew of its location, so it was not the safest place to hide things. He had to have been a boy the last time he looked at it, but his instincts itched to look inside.

He retrieved the key from the top drawer of his father's desk and then went to the strongbox. He opened it, reached inside, and retrieved a small wooden box. Holding his breath, he opened it.

Jewelry glistened inside. Gold rings and small silver and ivory trinkets.

His stomach fell as he thought of the jewelry that had been taken from Lanwyn Manor. Surely these were not any of those pieces.

Surely.

"Snooping?"

Isaac flinched at the suddenness of the words, but he did not move. Matthew.

"Or are you looking for something in particular?" Matthew's footsteps padded over the rug as he approached.

Refusing to delay the inevitable, Isaac picked up the topaz pendant and held it before him. "What's this?"

Not breaking his stride, Matthew stepped to the side table. "Don't know. Maybe it was Mother's? Haven't looked in there in ages." He held up the decanter of port. "Want some?"

Isaac stepped forward. "What's jewelry doing in here?"

Matthew's expression darkened as he uncorked the bottle and poured a drink. "Why exactly are you in my personal space, rifling through my things like some vagabond thief in the night? How would you like it if I came to the cottage and searched through your things?"

"I've nothing to hide," Isaac shot back.

"And I do?" Matthew's hazel eyes narrowed. "You know, I could have you thrown in the lockup for this."

Isaac smirked, unable to control the sarcasm slipping from his tongue. "Who then would run your mine?"

Matthew's nostrils flared, and for a moment Isaac thought his brother might strike him. He clenched his fists, ready to respond.

After several seconds engaged in a visual duel, Isaac said, "Miss Twethewey told me that an item fitting this description had been stolen from Lanwyn Manor."

"So you've been speaking with Miss Twethewey, have you? How interesting." A sly, almost sinister grin crossed his face. "Speaking of Julia, perhaps she'd take a fancy to that piece. Perhaps I should make it a gift."

"You'd be wise to stay away from her," Isaac said through clenched teeth.

"Ah." Matthew threw his head back in sardonic laughter. "'Tis happened at last. I knew it would. My little brother's taken a fancy to a young lady. And I commend your choice. But I hate to inform you that I'm the one who captured her heart. She told me as much when she was in my arms at the ball. Think on it, Brother. Do you really believe she'd prefer someone with little means? Bah. Tell yourself what you will, but I've captured her heart, and her uncle's mine." Matthew cocked his head to the side. "I hear the widow is available."

Isaac lunged forward. He stopped himself just before he slammed his fist against his brother.

"What, are you going to hit me? Like when we were boys?" Matthew challenged. "'Twas always your weakness, your inability to control those fists of yours. One would think you'd have outgrown such a habit."

Isaac had to stay calm. Matthew was luring him, baiting him as one would a fish.

"I'd like to think we've grown up from that," Matthew continued. "Besides, why are you calling my judgments into question? Need I remind you, I've seen you make a call or two that had a shade of dishonesty to it. Don't play the saint."

The brothers glared at each other.

Matthew shrugged. "I wondered when it would come to this."

"Come to what?"

"A division. We have managed to keep things civil since Father's death, and it has served us. You and I look alike. Sound alike. But we're hardly identical. Not at the core of who we are. I'm not surprised this cordial brotherly alliance of ours crumbled. Are you? It was based on loyalty to a man who expected more from both of us. So now that we're clear on that point, perhaps it would do you well to leave my property alone."

Anger seethed through him. Was his brother forcing him from the family home? In that moment he made a decision. "You are right, Brother. We are very different. In fact, I find I don't know you at all."

Isaac turned around to the open box, his body blocking Matthew's view. Instead of returning the pendant to where he found it, he slid it in his cuff. He then locked the safe, turned to toss his brother the key, and quit the study.

CHAPTER 44

With the exception of going to Jane's bedchamber, Julia did not venture far from her room over the course of the next several days. She didn't even take her meals in the dining room, nor did she go into the village to help with the sewing circle or the reading sessions. Not only was she fearful of encountering whoever wrote the messages, but Aunt Beatrice had all but forbade her from stepping foot out of doors.

Despite Aunt's insistence that Julia have no contact with anyone outside of the house, Matthew Blake had called every day. Julia could not avoid him, but with each encounter, she noticed subtle changes in him. He seemed pale. His hair, which was usually so tidy, was wild and curly. Dark circles shadowed his eyes. His speeches, which always had been grandiose and flattering, grew in their flamboyance.

It was impossible to see Isaac. The memory of his arms around her and his lips on hers had to sustain her for the time being. Even so, every morning she sat at her window, hoping to time it just right so that she might catch a glimpse of him on his way to the mine.

She believed him when he said he'd protect her. She had no doubt he was doing as he said—watching out for her. Trying to find out what was going on.

One morning, as she sat watching for a glimpse of him, a sharp, pain-laced cry sliced the predawn silence.

Julia bolted upright.

Another cry. Followed by, "Help. Someone help!"

Jane.

Julia leapt from the window seat and snatched her wrapper as she ran from her room. Legs still wobbly from lounging and sleep, she stumbled down the stairwell to the floor below, punching her hands through the sleeves with each step.

She burst into Jane's room. "What is it?"

Perspiration dampened Jane's face. Her hair clung to the side of her face. She gasped for air. "There's a pain. Here."

Julia hurried to the bed, gasping as her cousin suffered.

Was this her time? Surely not. She still had more than a month to go. "What can I do?" Julia inquired, wide-eyed, feeling helpless.

Jane reached out and gripped Julia's hand. "I think we must call Mr. Jackaby."

Before Julia could respond, Aunt Beatrice appeared at the door, hair wild and frizzy, and clad in a dressing gown. Horror reddened her round face, and immediately she tugged the bellpull next to the door to ring for Mrs. Sedrick. "Oh dear, oh dear! And with your father out of town."

Jane groaned and writhed.

"Mrs. Sedrick!" Aunt Beatrice shrieked, as if the bellpull was not enough to summon the woman. She nudged Julia aside so she could take her place at the bedside.

Caroline soon joined them in the chamber and, once inside, gripped Julia's hand, not taking her gaze off of her sister. "What if it's her time?"

"I'm not well versed in these things, but isn't it too early?" Julia responded. "The accoucheur said he was certain there was at least another month."

For the next several hours, frantic activity ensued. Mr. Jackaby and Uncle William were sent for, and the servants did everything in their power to make Jane more comfortable.

But Jane's distress did not diminish.

Aunt Beatrice had descended into hysterics and taken to her own bed.

Someone had to remain sensible. Someone had to take charge. All Julia could think of was the curse she'd heard about at church all those weeks ago—about no child surviving.

She could send word to Isaac or Matthew, or Miss Prynne or Miss Trebell, but all that would take time.

Julia turned to Mrs. Sedrick. "Send for the carriage and have it ready for me immediately."

Caroline popped her head around the corner. "Where are you going?"

Julia's movements slowed when she saw the look of disapproval in the housekeeper's eyes. "Jane is getting worse, and no one under this roof seems to know what to do."

"If the baby is coming, there are women here who have dealt with ladies who are in the family way," Mrs. Sedrick said.

"But it's too early. Something must be wrong." This was absurd. Julia pushed past Mrs. Sedrick and would call for the carriage herself. Julia ran to her chamber, retrieved her cloak, and encountered Caroline once more in the corridor.

"Try and keep Jane comfortable."

"How? And where are you going?"

"I'm going to get help."

CHAPTER 45

Julia pounded on Mrs. Benson's cottage door with her fist and stepped back, watching the door expectantly. After several seconds she arched her head to the side, looking for motion through the dark window.

Nothing.

She tapped her hand against her leg and sighed. The afternoon light seemed dark for the churning clouds, and frost plumed from her mouth with each breath. "Please be home."

Relief flooded her when, at length, noise echoed from inside, and the door opened just enough for a set of light eyes to peek out.

Julia's words rushed out at the first sight of the midwife. "Please, I need your help. My cousin is having her baby, at least I believe she is, anyway, and 'tis far too early. Something's not right and she's in a great deal of pain. She is—"

Mrs. Benson shifted to the side, and Julia's words caught in her throat.

Directly behind the midwife stood Isaac, his hazel eyes wide.

Julia stared at him for a moment, the shock of seeing him there momentarily robbing her of speech. Her heart tore. Isaac . . . and the widow?

The reality slammed against Julia, hard and fast. She'd heard the rumors herself but had almost forgotten them. They must be true.

The evidence existed right before her eyes. Her thoughts muddled and a fogginess descended over her.

She had to be strong. She had to. Her cousin could be dying.

Regaining her composure, she reached forward to touch the door so it wouldn't close. "P-please. She could die, and her accoucheur is in London. I beg you. My uncle can pay you for your services."

The widow pressed her lips together and looked over her shoulder at Isaac before she returned her attention to Julia. "Wait here. I'll get my bag." Mrs. Benson disappeared inside the house.

Careful not to look at Isaac, Julia leaned her back against the house to wait. She gritted her teeth, hoping—praying—that he would not step out to speak with her.

But that was just what he did, the breeze rustling his hair. "What can I do?"

She shook her head, fighting the feelings of betrayal, regardless of how unfounded they might be. "Nothing."

"Shall I call for the apothecary? Anyone?"

"Mrs. Benson will help us." She turned her back to him and started for the carriage.

"Surely I can do something." Isaac touched her arm.

She jerked her arm away.

"Julia, I can imagine what you think. I'm only here to deliver news that—"

"It doesn't matter," she snipped and paused to meet his gaze fully. "You owe me no explanation. On anything."

She continued her course to the carriage. She couldn't look back at him, not for another moment, for he might see every emotion. She knew too well the danger of letting a man monopolize her thoughts, and she'd not been careful enough.

Once at the carriage Julia paused and turned in time to see the widow emerge from the cottage and hand a bag to Isaac. In a flurry of activity, he assisted them both into the carriage and then, once they were settled, he said, "I'll send word to the physician in Cardow. Anything else, Margaret?"

Julia winced as the woman's Christian name passed his lips. Every moment seemed to offer fresh information confirming a relationship between the two—a relationship that, if it existed, would shatter the newfound hope her heart had fostered.

The widow leaned forward, partially blocking Julia's view of Isaac. "Ask the neighbor to watch Jory, will you? And fetch Miss Prynne and Miss Trebell and bring them to Lanwyn as quickly as you can."

With a nod and another glance in Julia's direction, Isaac closed the door and stepped back. The carriage lurched forward abruptly, as if the horses could sense their riders' urgency.

Almost immediately the midwife's voice rose sharply above the crunching of carriage wheels and pounding of hooves, "Tell me of her symptoms."

"She is c-crying in pain," Julia stammered, refocusing her attention on Jane. "Writhing."

"Is she bleeding?"

"Yes."

"Fever?"

"I think so."

The widow peppered her with more questions about Jane's condition, and as the carriage jostled back through the woods and over the bridge, Julia apprised the widow of everything she knew. When the carriage finally drew to a stop in front of Lanwyn Manor, Julia grabbed the midwife's hand. "Thank you. For coming."

Together the women hurried through the courtyard and the great hall and toward the tower stairs. In the time that Julia had been gone, Jane had been moved from her bedchamber to the lying-in chamber and was now dressed in a birthing gown. The curtains were drawn, the fires were blazing, and all was warm. Someone had plaited Jane's hair tightly against her head, and cries echoed from the stone walls.

Mrs. Benson wasted no time. She swept into the room and went straight to Jane.

Aunt Beatrice, already present in the chamber, jerked her head up at the intrusion. "Who is she?"

"Mrs. Margaret Benson," Julia explained. "A midwife."

"A *local* midwife?" Aunt Beatrice's voice rose two octaves. "Oh no. No, no, no. Not for my daughter. Absolutely not!"

"Have we a better solution?" Julia implored. "None of us knows what to do, and a midwife is the only one who has any experience in this. We're all frightened, and she might be our only hope."

Aunt sniffed and stepped aside, all the while glowering at the midwife.

"I will require hot water, blankets, and brandy," Mrs. Benson ordered. "Bring more candles and as many linens as you can find. Let's prepare to meet this little one."

Pulse wild and heart thumping, Isaac sprinted back to the mine's counting house.

He'd located Miss Trebell quickly and delivered her to Lanwyn Manor without delay.

Miss Prynne took much longer to locate. It was not until late in the afternoon he was able to find her at one of the cottages on Miner's Row, tending to Sophia's mother. He'd accompanied her to Lanwyn Manor.

He'd done what he promised to do. But he hadn't done what he *needed* to do.

He needed to talk to Julia. He saw it in her eyes—the mistrust.

The sting of perceived deception. He didn't know much about the man who had broken her heart, but he did know that he'd betrayed her for another. Isaac feared she might think he would do the same.

How he wanted to set the record straight, but he'd have to wait, even though each hour that passed with this obstacle between them would only breed more distrust. More pain.

His reason to be at Margaret's house was an honest one. He pulled the second letter from Richards from his pocket, advising them that he would soften his terms and set limits on costs. He would still require them to purchase materials exclusively from him, but the costs would be agreed upon beforehand.

It was a much more palatable offer, and with Matthew's recent odd behavior, collaborating with Edwin Richards might be the best option.

How did everything become so clouded?

How did his relationships become so complicated?

As he sat at the desk, hoping to divert his thinking, he assessed the untidy stack of papers. A small folded letter caught his eye. Sealed, with *Mr. Matthew Blake* scrawled across the top.

Isaac was in no mood for niceties, and his suspicion regarding his brother ran rampant. He ripped open the letter. Like the letter Matthew had thrown into the fire, it was short—just one word.

Tonight

HP

He tapped the letter against the desk. They were the same initials from the last letter. Isaac stood and paced as he studied the writing, wracking his brain to think of everyone he might know with those initials. And then it dawned on him.

He froze midstep.

He knew those initials.

He knew them very well.

Had he not been looking for her the entire day, he might not have made the connection, but suddenly the reality shifted into focus: *Harriet Prynne.*

Isaac shifted to the doorway and put his head out into the corridor. "Eliza! Eliza!"

The servant girl appeared around the corner, her eyes wide. "Yes, sir?"

"When did this letter arrive?"

She looked at the note in his hand. "About two hours or so ago."

"Who brought it?"

"A village boy. Lenken's boy, I believe. Shall I fetch 'im?"

"No. Thank you."

Tonight . . . Something was going to happen tonight, but whatever it was could not be good. Harriet Prynne was at Lanwyn Manor. It was not the time for speculation.

He needed to get to Lanwyn Manor.

Now.

CHAPTER 46

The story of the curse rang like clanging bells in Julia's mind.

Julia paused in her task of folding linens to wipe her forearm across her brow and glance around the birthing room. The afternoon had stretched into early evening. The curtains were drawn. A hearty fire sizzled in the hearth and candles lit every corner. The air in the room smelled stale and ill, thick with wood smoke and uncertainty.

It would be dusk soon, and yet Jane's agony continued. It was certain. The child was coming. With nearly every breath she breathed a prayer for Jane and the baby's safety.

As it was the accoucheur would not arrive in time. That much was clear. Julia had been impressed with how Mrs. Benson took charge, ordering the servants about, calling on the help of Miss Prynne and Miss Trebell. Julia was doing what she could, but now there was naught to do but wait and pray.

Aunt Beatrice had been in and out of the chamber. The heat and the sight of her daughter in such pain had broken her, and she needed to lie down to recover. But she'd returned, and despite her pallid coloring, disapproval pinched her expression.

Aunt glanced at Miss Prynne and then Miss Trebell. "Why are there so many people in here?"

"They are called gossips, Aunt." Julia patted her hand. "They are women who accompany the midwife to assist and help ease the mother."

"What are you giving her?" Aunt Beatrice demanded as Miss Prynne held Jane's head and helped her drink from a cup.

"Caudle. It supposedly eases the pain," Julia offered.

"This is not how it was supposed to be!" Aunt Beatrice moaned as she reclined on the settee in the lying-in chamber, garnering the attention of the women tending her daughter.

"Either you want me to help your daughter or you don't," Mrs. Benson snipped from her position by the bed, her face red from heat, her sleeves rolled up to her elbows. "If you want me to help you, we'll do this my way. I can leave."

"No, no." Aunt's eyes widened. "Stay. Do what you must. I'll say no more."

The hours dragged on. The servants bustled in and out, bringing supplies and taking away anything soiled. Julia sat in silence next to her cousin, dabbing a cool cloth on her brow, knowing full well it did little to ease the pain, but it made her feel useful, and it reinforced that she was here.

More than once the young mother-to-be called out for her husband. And it broke Julia's heart. How cruel love could be. Betrayals. Separations. Her own heart ached. The afternoon was so intense that she would forget about seeing Isaac in Mrs. Benson's house, but then something would remind her of it, and the pain would pierce afresh.

Julia lifted her head as Mrs. Sedrick appeared. "Mr. Isaac Blake is downstairs and has asked to speak with either Miss Twethewey or Mrs. Benson."

"Mr. *Isaac* Blake?" shot Aunt Beatrice. "What does he want here?"

"I'm obviously busy," Mrs. Benson blurted. "Tell him I'll speak with him later."

Mrs. Sedrick turned expectant eyes on Julia.

She could not turn him away.

Surprisingly, she realized she did not want to turn him away in spite of everything.

Besides, he'd done what he could and helped collect Miss Trebell and Miss Prynne. "I'll go."

Julia untied the apron from her dress and left the room. Cool, fresh air enveloped her as she hurried through the darkened corridors. She unrolled her sleeves and did her best to smooth her wild hair as she made her way through the ground-floor landing and dining room. She paused for a moment to take a deep breath before she stepped into the great hall.

He turned as she entered, and he dashed toward her, his face ruddy from the night's cold. He reached for her hands. "Julia, I—"

She pulled her hands back and stepped past him, maintaining her distance. Julia could feel his gaze on her. She thought she had buried the emotions far enough, but at the sight of his hazel eyes, the same sting she had felt while standing outside the Benson cottage resurfaced. She cleared her dry throat. "God willing, the babe will come tonight."

"And is your cousin well?"

"Mrs. Benson has said that we must prepare ourselves." Julia turned to look out the window into the darkened courtyard.

"I am sorry for her."

His steps approached, and Julia clasped her hands in front of her. Oh, she wanted to pretend that she hadn't seen him in Mrs. Benson's home. She wished her feelings could go back to what they were before. But wishing could not erase the memory.

"Why are you here?" Her words were sharp—much sharper than she intended. "I'm needed upstairs."

"I've intercepted a note. I fear something dreadful might happen tonight."

She jerked, surprised at his words, and turned. "What do you mean 'a note'?"

He retrieved a letter from his waistcoat pocket and extended it toward her.

She eyed it with suspicion for several moments before she accepted and unfolded it.

> Tonight
>
> HP

She frowned. It was certainly not in the same handwriting as the letters she had received, but it was disconcerting nonetheless. She flipped it over. "Why, this is addressed to Matthew." She snapped her head up to see his reaction.

He stepped closer, and Julia resisted the urge to shrink back.

"I told you I'd keep an eye on things and watch out for anything suspicious, and I think this fits that description. I don't know what it means, but I wanted you to be aware."

She huffed and handed the letter back to him. "Well, everyone's thoughts are not quite on jewels and strange noises and odd shadows in the night tonight. My cousin is fighting for her life and that of her child. If you'll excuse me—"

She started to push past him, but he reached out and caught her by the arm. He whispered, "Julia."

She stopped short at the touch and gasped. The sound of her name on his lips, the touch of his hand on her arm—it was all too much. Her heart jumped wildly to her throat, and the room grew warm. Much too warm. Tears threatened to let loose. They had been simmering below the surface all day, and now she doubted she had the strength to keep them at bay. She swallowed and forced her voice to be steady. "This has been a difficult day. It *is* a difficult day. Please let me go."

"I owe you an explanation. At least let me give you that."

"On the contrary, Mr. Blake. You don't owe me anything."

"Like I said before, nothing has changed, Julia."

She stabbed his hand on hers with a glare, then looked to his eyes. "Has it not?"

Did he think her a fool? A woman to be turned by an apology? Perhaps what she had heard was correct and not just rumors. He and Mrs. Benson were business partners, yes, but their relationship extended beyond that. Didn't it?

She was tired. Exhausted, really. Now was not the time for this discussion. She was needed upstairs.

She turned to leave, and as he moved to follow her, something clattered to the stone floor.

Julia looked down. A topaz brooch glistened on the floor.

———◆———

Isaac groaned as the brooch fell from his pocket to the great hall's stone floor. What a fool he'd been not to secure it further.

How was he going to explain this without betraying his brother? And since she'd seen him alone in Margaret's home, he feared Julia wouldn't believe a word he said.

Her eyes narrowed. "Is that . . . ?" She bent to retrieve it and held it before her, her hand covering her mouth. "It's my aunt's brooch!"

"Yes, I know."

"How do you know?" Her large eyes were wide with questions. "And how did you get it?"

He searched for words. "It's a difficult story, but I believe it has something to do with this note."

Her expression shifted and anger ruled. "I've been forced to bear the blame for these disappearances, and you nonchalantly have one of the items in your possession? Should I check you for the necklace as well?"

Her words smarted as if she'd smacked him across the face. "You misunderstand."

She fell quiet. The circles under her eyes seemed darker, her complexion paler. "I find that I don't know what to think or understand, Mr. Blake."

"Surely you don't think that I—"

"I don't know how or why you are in possession of stolen property. But I have the strong suspicion that you may not be the man I thought you were."

"Please, I—"

She held up her hand. "It's been a most exhausting day, Mr. Blake. Perhaps we can talk another time, but for now, my cousin needs me."

CHAPTER 47

All was quiet in the lying-in chamber. The gossips—Miss Prynne and Miss Trebell—had been shown to guest chambers for the night. Aunt Beatrice and Caroline, worn out from the day's excitement, had both retired to their respective chambers. Mrs. Benson sat in a chair next to the fire.

Julia alone remained at her cousin's bedside.

The silence was a refreshing reprieve from the groans and cries of pain. Even the late evening's darkness fit the mood. Finally calm. Finally peaceful.

"She's nothing short of miraculous," Julia whispered as she looked to the tiny baby slumbering in Jane's arms.

The perspiration had been wiped from Jane's brow, and a tired, happy smile replaced the earlier grimaces. "I only wish Jonathan were here to meet his daughter. He would think her darling, I'm sure."

"Of course he would," Julia cooed, smiling as the baby gripped her finger. "How could he not? Look at how sweet she is."

"I hope he'll not be disappointed she's a girl." Jane stroked her finger over the child's smooth cheek. "He always talked about wanting a son. Although she does have his dark hair."

After freeing her finger, Julia adjusted the swaddling around the baby's face. "Oh Jane, any man would be proud to have such a fine daughter."

"How odd that she's here, in my arms, and he doesn't even know," Jane exclaimed absently, as if to herself instead of to Julia. "He's not even expecting her arrival for weeks."

"Mrs. Benson said that happens sometimes—how easy it is to miscalculate."

Jane swiped a strand of her disheveled golden hair from her eyes. "I fear the entire day's made Mother quite distraught. She was so eager for the accoucheur and the monthly nurse, and now I've disrupted her plans. Where is Mother, by the way?"

Julia leaned back. "She's taken to her bed."

"Ah." Jane cast a glance toward Mrs. Benson. "I am grateful Mrs. Benson was able to come. I fear what might have happened if she had not."

"You mustn't even give that a thought now. Here. Let me put the baby in the bassinet. You must think about sleeping."

"But what if she wakes up?"

"There are women aplenty to help. Are you in much pain?"

Jane shifted uncomfortably. "I could pretend to be stoic, but I won't. Yes, I am in a great deal of pain. But one does not remember it—or so I am told."

"I don't want you to worry about a thing. I will write to Jonathan before I retire and tell him that he has a beautiful daughter and a very brave, strong wife. I'll assure him that everyone is well and eager to see him. Will that do?" Julia lifted the swaddled child from her mother's arms and cradled her in her own. "There now."

She paced the room for several moments as a warm silence fell over the room. She marveled at the tiny nose, the little eyebrows, the perfect lips. She could not help but smile. The Lambourne women had defied the curse. Mother and child were both well, and every indication was that Jane would fully recover.

As happy as she was at that blessed outcome, her heart ached at the memory of her interaction with Isaac. Could she have been so blind—again? She had allowed him to kiss her—fully believing his intentions were honorable. She'd trusted him with her concerns. Her thoughts. Perhaps he was telling her the truth about Mrs. Benson, but how could he explain the topaz brooch? Even if he had the most reasonable excuse, would it be worth it to risk her heart again?

With her thoughts running rampant, Julia placed the child in the cradle, then turned toward Mrs. Benson, who was now packing her bag. She'd been amazed at the woman's confidence and knowledge, her calmness and strength.

Awkward silence hovered, broken only by the crackling fire and the howl of the wind outside. At length Julia said, "We'll have quite a story to tell the child when she's older about the day she was born."

"Indeed, but no birth is without its own unique story." Mrs. Benson rolled down her sleeves. "It's my experience children born in strange conditions are born with fire in their veins. They are wild and bold."

"She will be more like her father than her mother, then."

Mrs. Benson removed her apron and set it aside. She was younger than Julia had thought when she first encountered her. Now, at this close distance, she noticed the opposite was true. She appeared not much older than Julia herself.

Julia leaned forward and lowered her voice. "I'm sorry for how my aunt treated you upon your arrival."

A faint smile—the first smile Julia had seen her give since she stepped foot in Lanwyn Manor—crossed her lips. "Don't be. Your aunt was frightened and only wants what she thinks is best for her daughter. Besides, I wasn't here for Mrs. Lambourne. I was here for Mrs. Townsend."

"Where did you learn to care for new mothers so?"

Mrs. Benson placed the jars and vials back into her bag. "My mother was a midwife. From the time I was very young, I'd assist her."

"It must be satisfying to be such a help to others. I do wish I had such a skill. I am quite envious."

Mrs. Benson chuckled, as if in disbelief. "You're envious of me?"

Julia nodded.

The widow looked over at the baby, and her stern expression softened. "I fear I owe ye an apology."

Julia stiffened. "You owe me nothing."

"On the contrary." Mrs. Benson bit her lower lip, crossed her arms over her chest, and turned to face Julia fully. "I owe you an apology for what I said to you that day in the village. It was wrong. I was wrong."

"Oh no." Julia waved a dismissive hand. "Please, don't think on it. 'Twas so long ago."

"It's not easy to lose someone you love, and I loved my husband, Miss Twethewey. I loved him with everythin' I am. It's easy to blame those around you when the world does not seem fair."

"I'm truly sorry for your loss." Julia offered her a smile. "You've done my family a great service today, and I'm so grateful. Come, the hour is late. I'll show you to a chamber where you can stay the night. I believe Mrs. Sedrick had one made up for you. I know you've said that you prefer to sleep in the lying-in chamber to be close to Jane and the baby, but you probably would like to freshen up."

They left the chamber, and the cooler air of the common landing embraced them. Julia lifted a candle and moved to the small bedchamber closest to Jane's room.

"You speak of being envious, when in truth it's I who am envious," Mrs. Benson said softly. "You have security. Lovely things. No doubt your life will go on as lovely."

Julia drew a deep breath. "No one escapes this life without tragedy or heartache. I fear your envy is misplaced, for I really have no security other than an aunt and uncle who care a great deal for me. Perhaps at one time I had a fortunate future, but it's gone, and my dowry consists of whatever my uncles scrape together. So there you have it. Insecurity."

The women shared a smile.

"Perhaps we are not as different as you think we are, Mrs. Benson."

"Perhaps not."

CHAPTER 48

Isaac stepped out of Lanwyn Manor's foyer into the frosty night air, and he lowered his hat against it.

Frustration fueled each step. It seemed every part of his life was hanging on by a mere thread—one second away from snapping.

What a disaster this day had been.

What a disaster everything seemed to be right now.

He cut across the courtyard, skirted around several of the outbuildings, and crossed Lanwyn Manor's west meadow toward the public road where he had met Julia so many times.

Oh, Julia.

There was no telling what she thought of him now. Her expression of confusion and hurt haunted him, and her angry tone rattled in his head. It was all a mistake, of course, an unfortunate misunderstanding, but he doubted she'd see it that way.

He tightened his coat as he approached the drystone wall—the very place where he and Julia had spent so many mornings talking.

Perhaps it was for the best, for in truth, a relationship between them was doomed from the start. He had little to offer her. She was not from their part of the country. She had said several times that she would stay until the baby was born and then what? She was going to return home to her life—away from Goldweth.

He prepared to climb the stile over the wall when something to the north near the Lanwyn stables caught his eye. He slowed his steps.

Two, maybe three shadows moved around the space, their hats outlined by the silver moonlight.

Isaac continued along the low wall. After all, he had every right to be on the public road. Then, as he drew closer, he recognized something odd about one of the men—long, greasy dark hair, free of a queue, with the same odd-shaped felt hat as the man who had brought the travel papers to his brother's study.

A fallen branch cracked under Isaac's boot, and one of the men turned. The man with the long hair glanced up, then approached him. "Thought you was inside. Somethin' go wrong?"

Isaac blinked, buying himself more time. Apparently this man thought he was Matthew again.

Isaac lowered his hat to guard his identity. If he wanted to find out what was going on, now was the time. "Inside?"

"Yeah. Thought you said you was comin' out the tunnel."

Tunnel? Isaac looked around, searching for words. "Uh, no. Everything's fine. Just wanted to go over the plan again."

The men exchanged glances.

Isaac groaned inwardly. He'd just said something that would never pass Matthew's lips. He held his breath until one of the other men spoke.

The man with the long hair leaned forward. "You changin' your mind? 'Cuz if you are, we—"

Isaac scoffed. "Of course not."

The man leaned forward and lowered his voice further. "Prynne was going to show you where to go. You get the chest, carry it out the tunnel, and we deliver it to Tregarthan quiet like. That still the plan?"

Isaac's blood pulsed through his veins. Had he heard correctly?

Miss Prynne was going to help Matthew take something from Lanwyn?

"Yes. It's still the plan. Let me see the tunnel again."

The men stepped inside, pulled aside a blanket of dead ivy, and revealed a door.

Isaac licked his lips and hid his shock, hoping he wasn't giving himself away. He'd never heard of a tunnel to Lanwyn, but after what Julia had told him about the hidden passageway to her tower chamber, he wasn't surprised.

One of the men opened the door.

Whether he liked it or not, he had engaged enough with these men that he could not turn back now, even if he wanted to.

Bricks lined the walls and curved up, forming a ceiling almost big enough for a man to stand in. If so much wasn't at stake, he might be fascinated by this find.

He weighed his options. He was in dangerous territory. They thought he was his brother, and if Matthew should appear, there would be no way to explain. But if Matthew were truly up to something, like these men suggested, perhaps there was still time to stop it.

"I'll be back." He picked up the lantern, stepped into the tunnel, and began walking.

CHAPTER 49

I t seemed that everyone was able to sleep—except Julia.

Even Mrs. Benson had returned to the lying-in chamber and had dozed off on the settee near Jane and the baby. Aunt Beatrice and Caroline had been abed for hours, and Miss Prynne and Miss Trebell were snug in their chambers.

Julia knew sleep would not come. The day's emotional strain had almost been too much, and her heart had been too disturbed by what she saw in Isaac's hand. The nauseating thought that perhaps he was not what he had seemed—and that she had misjudged yet another man—sickened her and made her head feel light.

Candle in hand, clad in her nightclothes and dressing gown with her hair down over her shoulders, Julia made her way to the study. She'd promised Jane that she'd write Jonathan on her behalf, but the inkwell in her chamber was dry. Once she arrived at the study door, she turned the knob, pushed it open, and stepped inside. No sounds save for the clicking of the case clock against the wall met her ears. She placed the candle on the large desk in the middle of the room and opened the drawer, looking for another inkwell.

Suddenly she froze.

Was that a whisper coming from the library?

Julia frowned. The midnight hours were upon them. No one

should be moving about the main living area, least of all in the secluded library.

Had Oscar gotten free perhaps?

She heard the voice again. Was that Miss Prynne? Julia recalled encountering her in this chamber once before.

Concerned, Julia stepped toward the library and poked her head through the doorway. All was dark inside, save for the moonlight sliding through the open curtains. An unexpected breeze swept over her, and she shivered as the icy air met her skin.

She'd been right—Miss Prynne stood near the far opposite wall, and next to her stood Matthew Blake.

A gasp rose in her throat. Her blood slowed in her veins.

They did not notice her. They were bent over the table studying something. Julia's mind raced to make sense of what she was seeing. Two people who should not be here. A stack of papers on the table.

"What's going on?" The words slipped out of her mouth before she had time to check them.

The pair both jerked up their heads.

"My child, what are you doing here?" Miss Prynne said in a frustratingly calm voice, as if they were meeting on Sunday at church instead of a private room in the middle of the night.

Julia ignored Miss Prynne's question. "Why are you here, Mr. Blake?"

Matthew stared at her, his eyes wide, and then stepped forward. "Go back, Julia. Forget you saw this."

"Forget I saw what? The two of you sneaking around my uncle's home in the middle of the night?"

He fixed a glare on her. "Leave. This doesn't concern you."

The condescension in his tone wore on her courage, and as he stepped closer, his overwhelming scent of tobacco and the outdoors smacked her senses. Her heart raced and she employed every ounce of willpower in her body not to look away from the directness of his glare.

"Of course it concerns me."

"The less you know, the better. Go back to your bed and . . ."

His words faded as she continued to assess what she saw. They seemed to have removed part of the wall.

And then she remembered—the hidden treasure.

Surely they weren't searching for it.

Surely.

And yet Miss Prynne had been in here. Did she know something?

Julia glanced over her shoulder, trying to put the pieces together. The tiny hidden door she had discovered her first day was open. Light glowed from it.

She moved that direction, and Mr. Blake grabbed her arm with surprising force. "I said go back to your chamber."

His eyes were hard, dark slits, and the candlelight cast odd shadows on his brow and cheekbones. It was almost frightening.

"And if you tell anyone what you saw here, *anyone* . . ." He produced a blade from his coat.

Her gaze followed the blade as he brandished it through the air, as if transfixed by the candlelight reflecting off the surface.

All the random pieces were circling around her. The warnings and the stares.

"This is not what we agreed on, Mr. Blake," Miss Prynne said, the protest shaky and small.

Julia swallowed her fright. "You wouldn't dare."

He sneered. "Dear Julia. I have plans. I tried to include you in them, really I did, but now I must look out for myself. I suggest you do the same."

"You're despicable."

He laughed again. "You're full of grit, aren't you? Unfortunately, that does not bode well for you. I've tried to be nice about this, but you leave me little choice." He took her by the arm and started to push her toward the door.

"Let go of me! Let go or I'll—"

He clamped his hand over her mouth.

Julia thrashed, kicking her leg out, but somehow in one quick motion, he whirled her around so her back pressed against his chest, and he held up the blade. Dangerously close. "Enough."

"Mr. Blake! Put that down this instant!" Miss Prynne's voice was sharper than before.

"Quiet, woman! Or you'll find yourself in the same situation as Miss Twethewey. Don't forget, you've as much to lose as I." He shoved Julia toward the short door and forced her inside. "Let's see how long it takes before someone misses you."

CHAPTER 50

Isaac had gone too far to turn back now.

Candles lined the tunnel. They were stuck in little grooves built into the bricks, giving it an eerily similar feeling to that of a mine. He was underground, he knew, for several yards into the tunnel he descended several stone steps, but instead of the jagged rock of a mine, smooth bricks formed a domed shape above him, and the same bricks formed a path beneath his feet. Someone had spent a great deal of time making this passageway.

He cast a glance backward, and the tunnel disappeared into a curve. From what he could tell, he was alone—and on borrowed time. The men at the entrance may not know he was Matthew's twin, but he didn't want to give them an opportunity to find out.

He walked for several minutes until another set of stairs led him upward, and then the tunnel ended at a closed wooden door. Perspiration beaded on his brow, and the overwhelming scent of candle smoke and damp earth surrounded him.

Pulse pounding, he pressed his ear against the door. Whatever was behind it was apparently very important to Matthew.

He listened a bit longer but heard nothing. He turned the handle so slowly that even if someone was on the other side, they might not notice. It was, surprisingly, not locked.

He had no weapon. No way to defend himself, should it come to that. But whatever reason Matthew had for sneaking into Lanwyn Manor could only bring him harm.

And Isaac had to stop it.

———◆———

Julia sucked a deep breath as the lock on the door clicked.

Panicked, she whirled and darted her gaze around the tiny room. She'd not come into this room since she discovered it all those weeks ago. Maps and tapestries still hung on the walls. A table still occupied the center.

Matthew was stealing something; she was sure of it. Somehow he'd employed Miss Prynne to assist. And now he'd threatened Julia. With a knife.

She heard them shuffling in the library. Every so often she'd hear Matthew curse or Miss Prynne whimper. He'd left her with no candle. The only light was the moonlight through the windows to the kitchen garden. Julia looked out, hoping someone might see her and come, but all was silent. Everyone was asleep. She sat at the table, trying to figure out the best course of action.

She was not sure how long she sat there. Perhaps fifteen minutes. Perhaps fifty. The shadows played tricks with her eyes, and fear manipulated her emotions.

Then she noticed it: one of the tapestries on the walls was moving.

Julia jumped up, nearly overturning her chair.

It continued to move, until it pushed outward. A door behind it was opening!

She pressed her back against the wall and held her breath as she waited for whatever, or whoever, might come out.

And then Isaac Blake peeked around the tapestry.

Frustration weighed down her already-weary heart.

At first neither spoke. Then he whispered, "What are you doing here?"

"What am *I* doing here?" she whispered back, arms folded tightly across her chest. "What are *you* doing here?"

He stepped through the door, candle first, and wiped his coat and looked around. "If you know, please tell me, where are we?"

"You don't know?" She eyed him.

"No, I don't know," he responded. "But I think my brother might be up to something, and I am trying to find out what it is."

"Your brother? The kidnapper?" she hurled. "You expect me to believe that you are not involved?"

"Involved in what?"

His innocent demeanor was convincing, but she was not certain. Not yet. She moved to the other door and rattled the handle, proving it was locked. "He locked me in here—he and Miss Prynne."

"HP," he breathed.

"And he has a knife. Isaac, I think Miss Prynne might be in danger."

"Please, Julia. You must trust me. I am trying to get to the bottom of this, just like you."

After several seconds she sighed. His actions might have hurt her, but in her heart of hearts she did not really believe him to be capable of anything criminal.

She drew a deep breath to organize her thoughts. "I'm not sure, exactly. They are searching for something. They've removed a portion of the wall in the library, which is just on the other side of the door."

He glanced at the door. "The treasure. The ridiculous treasure. That has to be it."

Isaac stared at Julia. Even though her face looked cool in the faint moonlight filtering through the tiny chamber's only window, her eyes flashed bright with indignation. Her long black hair hung in wild ringlets about her face. He'd give just about anything to see that softness return to her face—the gentleness, the joy he'd witnessed those mornings when they'd been alone.

They were alone now, as they had been then, and Julia stood before him, but how different things were.

He took a step in farther, hand extended, as if trying to soothe a frightened animal. "You've made it clear you do not want me here, and I understand that, but I'm here only to keep my brother from doing something he might seriously regret."

"It's far too late for that."

Despite her determined expression, she was frightened. He'd seen the look before—that night in the inn. He lowered his voice further. "If you'd but trust me—"

"I saw you with Aunt Beatrice's brooch, Isaac," she snipped. "I saw you with Mrs. Benson in her home. I'm not a fool, nor am I a child."

"I never meant to suggest you were either." He swallowed hard. "I'll tell you everything you want to know, if you'll only hear what I have to say. I found the brooch in my brother's house and was returning it. There's no use trying to defend Matthew anymore. Now my main priority is keeping him from doing significant damage and keeping the people I care for safe. And my visit with Margaret was only to discuss mine business. It was Charlie's wish to open Wheal Gwenna with me, and Margaret wants to proceed with it, for the sake of her son. We have a potential investor, and we were only discussing the wisdom of such a venture. You must believe me. Somehow the rest of this mess is all connected—from the attack at the inn, to the missing items, to this secret tunnel. And as far as Margaret goes . . ."

His heart raced as her expression softened. A tear balanced on her lower eyelid. Encouraged by the change in her demeanor, he took her hand in his. "She is a wonderful person, but oh, how she pales in comparison to you, my dear Julia." He brushed a curl away from her face. "Now is hardly the time for declarations and sentiment, but when we are out of this mess and all is settled, I'll tell you properly. But for now we must figure out what is going on once and for all."

CHAPTER 51

Isaac tightened his fingers around Julia's trembling hand.

"They're on the other side of this door," she whispered, her face close to his, her eyes wide and alert.

"And you have no idea what Miss Prynne is doing with him?"

"No, other than she seemed to be assisting him."

Isaac turned his full attention to the door's brass handle. "And you're certain it's locked?"

"Yes. I heard it click."

"What's on the other side?" Isaac whispered.

"The library."

He scoffed. "I didn't even know a library was here."

She nodded, leaning close, her long hair draping over his arm. "You access it through the study. That's the only way, I think. There are secret walls and doors all over this house—and outside, it would appear."

"The tunnel I came from had an entrance near the stables. The door was hidden in plain sight. I've lived in Goldweth my entire life and had no idea. If Matthew's been here, that's how he was coming and going."

"There have been times he seemed to materialize from nowhere. No one really ever questioned it. Now I know where he came from."

Isaac put his ear against the door. "Someone's out there, but I can't make out the words. Stand back." After a quick squeeze of her hand, he stepped in front of her, and using the heel of his boot he kicked through the lock.

Ancient wood splintered and shattered. Isaac burst through the door and quickly assessed the darkened chamber.

Miss Prynne was tied and gagged. Matthew and Mrs. Sedrick were removing a large wooden panel off the wall.

Without thinking, Isaac raced over to his brother and tackled him to the ground.

Miss Prynne grunted and thrashed from her chair. Mrs. Sedrick, in a flash, ran past them, shoved Julia into a bookshelf, and disappeared through the door from which they'd just come.

"Isaac!" Julia cried. "She's leaving!"

"Let her." He grunted, struggling to pin his stunned brother to the ground. His gaze swept the space and then landed on the table. "The pistol!"

Julia ran to the table and picked up the pistol. It looked ridiculously large in her small hands, but he'd never been so grateful to see one. He pushed himself off his brother and within two strides joined her. She quickly handed it over, as if it were made of fire rather than metal.

Weapon in hand, Isaac stepped in front of her and pointed the pistol at Matthew. Whatever was happening, whatever had happened, Isaac was about to get his answers.

Matthew glanced from Isaac's face, to the pistol, back to his face. Chest heaving from their grappling, a smile slid over Matthew's face—the same smile he'd employed so many times.

Even in this tense, precarious moment, when Isaac looked at Matthew, all he could see was his father's face. His own face. Staring back at him. A face he knew so well that he could see beyond the smile. See beyond the arrogance. He saw the boy.

But he also saw something else. Determination, raw and real.

Isaac straightened the pistol.

Perspiration beading, Matthew tossed his head to whisk the hair away from his forehead. "You wouldn't shoot me."

"You are attempting a robbery, Matthew. You may be my brother, but I'll not let you do this."

For several moments nobody moved.

"The treasure's mine. I'm going to take it, and you will let me."

"I see no treasure," Isaac challenged. "Besides, whatever is in this house now belongs to Lambourne."

Matthew's countenance darkened. "Nothing in this house belongs to him. It belonged to Rowe. To Goldweth. On his deathbed Rowe told Miss Prynne where the treasure was. He wanted her to take it."

"But why?"

"To help the villagers." A sinister grin slid over his sweaty face. "And I'm a resident of Goldweth, am I not?"

Isaac couldn't believe what he was hearing. "What possibly made you think that?"

Matthew guffawed. "Lambourne's a fool. You know as well as I that Rowe would turn in his grave at the thought of a man like him possessing the treasure."

"You were going to take the treasure and leave, weren't you?" Isaac deduced. "East Indies, is it? Your friend stopped by before you got to Tregarthan and I saw the travel papers. How could you do this?"

"Very easily. With a mine struggling to pay workers? With debt I can't escape from? Trapped in a life I never wanted or asked for?"

"So you'd take the coward's way out. And just leave." Isaac's gaze shifted to Miss Prynne. Tears moistened her eyes. She was trembling from head to toe. "Why did you have to involve her?"

Matthew extended his hands, as if declaring innocence. "She

came to me, not the other way around. Rowe told her of the treasure, and she thought I could help her. We tried to find it before the Lambournes arrived but failed. So with Sedrick's help we attempted to frighten them away. But then she came." He turned his eyes toward Julia.

Isaac's stomach dropped. "Tell me you did not have anything to do with the attack at the inn."

Matthew shrugged. "They didn't scare as easily as I thought they would."

Isaac thought he'd be sick. So that was how he knew where the watch was—and how he got it back so easily.

Matthew's air shifted, and he tossed an accusatory gaze toward the older woman. "Miss Prynne is involved as much in this as I. She was his special friend, wasn't she? She knew what room it was in, and she knew of the tunnel to get here, for it was how she got in here all the time to see Rowe."

At this Miss Prynne sobbed as much as the kerchief around her mouth would allow.

Julia scurried over to remove the cloth around her mouth and arms.

Isaac narrowed his gaze. "You are lucky then, Brother. Lucky it was I who figured this out and stopped you from what you were about to do. You'd be a criminal, and you may very well already be one for what you've done. You could hang for this. Caught in the act—not your name nor your position would save you from it. Word will be all over the countryside by dawn. I love you. But I'll not lie for you. Go, before I come to my senses and change my mind."

The brothers stared at each other for several moments, and then Matthew hurried from the space, through the door that led to the tunnel.

CHAPTER 52

Matthew was gone. The library was quiet once again, draped in the dark midnight hours, save for the candles Matthew and Mrs. Sedrick had been using to remove the heavy oak wall panels.

Julia stared at Isaac and he at her, and she tried to comprehend what she'd witnessed. As it was, books were scattered everywhere. Shelves had been pushed aside.

Julia turned her attention back to freeing Miss Prynne, and Isaac hurried to secure the door.

The knotted rag around her mouth finally fell free, and Miss Prynne cried, "He used me! I've known the boy his entire life. And this is what he does? To me? To all of us?"

"It's over now." Julia patted Miss Prynne's arm, trying to keep her voice soft and low. "Everything will be all right."

"All right? Nothing will be all right. Why, it's an abomination!"

Julia lifted her gaze to Isaac as he approached. His face twisted in a strange expression she'd never seen before. He was pale. Very pale. He knelt next to Miss Prynne. "Julia's right. It's all over now. You're safe and no one will hurt you."

"Oh, but the damage is done. Look around you!" Fresh tears cascaded down her wizened cheek. "That ridiculous treasure. Clearly there never was one. Mr. Rowe must have been talking in riddles. I see that now, but your brother could not. He *would* not."

Isaac took her other hand in his. "Tell us what happened."

Miss Prynne shook her head as if to clear cobwebs from her mind. "Now that I look back, I hardly know how we got here."

"Try."

"Oh, how I loved Elon Rowe." She sniffed and dabbed at her nose. "He was my life. My love. He always believed there was a treasure in this house, and after years of searching, he believed it to be in this very room. I never really believed the story, of course, but then on his deathbed, he asked me to find it and distribute it. He had such a heart for those in the village. Of course, I said I would. He said he'd discussed it at length with Matthew and suggested that I ask for his assistance. So I did.

"Your brother was immediately enthusiastic, but I truly believed his heart to be for the good. But the Lambournes arrived before we could find it. I'd accepted the fact that our opportunity had passed and that the treasure would remain hidden, but Matthew changed. Without my knowledge he somehow enlisted Mrs. Sedrick in his plans.

"He began trying to scare the Lambournes, subtly, to get them to leave. And then he attempted to woo Miss Twethewey to further gain access to the house. By the time I realized what he was doing, we had gone too far, and I was too involved.

"He was a man obsessed. He and Mrs. Sedrick began stealing the family items. Matthew convinced himself that the Lambournes did not deserve any of the wealth they had, and in his twisted mind he felt entitled to it. He told me that if I did not continue to help him, he'd inform Lambourne that I'd been the one stealing from them. I was so frightened."

The pieces slammed together in Julia's mind. Matthew did not want her. Nor did he care about the mines—any of them. He wanted this house and what was in it. "So that is why he would visit so often and why I found you in here."

"He's been manipulating us all, ever since Elon died."

"Did you ever find the treasure?" Isaac asked.

"No. No. It's nowhere." She gestured to the gaping hole in the paneling, and tears gathered afresh. "I believe now it was an old legend, one that time fanned to a flame. But Matthew kept saying that it was his only hope for a different life. His only chance."

Isaac stood. "We have to inform Lambourne right away. He has to know this was hidden in his home. That his housekeeper was involved. He has to know his family is safe."

Julia helped Miss Prynne to her feet. "We expect my uncle home anytime, for we sent word as soon as Jane's pains began, but nothing can be done now. Miss Prynne, you should try to rest. Tomorrow things can be sorted and made right."

"Can they?" she asked. "Nothing will be right ever again."

Julia smiled, the first real smile she'd felt in what seemed like forever. "Yes."

At length Miss Prynne returned to her chamber, shaken but unhurt, leaving Julia alone with Isaac.

As soon as her footsteps faded, Isaac reached for Julia and pulled her tightly into an embrace. She wrapped her arms around his waist and rested her cheek against the rough wool of his coat. His fingers smoothed her hair, and she could feel his heart thudding.

They stood there in silence, clinging to one another for several moments. It seemed now, in his arms, was the first time her tensed muscles relaxed. Her breathing slowed. She closed her eyes, memorizing the way he felt against her.

Finally he looked down at her.

What could be said in such a moment? How could one begin to address the pain—the betrayal—they both felt?

"What will happen now, I wonder?" she whispered. "Do you think Matthew will leave Goldweth?"

Isaac drew a deep breath, and the lines on his face tightened. "If he's smart he will, and he'll never return. Word of this *will* get out. How could he begin to explain what he's done?"

"But what about the mine? His house? Surely he can't just disappear."

"I saw the travel papers, Julia. A man delivered them just a few days ago. Matthew was planning to leave anyway. My guess is he thought he would get this treasure and escape."

"But it doesn't make sense."

"No, it doesn't." He smoothed her hair away from her face and let his finger linger on her cheek. "I am sorry he pretended to care for you. I hope it didn't distress you."

She gave a little laugh and leaned back into him. "I'm not sorry, for truly, you must know by now that my affections are aimed elsewhere."

He lowered his lips and kissed her, there in the darkened library. His touch made the cares of the day slide into the background of her thoughts, pushing her future to the forefront. How different this feeling was than what she'd felt with Percy. She felt whole. Complete. Trusting and true.

But even so, she detected a sadness behind his hazel eyes. She laced her fingers through his. "And you?"

His mouth eased into a half smile. "I suppose I have my answers too. I knew Matthew wanted to befriend your uncle, but I believed it was to strengthen our mine. It seems we've all been deceived."

She rested her head against his chest for several moments. Then he stepped back. "You should go to your chamber."

She frowned at the sudden sobering of his tone. "But I—"

"I'll be back in the morning. It's only right that I be here to explain what I know."

"But you are leaving now?" A sense of panic tremored through her. She wasn't ready for him to leave. Not yet.

He looked at her for several seconds. That strange twist returned to his face—not quite pain, not quite sadness, but a mixture that almost frightened her. "A lot has happened tonight. And I'm not sure I've entirely understood it all yet."

He offered her a weak smile and freed his fingers from hers. He placed his hands on her shoulders, stroked a finger down her cheek, and then went back through the tunnel door.

And Julia stood in the library alone.

CHAPTER 53

Isaac rarely felt nervous. But then again, he'd never told another man about how he'd been the target of an attempted robbery.

In spite of the storm brewing within his head and heart, the sunlight slid bright and fresh through the window behind him, and somewhere in the distance the newborn baby cried.

He'd not slept. How could he? His brother—his partner and, yes, his friend—had betrayed him.

Betrayed them all. And not just in a minor manner, but one that had the power to cause the entire community to crumble.

Yet Isaac held his head high and clasped his hands behind his back. He could say with all honesty he had no part in it—and he'd do what he could to make it right.

He glanced to his left. Julia, clad in a pale-yellow gown and with her hair bound loosely at her neck, stood next to Miss Prynne, whose tearstained face and swollen eyes told a story all their own.

He'd always considered Lambourne to be a little foolish and not much of a threat, but the unnerving, authoritative hardness in his blue eyes reminded Isaac that Lambourne was a businessman in his own right, and one capable of more than he'd thought. In one night the foundation of an entire family had been shaken, and the relationship between the Blakes and the Lambournes had been severed.

"And are you taking responsibility for this?" Lambourne demanded.

"No." Isaac fixed his gaze on the red-faced man, refusing to be the one to look away. "My brother acted independently. And I believe Miss Prynne is a victim as well."

Lambourne snorted, sarcasm twisting his tone. "I suppose Mrs. Sedrick is a victim too."

Miss Prynne's chin jutted in defiance, and her high-pitched voice squeaked with passion. "Mrs. Sedrick's an evil, vile woman capable of things even worse than Matthew Blake. I daresay you'll ne'er see sight of her again, for she knows what she's done."

Lambourne cast a dubious glance toward the older woman before he returned his attention to Isaac. "Do you know where he is?"

Isaac shook his head. "No. I went to Tregarthan last night and waited, but he never returned. I daresay he won't."

"So you admit Matthew is behind this all?"

"I'm afraid so."

Mrs. Lambourne jumped from where she was sitting, a fluster of purple silk and cream lace. "I always told you this place was a mistake. But would you listen?" She stomped to her husband's side. "I'll not stay here another day among these thieves."

"Consider, Aunt." Julia's voice was soft. "Jane cannot travel. She likely will not be able to travel for weeks, maybe months."

"I never trusted these people. Not for a moment." Mrs. Lambourne's cheeks shook with indignation. "Our housekeeper was stealing under our very noses. Our friends plotted against us. Mark my words, the Lambournes will never return to this godforsaken country. We're leaving as soon as arrangements can be made."

"My wife is right." Lambourne leaned back in his chair and rubbed his hand over his gray side whiskers as if in contemplation, then leaned forward with renewed vigor. "I'm loath to do it, but I admit defeat. This situation is beyond impossible, and it's time to cut my losses. I intend to write Elliot as soon as we are done here and accept his offer for Bal Tressa and Lanwyn Manor. He can have it, the whole mess of it, and good riddance, I say."

Isaac stiffened. So Bal Tressa would be in the hands of yet another outsider. But did it matter anymore? For what would become of Wheal Tamsen with Matthew gone?

With a condescending sniff, Mrs. Lambourne tossed her silver hair. "That's the most sensible thing I've heard in months. The more distance we can put between all of us, the better." She stormed past Isaac on her way toward the door, and he stepped back to avoid being trampled, her sharp lily-of-the-valley scent strong as ever.

He winced as the door slammed behind her. It was time to put an end to this once and for all. "I'm genuinely sorry my brother treated you so vindictively. I only hope my explanation will offer some answers, and I'll see to the costs to repair your library."

"You may not be responsible, Mr. Blake, but I think you will understand when I say that I want nothing from you."

Isaac slid a glance toward Julia.

"I think it best if you leave now," Lambourne growled.

Isaac nodded, gave a quick bow to the ladies, and turned to leave the room.

He felt sick. Was this how it would end?

He was retreating down the corridor when footsteps padded behind him. He turned to see Julia, small and pale, behind him. She'd been crying. There was no denying it. Her hair was wild about her face, and her eyes still glistened with tears.

"What will happen?" she whispered, her lower lip trembling.

The pain in her voice only emphasized the war within him. He could ask her to come with him, and she might say yes. But would she understand the cost, and would she be willing to pay it?

He wanted to tell her that he loved her. That she had touched a place in his heart he never knew existed. That she alone held the key to his happiness—his present. His future.

But how could it be now?

His brother—*his family*—had betrayed hers completely. The shadow of it would forever hang over them. Even if she could look past it, he feared he could not.

"I think it best, Julia, if you do what your aunt suggested."

"What?" Surprise colored her cheeks.

"This—you and I—'tis not good for you."

She shook her head, her brow furrowing. "But you said—"

"I know what I said." His throat tightened. "I know, and I meant every word. But after what has occurred—"

"No one blames you." She leaned forward and gripped his hands in hers. "I certainly don't. This will pass, this will—"

"He is my brother, Julia."

At this she dropped his hands. Pain replaced confusion. Her eyes narrowed.

"*My* brother—my family—did this to your family." He did not know what to say after that. Matthew had betrayed the Lambournes, yes, but he had also betrayed Isaac and the life he knew. And that fact twisted in him like a knife.

He cleared the emotion from his throat. "All I know is that I've no idea what's to happen next, but I cannot ask you to stay mixed in this odd, broken situation." He drew a sharp breath. "I think it best that you go with your aunt. For your sake."

Fresh tears sprang to her eyes.

"Please." He waited until he could trust himself to speak. "Don't cry."

Her jaw clenched, and she said nothing, only turned on her heel. Then she was gone.

CHAPTER 54

Two weeks later, Margaret stood at the mining house, her arms folded over her chest. "We can't put Richards off any longer. He's offered to pay for the pump. If we don't accept soon, he might retract his offer."

Isaac shrugged. With each passing day he saw his dream of opening Wheal Gwenna fade a bit more. Now that Matthew was gone, every ounce of his energy had gone into doing the work of two men—his and Matthew's. "At the moment my hands are full with Wheal Tamsen."

"Surely your brother will be back when this blows over. We don't want to pass up this opportunity."

"Matthew's not coming back." Conviction rang in his voice. "How can he? You know what he did. Everyone does."

"But Wheal Tamsen? The workers? Surely all the responsibility for it does not fall to your shoulders."

"The mine has enough money to see things through for now, and I can do his part until we figure out this mess."

She lifted her eyes and fixed them on Isaac. "I was out at Lanwyn Manor today to check on Mrs. Townsend and the baby. They are leaving for London at week's end."

As if this entire ordeal was not painful enough, the thought of Julia leaving the area for good was like a shot to the chest.

"I personally think it is far too early for Mrs. Townsend to be traveling," Margaret continued, "but Mrs. Lambourne will not be dissuaded."

"Can you blame them? Their home was invaded."

"No, I don't blame them," she said softly, and then eyed him carefully before she spoke again. "I heard rumors that Mr. Lambourne has officially sold Bal Tressa and Lanwyn Manor to a man from Falmouth. It's also said that he's to bring his own workers to run Bal Tressa."

Isaac forced his fingers through his hair and shook his head. "As far as I know, yes, it's true. While it's not ideal, Mr. Elliot is a revered miner. Perhaps in time he will open his mine to the local men. But only time will tell that, so that's why it is so important that Wheal Tamsen stay strong."

Margaret tilted her head to the side and toyed with the hem of her sleeve. "While I was at Lanwyn Manor the night the babe was born, I chatted with Julia Twethewey."

Heat rose beneath Isaac's collar. His jaw twitched. He'd managed to keep himself busy in an effort not to think of her. He'd taken another road to the mine every day. He'd stayed behind from church. It was best for her not to be involved in this embarrassment.

"Do you not want to know what we spoke about?" she asked.

He did not respond.

"I was wrong about her. I know that now." Margaret sat in the chair opposite the desk and tightened her shawl around her shoulders. "And she loves you. Any fool can see that. So that's why I don't understand you and what you're doing."

"You didn't see what I saw, Margaret. She may think she loves me, but she'd come to regret it. Matthew infiltrated their home. He used them. All of them. He—"

"That's it exactly. *Matthew* used them. *You* did not. Yes, what he

did was inexcusable. You saved the entire situation from becomin'
much worse. Do you not see it? La, men are such simple creatures. She
is in love with you, Isaac. Not Matthew. No doubt, to her, Matthew
is already gone. I think the real issue behind this all is that you are
hurting."

He huffed and leaned back in his chair. "Of course I'm hurt.
My brother does the unthinkable and leaves me here to defend the
indefensible."

"Don't let him do that to you. You have the power to stop it. Do
not let his crime become yours. Don't let his pain and dissatisfaction
become yours. Listen to me. You've been my friend for a long time,
and you have been there for me since Charlie died. You have not let
the gossips stand in the way of assistin' me. Julia Twethewey will be
there for you, and you're not givin' her a chance to make her own
decisions in this matter. You're a good man, Isaac Blake. Don't punish yourself for something Matthew did."

———◆———

For the first time since the night Matthew left, Isaac took the public
road to Anvon Cottage. He drew his horse to a stop next to the drystone wall and looked to Lanwyn Manor.

Julia was inside.

Perhaps she could see him from a window.

If he were so inclined, he could guide his horse to the courtyard.
Ask to see her. Whether or not she would agree to see him, he could
not tell. As he urged his horse forward once again, Margaret's words
rang loudly.

"*She loves you. Don't punish yourself for something Matthew did.*"

His gut twisted with the odd injustice of it all. He was suffering, yes, but her pain was twofold. She was also being punished for

Matthew's actions. He resumed his ride home, struggling to logically make sense of things. All he knew was that time was running out—for Julia. For Wheal Tamsen. For Wheal Gwenna.

He'd heard nothing from Matthew. Details of his perfidy had leaked to the community, and even if Matthew returned, the workers would not trust him. The miners were furious, unsettled, and rightfully so. Without their mine owner, what was to become of them?

He attempted to put the thoughts of Julia aside and guided his horse home, but when he arrived at Anvon's modest courtyard, a horse was tethered out front. Curious, he dismounted, secured his horse, and went inside.

There in his parlor sat Matthew's private solicitor, Mr. David Lead.

"Mr. Lead." Isaac swept his hat from his head and hung it on the hook. "I wondered when I'd be seeing you. I had a feeling you'd not be away for long."

"I'm here to inform you that your brother's bound for America," he said, expressionless. "I've the official word. His ship departed yesterday."

"I thought it was the East Indies." Isaac stepped in farther, making little effort to hide his sarcasm and forcing his fingers through his hair. "He's left quite a mess behind. If you have contact with him, be sure to tell him that."

Mr. Lead nodded and extended a leather portfolio toward him. "He paid me a call before departing and asked me to wait a fortnight before giving this to you. Here."

Isaac accepted the stack of bound papers and thumbed through it. "What's this?"

"Read it. It explains everything. I need to be on my way." His mouth twitched in a smile. "Congratulations, Mr. Blake."

Confused, Isaac shook the man's extended hand wordlessly.

Mr. Lead turned to leave but then paused. "Oh, and I almost forgot. He also asked me to give you this separate from the other documents."

Isaac took the sealed letter from the solicitor's gloved hand and tucked it against the portfolio. "Thank you, Mr. Lead. Would you stay for a meal before you depart?"

"No, no. I must be going. But if you have any questions, you know how to reach me."

Isaac watched the man's lanky form as it retreated from the house and through the courtyard. When all was once again silent, he retrieved the letter. He stared at it for several seconds—at the familiar handwriting and the familiar wax seal. Part of him wanted to hurl the missive into the fire. Weeks had passed and his brother's betrayal stung more than he cared to admit. But another emotion simmered below the surface—curiosity.

Isaac,

By now you know. I'm going to America. Miners are in demand. Whether I care to admit it or not, my knowledge might serve me well.

There is the matter of Tregarthan Hall and Wheal Tamsen. I'm signing them over to you. You are now legal owner of both.

This seems as if it is the way Father would have wanted it, after all. They were really both more yours than mine, weren't they? Ever since we were children, you saw yourself as part of the history. I saw it as a noose tied around my neck.

One never knows how to end such a letter. I made a mess of everything. There is no explanation I can give, no words to erase it. Even if I wanted to, it would be impossible for me to return to England, let alone Cornwall—not and keep my freedom. Perhaps it is the coward's way out. Perhaps it is the wise way out. But I've bid my homeland farewell for the final time.

I will let you know where I settle. In spite of all, I wish you happiness, Brother. Perhaps one of us will restore honor to the family name, and as for me, I regret my part in tarnishing it.

I was blinded. Blinded by desire to leave Cornwall with as much money as possible. It was never about Bal Tressa or Wheal Tamsen for me. It was always about the escape. I hope you will treat our legacy better than I did.

Farewell. I do hope our paths will cross again, but for now, I accept things as they are. I am happy for you, Brother. You will do great things.

CHAPTER 55

Julia placed her silk gown in the traveling chest. It seemed like only yesterday she had packed her trunks to leave Penwythe Hall to come to Lanwyn Manor. Her heart had been broken then, just as it was broken now. But for a very different reason.

She sniffed and handed Caroline another gown to add to the chest.

"I can hardly wait to get to London!" Caroline giggled, holding the dress before her and gazing into the looking glass. "Just think, we will leave this wretched place, and with any luck we will never return."

Julia forced a halfhearted smile. For her cousin, she'd smile. She'd be happy. But how her heart ached for Isaac.

Absently, she gazed down the public road on the far side of the drystone wall. He was not there, of course. She'd watched for him for days, hoping to catch a glimpse of him. But he no longer took the road. Could it really be true that she would never see him again? That she would never again laugh with him? Smile with him? Be held in his arms again?

She sighed and refocused her attention on her cousin and the pile of clothes before her.

"He will be there to greet us, you know," Caroline continued, oblivious to the war raging within Julia. "I feel almost giddy. Imagine, in just a few short days, I will be by Roger's side once more. Life will finally begin for me."

Julia nodded absently, for indeed she was happy that her cousin anticipated the reunion so. But a part of Julia's heart—a desperate part that had broken free—would remain here in Goldweth.

"I still can't believe Matthew Blake. The scoundrel. But mark my words, London is the place to find a husband, my dear Julia. All this will soon be a distant nightmare and someone far more fetching will take Mr. Blake's place in your heart. And we will be arriving in time for the season. Oh, you will adore it!"

Julia stiffened. *Matthew Blake.*

All this time Caroline and her aunt still believed she had underlying feelings for the man. She never corrected them, and she probably never would. For what good could come of it? Isaac had severed his tie with her. It would do no good to comment on a topic that was dead and gone.

Caroline scurried back to her own chamber, leaving Julia alone with her thoughts. She moved to her desk to write her final letter to Aunt Delia from Lanwyn Manor. As she lifted her quill, she struggled with what to write. She could not tell anyone about her true feelings. Another broken heart? She could scarcely face the truth herself.

She looked up to see Jane in the doorway, the baby cradled in her arms.

"Jane! You should be abed." Julia stood and hurried to her cousin's side. "Oh, but I am glad to see you. And how is the little one today?"

"Please don't scold me about being on my feet. After being in bed for so many months, I am aching to walk and stretch my legs. And my little angel is as happy as can be this morning." She nodded toward the desk. "What are you doing?"

"Writing my aunt Delia."

"I suppose you have a great deal to share with her."

"Do I?" Julia could not resist a slight laugh. "What part of this unbelievable story should I share with her?"

Jane stepped farther into the chamber and lifted a gown lying on the bed. "Yes, it has been a rather strange sequence of events over the past several weeks. And what of Mr. Isaac Blake? Have you had any word from him?"

Julia considered Jane's words as she followed her to the bed. Just as it had been when she first arrived, there was no need to hide the truth from Jane. She was the only one who realized that Julia had developed feelings for Isaac.

Julia stiffened. "No. No word."

"How sad it must make you. I'm sorry."

"It was not meant to be." Julia shrugged, feigning nonchalance. "I must accept it."

Jane tilted her head to the side. "And still, I wonder."

Julia recalled the indifferent expression in his hazel eyes when they last spoke. "You did not hear him. *See* him. He wants nothing to do with me. I was a fool to even entertain the thought that it might be otherwise."

"No, I did not hear him. But consider, Julia. He essentially lost his brother. Furthermore, I'm sure he feels that his brother's actions cast shame on the family name. Is it any wonder he withdrew?"

Julia's chest tightened. "But what's to be done? I can hardly go to him. I made my thoughts clear—much clearer than I ever should have, in hindsight. When will I learn, Jane? When will I guard my heart more carefully?"

"The heart freely given is a heart that is open to pain. But it is also open to the joys."

Unsure of how to respond, Julia rose and took the baby from

Jane. "Let's hope you have more sense about you than your silly cousin Julia." She softened as the baby cooed up at her. "Are you ready to depart tomorrow?"

"I can't imagine how dreadful the carriage ride will be, so bumpy and jolty, but yes, we are ready. We will be that much closer to Jonathan's family, so I am hopeful we can grow closer. Perhaps that will make him feel not so far away."

With Jane's help Julia continued to pack up her gowns and slippers, her letters and her ribbons. All had contributed to her life here, and it seemed so strange that in just a few short days her life would begin again in London.

But there would be one missing piece.

A part of her heart would remain behind in the walls of Lanwyn Manor, and she feared it would not be easily repaired. For it now belonged to Isaac Blake, whether she cared to admit it or not, and only time would tell if it would ever be whole again.

———◆———

Isaac bolted upright in his bed. Perspiration dripped from his forehead. Silence and darkness surrounded him, and he swiped his damp hair away from his face.

The dream he'd had every night for the past week haunted him. Again.

His father.

The day Wheal Gwenna flooded.

His mother's bedchamber shrouded in black after her feverish, sudden death.

The mournful sight of his father in tears at her burial—the only time Isaac ever saw him show any emotion.

Julia was in the dream too. She was roaming the halls of Tregarthan, searching for something. He kept asking her what she was looking for, but she couldn't see him. Couldn't hear him.

Isaac swung his legs over the side of the bed and sat on its edge for several moments, struggling to put the pieces together.

He dragged his hand over his face, stepped over to his window, and turned the latch to open it. Icy air swirled in, and he stared into the blackness and breathed the frosty night air.

The pain and the fog of the dream still pressed on him.

It was as if he could feel his father's grief. Feel the loss. Feel the loneliness.

He reached for his father's pocket watch and looked at the hour. Four in the morning. Today was the day the Lambournes were to leave for London—the day Julia would forever be out of his life.

He squeezed his eyes shut. What had he done?

Suddenly the threads of his dream slammed together. The dream was about loss of love. Loss of purpose.

Sleep's fog fell away, slowly at first, but then increasing clarity materialized.

He was about to lose Julia. And his own actions—his own fears—were to blame.

He yanked on his breeches in the dark and donned his waistcoat. His fingers trembled as he fastened the buttons. Margaret's words echoed loudly in his mind.

"I fear you are not giving her a chance to make her own decisions in this matter."

It was true. For the past few weeks he'd been miserable. He suspected she had been as well. But in Margaret's view, it was preventable. He wasn't miserable because of what Matthew did. He was miserable because Julia wasn't in his life.

As soon as dawn broke silver and clear in the eastern sky, he mounted his horse and made his way to the circle drive before Lanwyn Manor's gatehouse. Even at this early hour, two carriages stood at the ready. Footmen, drivers, and guards milled around, loading crates and trunks and calling instructions to each other.

He was not surprised that they would make such an early start. He only hoped he hadn't waited too long.

He cantered his horse through the gatehouse archway into the courtyard. His heart raced at the sight of the family assembled.

There is still time.

Mr. Lambourne noticed him first, and then they all turned.

His eyes latched onto Julia, and her mouth fell open at the sight of him. He slid from his saddle.

"Blake." Mr. Lambourne furrowed his brows. "What are you doing here?"

Isaac ignored him. His attention was drawn to her, and everything else paled. She was clad in a traveling gown of blue velvet. Her dark hair was gathered at the nape beneath a bonnet. The cool air pinked her cheeks.

Beautiful.

He cleared his throat. "I would like to speak with Miss Twethewey. Alone, please."

The Lambournes exchanged glances, but Julia stared at him.

For several seconds he thought she was not going to move, but then she handed a small bag to her cousin and stepped toward him, questions bright and brimming in her eyes.

He guided her toward a small arch where they could talk in privacy. Once they were out of earshot and out of sight, he turned to her and gripped her hands. "I've been a fool."

She drew a sharp breath.

Her silence spurred him on. "I was wrong. I know that now. I don't know what came over me that day after Matthew left, and I'm so sorry. All I know is that I can't let you get in that carriage without telling you that I love you."

She stared at him with those wide blue eyes. And yet her silence was jarring.

"I don't expect you to understand. I know I hurt you, and I promise if you, if you will forgive me, I will never, ever hurt you again. Please, Julia. I've come to ask you to stay."

Tears glossed her eyes, and she stammered, "But I c-can't stay. My family is leaving. I'll be alone, and I—"

"Then marry me," he blurted. "Marry me. Stay here with me."

She snatched her hand back, and it flew to her chest. "What did you say?"

"Marry me." He could not prevent the smile that spread over his face. He placed his hands on her shoulders and stepped closer. "Oh, darling Julia, if these last few weeks have taught me one thing, it is that I never want to be separated from you. I've been miserable, and I realized my sadness came from being without you. I love you, Julia. Please, don't get in that carriage. Don't go away."

Tears filled her eyes, and her full lips parted as if in surprise. She stepped closer, glanced over her shoulder to make sure no one was watching, then returned her gaze to Isaac. A smile curved the corners of her lips. "Ask me again."

His heart raced as optimism swirled. "Julia, my love, will you marry me? Will you become my wife?"

Julia gripped Isaac's hands and snuck a glance up at the man next to her as they stood before her aunt and uncle. Her heart leapt at the sight.

How things could have ended differently. Had he arrived just fifteen minutes later, she would have already boarded the carriage for London. And then where would they be?

But now his hazel eyes were fixed confidently on her uncle, awaiting his response. Even the harnessed horses behind them seemed eager for an answer, for they pawed at the earth.

And yet her uncle said nothing.

Aunt Beatrice's shrill voice shattered the silence. "A miner's wife?" Her hand flew to her bosom in horror. "But, Julia, consider. London awaits!"

She tightened her grip on his work-worn hand. "My mind is made up, Aunt. I am not going to London. I'll stay here."

The morning wind caught the ribbons of her aunt's ostentatious bonnet and whipped them around her face. "I cannot allow it. What will your uncle Jac and aunt Delia say?"

Julia's confidence soared. "They'll say that if I have found the man I love, then they are happy for me. Please, I hope you will be happy for me too."

"Love? You speak of love?" Aunt Beatrice scoffed. "And you love him? This I cannot believe."

"I do, Aunt."

"Consider his family." Aunt Beatrice shifted her gaze to make sure the servants were not about and lowered her voice. "Consider what they have done to us! Surely you cannot overlook it."

"That was Matthew. Isaac is not his brother."

"But how will you provide for her?" Mr. Lambourne interjected. "With your brother gone, surely the mine will be undergoing changes."

"You are quite right, Mr. Lambourne. A great deal of changes are afoot. The biggest one is that my brother has relocated to America. He has signed over ownership of Tregarthan Hall and all of his holdings to me—including Wheal Tamsen."

Julia jerked her head upward at the news. After all the pain and hardship, how happy she felt to know that Isaac's home was returning to him.

"But he's up to his neck in debt," Uncle William stated. "Surely that will fall to you. A terrible situation, if you ask me."

"No, it's not ideal." Isaac nodded in agreement. "It won't necessarily be easy, but I like to think I've a level head on my shoulders. Surely it is not beyond repair. And I've a bit set aside on my own. Perhaps you've forgotten that I also own Wheal Gwenna. We are not without options. Far from it."

"Well, that does shed a different light on the matter," Aunt Beatrice said. "Security is vital, as I've told you many times, Julia."

"So you understand my decision not to accompany you?"

Aunt Beatrice eyed Isaac skeptically. "There's no need for such a rush! You are an unmarried woman. Betrothed or not, it will not do for you to stay behind, alone, without a chaperone. No, no. Your uncle Jac left me in charge of you, and I must insist."

A thread of panic twisted through her. "If I need to, I'll return to Penwythe Hall for the time being, but my mind is set."

Jane stepped forward, her baby in her arms. "I will stay behind," she blurted. "I am a married woman, and a mother at that. I would be happy to serve as her chaperone."

Less than an hour later, Jane's and Julia's trunks had been removed from the carriage. Julia and Isaac had walked out to the drystone wall to see the carriage off. They stood at the tree line, their tree line, and stood hand in hand, the carriages growing smaller as they disappeared down the road.

Isaac wrapped his arms around her, and she melted into his embrace. He'd become a stronghold for her—a place of protection, a place of rest. She no longer regarded him as she did when she'd first arrived. The feelings he had awakened in her were far stronger than any

Percy was ever able to reach in her heart, and that realization was as frightening as it was thrilling.

She snuggled tighter in toward him. He smelled of winter and horses, of smoke and cold, and she pressed her cheek against the broadcloth of his caped greatcoat. They stood there in silence, locked in an embrace, and for those several moments Julia felt safe. No one could touch her, no one could hurt her.

"See it there, between the trees?" He tightened his arms around her.

"See what?" she asked, drawing her brows together.

"Tregarthan Hall."

She lifted her gaze and saw it—a tall, gabled slate roof rising above the morning mist. She could almost laugh. Aunt Beatrice had wanted so badly for Julia to be mistress of the fine house. And now she was about to become just that.

"It's beautiful, but I understand if you don't want to live there, Isaac. Your brother treated you—us—vilely. If it brings back memories—"

"No. He will not taint it for me. It is the house my father built. And now I can't wait to share it with you."

She smiled, sank back against him, and looked to Lanwyn Manor. Much had been stolen from it over the past few months, but in spite of all that had been lost, so much had been gained—the freedom to love. The sense of worth in herself. The pursuit of happiness. There might not be real treasure of silver and gold hidden in the walls, as the legend had claimed, but with Isaac's arms around her, Julia realized this was the treasure her heart had sought all along.

ACKNOWLEDGMENTS

I am eternally grateful to those who have supported me and cheered me on while I was writing *The Thief of Lanwyn Manor*.

To my incredible family: If it weren't for your encouragement and inspiration, this book would never have been written. You are such a blessing to me!

To my agent, Rachelle Gardner: Your support, friendship, and guidance mean more than you know. Thanks for rolling up your sleeves and coming alongside me!

To my editor, Becky Monds, and to my line editor, Julee Shwarzburg: Thank you for helping me transform this story from an idea to a finished novel. I am so grateful for you! And to the rest of the Harper Collins Christian Publishing Team: From marketing to design to sales and everything in between—thank you for all you do!

And finally, to KC, KBR, and the other writers I am lucky enough to call friends: You are a treasure! Thanks for the brainstorming chats, phone calls, and for sharing this journey with me. I am so blessed!

DISCUSSION QUESTIONS

1. These characters were such fun to write! Did you have a favorite? Who was it, and what did you like about them? Who was your least favorite character?

2. If you could give Julia one piece of advice at the beginning of the book, what would it be? What advice would you give her at the end?

3. When Julia leaves her home at Penwythe Hall, she is escaping certain events that she would rather forget. Have you ever made a drastic move to remove yourself from a certain situation?

4. Let's talk about Miss Prynne. Do you think she is a villain or a victim? Why or why not?

5. Growing up, Isaac always knew what was expected of him—he was expected to help run his family's mine. Have you ever been expected to take on a specific role? What was it? Did you take on the role? If so, how did it change the course of your life?

6. Do you think Beatrice Lambourne was a good person? What was her best quality? What was her worst? Do you

think she had Julia's best interests at heart? What about William Lambourne?

7. It's your turn! What comes next for Julia and Isaac? If you could write the sequel to their story, what would happen?

DON'T MISS SARAH LADD'S TREASURES OF SURREY NOVELS!

RT Book Reviews calls Sarah Ladd a "superior novelist" and the Treasures of Surrey novels "Regency romantic suspense at its page-turning best."

THOMAS NELSON
Since 1798